P9-CNH-349

HEAT LIGHTNING

ALSO BY JOHN SANDFORD

Rules of Prey

Shadow Prey

Eyes of Prey

Silent Prey

Winter Prey

Night Prey

Mind Prey

Sudden Prey

The Night Crew

Secret Prey

Certain Prey

Easy Prey

Chosen Prey

Mortal Prey

Naked Prey

Hidden Prey

Broken Prey

Dead Watch

Invisible Prey

Phantom Prey

KIDD NOVELS

The Fool's Run

The Empress File

The Devil's Code

The Hanged Man's Song

VIRGIL FLOWERS NOVELS

Dark of the Moon

HEAT LIGHTNING

JOHN SANDFORD

G. P. Putnam's Sons

New York

PUTNAM

G. P. PUTNAM'S SONS
Publishers Since 1838
Published by the Penguin Group
Penguin Group (USA) Inc., 375 Hudson Street, New York, New York 10014, USA • Penguin Group (Canada), 90 Eglinton Avenue East, Suite 700, Toronto, Ontario M4P 2Y3, Canada (a division of Pearson Canada Inc.) • Penguin Books Ltd, 80 Strand, London WC2R 0RL, England • Penguin Ireland, 25 St Stephen's Green, Dublin 2, Ireland (a division of Penguin Books Ltd) • Penguin Group (Australia), 250 Camberwell Road, Camberwell, Victoria 3124, Australia (a division of Pearson Australia Group Pty Ltd) • Penguin Books India Pvt Ltd, 11 Community Centre, Panchsheel Park, New Delhi–110 017, India • Penguin Group (NZ), 67 Apollo Drive, Rosedale, North Shore 0632, New Zealand (a division of Pearson New Zealand Ltd) • Penguin Books (South Africa) (Pty) Ltd, 24 Sturdee Avenue, Rosebank, Johannesburg 2196, South Africa

Penguin Books Ltd, Registered Offices:
80 Strand, London WC2R 0RL, England

ISBN 978-0-399-15527-7
Printed in the United States of America

BOOK DESIGN BY NICOLE LAROCHE

For Benjamin

ACKNOWLEDGMENTS

Heat Lightning was written in cooperation with my old friend and hunting partner Chuck Logan, the author of a terrific bunch of thrillers of his own—the latest being *South of Shiloh* from HarperCollins. Chuck and I have shared a number of adventures that later turned up in our books, and that taught us about things like tracking blood trails through the North Woods. . . .

—John Sandford

HEAT LIGHTNING

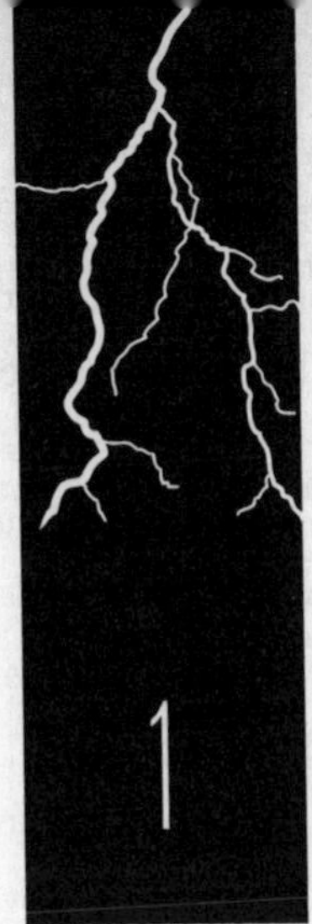

1

THE MIDNIGHT SHIFT: the shooter was going to work.

He jogged through the night in a charcoal-colored nylon rain suit and black New Balance running shoes, with a brilliant reflective green strap over his shoulders, like a bandolier. With the strap, he jumped out at passing cars; nothing furtive here, nobody trying to hide anything. . . .

He ran carefully, taking his time. The old sidewalk, probably laid down in the first decades of the twentieth century, was cracked and shifting underfoot. A wrong step could leave him with a sprain, or worse. Not good for a man with a silenced pistol in his pocket.

The night was hot, cloudy, humid. Lightning flickered way off to the north, a thunderstorm passing by. The tempest would miss by ten miles: no relief from the heat, not yet. He ran through the odor of summer flowers, unseen in the darkness—nice houses here, well-maintained, flourishes of Victorian gingerbread, fences with gardens, flower heads pale in the dim ambient light.

Stillwater, Minnesota, on the bluff above downtown, above the St. Croix River. Third Street once had so many churches that it was called Church Street by the locals. The churches that remained pushed steeples into the night sky like medieval lightning rods, straining to ward off the evil that men do.

THE SHOOTER passed the front of the redbrick historic courthouse, which was guarded by a bronze Civil War infantryman with a fixed bayonet and a plaque. He paused next to a hedge, behind a tree trunk, bent over with his hands on his knees, as if catching his breath or stretching his hamstrings, like runners do. Looked around. Said quietly, "On point."

Dark, silent. Waiting for something to happen. Nothing did. After a last look around, he pulled off the reflective strap and stuffed it in a pocket. When he did that, he vanished. He was gone; he was part of the fabric of the night.

Across from the courthouse, just downhill, a metal spire pushed up from a vest-pocket park, illuminated by spotlights. Ten-foot granite slabs anchored the foot of the needle. On the slabs were more bronze plaques, with the names of the local boys who didn't make it back from all the wars fought since Stillwater was built. A blank plaque awaited names from Iraq and Afghanistan.

The shooter slipped across the street, to the edge of the memorial. The brilliant spotlights made the nearby shadows even darker. He disappeared into one of them, like an ink drop falling into a coal cellar. Before he went, he pulled back the sleeve of the running suit and checked the luminous dial of his combat watch.

If Sanderson stuck to his routine—or the dog's routine, anyway—

he'd walk down the west side of Third Street sometime in the next ten minutes. Big German shepherd. Shame about the dog.

CHUCK UTECHT had been the first man on the controller's list. He'd been a smooth white egg of a man, whose insides, when he cracked, flowed out like a yellow yolk. He'd given up three names. He'd given them up easily.

"I only did one bad thing in my life," he cried. "I've been making up for it ever since."

His final words had been "I'm sorry," not for what he'd done, but because he knew what was coming and had peed his pants.

The scout could extract only so much information from a man who accepted his own execution, who seemed to believe that he deserved it. They had not been in a place where the scout could use pliers or knives or ropes or electricity or waterboards. All he had was the threat of death, and Utecht had closed his eyes and had begun mumbling through a prayer. The scout had seen the resignation; he looked at the shooter and nodded.

The shooter shot him twice in the back of the head, halfway through the prayer.

Now he waited for Sanderson and the dog.

They needed two more names.

The scout said in the shooter's ear, "He's coming."

BOBBY SANDERSON strolled down Third Street with the dog on the end of its lead, a familiar nighttime sight. The dog was as regular as a quartz watch: took a small dump at eight o'clock in the morning, and a big one at eleven o'clock at night. If it wasn't out on the street, it'd be somewhere in the yard, and Sanderson would step in it the next day, sure as God made little green apples. So, twice a day, they were on the street.

Sanderson was preoccupied with an argument he'd had with his girlfriend. Or maybe not an argument, but he didn't know exactly what else you could call it. She didn't want him out at night; not for a while. Not until they found out whether something was going on.

"If you're scared enough that you have meetings, then you ought to be scared enough to stay inside at night," she'd said. She'd been in the kitchen, drying the dishes with an old square of unbleached muslin. She smelled of dishwashing liquid and pork chop grease.

"You know what happens with the dog if he don't get his walk," Sanderson said. "Besides, who's going to mess with Mike?"

But before he'd gone, he'd stepped back to the bedroom, as though he'd forgotten something, had taken the .38 out of a bedroom bureau and slipped it into his pocket. He was not the kind of guy to be pushed. If somebody pushed, he'd push back, twice as hard.

Sanderson was fifty-nine, five-six, a hundred and sixty pounds. A short man, with a short-man complex. You don't fuck with me. You don't fuck with the Man.

He thought like that.

He thought like a TV show.

THE SHOOTER was waiting behind a rampart of limestone blocks next to the monument. Not tense, not anything—not thinking, just waiting, like a rock, or a stump, or a loaded bullet. Waiting . . . Then two words in his ear: "He's coming."

He heard first the click of the dog's toenails on the sidewalk. The animal probably went a hundred pounds, maybe even one-twenty. Had to take him smoothly. . . .

Close now.

The shooter's hand was at his side, with the pistol dangling from it. When they'd scouted Sanderson on a previous walk, they noted that the dog was always on a long lead—there'd be some distance between the dog and Sanderson. The dog didn't seem particularly nervous, but might well sense a man waiting in the night.

Comes the dog.

The shooter went into his routine, squaring his feet, the deep breath already taken. He exhaled slowly, held it, and the dog was there, ten feet out, turning his big head toward the shadow—the alarm, or curiosity, or something, in his eyes, he knew *something.*

THE SHOOTER was in his shooting crouch, arms extended, and the gun recoiled a bit. There was a fast *snap* sound, like an electrical spark, and a mechanical ratcheting as the gun cycled. The dog dropped, shot between the eyes, and the shooter vaulted from the shadows, moving fast, right there in Sanderson's face in a quarter second.

This was no TV show, and you *do* fuck with the Man. Sanderson's eyes just had time to widen and his hand went to his pocket—he never really thought he'd need the pistol.

Never really thought.

The shooter had reversed the pistol in his hand and now held it by the silencer, so that it functioned as a hammer. He chopped Sanderson on the left ear and Sanderson staggered, falling, and put down his gun hand, no gun in it, and the gun pocket hit the ground with a *clank,* and the shooter, realizing that he hadn't hit him quite hard enough, hit him again, and this time, Sanderson went flat.

Not a killing blow.

They needed those names.

THE SHOOTER was trained, the shooter was a killing machine, but he was still human. Now, breathing hard, he tasted blood in his mouth like you might after a tough run; and all the time, he was looking for lights, he was looking for an alarm, a cry in the dark.

He said into the mouthpiece, "Come now."

He yanked the dog lead off Sanderson's wrist, dragged the dog's body into the darkness under the limestone blocks. Moved Sanderson next, the man twitching, trying to come back, but the shooter, gripping him by the shirt collar, moved him effortlessly into the dark. Another look around.

The scout came, all of a sudden, like a vampire bat dropping from the sky. He took a loop of rope from his pocket. The rope was a short noose, with a twisting handle, like the handle on a lawn mower starter-rope. He slipped the noose around Sanderson's neck, twisted the handle until the rope was not quite choking the semiconscious man.

He knelt then, his knees weighing on Sanderson's chest, pinning him, and he shined an LED penlight into Sanderson's eyes. Sanderson moaned, trying to come back, then turned his head away from the burning light, his feet drumming on the ground.

"Listen to me," the scout said. "Listen to me. Can you hear me?"

It took a moment. Though the shooter had been careful, even a mild concussion is, nevertheless, a concussion. "Mr. Sanderson. Can you hear me?"

Sanderson moaned again, but his eyes were clearing. The scout turned the choke rope so that Sanderson could feel it, so that he couldn't cry out.

Slapped him, hard: not to do further injury, but to sting him, bring him up. He put his face next to Sanderson's, while the shooter watched for cars, or another runner. The scout said, "Utecht, Sanderson, Bunton, Wigge. Who were the other two? Who? Who is Carl? Mr. Sanderson . . ."

Sanderson's pupils narrowed: he was coming back.

"Mr. Sanderson, who is Carl?" The scout's voice was soft, and he loosened the noose. Sanderson took a rasping breath. "It wasn't me. It wasn't me. Not me. Not me."

"Who is Carl? We know Ray Bunton, we know John Wigge, but who's Carl?"

"Don't know his name . . ." The desperation was right there, on the surface. The scout could hear it.

"But you knew Utecht," the scout said, persisting, pressuring. "Bunton and Wigge were at your house two days ago. I watched you argue. Who was the man in the car?"

"Some pal of Wigge's. I don't know, I don't know." He strained for air, feet beating on the ground again.

"There was a sixth man. Who was the sixth man?"

"Don't . . ." Then Sanderson's eyes reached up toward the scout's and he seemed to recognize him, what he was, why he was there; with the realization came the knowledge that he would die. "Ah, shit," he said, the sadness thick in the words. "Sally will be hurt."

The scout saw the death in Sanderson's eyes. Nothing more here. He stood up, shook his head. The shooter extended the gun and, without a further word, shot Sanderson twice in the forehead. He caught the ejected .22 shells in his off hand.

The shooter could smell the blood. The odor of blood sometimes nauseated him now. Didn't happen before. Only the last couple of years. He slipped a lemon from his pocket, scraped it with a fingernail, and inhaled the odor of the lemon rind. Better. Better than blood.

Then he bent, pushed down Sanderson's jaw, shoved the lemon into his dead mouth.

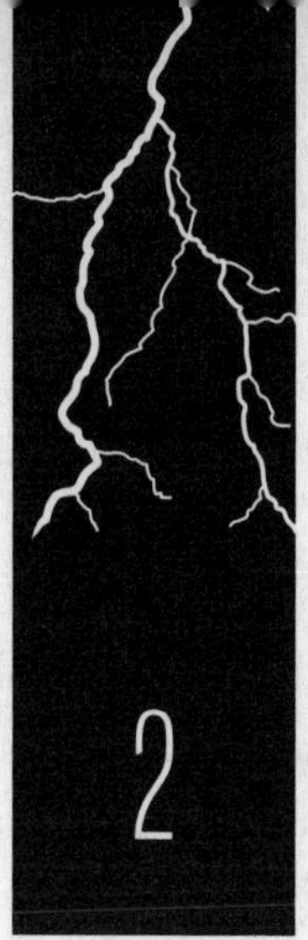

2

EVERY NIGHT, before he went to bed, Virgil Flowers thought about God.

The practice was good for him, he believed, and saved him from the cynicism of a cop's life. Virgil was a believer. A believer in God and the immortal soul, though not in religions—a position that troubled his father, a Lutheran minister of the old school.

"Religion is a way of organizing the culture, your relationship to God and the people around you," his father argued the last time Virgil went back home. "It's not a phone booth to God. A good religion reaches wider than that. A good religion would be a value in itself, even if God didn't exist."

Virgil said, "My problem with that is I don't believe God cares *what* we do. Everything is equally relevant and irrelevant to God. A religion is nothing more than a political party organized around some guy's moral views, Confucius, Buddha, Jesus, Mohammed, like conventional political parties are organized around some guy's economic views. Like Bill Clinton's."

His father disdained Bill Clinton, but he took the shot with appreciation.

So they'd argued around the breakfast table in the kitchen, enjoying themselves, the odor of breakfast rolls lingering in the air, cinnamon and white frosting and hot raisins, and coffee; and mom humming in the background. Though he and his father had the usual growing-up troubles, they'd become closer as Virgil got into his thirties, and his father began dealing with sixty and the reality of age.

His father, Virgil understood, appreciated that his son believed in the immortal soul and that he actually thought about God each night. He may have also envied the fact that his son was a cop; the preacher thought of himself as a man of peace, and he envied the man of action.

The son didn't envy the father. Virgil had been raised in a church, and the problems his father dealt with, he thought, would have driven him crazy. It's relatively easy to solve a problem with a gun and a warrant and a prison; but what do you do about somebody who is unloved?

Better, Virgil thought, to carry a badge, and maintain your amateur status when it came to considering the wonders of the universe.

ON THIS HOT, close night, Virgil's consideration of the wonders of the universe were discomfited by the proximity of Janey Small's naked ass, which, in Virgil's opinion, *was* one of the wonders of the universe. Like a planet. A small, hot planet like Mercury, pulling you both with its heat and its gravity.

Janey was asleep on her side, snoring a bit, her butt thrust toward him, which Virgil believed was not an accident. They'd already gone around twice, but Janey was fond of what she called "threesies," and Virgil had been married to her long enough to understand the signal he was getting. Married to her second; that is, between his first and third wives. And before her third and fourth.

Janey Small had been a rotten idea. Virgil had been in town, had dropped by the Minnesota Music Café to see what was up, and there she was, leaning on the bar, the wonder of the universe packed into a pair of women's 501s.

One thing led to another—it wasn't like they were sexually incompatible. *That* hadn't been the problem. They'd just been incompatible in every other way, like when she became webmaster of a Celine Dion fan site, or decided that fried tofu strips were better than bacon, or that fish felt lip pain.

Janey.

A problem. He liked her, but only for a couple hours at a time.

Maybe if he could slide really slowly over to the edge of the bed . . . his jeans and boots and shirt were right there on the floor, he could be halfway to the door before she woke up.

Virgil was making his move when the cell phone went off on the nightstand, and Janey woke with a start and rolled flat and said, "You left the cell phone on, you goddamned moron."

Not like she had a mouth on her.

Virgil fumbled for the phone, peered at the view-screen, hoping against hope that the call was from an 888 number, but it wasn't.

Lucas Davenport. Virgil said aloud, "It's Davenport."

"That's not good," Janey said. She was a cop groupie and knew what a late-night call meant. Her last husband, Small, worked vice in St. Paul. Janey said he'd picked up some entertaining tips on the job, but unfortunately was deeply enmeshed in his model-train hobby, and when he began building the Rock Island Line in the living room, she moved out.

In any case, she knew Lucas. "So answer it."

He did. "Yeah, Lucas," Virgil said into the cell phone.

"You sound like you're already awake," Lucas said.

"Just getting ready for bed," Virgil said. "I'm kinda beat up."

"No, he isn't," Janey shouted. "He's over here fuckin' me."

"Who was that?" Lucas asked. "Was that Janey Carter?"

"Ah, man," Virgil said. "It's Janey Small now. She got married to Greg Small over at St. Paul. They broke up."

"There's a surprise," Lucas said. "Listen: get out to Stillwater. The Stillwater cops have a body at a veterans' memorial. With a lemon."

"What?" He swung his feet over the edge of the bed. "Two shots to the head?"

"Exactly," Lucas said. "They'd like to move the body before the TV people get onto it. It looks exactly like Utecht, and you're the guy. Tom Mattson is the chief out there, he called operations and they yanked me out of bed."

"Okay, okay," Virgil said. "I might need some backup. This could get ugly."

"Yeah, I know—and I'm heading into D.C. tomorrow for more convention stuff. Del's going with me, the feds are briefing us on the counterculture people. You can have Shrake and Jenkins if you need them. I'll be on my cell phone if you need some weight, and I'll leave a note for Rose Marie."

"Okay."

"You gotta move on this," Lucas said. "Take your gun with you."

"I'm on my way. I'm putting on my boots," Virgil said. "I got my gun right here."

"Stay in touch," Lucas said, and he was gone.

Janey said, "Don't let the door hit you in the ass."

THREE-THIRTY in the morning, running not that late, he thought, ninety-five miles an hour east out of St. Paul, on an empty I-94, his grille lights flashing red and blue, hair wet from a shower, but feeling tacky in yesterday's T-shirt, underwear, and jeans. Thumbed his cell, ramped up the exit onto I-694, got the operations duty guy, got a phone number for the Stillwater chief of police, punched it in, got the guy at the scene.

"Mattson," the chief said.

"Hey—Virgil Flowers, BCA. I'm getting there fast as I can. I'm on 694 coming up to 36. You shut down the scene?"

"Yeah, we shut off the whole block," Mattson said. "No TV yet, but there probably will be. People are coming out of their houses."

"Was the guy on the ground, or do you have some kind of display?"

"He's sitting up, leaning back against one of these memorial slab-things," Mattson said. "We put a construction screen around him so there won't be any photos. I guess Davenport probably told you about the lemon."

"Yeah, he did," Virgil said. "Who found him?"

"One of our guys. Sanderson—victim's name is Bobby Sanderson—

went out to walk the dog and didn't come back," Mattson said. "His old lady got worried and called in and we rolled a car around his route. Not like he was hidden or anything. He was right there, in the lights. Something going on with his old lady, though. She's got a story you need to listen to."

"All right," Virgil said. "You think she had a hand in it?"

"No, no. I'm sure she didn't," Mattson said. "She's a pretty messed-up ol' gal. But something was going on with Sanderson. He might've known the killer."

"Be there in ten minutes," Virgil said. "You're up on the hill, by the old courthouse?"

"Right there. We got coffee coming."

VIRGIL WAS MEDIUM-TALL and lanky, mid-thirties, weathered, with blond hair worn on his shoulders, too long for a cop. He'd once sported an earring, but after two weeks decided that he looked like an asshole and got rid of it.

He'd been a high school jock, and played university-level baseball for a couple of years. When he didn't show up for the third year, the coaches hadn't beaten his door down. Good on defense, with a strong arm from third base, he just couldn't see a college-level fastball, and was hitting .190 at the end of his second season.

He'd also picked up on the fact that the slender, brown-haired, big-boobed literature students, the ones who turned his crank, didn't give a rat's ass about baseball, didn't know Mike Schmidt from Willie Mays, but could tell you anything you wanted to know about Jean-Paul Sartre or those other French guys. Derrida. Foucault. Whatever.

Virgil drifted through college, changing majors a couple of times, and wound up with a degree in ecological science. The demand for ecologists wasn't that great when he got out of school, so he volunteered for Army Officer Candidate School. He'd been thinking infantry, but the army made him an MP. Got in some fights, but never shot at anyone.

Back in civilian life, there still wasn't much demand for ecologists, so he hooked up with the St. Paul cops. After a few years of that, he moved along to the Bureau of Criminal Apprehension, pulled in by Lucas Davenport, a political appointee and the BCA's semi-official wild hair. When he came over, Davenport had told him that they'd put him on the hard stuff. And they did.

VIRGIL WAS A WRITER in his spare time; or, on occasion, got his reporting done by taking a few hours of undertime.

A lifelong outdoorsman, he wrote for a variety of hook-and-bullet magazines, enough that he was becoming a regular at some of them and was making a name. He told people it was for the extra money, but he loved seeing his byline on a story, his credit line on a photograph—and he loved it when somebody came up at a sports show and asked, "Are you the Virgil Flowers who wrote that musky article in *Gray's*?"

He loved pushing out on a stream, or a lake, at 5:30 on a cool summer morning with the sun on the horizon and the steam coming off the still water. He liked still-hunting for deer, ghosting through the woods with the snow falling down around him, shifting through the pines. . . .

Virgil's home base was in the south Minnesota town of Mankato, and he worked the counties generally south and west of the Twin Cities metro area, down to the Iowa line, out west to South Dakota. That had been changing, and Davenport had been pulling him into the metro area more often. Virgil had an astonishing clearance rate with the BCA, as he'd had with the St. Paul cops.

Nobody, including Virgil, knew exactly how he did it, but it seemed to derive from a combination of hanging out on the corner, bullshit, rumor, skepticism, luck, and possibly prayer. Davenport liked it because it worked.

THIS CASE HAD BEGUN in the town of New Ulm, right in the heart of Virgil's home territory, when a man named Chuck Utecht had turned up dead and mutilated at the foot of the local veterans' monument. He had a lemon in his mouth and had been shot twice in the head with a .22-caliber pistol. The .22 was a target shooter's piece, or a stone-cold killer's. It was not the kind of gun that a man would keep for self-protection or as a carry weapon. That was interesting.

Virgil had spent much of the two weeks going in and out of the Brown County Law Enforcement Center, working with the New Ulm cops and Brown County sheriff's deputies, doing interviews, pushing the little bits of evidence around, looking for somebody who might hate Utecht enough to kill him. At the end of the two weeks, he'd been thinking about checking out the local food stores, to see who'd been buying lemons—at that point, he had zip. Nada. Nothing. Utecht had run a title company; who hates a title company?

He'd talked to Utecht's wife, Marilyn, three times, and even she didn't seem to have a strong opinion about the man. His death had been more of an inconvenience than a tragedy, although, Virgil said to himself, that might be unfair. Marilyn may have been in the grip of some strong, hidden current of emotion that he simply hadn't felt.

Or not.

Death had a strange effect on the left-behind people. Some found peace and a new life; some clutched the death to their breasts.

VIRGIL HAD KILLED a man the year before, and hadn't quite gotten over it. He spoke with God about it some nights. He wasn't sure, but he thought the killing might have made him a bit more sober than he had been, might have aged him a little.

On the other hand, here he was, tearing through the night, wearing a Bif Naked T-shirt and cowboy boots, with a guilty, semi-chafed dick. He made the turn on 36 and ran it up to a hundred and five. Willie Nelson came up on the satellite radio with "Gravedigger," one of Virgil's top-five Willie songs of all time, and he started to rock with it, singing along, and not badly, burning up the highway toward the lights of Stillwater.

HE GOT OFF AT Osgood Avenue and headed north, past the cemetery, through the dark streets, through a stop sign, without hesitating, over a hump toward a barricade and all the lights of the cops beyond. At the barricade, he held up his ID and a cop came over and looked at it, said, "It's a mess," and let him through. He rolled down a slope, found a hole in the pile of cop cars, stuck the truck into it, and climbed out.

There were cars from Washington County, Stillwater, Oak Park

Heights, a fire truck, and even a cop car from Hudson, across the river in Wisconsin. No sign of the crime-scene van. Though it was coming up on four o'clock in the morning, local residents were clustering around the police barricades, chatting with the cops and each other, or standing on front lawns, looking down at the memorial. A number of them were carrying coffee cups, and when he got out of the truck, Virgil could smell coffee on the night air.

The courthouse was an old brown-brick relic with an Italianate cupola, sitting on a bump on a hill that looked down on the old river town. Virgil had been there once before, for a wedding out on the lawn—Civil War statue to one side, spires of the churches poking through the trees, narrow streets, clapboard houses from the days when the river was clogged with logs and made Stillwater temporarily rich.

Slightly down the bump from the courthouse, and across the street, the sixty-foot stainless-steel veterans' memorial was glittering in the work lights set up by the firemen. In the middle of it, under a spear-pointed shaft reflective of the steeples down the hill, a gated fence, like the kind that gas-company workers set up around manholes, shielded the body from the public eye. Virgil walked on down, picked out a clump of big thick-chested men who looked like the local authority, and headed toward them.

One of the men, a square-shouldered fifty-year-old with a brush mustache, dressed in a rumpled suit, nodded at him, and asked, "You Virgil Flowers?"

"Yeah, I am," Virgil said.

They shook hands, and the man said, "Tom Mattson," and then gestured to the two men he'd been standing with and said, "Darryl Cunningham, Washington County chief deputy, and Jim Brandt, my assistant chief."

Virgil shook their hands and noticed all three noticing his Bif Naked T-shirt and he didn't explain it, because he didn't do that. If they wanted to know, they could ask. "Where's the crime-scene guys?"

Mattson shook his head, and Cunningham said, "There might have been some miscommunication. They didn't get rolling as quick as they could."

"A fuckin' clown car would have been here by now," Brandt fumed.

Cunningham said, "Hey, c'mon . . ." He was really saying, *Not in front of the state guy.*

"It happens," Virgil said, letting everybody off the hook. "Mind if I take a look?"

THEY WALKED DOWN to the utility fence as a group, Mattson filling him in on how the body had been found. "He was out walking his dog, a German shepherd. The dog was shot right between the eyes. It's down below, there."

"Takes a good shot to kill a big shepherd with one round," Virgil said.

"Especially since, if you missed, the dog would eat your ass alive. The girlfriend says it was security-trained."

The utility fence was hip-high and consisted of two overlapping C-shaped metal frames covered with canvas panels. A space between the Cs allowed the cops to come and go. The fence was ten feet back from the body. Virgil stepped through the space between the two arcs of fence, watching where he put his feet, and eased up close enough to see the bullet wounds in Sanderson's head; bullet wounds with some burn and debris. The muzzle of the gun hadn't been more than an inch or two from Sanderson's forehead.

A quarter of a lemon was visible between the victim's thin lips, clenched by yellowed teeth. Sanderson looked like he was in his late fifties or early sixties. He had rough, square hands; a workingman's hands.

The killing looked exactly like the Utecht murder. Virgil stared at the body for another ten seconds, was about to turn away when he noticed a hard curve in the jogging suit, slightly under the body.

He looked back over his shoulder: "So the crime-scene guys know, I'm going to touch his suit." He checked the concrete between himself and the body to make sure he wouldn't disturb anything, then duck-walked forward a couple of feet, reached out, and touched the hard curve. Shook his head, stood up.

"What?" Mattson asked.

"He's got a gun in his pocket," Virgil said.

"Are you shitting me?"

"No. I could feel the cylinder cuts," Virgil said. "You might want to check and see if he's got a carry permit, and if he does, when he got it."

"That means . . . he knew something was coming."

"Maybe," Virgil said.

"CRIME SCENE'S HERE," Cunningham said, looking back up the street.

Virgil stepped away, back to the fence, and out, and Mattson asked, "What do you think?"

"Same as New Ulm. The gunshots look identical. A .22, from two inches. One difference—Sanderson's got some abrasions on his neck, like he was choked. Didn't see that at New Ulm. But the lemon's not public, yet, and that pretty much ties it up."

"Some of the media know about the lemon," Mattson said. "I had Linda Bennett from KSTP, she asked me if there was a lemon in his mouth."

"Yeah, some of them know. We asked them not to report it. But they'll be connecting the dots, the veterans' memorial," Virgil said, looking up at the hoops and struts of the memorial. "I hope we can hold the line on the lemon. Don't need any copycats."

"You actually know of any copycats?" Cunningham asked. He seemed genuinely curious.

Virgil grinned and said, "No, but I've seen them on TV shows."

"Speaking of which," Mattson said. Virgil looked up the hill and saw a white SUV do a U-turn at the barricade. A logo on the door said WCCO.

"I'm surprised they took so long," Virgil said. "You guys ought to take five minutes to think about who's going to say what. The whole bunch of them will be down here, and they'll be all over you."

They all looked over the fence at the body, which looked a little like a scarecrow, deflated and dead, and Brandt asked, "What the hell's going on?"

"Wish you could tell me," Virgil said. The crime-scene van was squeezing down the hill, and a cop car had to be moved so it could get past.

"You all through here?" Cunningham asked.

"Yeah—nothing much for me to do," Virgil said. "I ain't Sherlock Holmes."

Cunningham said, "I talked to Jimmy Stryker at the sheriff's meet last month, and he thinks you are."

Virgil said, "Well, we're friends."

"He said you were friends with his sister, too—for a while," Cunningham said.

Virgil nodded at him, sharp and quick. "Ships passing in the night, Sheriff." He wasn't going to step into that bog. "I *would* like to talk to Sanderson's girlfriend. We need to know why he was carrying a revolver."

Mattson nodded. "She's available."

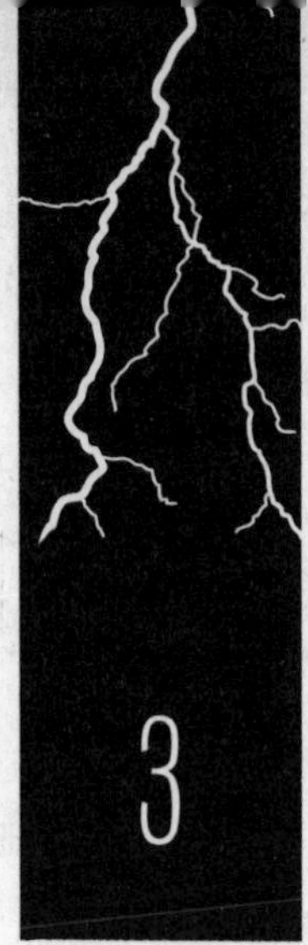

3

SANDERSON HAD lived three blocks from the veterans' memorial, up the hill, past the courthouse, and down a dark side street. Brandt walked along with him, to show him the way and to fill him in on the dead man's background.

"We all knew him," Brandt said. "He used to be a building inspector for the city. He was a carpenter before that. He was around all the time."

"Nice guy? Bad guy?"

"You know—had a little mean streak, but wasn't too bad when you got to know him. Short-guy stuff," Brandt said. "He'd get in your face. But nobody, you know, took him all that seriously. Never knew him to actually get in a fight or anything. You'd see him, you might stop and chat. One of the guys around town."

"So . . . you said he used to work for the city," Virgil said. "What was he doing now?"

"He retired, took the pension, started rehabbing these old Victorians. He'd buy one, live in it, and rehab it," Brandt said. "That's how he met Sally. His girlfriend's Sally Owen, she's a decorator in one of the shops downtown."

"Younger woman?"

"No, they must be about the same age. Sanderson was fifty-nine. Sally might even be a year or two older. Her husband was a contractor, died of a heart attack maybe three, four years ago. She and Bobby hooked up a couple of years back."

"Building inspectors have a reputation, sometimes, for taking a little schmear here and there," Virgil said.

Brandt shook his head. "Never heard anything like that about him. Didn't have that smell. He'd tag a site, but I never heard that he was taking money."

"So, just a guy," Virgil said.

"Yeah, pretty much."

"A veteran."

Brandt's forehead wrinkled. "Yeah. We asked Sally when we talked to her. Two years in Korea, during the Vietnam War. Drafted, got out as quick as he could. We could check, to pin it down, but that's what she said."

"Probably need to check," Virgil said.

"The guy in New Ulm—he was a vet?"

"Nope. No, he was the right age for the draft, but he had a heart murmur or something," Virgil said. And it bothered him—why had a nonvet been left at a veterans' monument?

WALKED ALONG A BIT. Then Virgil asked, "You find anybody who heard the shots? Three shots?"

"Nope. That's unusual. Every time a car backfires, we get calls," Brandt said. "Even a .22 is pretty noticeable, especially in the middle of the night. We're still knocking on doors, but the further away we get from the scene, the less likely it is that somebody would have heard anything."

Virgil thought: *Silencer?* Silencers were so rare in crime circles as to be almost mythical. A few leaked out on the street from military sources, but that was almost all on the East Coast, and people who got them were usually jerkwaters showing off for their gun-club pals. Still, somebody should have heard a shot on a quiet street, with houses only a couple hundred feet away.

A professional assassin might have a silencer . . . but the only professional assassins he knew about, other than one that Davenport had tangled with, were like copycat killers—on television.

SANDERSON'S HOUSE was an 1890s cream-and-teal clapboard near-mansion that had been reworked into a duplex, set back and screened from the street by a hedge of ancient lilacs. A scaffold was hung on one side of the house, with a pile of boards set up on two-by-sixes, and covered with a plastic sheet, on the ground below it.

As they passed the driveway on the way to the front walk, Virgil could see a pickup truck and, behind it, the dark rounded shape of a fishing boat. A Stillwater cop answered the doorbell. They stepped inside to heavy-duty air-conditioning that made the hair prickle on Virgil's forearms.

Sally Owen was sitting on a bar chair next to a work island in the kitchen. The kitchen had been recently refurbished with European appliances with a deep-red finish and black granite countertops. Virgil could smell fresh drywall, and the maple flooring was shiny and unblemished by sand or age.

"Miz Owen," Brandt said. "This is Virgil Flowers, he's with the state Bureau of Criminal Apprehension, he's going to be handling this . . . incident. Uh, he wanted to chat with you. . . ."

"You don't look like a police officer," Owen said, with a small sad smile. "You look like a hippie."

"I was out dancing last night," Virgil said. "I came on the run."

"I'll leave you to it," Brandt said. "I gotta get back."

When he'd gone, Owen said, "So. You're telling me that you got rhythm?"

"Hard to believe, huh?" Virgil said. There was another bar chair across the counter from her, and he pulled it out and slid onto it.

"Hard to believe," she said, and then she turned half away and her eyes defocused, and Virgil had the feeling that he wasn't really talking to her at that instant, she'd gone somewhere else. Owen had short brown hair with filaments of gray, and deep brown eyes. She'd never been a beautiful woman, but now she was getting a late-life revenge on her contemporaries who had been: she had porcelain-smooth skin, with a soft summer tan; slender face and arms, like a bike rider's; an attractive square-chinned smile.

Virgil let her go for a moment, to wherever she'd gone, then brought her back. "Did you know that Bobby took a gun with him tonight?"

Brown eyes snapped back: "No . . . are you sure?"

"Yes. You knew he had a gun?"

She nodded. "He has some hunting rifles, but there's only one pistol . . . it was a pistol? It must have been."

"Yes."

She stood up. "Let me look." She led him back through the house, to the bedroom, a neat, compact cubicle with a queen-size bed, covered only with sheets, with a quilt folded back to its foot, two chests of drawers, and a closet with folding doors. Owen knelt next to one of the bureaus, pulled out the bottom drawer, pushed a hand under a pile of sweatshirts, and said, "It's gone."

She stood up and shook her head. "He never took it before. I would have known."

"Chief Mattson said you had a story about Bobby," Virgil said. He drifted back toward the kitchen, pulling her along as if by gravity. "What happened the other night?"

She busied herself, getting coffee. "All I've got is instant. . . . I told him not to go out."

"Instant's fine," Virgil said. "Why shouldn't he walk the dog?"

"Something was going on, and he wouldn't tell me about it. Two nights ago, some men came to see him—they were talking in the street. Arguing."

"Was he afraid of them?"

She paused with a jar of instant coffee, a puzzled look on her face. "No, no, he wasn't afraid of *them*. Whatever it was, whatever they were talking about, that's why he took the gun with him. He was really upset when he came back in."

"What did the guys look like?" Virgil asked.

"I only saw one of them clearly—I didn't know him, but he looked like a cop," Owen said. "Like a policeman. He had that attitude. He was always hooking one thumb in his belt, like you see cops do. I don't know—I thought he was a cop."

Virgil took his notebook out of his jacket pocket. It was a black European-style notebook called a Moleskine, with an elastic band to keep it closed. He bought them a dozen at a time, one for each heavy case he worked. When he was done with a case, he put the notebook—or several of them sometimes—on a bookshelf, a vein to be mined if he ever started writing fiction.

He slipped the elastic on the cover, flipped open the notebook, wrote, "cop."

"You couldn't see the other guy?" he asked.

"No. Not very well. But I got the feeling that he might have been an Indian."

"You mean, like, a dot on the forehead? Or an American Indian?"

"American Indian," Owen said. "I couldn't see him very well, but he was stocky and had short hair, but there was something about the way he dressed that made me think Indian. He was wearing a jean jacket and Levi's, and I think he came on a motorcycle and walked down here, because I heard a motorcycle before Bobby went out, and then, when he came back in, I heard a motorcycle pulling away. The cop guy came in a car."

"What kind of car?"

She showed a small smile. She knew the answer to this one: "A Jeep. I had one just like it, my all-time favorite. A red Jeep Cherokee." Then she turned away from him again, like the first time he lost her, and she said, "God, why did this happen?" and she shook a little, standing there with the coffee in her hands.

"You okay?" Virgil asked after a moment. He wrote "red Cherokee" in his notebook, and "Indian/motorcycle."

"No, I'm not," she said.

"I'm sorry," he said. "You okay for a couple more questions?"

"Yeah, let me get this coffee going." She spooned coffee into two china mugs, filled them with water, stirred, and stuck them in a microwave; the whole procedure was so practiced that Virgil would have bet she did it every morning with Sanderson. "Something else," she said. "It's possible that the Indian's name is Ray. I don't know that, but it could be."

"Why Ray?" The microwave beeped and she took the cups out, and slid one across to Virgil. They both took a sip, the coffee strong and boiling hot, and Virgil said again, "Ray?"

Ray was an Indian, an Ojibwa, a Chippewa, from Red Lake. She'd never met him, but he was an old pal of Sanderson's—Bobby never explained how they met—and the past three weeks they'd been going to vet meetings in St. Paul.

Virgil perked up. "Vet meetings?"

"Yes. Bobby didn't tell me about those either. I mean, it's starting to sound like he didn't tell me about anything, but that's not true. He could be a talkative man. But these men in the street, these meetings . . . it's like he couldn't talk to a woman about them. This was man stuff, like maybe it went back a long time."

Virgil wrote "Ray/Indian" in his book, and "vet meetings."

"When you say vet meetings," he asked, "did you get the impression it was just a bunch of guys, a bull session, or was it more like group therapy or what?" Virgil asked.

"Group therapy. Maybe not exactly that, but more than a bull session." She squinted at him across the work island. "I don't know why Bobby would need vet's therapy, though. He worked in a motor pool for some obsolete missile battalion. He said they'd shoot off their missiles, for practice, and they couldn't hit this mountain that they used as a target."

"In Korea."

"Yes. Someplace up in the hills," she said. "Chunchon? Something like that."

"You know which vet center?" Virgil asked.

"I don't know exactly, but it's on University Avenue in St. Paul. He said something about parking off University."

The meeting in the street, she said, had involved the cop-looking guy, the Indian, Sanderson, and a man who never got out of the car.

"The weird thing about that was, he was sitting in the backseat. Like the cop guy had chauffeured him out here. Like he was some big shot. Anyway, at one point, the window rolled down, the back window, and the cop guy got Bobby's arm and tried to pull him over there, and the Indian guy pushed the cop guy away," she said.

She was becoming animated as she remembered. "I thought there was going to be a fight for a minute; but then they all quieted down and they were looking around like they were worried that they disturbed somebody. Then they finished up and the Indian man went down the street, and the cop got back in the car and Bobby came in, and I said, 'What the heck was all that?' and he said, 'Nothing. Some old bullshit. I don't want to talk about it. Tell you some other time.' That's what he said, exactly. He was harsh about it, so I didn't want to push him about it. I should of pushed."

Virgil wrote it down, exactly.

Owen had an extra photograph of Sanderson, taken standing next to his boat, wearing a T-shirt and shorts. "I don't need it back," she said.

They talked for a few more minutes, but she had only one more thing, having to do with the bowel regularity of the dog. "It was like the train coming through town," Owen said. "They were out the door every night, same time, within five minutes. Walked the same route. If you knew him, if you wanted to kill him . . ."

"I understand the dog was security-trained," Virgil said.

"Sort of. You know, one of those Wisconsin places where they say their dogs are all this great, but you think, if they're so great, why are they so cheap? I liked him, he was a good dog, but he wasn't exactly a wolf."

HE LEFT HER in the kitchen, staring at the future, went out the side door, took a look at the boat. Boats had always been big in Virgil's life, and this was a nice one, a Lund Pro-V 2025 with a two-hundred-horse Yamaha hanging on the back, Eagle trailer, Lowrance electronics, the ones with the integrated map and GPS. Sanderson had fitted it with a couple of Wave Whackers, so he did some back-trolling; walleye fisherman, probably. Nice rig, well-kept, well-used.

Seemed like Sanderson had a nice life going for himself; nice lady, nice job, nice truck, nice fishing rig.

Virgil moved back toward the front of the house, saw a big man in a Hawaiian shirt coming along the street, limping a little. "Shrake?"

The big man stopped, peered into the dark. "Virgil?"

"You're limping," Virgil said, moving into the light.

"Ah, man." Shrake was a BCA agent, one of the agency's two official thugs. He liked nothing more than running into a bad bar, jerking some dickweed off a barstool in midsentence, and dragging his ass past his pals and into the waiting cop car. "I think I pulled a muscle in my butt."

"Christ, you smell like somebody poured a bottle of Jim Beam on your head," Virgil said.

"That fuckin' Jenkins . . ."

Virgil started to laugh.

"That fuckin' Jenkins set me up with a hot date," Shrake said, hitching up his pants. "She was already out of control when I picked her up. Smelled like she'd been brushing her teeth with bourbon. She drank while she danced . . . then she fell down and I stupidly tried to catch her. . . . Anyway—what should I do?"

"I don't know," Virgil said. And, "Why are you out here?"

"Davenport called me up, said you might need some backup." Shrake cocked his head. "He said you were banging Janey Carter when he called."

"Actually, it's Janey Small . . . ah, never mind. Listen, there's not much to do. The locals are knocking the doors, we're waiting for the ME—"

"The ME's here," Shrake said.

"Okay. But to tell you the truth, and I hate to say it, it looks professional," Virgil said. "There ain't gonna be much."

"Yeah?" Shrake was interested. "Same guy as that New Ulm killing, you think?"

"Same guy," Virgil said. "From looking at it, I'd say our best hope is that he only had two targets. I've got some stuff to check out in the morning, but this is gonna be tough."

"Well, you know what they say," Shrake said. "When the going gets tough, try to unload it on that fuckin' Flowers."

The problem with a pro was that there'd be none of the usual skein of connections that tied a killer to a victim. The crime scene would be useless, because a pro wouldn't leave anything behind. If a bunch of bodies added up to a motive for some particular person—the person who hired the pro—that person would have an alibi for the time of the killings, and could stand silent when questioned. The pro, in the meantime, might have come from anywhere, and might have gone anywhere after the killings. With hundreds of thousands of people moving through the metro area on any given day, how did you pick the murderous needle out of the innocent haystack?

VIRGIL AND SHRAKE walked together back to the veterans' memorial. The TV trucks had all come in, and Mattson was standing in a pool of light, talking to three reporters. Brandt came over and asked, "You done with Miz Owen?"

"For tonight. If you could find a friend . . ."

"Got her sister coming over. She lives in Eagan, it'll take a while, but she's coming," Brandt said.

"Good," Virgil said. He nodded toward the monument. "The ME's guys say anything?"

"Yeah. He was shot twice. In the head."

"Well, shit, what more do you want?" Shrake asked. Brandt's nosed twitched, picking up Shrake's bourbon bouquet, and Shrake sidled away.

Brandt said to Virgil, "The mayor would like to talk to you."

"Sure," Virgil said. "Where is he?"

BRANDT TOOK THEM OVER, Shrake staying downwind. The mayor was a short, pudgy man, a professional smiler and a meet-your-eyes-with-compassion sort of guy, whose facial muscles were now misbehaving. He said to Virgil, "What-a, what-a, what-a . . ."

Virgil knew what he was trying to ask, and said, "This doesn't have anything to do with your town—I think Mr. Sanderson was a specific target. The same man killed another victim down in New Ulm. That's what I think. You don't have much to worry about."

"Thank you for that," the mayor said. He rubbed his hands nervously, peering about at the crime scene. "I feel so bad for Sally. Gosh, I hope she gets through this okay." He seemed to mean it, and Virgil nodded and said to Shrake, "We oughta head back. We need to get at some computers."

Shrake nodded. Virgil said a few more words to the mayor, gave his card, with a couple of spares, to Brandt, and told him to call if *anything* turned up. "The guy had to get here somehow. If anybody even thinks they might have seen a car, or a guy . . ."

"We're doing it all, man," Brandt said.

The mayor said to Brandt, "And *good for you*. Good for you, *by golly*."

On the way back to his car, Virgil asked Shrake if he knew anything about a veterans' center on University Avenue.

"Sure. Something going on there?"

Virgil told Shrake about Sanderson and the therapy group, and Shrake said, "Sounds right. That's what they do there."

"E-mail me an address or something," Virgil said. "I gotta get some sleep before I go back out."

"Me, too," Shrake said, and yawned.

Virgil felt somebody step close behind him and then a small hand slipped into his back pocket, tight inside the jeans. He twisted and looked back over his shoulder: Daisy Jones, blond, slender, a little tattered around the eyes, glitter lipstick with tooth holes in it.

"Virgil Flowers, as I live and breathe," she said, moving close, letting the pheromones work on him. "I was laying in bed tonight . . ."

"Laying? Really? Not lying?" Virgil said. She did smell good. She only used the choicest French perfumes, which reached out like the softest of fingers.

She ignored him, continued: ". . . when I felt a kind of feminine orgasmic wave cross over the metro area. I said to myself, 'Daisy, girl, that fuckin' Flowers must have come back to town.'"

"That was me," Virgil admitted.

"I got my sap," Shrake said to Virgil. "We could whack her, throw her body in the lilacs."

"Shrake, you gorgeous hunk, I get so *aroused* when you talk about my body," Jones said. She pressed her hand against Shrake's chest, lightly scratching with long nails, and made him smile. "Is it true that this murdered man had a lemon in his mouth, and was shot twice, an identical killing to the one in New Ulm?"

"Goddamnit, Daisy, we don't need that lemon stuff out there," Virgil said.

"Oh, horseshit," she said. "The killer knows he does it. You know he does it. I know he does it. The only people who don't know he does it are the stupes. So I'm going to put it on the air, unless you give me something better."

"Okay, here's something better," Virgil said. "Yes."

"Yes, what?"

"The killings are virtually identical," he said. "The same guy did them both."

"Can I quote you?" she asked.

"You can say that you spoke to me briefly, and that I acknowledged that there were striking similarities between the two," Virgil said.

She stuck out a lower lip: "I'm not sure that's enough to kill the lemon angle. The lemon has a certain . . . interest about it."

"A lemon twist," Shrake offered.

"Oh, shit! That's my lead," Daisy said. "Thank you, Shrake."

"Okay. You're gonna use it," Virgil said. He stepped toward the TV lights. "I'll go over and go on camera with these other guys, and give them my opinion about the killings. . . ."

"Virgil—don't do that," she said, hooking his arm.

"Daisy . . ."

"*All right*. But if anybody else squeals *lemon*, I'll be five seconds behind them."

"If you use my name on the air," Virgil said, "mention that thing about the orgasmic wave, huh?"

As they walked away from her, Shrake said, "I think she's getting better as she gets older."

"Yeah."

"Did you ever . . . ?"

"No, I did not, for Christ's sakes. I don't . . . Never mind."

"You mean, fuck everybody?" Shrake was enjoying himself.

"Shrake . . ."

"Davenport tried to do that, you know, before he got married. You guys are somewhat alike."

"Bullshit. I'm a *lot* better-looking."

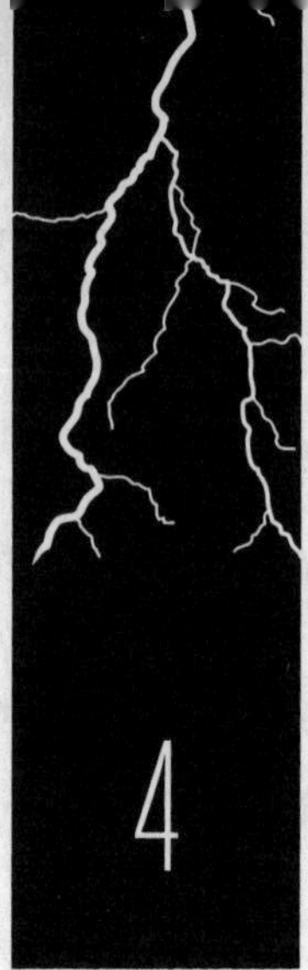

4

VIRGIL WAS staying at the Emerald Inn, made it back about a hundred feet in front of the first rush-hour car, went to his room, got undressed, set the alarm, and fell facedown on the bed.

Too much.

Four Leinie's at the club, bedtime with Janey, then the murder. He'd started the day at five o'clock in the morning in Mankato, eighty miles south of the Twin Cities, and now was twenty-five hours down the line, with a hard day coming up.

He would have been asleep in forty seconds, except thirty seconds after he landed facedown, the nightstand beeped at him. Beeped again thirty seconds later; again thirty seconds after that. No point in resisting: it wasn't going to quit.

He pushed up on his elbows, looked at the nightstand. Nothing there but a pile of dollar bills, the clock, and the lamp. Another beep. Had to be the clock, which had gone nuts for some reason. There was nothing to turn off except the alarm, and he needed the alarm, so he put the clock on the floor, pushed it under the bed, and dropped back on the pillow.

Another beep, right next to his ear.

Groggy, he looked at the nightstand. Nothing now but a pile of dollar bills and the lamp. He pulled open the only drawer, found a Gideon's Bible, which he opened. The Gideon was not beeping him.

Another beep. The lamp beeped? With the feeling that he was actually going insane, he inspected the lamp but could find no sign of anything that might beep. He'd just drawn back from it, looking at his pillow, when it beeped again.

He was losing it, he thought. There was nothing there; the beep was in his head, and it would never go away. He flashed on a scene with himself at the Mayo Clinic, surrounded by shrinks, shaking their heads at the syndrome now known as Flowers's Beep.

He reached out to the stack of dollar bills . . . and found his cell phone beneath them, thin enough to be invisible. The low-battery warning. Jesus. He staggered over to his briefcase, got out the charger, plugged it in, and thought later that he must have passed out while hanging in midair over the bed, falling onto the pillow.

WHEN THE ALARM went off at nine o'clock, he woke bright-eyed, but in the bright-eyed, dazed way that means he'd feel like death at two o'clock in the afternoon. He cleaned up, staring at himself in the mirror as he shaved, and then said to his own image, "You're too old for that Janey thing. You gotta wake up and fly right, Virgil. This is the first day of the rest of your life. You don't have to *be* this way."

He wasn't convinced. He got dressed, and spent a moment choosing a T-shirt that would go with his mood—eventually choosing one that said "WWTDD." He pulled on a blue sport coat, stuck his notebook in the pocket, smiled at himself in the mirror.

Not bad, except for the black rings under his eyes. He checked his laptop, which was hooked into the motel's wireless system, and found an e-mail from Shrake with the vet center's address. Shrake had also run Sanderson through the FBI's National Crime Information Center, and the feds had come back with two hits, both DWIs in the 1980s.

After pancakes and bacon and a glance at the *Star Tribune* at a Country Kitchen, Virgil rolled along behind the last car in the rush hour, west on I-94, got off at 280 and then immediately at University Avenue. The vet center was in a long, old, undistinguished brown-brick building, between an art studio and an architect's office. Virgil dumped the truck on the street and went inside.

THE WOMAN AT THE reception desk took a look at his ID and called the director, listened to her phone for a couple of seconds, then pointed Virgil down the hall. The director was a Vietnam-era guy named Don Worth. He must have been coming up on retirement, Virgil thought, mild-looking with his gray hair in a comb-over, brown sport coat and khakis with a blue button-down shirt, brown loafers. He shook Virgil's hand after looking at his ID, pointed him at a chair, and said, "You need . . ."

Virgil took the photograph of Sanderson out of his briefcase and passed it across the desk. "He was murdered last night. Another man was murdered a couple of weeks ago in New Ulm, in exactly the same way. The bodies were left on veterans' memorials. We think Mr. Sanderson was coming to a veterans' discussion group, or therapy group, with a man named Ray."

He explained briefly about the scene in the street and that Sanderson had suddenly started carrying a gun. He didn't mention that the New Ulm victim was not a veteran. "So what I need is Ray's name, and the names of the other people in the group."

Worth leaned back in his chair and said, "The way the VA views these kinds of things is, all the information belongs to the veterans themselves, including names, and we're not allowed to release it."

"Under the circumstances . . ." Virgil began.

Worth picked up his sentence: "I'd be an asshole not to give you something. I don't know Ray, but I think I've seen him. I don't know what group he's in, either. But we have a volunteer coordinator named Chuck Grogan who could tell you. Chuck owns Perfect Garage Doors and Fireplaces. It's about two miles from here, on Snelling."

PERFECT GARAGE DOORS was a storefront with parking in what looked like a burned-out lot next door; part of a brick wall still stuck up out of the ground in back, and had been thoroughly tagged by artists named Owl and Rosso. Virgil walked in, under a jingling bell, and found Grogan peering at an old paper wall-map of the Twin Cities. "You know what the trouble is," Grogan said without preamble, "is that the roads aren't always where the maps say they are."

"That is one of the troubles," Virgil agreed. Grogan was a square man with a gray mustache and sideburns, a big gut tucked into jeans, and motorcycle boots. If there wasn't a Harley in his life, Virgil would have been astonished. He held up his ID: "I'm looking for a guy named Ray. . . ."

THEY SAT IN Grogan's office, a drywall cube ten feet on a side, in squeaking office chairs, garage-door-opener parts in the corners, and Virgil told him about it. Grogan couldn't believe that Sanderson had been killed. "Like assassinated? Holy shit. What do you think happened?"

"I don't know. That's why I want to talk to Ray, and the other guys in the group," Virgil said. "See if anything came up in the group."

Grogan was shaking his head. "I'm the moderator of that group. Bob was only there three times, I think. He came with Ray. Didn't say much, asked some questions."

"Why was he there, then?"

Grogan made his hands into fists and looked down at them, turned them over, then said, "I think . . . he had a problem. In Vietnam. What it was, I don't know. We don't push that. If it's going to come out, it'll come out. And it usually does, you know? Even with these hard guys."

"You mean, like, atrocities or something?" Virgil asked.

"No, no. But seeing death, seeing dead people, having people trying to kill you, maybe trying to kill other people. All the stress. We had one guy, a supply guy, flew into Vietnam as a replacement, trucked up to an advance base, fairly big base, never stepped off it in thirteen months. But once a day, some Vietcong with a mortar would fire one round into the base. That guy says when he got up in the morning that he'd start praying that he didn't get hit that day, and he'd pray all day until the mortar came in, and then he'd stop praying until he got up the next morning. Literally prayed until his lips got chapped. Went on for a year . . . That'll fuckin' warp your head."

"Sanderson was in the Army, but he was never in Vietnam," Virgil said. "He was in Korea, with some kind of missile unit."

Grogan frowned, leaned back. "You sure? This was a Vietnam vets group."

"That's what his girlfriend says," Virgil said. "The other guy, in New Ulm, wasn't in the military at all."

"You checked all that?" Grogan asked.

"Not really. Not with the government . . ."

"Maybe there's something you don't know," Grogan said. "Some kind of black ops."

Virgil shook his head. "I was an MP. I met every kind there was in the Army, most of them when they were drunk. These guys weren't operators. Sanderson was a mechanic. Utecht ran a title service, and before that, he worked for State Farm."

Grogan said, "Huh. Well, then, you better talk to Ray. But I'll tell you what, I think Sanderson was in Vietnam. He seemed to . . . know shit."

Ray's last name was Bunton, Grogan said. "He's part Chippewa and he's got family all over. He's got a place up in Red Lake. If he's down here, he's probably crashing with one of his relatives."

"He was in Vietnam?" Virgil asked.

"Yeah, he was pretty hard-core infantry," Grogan said.

"And he brought in Sanderson."

"Yeah. Don't know why he'd do that, though, if Sanderson wasn't in-country. That was part of the deal for this group," Grogan said.

"Thanks for that," Virgil said, standing up.

Grogan scratched his head and said, "You know . . . you probably want to talk to this professor who came to some of the meetings. The guys voted to let him in. I saw him—the professor—talking to Ray and Bob after the last meeting, out on the street. They were going at it for a while."

"Who's the professor? You say they were arguing?"

"Not arguing, just kinda . . . getting into it. One of those Vietnam discussions, where not everybody sees things the same way."

"I need that," Virgil said. "What's the guy's name? The professor's? Is he really a professor?"

"Yeah, he is. University of Wisconsin at Madison. Mead Sinclair. He's doing research on long-term aftereffects of the Vietnam War, is what he says," Grogan said. "This last meeting, we were pushing him, and he said he actually was an antiwar guy during Vietnam, and *then* he says he was in Hanoi with the Jane Fonda group during the war."

"Bet that made everybody happy," Virgil said.

"A couple guys wanted to throw his ass out on the street—but most of them, you know, say, *whatever*. Jane Fonda's old and that was a long time ago. Anyway, he sort of got into it with Ray and Bob. Maybe something came up. . . ."

"That's Mead Sinclair." Virgil wrote it in his notebook.

"Yep. Pretty snazzy name, huh?"

Two names: Mead Sinclair, Ray Bunton.

Virgil was out the door, halfway to his car, when Grogan called, "Hey, wait a minute. I might have something for you." Grogan walked up the side of the building to an ancient Nissan pickup, popped open the passenger-side door, and took out an old leather briefcase. He dug around inside it for a moment, then pulled out a sheaf of xeroxed papers, stapled together. "When the professor asked if he could sit in, he sent me a paper he wrote on Vietnam. . . . I never read it. Maybe it'd be of some use."

He handed it over: a reprint from *Mother Jones* magazine, "The Legacy of Agent Orange."

BACK ACROSS TOWN to BCA headquarters. Virgil left the truck in the parking lot, climbed the stairs to Davenport's office, asked his secretary, Carol, where he could sit with a computer.

"Lucas said you can use his office until he gets back. After that, we'll find something else," she said. "He said not to try to pick the lock on the gray steel file. Nothing else is locked."

"The gray steel one," Virgil said.

"Yeah. It's got employee evaluations and that sort of thing in there," she said. Carol was one of the rubbery blondes who dominated the state bureaucracy; sergeant-major types who kept the place going.

"Okay. I won't," Virgil said.

He sat in Davenport's chair, took a good look at the lock on the gray steel cabinet, and Carol asked from over his shoulder, from the doorway, "What do you think?"

"Not a chance," he said. "If it was standard file, I could pop it. This is more like a safe. Lucas's idea of a joke."

"I've never figured out where he keeps the key," she said.

"Probably on a key ring."

"Huh. I doubt it. A key ring would break the line of his trousers." She did a thing with her eyebrows, then said, "Ah, well," and, "Rose Marie's in the building."

"She's not looking for me?" Rose Marie was the state commissioner of public safety, the woman who got Davenport his job, with overall responsibility for the BCA and several other related agencies, like the highway patrol.

"Hard to tell," Carol said, and she went back to her desk.

Virgil turned to the computer, wiggled his fingers, called up Google, and typed in *Mead Sinclair.*

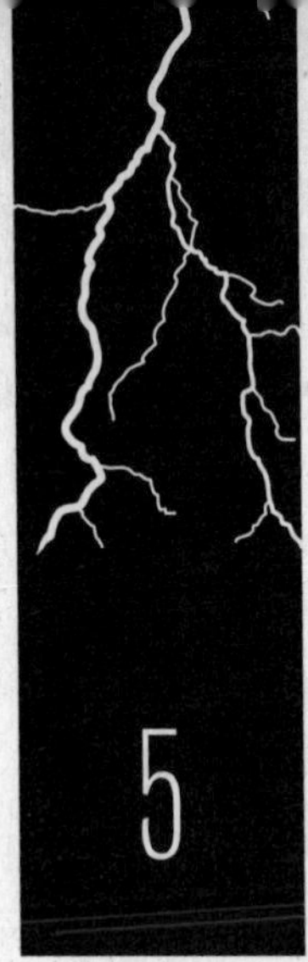

5

THE SCOUT sat at a laptop and worked over the photographs he'd taken outside Sanderson's house two nights before the killing. The photos had been taken with a Leica M8 with a Noctilux 50mm lens, with no light but that from nearby windows and, in two shots, from the headlights of a passing car.

He'd taken them in the camera's RAW format, which would allow him to enhance them in a program called Adobe Lightroom. He had a problem: the reflectivity of the 3M paint used in Minnesota license plates was too strong.

He had been exposing for the extreme low light, and the passing car had caught him by surprise. The direct light, from the headlights, had blown out the plates, leaving nothing but white rectangles on the back of the car. He hadn't had a chance to reduce the exposure before the passing car was gone.

Actually, he admitted to himself, he *did* have time, but hadn't thought to do it in the few seconds before the opportunity was gone.

The scout knew cameras, but he was not a photographic professional. He was, however, a professional in his own fields of reconnaissance and interrogation, and unrelentingly self-critical. Self-criticism, he believed, was the scout's key to survival. He'd not done well with the photography. He would work on it when he had a chance.

He worked through Lightroom's photo library, enlarging one shot after another, looking for the one shot that might have caught light from the passing car as it turned a corner, or light reflecting off the houses as the car went past, enough light to bring up the number, but not so much that it blew it out.

And he stopped to look at faces.

Three men, arguing on a T of concrete, where Sanderson's front walk met the public sidewalk, in a shaft of light from the door of Sanderson's house, with a little additional light from two front windows over the porch.

The tough-looking man in beaded leathers, who'd come in on a motorcycle, must be Bunton. He'd left the bike the best part of a block away—the scout had heard it but dismissed it, as its growl died away. Then, a couple of minutes later, Bunton showed, ambling down the sidewalk, looking like an advertising prototype of the aging Harley-Davidson dude.

He'd left the bike in the dark somewhere, the scout realized, and done a recon on foot. Bunton was being careful for some reason. The Utecht killing? The scout hadn't expected the targets to get worried until the second man went down. Of course, the lemon, if they knew about the lemons . . .

The blond man arguing with Bunton and Sanderson could be John Wigge, the third man named by Utecht. Or Wigge could be the man who hadn't gotten out of the car. That man, from the scout's angle, had never been more than a smear of white face in the back of the Jeep.

The scout hoped that Wigge was the man in the backseat. If he was, then the man on the sidewalk would be one of the unknowns, and that man had been driving the Jeep. If he could get the plate number, he might have one of the two missing names, he thought.

He let the license plate go for a moment and carefully snipped the face of the blond man from a half-dozen shots, brought them up one at a time, played with exposure and fill light, with brightness and contrast, with clarity, moving the sliders this way and that. When they were as good as they'd get, he added a bit of noise reduction and sharpening, and finally sent the pictures off to a diminutive Canon printer that pooped out photos like eggs out of an aluminum chicken.

When he was done, he collected the six four-by-sixes, spread them under the desk lamp, and inspected them. They'd never be accepted as passport photos, but they were good enough. When he saw this man again, he'd recognize him.

Hoped that the blond was one of the unknowns—but had the feeling that he was Wigge. Wigge had been a policeman, and the blond on the sidewalk had smelled of the police.

Back to the license plates. He went through each exposure with maximum care, and then, laughing quietly at his own obtuseness, realized that he didn't need to read all the numbers from one shot. First he'd had a problem with the simple photography, and now this. Getting old, scout?

He went back, found a leaf of light on one part of the plate, brought it up, played with the software sliders, got two and maybe three letters—he thought the third one was a *Z,* but it could have been a *2.* Found another plate, more fiddling, confirmed the *Z,* got a *5* from the other side of the dash. Could have been an *S,* but that wouldn't fit with what he'd seen of Minnesota license-plate style. Three numbers, three letters.

More looks, more sliders, he needed two more letters . . . and got them, first a *Y,* and then a *K,* and with another shot, he confirmed the *5* and got a *7.*

Couldn't get the last number: Had 5(?)7 YKZ, but also the make and color of the vehicle. Should be enough, because he also had a man who could get into the state automobile registration computer.

The scout picked up the phone, which he'd bought a week earlier at a Wal-Mart, and dialed the number.

A man's voice, quiet, cultured. "Yes." Nothing more.

"I have a license plate number. I need the name that goes with it."

"Give it to me." The scout read the number, and the man said, "Hold on."

A moment later, he was back. "The car is registered to a John Wigge."

"Ah."

"Good?"

"No. I'd hoped for another name. Is there a house number with this registration?"

"Of course."

The scout took the number, said, politely, "Thank you," and hung up.

Two names, then: Ray Bunton, John Wigge. Names they already had.

If he did not get more names from the two of them, then his mission would be done, and unsuccessful. He needed to spend some time with one of the men.

Spend some time with a knife . . .

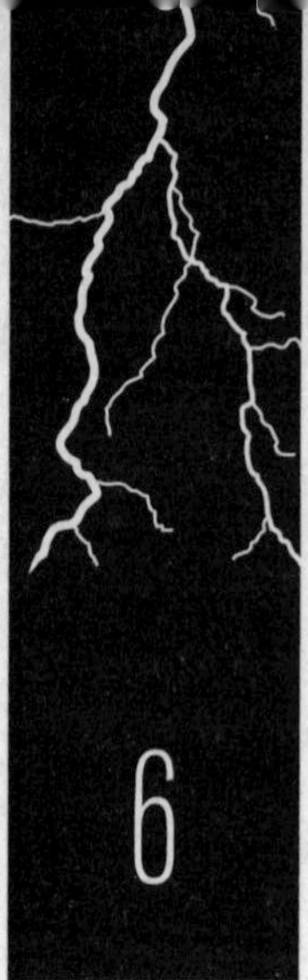

6

VIRGIL SAT back in the chair, feet up on Davenport's desk, and clicked.

Mead Sinclair never let any grass grow under his feet: Google dredged up stories about him that went back forty years before Google was invented.

Born in 1943, Sinclair had gone to South America as a high school senior, on a trip sponsored by a lefty educational foundation, to study the economic development of third-world countries. He later spent four years at Michigan, studying economics, then took a PhD at Harvard in economic history.

He'd apparently dodged the draft.

As an Ivy League grad student and later as an assistant professor at the University of Wisconsin at Madison, he'd taught summers during the 1960s and '70s at a variety of peace camps and academic conclaves.

He'd also gone to Hanoi during the Vietnam War, ostensibly as a stringer for *Ramparts* magazine, a latter-day John Reed.

According to the Google reports, he'd been wounded in a B-52 strike while touring the southern part of North Vietnam, and, recovering in a Hanoi hospital, he had written a long story about the use of acupuncture in wound care. Back in the United States, he married a Vietnamese-American woman whom he met at a rally in Madison. Their daughter, Mai, was born in Madison.

Later, because of his connections in Hanoi, he served as a go-between to negotiate the return of the remains of U.S. servicemen killed during the war. He was mentioned in several articles about Vietnamese tourism, and did some work with a consortium of U.S. and Australian hoteliers who wanted to build a new Asian Gold Coast south of Hanoi.

He wrote the study on the use of Agent Orange in Vietnam, and published it in 1990. The study was attacked online by another academic, from the conservative Heritage Foundation, who dismissed it as an overreaction to Sinclair's wife's death from cancer in 1988.

In 2004, Sinclair had been ordered to leave Vietnam for supporting a dissident Vietnamese academic. After that, nothing but a lot of references to academic papers and disputes.

Interesting guy; and his name, together with the Agent Orange paper, rang a bell in Virgil's memory. He took a look at the paper that Grogan had given him, skipping through it. *Kudzu*, he thought after a while. *This was the kudzu paper*.

In an effort to recover from the effects of the defoliant, the Vietnamese had decided to try kudzu, as a fast-growing, hardy perennial. The plant was hardy, all right: in ten years, with no natural enemies, it was burying the country. The Viets had been fighting the kudzu ever since, and were losing. Shouldn't fuck with Mother Nature; or if you did, Virgil mused, you should do it in somebody else's country.

The paper had been assigned reading in his ecological sciences senior seminar. He remembered the arguments about it—the first time he realized that even scientists would throw science overboard when it conflicted with their politics.

Huh.

He looked online for a local phone number or address, checked with directory assistance, and finally called, "Carol?"

She stuck her head in. "Yeah?"

"I need to find a guy—moved here last year, I can't find anything on him."

"Gimme his stuff. I'll get it to Sandy, she'll find him." Sandy was a part-time staff researcher, part of Davenport's team.

SINCLAIR HAD LED a prominent but fairly opaque life. Virgil read a number of profiles and found out only that he'd been sandy-haired and slender in the eighties; and one article mentioned that he was a poker player. That was it, on the personal level. Everything else was politics and left-wing infighting.

With Bunton, the opposite was true. Nothing on the Internet, not even his name. But in the state records . . .

Virgil first checked the criminal records, since Bunton was a biker and a tough guy. Got immediate hits: two thirty-day jail terms in Beltrami County in the late seventies, on assault and public drunkenness charges. Forty-five days in the Hennepin County Jail for drunk and disorderly and resisting arrest without violence, which is what cops charged you with when you'd done something to piss them off.

He'd been served a writ by an ex-wife to keep him away from her, and had protested that the wife was stealing and signing his veteran's disability checks. That meant that he'd suffered some kind of job-related injury in the military. Given his age, Virgil thought, it was possible that he'd been wounded in Vietnam. Northern Plains Indians were known for their willingness to volunteer for the toughest infantry jobs.

Bunton had been implicated, but not charged, in a fencing sting involving stolen car parts; had been arrested twice for simple assault; and had spent two weeks in the Ramsey County Jail on outstanding, unpaid traffic tickets. That had been four years earlier, and he'd stayed clear of the law since.

Getting old, Virgil thought. Probably still full of the piss, but not the vinegar.

Altogether, he knew exactly what Bunton would be like, but nothing about what he did for a living. It was possible, Virgil thought, that he didn't do anything.

CAROL STUCK HER head in. "Sandy got the Sinclair guy. Phone number and address."

"Excellent. Now I've got another guy I need to look for . . ."

He gave her the information on Bunton.

ON THE PHONE, Sinclair had a straight, clear teacher's voice, a classroom voice. He hadn't known about the Sanderson murder, he said, because he didn't watch much TV, and hadn't gotten into the habit of reading the local papers. "I get most of my news online," he said.

"But you knew Robert Sanderson," Virgil said.

"I knew who he was, but I didn't actually *know* him," he said. "We talked for a few minutes the other night, after the meeting . . . had a little debate about American actions in Vietnam."

"I'd like to come over and talk to you about the whole meeting," Virgil said.

"Come on over—but get something to eat first. We're just sitting down to lunch here, and I'm afraid there's not enough for three."

Sinclair gave Virgil a street address on Lincoln Avenue, one of the better parts of St. Paul, two or three miles west of the BCA office, up the hill from downtown. Having been disinvited from lunch, Virgil went to an I-94 diner and had a chicken potpie, with roughly a billion calories in chicken fat, which added flavor to the two pounds of salt included with the pie. He cut the salt with three Cokes, and left feeling like the Hindenburg.

SINCLAIR LIVED IN A liver-colored Victorian with a wide porch and—Virgil counted them, one-two-three-four—mailboxes. A condominium, then, or an apartment. He left the car under an elm, or, as a good ecological-sciences guy would say, a *doomed* elm, climbed the porch, and looked at the mailboxes. Sinclair was in apartment 1. The outer door was locked, but there were four doorbells next to a speaker disguised as a wooden eagle.

He pushed *1*, and a moment later a female voice said, "Yes?"

and Virgil said, "Virgil Flowers, BCA. I called Professor Sinclair an hour ago."

The door lock buzzed and Virgil let himself into the interior hallway. A sweeping stairway curved up to the left, protected by a walnut banister with gold-leaf accents. *Top floor must be 3 and 4,* Virgil thought. He stepped down the hall to his right, saw a *1* on a white door, and knocked.

The door was answered by a young Asian woman, tall and slender, with an oddly asymmetrical face and a chipped central incisor. Her forehead was flecked with three inch-long white scars, like knife cuts, halfway between her hairline and her right eyebrow. They almost looked like initiation scars, or tribal scars, Virgil thought, although everything he knew about tribal scars could be written on the back of a postage stamp.

"Dad's on the porch," the woman said. Nothing Asian about her accent. She sounded like she might have come from milking the local cow. "Come in."

Not pretty, he thought, but attractive. Tough upper lip; soft brown eyes.

On the way through the apartment, she chattered away, friendly, loose: "Virgil Flowers. I like that. Classical and corny at the same time—like *way* out in the country. Do all the cops here wear cowboy boots? They don't in Madison. . . . Did you ever go undercover as a singer or something? What does your shirt say? WWTDD? Is that a music group?"

"I can't talk about it, ma'am," Virgil said.

"Some kind of cop thing?"

The condo had a glassed-in back porch, looking out on a square of lawn, and Sinclair was out there, a lanky older man with still-blond hair, gray stubble on his chin. Women of a certain age would go for him in a big way, Virgil thought. He looked a little like the actor Richard Harris, in a loose white cotton dress shirt, the sleeves turned up, a gold tennis bracelet glittering from one wrist. He was sitting at a table, clicking at a laptop, with a glass of lemonade next to his hand.

When he saw them coming, he stood up and offered a soft, scholarly hand: "Mr. Flowers." He was six-three, Virgil thought, a couple inches taller than he was, with broad shoulders and a still-narrow waist.

"Mr. Sinclair," Virgil said. Virgil turned to the woman and said, "You never mentioned your name."

"Mai."

"Mai Sinclair?" Virgil asked.

"Yes. Not married. Unlucky in love, I guess," she said.

"Well, good," Virgil said. Sinclair was smiling at them, sat back in his chair, pointed Virgil to the other one.

"Do you handle homicides on a regular basis, Mr. Flowers?" he asked.

"Call me Virgil," Virgil said as he sat down and stretched out his legs. "Most of my homicides are pretty irregular. Damnedest thing. I'd give anything for a good old beer-bottle domestic. I sometimes get so confused, I don't know what to do next."

"Well . . . Consider what each soil will bear, and what each refuses," Sinclair said.

Virgil laughed and clapped his hands. "You looked that up before I got here. You didn't just pull that out. . . ."

Mai had lingered, and asked, looking between them, "What?"

"He's quoting Virgil at me," Virgil said. "That's never happened before, and I've talked to some pretty smart fellas."

Sinclair, surprised that Virgil had recognized the line, said, "Well."

Mai said to Sinclair, "He won't tell me what his T-shirt means. The 'WW' is 'What Would,' and the last 'D' is 'Do,' but he won't tell me the rest."

"We can't talk about it," Sinclair said. "That's the first rule."

"The first rule of what?" she asked.

"Can't talk about it," Virgil said, nodding to her father.

"What?" Hands on her hips.

"Can't talk about it," Sinclair repeated, looking up at his daughter, shaking his head.

She took them in for a moment, then said, "Well, poop on you both. I'll go iron my underwear."

"You wrote a paper, about twenty years ago, about Agent Orange, and how the Vietnamese tried to refoliate with kudzu," Virgil said.

"So you looked up my vita on the Internet," Sinclair said.

"I did," Virgil said. "But I also read the paper in my senior seminar—I majored in ecological science—and I remembered it when I looked it up. We talked about it for quite a while; about the unexpected effects of good intentions."

Sinclair was pleased. "The paper was controversial, but shouldn't have been—it was a good piece of work," he said. "But we were coming out of the Reagan years, and the triumphalism, and nobody wanted to hear about the collateral damage we'd caused around the world with these crazy military adventures." He leaned forward, intent now, jabbed his finger at Virgil in a professorial, mentor-to-student way. "I'll tell you, Virgil, what this country needs more than anything in the world—more than anything—is a sane energy policy. That's what I'm writing about now. Energy, environment, it all ties together. Instead, we get wars, we get military adventures, we spend two years fighting about whether a president got a blow job, a little squirt in the dark? I mean, who could really care? This country does everything but take care of business. We just . . . ah, that's not what you're here for. . . ."

He settled back, looked tired. "So. What're you here for?"

"I mostly agree with everything you just said, to get that out of the way," Virgil said. "But. Robert Sanderson got himself killed in a pretty unpleasant way, and his body was dropped on a veterans' memorial. . . ."

Virgil detailed the Sanderson killing, and then the Utecht murder, pointing out the similarities, and how, two nights before the killing, Sanderson was seen arguing with two men in the street outside his house.

"At least one of them was Ray Bunton. We're looking for him, but haven't found him yet. When we went down to the vet center to inquire, they told us that you'd been sitting in on their therapy sessions, the talk. And that you'd spoken to Bunton and Sanderson afterward. We're wondering if they might have said anything that would cast some light on this murder."

Sinclair made a moue and, after a moment's consideration, said, "I have to tell you, Virgil, it runs against the grain to talk to the police about people who aren't around to defend themselves."

"This is not a political deal," Virgil said.

"Well, it probably it is, at some level. The veterans' memorials and all." Sinclair leaned back in his chair, hands behind his head, fingers interlaced. "But I recognize what you're saying. I can tell you that there was something strange, something . . . tense going on between Sanderson and Ray Bunton. Did you . . . do you know if Sanderson ever *went* to Vietnam? Was he in combat?"

"Not unless he was some kind of special forces guy, undercover. As far as we know, he worked in a headquarters company in Korea as a mechanic. I can't believe . . . I mean, he was pretty young at the time. I don't see how he could have gotten trained enough, important enough, to have a heavy cover that would have been kept all these years. So I don't think he was there. His records say Korea, and that's what he told his girlfriend. On the other hand, he was at this vets' session . . ."

"And he said something about the Viets being a bunch of frogs . . . meaning Frenchmen . . . that made me think he'd been there," Sinclair said. "He said it in a way . . . I don't know. Anyway, at that point, Bunton was staring him down, and Sanderson saw it and shut up. On the street, I was just coming out the door, and they were already out there, and I heard Bunton say something about 'keeping your mouth shut.' I was curious, I dug around, but they told me to take a hike. I'd let that Fonda shit out . . ." He grinned wryly. "Some of those guys'll never forget. If Jane doesn't outlive them, her gravestone's gonna have urine stains all over it."

"Huh," Virgil said.

"Are you going to ask me where I was last night?"

Virgil yawned and said, "Sure. Where were you last night?"

"Asleep." He laughed. "Mai and I ordered out, ate in—around eight o'clock—and I did some correspondence on the Internet, and Mai and I had a little talk about my health . . . and then we went to bed."

"Your health?"

Sinclair tapped his chest. "Had a nuclear stress test yesterday morning. Starting to show what the cardiologist calls 'anomalies.' I eat eggs, I eat bacon, I drink milk. They want me to eat air with some plastic spray on it."

"So how bad? Bypass?" Virgil asked.

"Not yet—but that could be down the road. We're gonna do an angiogram and figure out what to do. They could put a stent in," he said. "That's why Mai's up here—she's trying to get me to go home to Madison, where she can keep an eye on me."

"Hmmph. Makes me nervous just hearing about it. I do like my bacon," Virgil said. Then he asked, "Why are you here, anyway? In St. Paul? You're a big shot in Madison."

"A couple reasons. Teaching, mostly. I was drying up in Madison. I had this gig, I'd do my gig, and it was like I was teaching from reflex. Grad students, small classes." Virgil was listening, but thought it all sounded rehearsed. Scripted. Sinclair was saying, "So I had this seminar, and one day we sat working through class, and every one of the students yawned at one time or another. I started noticing. So—I took a year's leave. Got a teaching job here: I teach nothing but freshmen and sophomores, they ask off-the-wall questions, they push me around, they've got no respect. It's working—it's like fresh air."

"Why would the University of Minnesota be any different than Wisconsin? Except that we don't smoke as much dope?"

"I'm not teaching at Minnesota. I'm teaching at Metro State," Sinclair said, amused. "I went *way* down-market."

"All right," Virgil said. "You said a couple of reasons. What's the other one?"

"You know Larson International, the hotels? Headquarters down in Bloomington?"

"Sure. I've got a frequent-guest card for Mobile Inn," Virgil said. "Owned by Minnesota's fourth-richest billionaire."

Sinclair nodded. "They're trying to build some big resort hotels in Asia—Vietnam, Thailand, maybe even China. I'm consulting with them on the Vietnam project. I've still got a bit of a reputation there. The idea is, I can help them with government contacts and so on."

"Can you?"

"Yes. I speak the language and I know how things work," Sinclair said. "You know, who gets greased, and how heavily. So they get their money's worth."

MAI CAME BACK and took a chair, swiveled it back and forth with her excellent legs. "I looked it up on the Net—WWTDD. What Would Tyler Durden Do. Fight Club. The first rule of Fight Club is that you don't talk about Fight Club."

Virgil and Sinclair looked at each other, then Sinclair turned back to his daughter, a puzzled look on his face. "What are you talking about?"

"Aww . . ." She looked at Virgil. "I really need to go dancing," she said. "I signed up for a dance class here, but it's all . . . dance. I need to go to a club. You know the clubs?"

"I know a few." Also a few that he'd have to stay away from, like the ones that Janey went to. "You ever do any line dancing?"

She was stricken. "Oh, no. You are *not* serious. . . ."

VIRGIL GOT AROUND to asking Sinclair where he was the night of Utecht's murder, and Sinclair got up, came back with a leatherette calendar, put on a pair of reading glasses, paged through it, and said, "Same thing as with last night's. I was here, asleep."

"The best alibi of all," Virgil said.

"Why's that?" Sinclair asked, his crystal blue eyes peering over the top of the half glasses.

"Because it can't be broken," Virgil said.

Sinclair looked at Mai. "He's smarter than he looks."

"Thank God," she said. "He looks like he ought to be waxing his surfboard. If they've got surf in Iowa."

Virgil laughed again, said, "Y'all are pickin' on me."

"I like the way that hick accent comes and goes," Sinclair said to Mai. "It's like a spring breeze—first it's here, and then it's gone."

"Okay. The hell with it. I don't even know why I'm talking to you." Virgil pushed off the chair, but Sinclair held up a hand. "So Sanderson and this other man were executed? Is that what you're saying?"

"That's what it looks like." Virgil hesitated, then said, "One other thing—they both had lemons stuffed in their mouths."

"Ah . . . shit." The word sounded strange, and peculiarly vulgar, coming from Sinclair, with his aristocratic manner.

"What?"

Sinclair glanced at Mai. "When the Vietnamese execute a prisoner—a political prisoner, or even a murderer—they'll gag him by stuffing a lemon in his mouth. Hold it there with tape. Duct tape. Keeps them from talking while they're walking out to the wall."

"That's pretty goddamn interesting," Virgil said.

Mai rolled her eyes. "And probably an urban myth."

"What would you know about it?" Sinclair snapped.

His daughter turned her face, embarrassed by the sudden pique. "It's too dramatic, it's too weird. Why would anybody do something like that? It's got the earmarks of a legend; if you'd studied literature, you'd know that."

"Ahh . . . They did it, take my word for it," Sinclair said irritably. To Virgil: "*We* don't have anything to do with any of this, but it sounds to me like it goes back to Vietnam. Somehow. I'd take a good close look at Sanderson. See what unit he was in. See if there's anything blacked out in his file. Some of these Vietnam vets, they're crazier than a barrel of wood ticks. They're getting old and ready to die. You might have an old rogue killer with an agenda. He might be good at it, if he was Phoenix, or something. . . ."

"I heard about Phoenix when I was in," Virgil said. "You'd hear about it from these old sergeants-major. Sounded like there was an element of bullshit to it."

"Of course there was! Of course there was!" Sinclair said, leaning forward and rapping on the table with his knuckles. "But there's a core of reality to it, too. We *did* have assassins. We *did* murder people in their homes. We *did* hire men with silencers and guns and no useful skill but murder. We even had a name for it—wet work! Look it up! Look it up!"

Virgil exhaled, stuck his notebook in his hip pocket, and said, "I better find Ray."

Sinclair relaxed, suddenly affable again, and he smiled and said, "Good luck to you."

MAI TAGGED ALONG to the front door, walking close to Virgil's side. He said, "I would be delighted to take you dancing anytime you want, ma'am, except not tonight, because I gotta find this guy." His words were tumbling out, a little confused, but that was one of his more endearing traits, he'd been told, so he worked it. "I can't make any promises about tomorrow or any other night, because of this murder thing, but if I could call you about six o'clock, some night when I'll know what I'm doing . . ."

"I'm usually home by then," she said. "You're a good dancer?"

"I gotta couple moves," Virgil said. He tried to look modest.

"I noticed that, but I was talking about dancing," she said. They both laughed and Virgil said, "I got your number someplace."

"Here." She stepped over to an entryway table, pulled open a drawer, and took out a pen. Taking Virgil's hand in hers, she wrote a number in his palm, a process so erotic that Virgil feared erective embarrassment. He left hastily, Mai in the doorway, watching him all the way through the front door, smiling.

If Jesus Christ had a girlfriend, Virgil thought, that's what she'd look like.

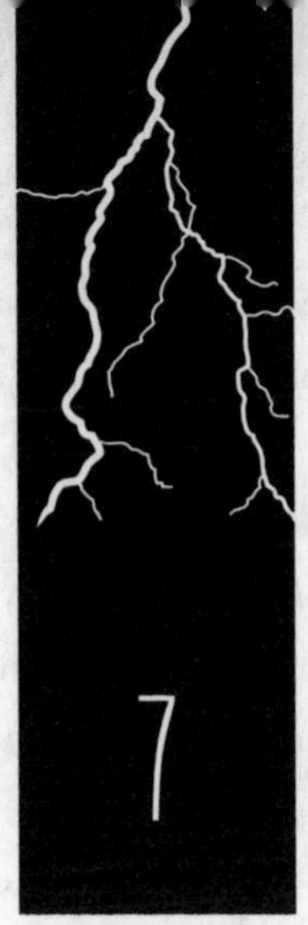

VIRGIL WALKED down to his truck, climbed in, thought about it for a minute, then drove around the block so the back of the truck was looking down at the Sinclairs' condo. He shut the truck down, got his laptop, phone, camera, and an oversized photography book called *Photojournalism*, and crawled into the back.

Minnesota allows only a certain level of window tinting in cars, so that highway patrolmen won't walk into a gun they can't see. Virgil's was twice as dark as the permissible tint, which was okay for police vehicles used for surveillance. Virgil didn't use the 4Runner much for surveillance, but since it was always full of fishing tackle or hunting gear or camera equipment, the heavy tint worked as insurance, keeping the eyes of the greedy out of the back of his truck.

And it also worked for surveillance, as intended.

Sitting in the back, he was invisible from the outside, and a camping pillow made a comfortable-enough seat. If he'd jolted Sinclair in any way, then he might make a move. If not, he had things to do, which could be done from the back of the truck.

He called Carol and asked, "So where's Ray Bunton?"

"Can't find him. The cops at Red Lake are all out working, there's nobody to talk to us. But they're gonna call back," she said.

"Check them every five minutes," Virgil said.

That done, he opened the photojournalism book to the section called "Techniques of the Sports Shooter" and settled in for a little study, trying out things with his new Nikon as he did it.

The good thing about the new digital cameras, like his D3, was that you could see the shot instantly. He was working on his panning technique, shooting the occasional passerby, when Mead Sinclair walked out of his house, looked both ways, and then turned toward Virgil's truck.

Virgil took a shot or two as Sinclair came up—couldn't hurt to have a couple of current shots—and went on past. Sinclair never looked at the truck. He seemed to be talking to himself, or maybe singing to himself, and he had a hand-sized spiral notebook in one hand, with a pen clipped to it, and up the block, he stopped and made a note, then continued on. An intellectual, Virgil thought.

At the end of the block, Sinclair crossed the street and started along the next block, and Virgil watched him through the windshield. At the end of the second block, he wrapped around to his right, headed out to Grand Avenue.

Virgil followed in the truck, crossed the street that Sinclair had taken, saw him walking up the block. Virgil took the opportunity to back up a bit, watched him in a narrow gap between the edge of a house and a tree trunk. Sinclair crossed the street at the corner, carefully looking both ways before he crossed, and a moment later was out of sight again.

He could lose him right there, but Virgil took the chance and drove on another block, then right, to the end of the block, and eased out, looking down the block, and saw Sinclair crossing Grand, heading into a restaurant.

Sinclair had just eaten, he'd said. Virgil hadn't been invited. . . . So why the restaurant? Virgil parked, waiting to see who he might come out with—or who might come out that was interesting.

Nobody came out but Sinclair, a minute or so after he went in. He recrossed the street, then turned away, down the block, retracing his steps: might be headed home. Virgil made a quick turn, went down to the end of the block, found a bush he could stop behind. A minute later, Sinclair appeared a block away, crossed the street again, and headed back toward his house.

Virgil said, "Shoot," and wrestled the truck in a quick U. Had he missed somebody? He should have waited outside the restaurant.

Nobody came out for ten minutes, and then it was two elderly ladies. Another five minutes, and two fat guys in golf shirts, one picking ferociously at his teeth with a toothpick. They got into a Cadillac and drove away; they seemed unlikely.

Virgil decided to look for himself. Walked down to the restaurant, stood at the hostess stand for a moment, checking out the ten or twelve people in the booths. They all looked unremarkable, and seemed focused on food or conversation. The hostess, who might have been a college girl from Macalester, came over and said, "One?"

"Ah, I was here to meet a guy, but I'm late, and I'm afraid I might have missed him. Good-looking older guy, still blond . . ."

"Oh—the professor?"

"Yeah. That's him," Virgil said.

"He was here, but made a call and then he left again. He might be trying to call you."

"Thanks," Virgil said. He backed away, glanced toward the restrooms, saw the old-fashioned black coin phone on the wall. "I'll try him again on the phone."

He went back and looked at it: the phone dial showed a number, and he jotted it down in the palm of his hand, under the number that Mai had written there.

Outside again, he thought about it. Sinclair had just walked four blocks to a cold phone to make a call. Interesting. . . .

He noted the time and called Carol. "See if you can get a subpoena for the phone records for a pay phone at Stern's Café, on Grand. Here's the number . . ."

"You want me to check informally first?" She meant that Davenport knew a guy who could tell them whether a subpoena would be a waste of time.

"If you could. Get in touch with Red Lake?"

"Not yet; still trying."

VIRGIL RANG OFF, looked at the phone for a moment, groped in his briefcase for his black book, punched in a number.

"Harold; it's Virgil Flowers in Minnesota."

"Yeah, Virgil. What's up?"

"I got a killer who's executed two older guys, left their bodies on vet memorials, with lemons stuck in their mouths. Killed them with a .22, two shots, maybe silenced. You ever hear of anything like that, with the cartels, the mob, or anybody?"

"New one on me," Harold Gomez said. He was an agent with the DEA. "You got weird shit up there. I always said that."

"If you have a line into the FBI, into that serial-killer unit, whatever it is . . . could you check the lemon thing? Without burning up any of your personal credit?"

"Sure. I know a guy who knows those guys," Gomez said. "How fast you need it?"

"Well, if you get a hit, I need to know right away," Virgil said. "The killer guy, we don't know that he's left town. If he's crazy, if it's business, or what it is. If he's got a list, it could get ugly."

"I'll call—but to tell you the truth, it sounds more like some kind of goddamn Russian thing or Armenian or Kazakh. They're into the rituals and warnings and shit. The mob, those assholes just shoot your ass and bury you in the woods with Jimmy."

"Jimmy?"

"Hoffa."

"Oh, yeah. Listen—another guy told me that the Vietnamese executioners sometimes stick lemons in the mouths of the people they're going to execute," Virgil said. "Like gags. If you can find any reference to that . . . maybe old Vietnam guys or something?"

"Sounds kinky. Let me check," Gomez said. "You on your cell phone?"

"I am. One more thing, Harold? See if the guys in the serial-killer unit are looking at any chain of old veteran deaths. Even without lemons and memorials."

"Sure."

"I owe you, Harold."

HE CLICKED OFF, got ready to move, but Carol called back.

"We talked to a guy in Red Lake who knows Bunton, and they're out looking for a guy to call you back. Sandy dug up some pictures of him, she e-mailed them to you, along with every file she can find on him. Income tax, all of that. She can't get into the military records, but there's a reference in one of his DWI files that he was treated for alcoholism at the Veterans Administration Hospital, and that he did service in Vietnam . . . so he's ex-military."

"All right. I sort of knew that, but it all helps."

HE WAS FIVE MINUTES from a Starbucks, where he had an online account. He got a white chocolate mocha Frappuccino, found a table, and brought the computer up as he sipped.

The photos of Bunton showed a hard, square-looking man, always in T-shirts. In one photo, he glared at the camera, a headband tight around his forehead, an eagle feather dangling over one ear. With his pale eyes, he didn't look particularly Indian, Virgil thought—more like an IRA dead-ender. Was Bunton an Irish name? Or maybe Scots? Didn't sound a hell of a lot like Ojibwa.

Whatever.

The rest of the Bunton file told him what he'd already guessed—Vietnam, hanging out, motorcycles, alcoholism, dope, and sporadic employment involving automobile parts.

When he finished, Virgil shut down the computer, looked at his watch.

Goddamn Bunton.

He stood up to leave, but his phone rang. Carol. He sat down again, flipped it open, and said, "Yeah?"

"Informally, the phone call went to the Minneapolis Hyatt. I've got the number, but not the room. . . ."

THE MINNEAPOLIS HYATT is all tangled up in the Skyway system, and Virgil, operating on Kentucky windage, put his truck in the wrong parking ramp and debouched into the Skyway, not realizing that he wasn't where he thought he was. He spent ten minutes running around like a hamster in a plastic habitat, before he found a map and realized his mistake.

The hotel's lobby was empty, but the Hyatt desk was being run by a young woman who was far too sophisticated and generally *out there* to be running a hotel desk. Virgil had the uneasy feeling that if he asked her to connect a phone number to a room and a name, she'd call a manager, who might want to see a subpoena . . . blah-blah-blah.

He looked around and saw an elderly rusty-haired bellhop sitting on a window ledge, reading a sex newspaper called *Seed*, which, Virgil happened to know, was the publishing arm of an outlaw motorcycle gang.

Virgil went over and sat down next to him. The bellhop looked like a model for the next Leprechaun horror film, with a nose the size of a turnip and a bush of red hair shot through with gray.

He glanced at Virgil and said, "You look like a hippie, but you're a cop." He was wearing a tag that said *George*. "Looking for hookers?"

"Nope. I'm trying to find out which room is connected to a particular phone number without having to go through a lot of bureaucratic bullshit," Virgil said. "The girl behind the desk looks like she lives for bureaucratic bullshit."

The bellhop looked at the girl behind the desk and said, "Somebody turned me in for smoking in the stairwell last winter. It was about a hundred below zero, which is why I was there instead of outside. I think she's the one. She's like this no-smoking Nazi. When I was bitching about it, she said it was for my own good. I said, 'What, getting fired?' Bitch."

"You think you could work this sense of anger and disenfranchisement into a room number? And a name?" Virgil turned his hand over; a folded-over twenty-dollar bill was pinched between his index and middle fingers.

"What's the number?" George asked as he lifted out the twenty.

"Atta boy," Virgil said. He wrote the number on a slip of paper and passed it over.

The bellhop disappeared into the back and a moment later was back. "Got the number and the names. It's Tai and Phem, a couple of Japs."

"Japs?" Virgil was puzzled. "The names sound Vietnamese."

George shrugged. "Whatever. I'll tell you what, though, they are bad, bad tippers. The other night, Tai—he's the tall one—orders a steak sandwich and fries at midnight. They don't give those things away, that's a thirty-dollar meal. He gave me a fuckin' buck."

"What else you got?"

"Well—just what everybody knows," George said. "They're Canadian."

"Canadian?"

"Yeah. They've been here, off and on, mostly on, for three months.

They're supposedly working on a big deal with Larson International to build hotels."

"Larson," Virgil said.

"Yeah, you know."

"I know." The chain that Sinclair worked for. "So they're high-fliers."

"Well, if they are, somebody's got them on a pretty friggin' tight expense account—either that, or they're putting down twenty percent for tips and keeping the cash."

"They're that kind of guys?" Virgil asked.

"They're, uh . . . They're some guys I wouldn't fuck with," George said.

"You're fuckin' with them now," Virgil said.

The bellhop looked startled. "You're not going to *tell* them."

"No. I just wanted to see if you'd jump," Virgil said, standing up, stretching. "You did, which means, you know, maybe you're not bullshitting me."

"You watch yourself, cowboy," the bellhop said. "Them Japs is some serious anacondas." He made a pistol shape with his thumb and forefinger, poked Virgil above the navel, and shuffled away.

VIRGIL HAD SPENT a good part of his life knocking on doors that had nobody behind them, entering rooms that people had just left, so he was mildly surprised when a slender man with longish hair, combed flat over the top of his head, and apparently nailed in place with gel, opened the door and said, pleasantly, "Yes?"

"Virgil Flowers, Minnesota Bureau of Criminal Apprehension," Virgil said, flipping open his ID. "I talked to Mead Sinclair a while ago, he said you might be able to help me with some Vietnam-related stuff. Are you Mr. Tai?"

"Yes. Well . . . Okay, come in," Tai said. He was thin, with a face that was delicate but tough. The splice lines of a major scar cut down his forehead, another white scar line hung under his left eye, another below his lip. "We're working right now, it's coming up on early morning in Vietnam, the markets are opening . . ."

"Just take a couple of minutes," Virgil said.

He followed Tai into the suite's main room, where another Asian man sat on a couch, with a laptop on his knee and a telephone headset on his head. He was shoeless, wearing a T-shirt and blue silky gym shorts. "My partner, Phem," Tai said.

Phem didn't look up from his laptop but said, "What's up, eh?"

He said the "eh" perfectly: Canucks, Virgil thought, not Vietnamese.

Tai pointed at a chair, and Virgil settled in and said, "Have you ever heard of the Vietnamese, uh, what would you call it . . . custom? The Vietnamese custom of putting a lemon in a man's mouth, as a gag, before they execute him?"

Tai had arranged his face in a smile, which vanished in an instant. "Jesus Christ, no. What's up with that?"

"You guys are from . . ."

"Toronto," Tai said. "Born and raised."

"But your parents must have been from Vietnam?"

He nodded. "Saigon. Got out just before the shit hit the fan. I spoke Vietnamese until I was three, lucky for me. Hard language to learn later on," he said. "It helps when you're running around the rim. Phem the same, except he started English a little later."

"The rim?"

"The Pacific Rim," Tai said.

"Ah . . . so . . . well, heck, I just about used up my questions," Virgil admitted. "That lemon thing is really bugging me. Have you seen the stories on TV, or the papers, about the guys who were murdered and left on veterans' memorials?"

"Something about it, but we usually mostly read the financial pages."

Phem nudged Tai, tapped his computer screen. Tai leaned over to look and said, "No way," then turned back to Virgil.

"There's some connection with Vietnam," Virgil said. "One of the murdered men was going to meetings with a Vietnam vet group, and he'd talked to Sinclair, and I know nothing about Vietnam. Hell, I've never been much further away from here than Amarillo, Texas."

Tai said, "Amarillo? You ever have the chicken-fried steak at the Holiday Inn?"

"Oh, Lord, I *have*," Virgil said. "That one right on Interstate 40?"

"That always has some soldiers hanging around?"

"Ah, man, that's the one. . . ."

They talked about the effects of the chicken-fried steak for a minute, the effects lasting, depending on which direction you were going, at least to Elk City, Oklahoma (east), or Tucumcari, New Mexico (west).

When the talk died down and he couldn't think of any more sane questions, Virgil stood up, took out a business card, and handed it to Tai. "Well, shoot. If you have the time, ask some of your Vietnamese friends about lemons. Give me a call."

Tai tilted his head back and forth. "Mm. I think that would be . . .

inappropriate . . . for people in our position. But I'll tell you what you could do. You could call a guy named Mr. Hao Nguyen at the Vietnamese embassy in Ottawa, and ask him. Don't tell him you got his name from me, for Christ's sakes."

"Who is he?"

"The resident for the Vietnamese intelligence service," Tai said. He stepped across to the telephone desk, picked up a small leather case, took out a business card, wrote on the back with a gold pen, and passed it to Virgil. He'd written, *Hao Nguyen*.

"Really? You know that sort of stuff?" Virgil asked.

"The embassy isn't that big," Tai said. "You go through a process of elimination, figuring out who is really doing what. Whoever's left is the intelligence guy."

"Really."

Tai was easing him toward the door. "No big secret. Don't tell him you talked to me. That would hurt. I would be interested in his reaction." He giggled. "Really get his knickers in a bunch."

"I'll give him a jingle," Virgil said.

Just before he went through the door, he let Tai see that he was checking the facial scars: "Play a little hockey?"

"High school goalie. Started my last two years," Tai said.

"A Patrick Roy poster above the bed?"

Tai smiled and shook his head. "There are actually several cities in Canada, Mr. Flowers. Pat Roy was a hell of a goalie, but he played for Montreal. If I'd put up a Pat Roy poster, I'd have been strangled in my sleep. By my brother."

"Shows you what I know about hockey," Virgil said as the door closed behind him. The lock went *snick*.

"And don't let the door hit you in the ass," Virgil said to the empty corridor.

As he was going down in the elevator, he realized that Phem had said three words to him: "What's up, eh?"

Back in the truck, Virgil looked at the business card: Nguyen Van Tai, Bennu Consultants. An address on Merchant Street in Toronto.

DIDN'T WANT TO do it; did it anyway.

Mai Sinclair said she went to a dance studio in the evening.

It was almost evening.

He parked two blocks down from the Sinclairs' condo, half the truck behind a tree. He could see the front porch clearly. He settled down, took out his cell phone and called the information operator, and got the number for the Vietnamese embassy.

A woman answered, and Virgil said, "Could I speak to Mr. Hao Nguyen? I'm not sure I'm pronouncing that quite the right way."

"I'll see if Mr. Nguyen is in." No problem there.

Nguyen came on a moment later, a deep voice with a heavy Vietnamese accent: "Mr. Nguyen speaking."

"Mr. Nguyen, my name is Virgil Flowers. I'm a police officer with the state of Minnesota down in the U.S. I was told that you might be able to help me with a question."

"Well . . . Officer Flowers . . . I'm a cultural attaché here. I'm not sure that I'm the person . . ."

"You should know," Virgil said. "What I need to know is, when the Vietnamese execute a criminal, or whatever, do you guys stick a lemon in his mouth to keep him from protesting?"

"What?"

"Do you stick a lemon . . ."

"Is this a joke?"

"No, no. We've had two murders down here, that I'm investigating, and both of the dead men had lemons stuck in their mouths," Virgil said. "I was told that Vietnamese executioners sometimes did that, you know, like firing squads, to keep the man quiet."

"Why would I know something like that? Who told you to call me?"

"Well, I was told that you're really the resident for Vietnamese intelligence, and that it's something you would know."

"What? Intelligence? Who would tell you such a thing?"

"Just a guy I met down here," Virgil said.

"I don't understand a single thing you are saying. I am hanging up now. Good-bye." The phone banged down.

"Sounded like a big 'Yes' to me," Virgil said aloud.

HE KILLED MORE TIME with his camera, and was looking through a long lens at the Sinclair apartment when Mai came out, forty-five minutes later, carrying a gym bag. Watched her walk away.

He let her get another block down the street, then started the truck, eased onto Lincoln. She walked four blocks, then over to Grand, where she became involved in a curious incident.

Two skaters turned the corner, slipping along on their boards, hats backward, long shirts, calf-length baggy pants, fingerless gloves, nearly twins except that one was black and one was white.

The white kid said something to her, with a body gesture that was right next to a smirk, and Mai stopped and said something back to him, and held up a finger; and said something else, and waited; and the two boys turned away, got off the sidewalk, and slipped on down the street.

Virgil eased the truck back behind the corner before Mai could turn far enough to see it. When he eased forward again, she'd gone on, taking a left on Grand. He went up to the corner, looked left, and saw her turn at a tan-brick building with the red scrawl of a neon sign in the window. He was at too sharp an angle to read the sign, but it looked like a dance studio.

He thought about going back after the kids, to ask what she'd said to them, but there'd be a risk in that if they were local, and if she should encounter them again.

Besides, he didn't really need to. He knew what had been said.

Something close to:

"Hey, mama, you wanna feel a *really* hard muscle?"

And she'd said, "Go away, little boys. You don't want to mess with me."

They'd gone, because they'd seen the same thing that Virgil saw.

Virgil didn't know a hell of a lot about karate or kung fu or jujitsu, but standing there, Mai had looked like one of the sword women in the Chinese slasher films that Virgil had seen three of, with titles like *The Pink Flowers of Eternity and Swords & Shit.*

A certain pose that didn't say dance, but said, instead, "I'll pluck your fuckin' eyeballs out."

You find out the most interesting things by spying on people, Virgil thought. Especially if you're a cynical and evil motherfucker.

Just take the girl dancing, Virgil.

DAVENPORT CALLED AS VIRGIL was driving back toward the motel.

"What're you doing?" Davenport asked.

"Nothing much. How about you?"

"Nothing much here," Davenport said.

"Okay. Well, talk to you tomorrow," Virgil said.

"Virgil . . . I'm too tired. Just tell me."

Virgil gave him a recap of the day, and when he finished, there was a moment of silence, then Davenport said, "Good."

"One thing. These guys, Tai and Phem—you know anybody in the Mounties who might take a peek into a computer, see what's up with them?"

"I don't, but Larry McDonald up in Bemidji, he works with them all the time. I got his number here."

Virgil jotted the number on his pad, on the seat beside him, and the car on the left honked as he swerved slightly into that lane. "Fuck you," he muttered.

"What?"

"Not you. Guy just honked at me," Virgil said. "Road rage. Okay, I'll jack up McDonald, but I think my best bet is Bunton. I can't find anybody to tell me about him."

"Be patient; you'll have him by noon tomorrow," Davenport said. "The big question is, are there more targets? It'd be sort of a Bad Thing if another body turned up."

"Thank you, boss."

McDonald, an agent in the BCA's northern Minnesota office, was in the middle of dinner, which he mentioned in passing, and which Virgil ignored. He explained what he needed, and McDonald said, "I can do that—but my guy up there, the computer guy, won't be in until tomorrow morning."

"Anything we can get," Virgil said. "People are starting to grit their teeth down here."

Another phone call from Carol. "The Sinclair guy just called, and he's pissed."

"Did he say what about?"

"He said something about some Vietnamese . . ."

"I'll call him."

He did.

Sinclair said, "Why did you tell Phem and Tai that I gave you their names? They think you're investigating them. I could be out of a job. How in the hell did you even know about them?"

"Asked around," Virgil said. "You mentioned working for Larson on the hotels that they want to build in Vietnam, and I thought, well, maybe there'd be some Vietnamese I could talk to. Turns out they're Canadian."

"Goddamnit, Flowers, it's gonna take forever to paper this over."

"I could give them a call," Virgil said.

"But you *lied* to them," Sinclair said. "What could you tell them this time?"

"That I misspoke?"

Sinclair said, "Ah, man." Then, "Listen, you want to talk to them again, don't bring my name into it, okay? I mean, you're really messing me up here."

VIRGIL APOLOGIZED one last time as he rolled into the motel parking lot. He had one foot out of the truck when Sandy, the researcher, called.

"I had to tell some lies," she said.

Cops all lie, Virgil thought. But he said, "Let's meet at the cathedral. I'll sprinkle some holy water on your ass."

"Sounds like a deal," she said, with a slender note of invitation in her voice. She paused, looking for a reaction.

"Sandy!" He was shocked. Sandy was the office virgin, though, he'd noticed, from a move he'd seen with another guy in a hallway, actual virginity was unlikely.

"Chicken," she said. "All right, what I got is this. If Ray Bunton got an unexpected tax refund, and it was sent to an old girlfriend, and the girlfriend called his cousin up in Red Lake and asked where she could send the check, she'd get a phone number to call. The phone number is attached to an address in south Minneapolis, off Franklin."

"Atta girl."

"That's what I need. More atta girls." And she was gone.

Ray Bunton: Virgil looked up at the motel, sighed, and got back in the truck.

BUNTON WAS living in a ramshackle place off Franklin Avenue south of the Minneapolis loop, a house that hadn't been painted in fifty years, a worn-out lawn that had been driven on repeatedly, dandelions glowing from patches of oily grass.

Virgil left the truck a few doors down so he could look at the house for a moment as he walked along; and after he stepped into the street, he thought about it for a moment, reached under the seat, got his pistol in the leather inside-the-belt holster, and stuck it in the small of his back, under his jacket.

As he headed down the street, he could hear somebody playing an old Black Sabbath piece, "Paranoid," pounding out of a stereo or boom box. From the end of a cracked two-strip driveway that squeezed between the close-set houses, he could see a garage in back of Bunton's place. A guy was lying under a rusted-out Blazer, which was up on steel ramps. A couple of work lights lay on the floor, shining on the underside of the car. A motorcycle, slung like a Harley softtail, sat on the drive in front of the garage.

Virgil watched for a few seconds, then wandered up the driveway. As he came up to the back of the house, the man pushed out from under the truck and wiped his hands on a rag. Virgil recognized him as Bunton. He walked up to the lip of the garage, hands in his jeans pockets, and stood there for a moment, until Bunton felt him and turned his face up, and Virgil said, "Hey."

Bunton held up a finger, crawled across the floor to the boom box, and poked a button on it; the silence seemed to jump out of the ground.

Bunton asked, "You a cop?"

"Yeah. BCA. Trying to figure out what happened to Bob Sanderson," Virgil said.

Bunton dropped his chin to his chest, then shook his head, crawled a few more feet across the garage, got a jean jacket, and shook a pack of Kools and a beat-up Zippo out of the pocket.

Bunton was gaunt, with bad teeth colored nicotine-brown under the brilliant work lights. Once-muscular arms, now going to flab, showed purple stains that had been tattoos. He lit a Kool after flicking the Zippo a few times, and the stink of lighter fluid sifted over to Virgil. Bunton took a drag and said, "Bob's time ran out, you know. What the fuck."

"You got any ideas why? Or who stopped his clock?" Virgil asked.

"No, I don't, but I'd like to."

"You know a guy name of Utecht from down in New Ulm?" Virgil asked.

"Ah, Christ, if it ain't one thing, it's another," Bunton said, and Virgil felt the spark. Bunton knew Utecht: a connection.

Bunton stood up and stretched, and Virgil noticed that he was wearing a leg brace. These were old guys: these guys were older than Virgil's father. "Somebody told you that we were going to meetings together, huh? Me 'n' Bob?"

"Somebody," Virgil said. "This all have something to do with Vietnam?"

Bunton laughed, and then coughed, a smoker's hack. When he finished, he patted himself on the chest with his cigarette hand and said, "Tell you what, pal—what's your name?"

"Virgil Flowers."

"No shit? Good name. But tell you what: I went to Vietnam when I was nineteen, and since then, *everything* has something to do with Vietnam. Lot of people like that, you know? They even go back there, like tourists, to see if it was real."

Bunton might have been part Indian, Virgil thought, but not too much: as in his photos, he looked more Scots than Indian—and a little like the Cowardly Lion in *The Wizard of Oz*.

"Okay, I don't understand that," Virgil said. "I was in the military, but not in heavy combat. But I believe you."

"That's nice of you," Bunton said.

"The thing is, I understand that Sanderson wasn't in Vietnam," Virgil said. "He was in Korea. Some guys have suggested I try to find out if he was in some kind of intelligence outfit and Korea was just a cover."

"Ah, jeez. Not Bob. Bob was . . ." Bunton had a wrench in his hand, and he dropped it into an open steel toolbox and interrupted himself to say, "Hand me that other wrench there, will you?"

Virgil was standing beside the truck fender a couple feet from the old man, and he turned and looked at the hood and realized that there wasn't a wrench there, and then he was hit by lightning.

The impact was right behind his ear, and he went down. No pain, no understanding of what had happened, it could have been an electrical shock. He hadn't quite understood that Bunton had sucker-punched him, and he tried to push up to his hands and knees, and then Bunton hit him again.

There was a confused space.

He heard the motorcycle start up, he remembered later, and then it was quiet, and then there was some talk, and then he tried to get up and there was another old man there, who said, "What happened, buddy? What happened?"

And he fell down again and he heard the old man shout, "I think he's having a heart attack or something. Call 911." And the old man asked Virgil, "Where's Ray?"

THE AMBULANCE took him to Hennepin Medical Center, and he woke up in a bed with a bunch of cops around, including Shrake and Jenkins. Virgil asked, "What happened? Was it that fuckin' Bunton?"

Jenkins looked at Shrake and said, "He's back."

Maybe he was back, but Virgil's head felt like it was in New Jersey. "What do you mean, I'm back?"

"For the past hour, you've been asking, 'What happened?' and we'd tell you, but the needle was stuck, and after we told you, you'd say, 'What happened?'"

"Ah, man," Virgil groaned. "That goddamned Bunton. Did he get my gun?"

"Nope. You've got your gun, you've got your wallet, got your ID—which is why we're here," Shrake said. "You got a lump on the back of your head and a contusion and a bruise, like you were sapped."

"What happened to my truck?" Virgil asked.

"I don't know," Shrake said. "Where'd you leave it?"

"Ah, man . . ."

A nurse stuck her head in. "He's back?"

"He's back," Jenkins told her. "Get the doc."

"I've been out?" Virgil asked.

"Not exactly out," Shrake said. "The lights were on, you know, but nobody was home."

"Not the first time you heard that, huh?" Jenkins asked. "So: who do we kill?"

"Hey—I'm naked under here," Virgil said, peering under the sheet that covered him.

"That's cool—don't have to show us," Jenkins said.

The doctor came and told him that he'd suffered a concussion of modest severity—"Not terrible, but not nothing, either. You got hit pretty damn hard. You remember the MRI?"

"No."

"Well, we did an MRI," the doc said.

"I remember a loud noise. . . ."

"That was it. Anyway, there's no fracture, and we didn't see any real organic damage, no bleeding, but you took a hit and got your circuits scrambled. We want you here overnight, to make sure that everything continues to work. Make sure that a clot doesn't pop out of the woodwork."

"Is that likely?" Shrake asked.

"It's getting less likely the longer it goes, but he doesn't want to be out in a canoe somewhere if it happens," the doc told Shrake. To Virgil: "So, stay overnight, and we'll look at you tomorrow morning and then you can go home."

"My head hurts. . . ."

"We can fix that," the doc said. "You could use some sleep, too."

He woke early, feeling tired, drugged, and disoriented. A nurse looked in on him, gave him a piece of paper, and asked him to read the small type. He did. She said, "What do you want for breakfast?" He ate and went back to sleep.

Davenport called from Washington and said, "Sounds like you're making progress. I told you that you'd find him."

"Is that what you thought when you got your ass shot? That you were making progress?"

Davenport laughed, then said, "Wasn't my ass, it was my leg. Anyway—are you okay? You sound okay."

"Got a headache, but I'm not gonna die," Virgil said. "Can't say the same for fuckin' Bunton when I find him."

"Don't shoot him right away," Davenport said. "Ask him some questions first. Find out if he did Sanderson and Utecht."

"Ah, I don't think he did—but I think he knows why they were killed. I gotta get outa here, he could be anywhere by now."

"Jenkins and Shrake called me last night after they talked to you. They've been tracking him—or trying to. They oughta be coming by to tell you what they've got. You still got your cell?"

"Yeah."

"All right. You're doing good, Virgil," Davenport said. "Keep it up. I want this cleared out before I get back there."

TEN O'CLOCK: he had to wait until the doc got to him before he could check out, and the doc took his time. After a perfunctory check, he told Virgil to take it easy for a couple of days and to stay away from aspirin for a few more.

"What happens if I don't take it easy?" Virgil asked.

"Probably nothing, except that your head will hurt more," the doc said.

Virgil was getting dressed when Jenkins stuck his head into the room. "You okay?"

"I'm good to go," Virgil said. A headache lingered, but he ignored it. "Just signed the insurance papers. What about Bunton?"

"That house you were at? It belonged to Bunton's father's step-brother, so he's like a step-uncle, if there is such a thing. He's the guy who called the ambulance. We landed on him pretty hard, and what we got is, Bunton is running around somewhere on a Harley. We've got the plates, we've got the description, we're stopping half the Harleys in the state. Haven't found him yet."

"What about my truck?"

"Shrake and I moved it up here, across the street in the parking garage. I'll walk you over."

"Thanks, man." Virgil pulled on his boots. "That fuckin' Bunton. Wonder what the hell was going through his head?"

"Maybe nothing," Jenkins said. "I looked at his file—he ain't exactly a wizard."

"He'd know better than to whack a cop," Virgil said, standing up, tucking in his shirt. "If he goes to Stillwater for ag assault on a cop, he might not get out."

"So what're we doing?"

"I'm gonna go back and talk to this uncle; make some things clear," Virgil said.

BUNTON'S STEP-UNCLE, whose name was Carl Bunton, had been laid off by Northwest Airlines, Jenkins said, and was working as a clerk in a convenience store. Virgil got his truck and followed Jenkins out of the parking garage, down south through the loop, to a no-name food shop on Franklin. A kid, maybe twelve, came running out of the shop, carrying a pack of Marlboros, as Virgil and Jenkins crossed the parking lot. A man's face floated behind the dark glass, looking out at them; saw them checking out the kid.

"He didn't buy them," the man said to Jenkins as they came through the door. He was standing behind the cash register, worried. "His pa is handicapped. He just came to pick them up."

Jenkins poked a finger at the guy and said to Virgil, "Carl Bunton."

Virgil nodded and said, "I wanted to thank you for helping me out last night."

"Glad to do it," Bunton said. "But I don't know where Ray went—he's a goof, and I'm not responsible."

"He's got to be hiding somewhere," Virgil said.

"Up at the res," Bunton said.

Jenkins shook his head. "It's six hours up there. We were looking for him an hour after he left here. He didn't get to Red Lake without being seen. There's not enough roads."

"He knows every one of them, though," Bunton said. "Once he gets back on the res, you ain't getting him out. They got their own laws up there."

"But he ain't up there," Jenkins said.

"Have any friends down here? People who'd put him up? More relatives?"

"Ray's got friends all over—I don't even know who. He's been a biker for fifty years, pretty near. They don't give a shit about cops."

"Huh," Virgil said. "And you don't have any idea . . ."

Bunton shook his head. "No. But I can tell you, he's going to the res. No doubt about that. Once he gets up in them woods, he's gone."

THEY STOPPED AT Bunton's house, and Virgil walked back along the driveway and peered through a garage window. The Blazer was still there, still up on the portable ramps. Virgil thought Ray Bunton might have snuck back in the night to get the truck, but he hadn't. Back at the curb, he said good-bye to Jenkins—"See you at the office"—then called Sandy.

"How bad were you hurt?" she asked.

"Ahhh . . . Anyway, this Ray Bunton guy. Check his latest arrests, see if anybody else was arrested with him. I'm looking for friends. I'm especially looking for a friend who might be able to get him a car, or loan him one."

By the time he got back to the office, Sandy had five names, with more to come. Virgil started calling local law-enforcement agencies, asking them to send cops around to check for Bunton. Nothing happened, and Virgil kept pressing until evening.

McDonald, the cop from Bemidji who knew some Mounties, called halfway through the afternoon with information about Tai and Phem, the two Vietnamese-Canadian businessmen.

"Unless you've got a specific string to pull, they're pretty much what-you-see-is-what-you-get. Both were born in the Toronto area, no known criminal or histories, both have worked with the Canadian government in dealings with the Vietnamese, and because of that, they've both undergone security checks and have come up clean. Not that they're perfect—they've both been involved in disputes with Canada Revenue. That's the Canadian IRS. But the disputes are civil, not criminal."

"So they're clean."

"That's not what I said. What I said is, nobody knows the illegal stuff that they've done."

"You're a cynical man, McDonald."

At six o'clock, with nothing moving and the office emptied out, he took stock: he smelled bad, he thought, his head still hurt, he wasn't allowed aspirin or alcohol or caffeine, and he wasn't finding Bunton. He had a dozen police agencies checking Bunton's friends, and they all had his phone number; driving aimlessly around in the streets wouldn't help. He fished Mead Sinclair's card out of his pocket, stared at it for a moment, then dialed.

Sinclair answered, and Virgil identified himself and asked, "Your daughter around?"

"Oh, for Christ's sakes." Then Virgil heard Sinclair shout, "Mai—it's the cops."

VIRGIL WENT BACK to the motel, cleaned up, put on fresh jeans and an antique Hole T-shirt and a black sport coat. With his usual cowboy boots and his long blond hair, he did look a little country, he thought, and not too drugstore, either. He'd told her jeans were appropriate, and whatever else she had.

ON THE WAY to Sinclair's place, his contact at the DEA called: "I got nothing. I talked to the FBI guys, and they got nothing. Nothing about lemons, nothing about serial vet murders. The guy I talked to wants you to drop him a line."

"You got my e-mail?" Virgil asked.

"I do."

"Give it to the FBI guy, tell him to e-mail me. I'll pop something back to him."

MAI HAD GONE WITH a man's white dress shirt, unbuttoned about three down, jeans, and sandals, and had pulled her hair into a ponytail.

She looked terrific, her heart-shaped face framed by the white collar, and country enough.

"Dad's writing," she said, quietly, at the door. Most of the lights in the apartment were out.

"He works at night?" he asked. He always asked when other writers worked.

"And early. He gets up at dawn. Always has. He says he can get five hours of work done before anybody else is up. He's still really angry with you, by the way. He doesn't believe you found those Vietnamese by calling Larson."

"Well—suspicious old coot."

THEY TALKED ABOUT personal biography in the truck—growing up in Madison, Wisconsin, for her, in Marshall, Minnesota, for him. She told him about working as her father's editorial assistant, about looking for work as an actress, as a dancer. He told her about being a cop; about killing a man the year before.

"My father hates killing," she said. "He spent his life fighting the idea of killing as a solution to anything."

"I hope he doesn't find out about me calling up the intelligence guy," Virgil said.

"What? You called the CIA?" Eyebrows up.

"No, no," Virgil said. "I called the Vietnamese intelligence guy at their embassy in Ottawa. You know—their spy guy."

"Oh . . . you did not."

"Yes, I did," Virgil said, glancing over at her. "His name was something like, you know, Wun Hung Low."

"It is not, and that's racist," she said.

"Sorry. His name was, uh, Hao Nguyen," Virgil said. "He was pretty surprised to hear from me, I can tell you."

She brushed it off. "You called a *spy*?"

"Yup. He told me to get lost."

She had her phone out, dialed, waited a minute, then said, "Hey, Dad. Virgil and I are on the way to the dance club. He just told me that he called some spy up in the Vietnamese embassy in Ottawa. About you. Yeah. He said 'One Truck Load' . . . No, no, he said, Hao Nguyen. Yeah. Yeah, I bet. Okay, I will."

She hung up, and Virgil said, "Boy, I sure hope he doesn't hear about that."

She said, "Now he's *really* pissed."

"You said, 'I will.' What was that?"

"He wants me to see what else I can worm out of you," she said.

"Well, hell," Virgil said, "I am the talkative sort."

HE TOOK HER TO One-Eyed Dick's Tejas Tap in Roseville, where they had dancing and live music. They lucked into a booth, she got a Corona with a slice of lime, he ordered a lemonade. "You have a problem with alcohol?" she asked.

It took him a second, then he said, "Oh. No. Not that way. I got whacked on the head last night."

He told her about it, dramatizing a little because she looked so good, and she said, "The same guy you were telling Dad about? The Indian guy?"

"Yeah. I don't know what's up with him. He figures in here

somehow. Anyway, he's running. I'll find him." He took a sip of lemonade.

"Why are you wearing a shirt that says, 'Hole'?"

"Just another band," he said. "C'mon. Let's dance."

So they danced, cheek-to-cheek, and she was a perfect dancer, like a warm, well-rounded shadow. He wasn't bad himself, he thought. One-Eyed Dick's didn't do much in the way of line dancing, a fad that had faded, but still did some, including a beginner's electric slide, and she caught on instantly and he had her laughing hard with it, dark eyes sparkling. Watching her, he thought he might give quite a bit to see her laughing over the years. But then, he'd had that same thought with three other women.

While he was at the bar, getting another lemonade and beer, he watched her talking excitedly on her cell phone. She was putting it away when he got back, and she said, "Girlfriend from Madison. She found my perfect life-mate."

"Dancer?"

"Psychiatrist," she said, and they both laughed, and she said, "She was serious, too."

She probed on murder investigations: how he did them, why he did them. Asked if cops still beat people up to get information.

"I wouldn't," he said. "It's torture. Torture's immoral."

"The CIA doesn't seem to think so."

"No, no." He wagged a finger at her. "*Some* people in the CIA think it *is* immoral. Maybe some don't."

"What about with things like 9/11, where you've got terrorists blowing up buildings?"

He shrugged. "Are you going to torture people because you *suspect* they might be up to something? Somebody's *always* up to something. What about a guy you suspect is killing little children? Do you torture him because of what you suspect? If you torture people you suspect of being criminals, where do you stop? Who do you trust to do the suspecting? And if you don't want to torture people in advance, then do you torture them afterwards? For what? For revenge? That doesn't seem like something civilized people would do."

"What about capital punishment?" she asked.

"Don't believe in it," Virgil said.

"You're a weird cop," she said.

"Not really—a lot of cops don't believe in it. Torture, anyway. The problem isn't what it does to the victim, it's what it does to the people who do it. Messes them up. Turns them into animals. I'll tell you something—you show me an executioner, and I'll show you a screwed-up human being."

"But you killed a guy last year . . ."

"Who was trying to kill me. I *do* believe in self-defense," Virgil said. "But torture and cold-blooded execution . . . those things are sins."

They danced some more, and the music and the lights began to jiggle his brain around, and finally she put a hand on his chest and asked, "Are you okay?"

"The headache's coming back. It's the lights," he said.

"So we can dance anytime. Why don't you take me home and get some rest? Or, better yet, you can take the Mai Sinclair instant concussion cure."

"What's that?"

"Can't be explained, only shown," she said.

Back at her apartment, she put a finger to her lips, said, "Quiet—if he wakes up, he'll never get back to sleep." They crept inside, across the living room to the glassed-in porch where Sinclair did his writing; on the way, Mai got a pillow from a couch.

On the porch, a six-foot-long Oriental carpet spread out behind Sinclair's writing chair. After Mai had closed the porch door, she said, "I want you to lie down on the carpet, arms above your head, folded, fingers touching, forehead on the pillow. Facedown, so your spine is straight."

All right. Virgil sprawled facedown on the carpet, moved his hands around until she was satisfied that his body was squared up; then she straddled him, sitting in the small of his back, probed his neck with her fingertips, as if looking for something, then suddenly dug in. The pain was like an electric shock, and he arched his back and yelped: "Ah."

"Shhh," she whispered. "Relax. I'm going to do that again, but it won't hurt as much. Your neck muscles are like wood—that slows down the blood flow you need. So relax . . ." Her voice lulled him, and she dug in again, at the instant he no longer expected it, and the shock was as bad as the first: "AHHHH."

"Easy, easy . . . that's the last shock. Now I'm going to pull some of the muscles apart." She did, and it still hurt; but the pain gradually ebbed, to be replaced by a surging warmth, and he went away for a while, only to come back when she stood up, slapped him on the butt, and said, "You're cured, cowboy."

He sat up, a little dizzy. "Ah, jeez . . ." But he felt good—though tired—and the headache was gone.

"You need to go home and get some sleep," she said. "Tomorrow morning, you'll feel good. If you get some sleep."

"Hmm." He ran his hands through his hair, shaking it out. "All right. What'd you just do? Some kind of massage therapy?"

"Something like that—a little like acupuncture, too," she said. "Dancers learn that stuff. We've always got aches and pains."

She was moving him toward the door, he realized. He wasn't going to get any further this night; better to go with shyness, or politeness, than to make a grab at her. "I appreciate it. Jeez, I'd like to take you dancing again."

"Give me a call," she said at the door. She kissed a fingertip and pressed it against his nose, and closed the door.

Second time that happened. Just like with the Vietnamese guys: don't let the door hit you in the ass, Virgil.

He was back in his truck when he became aware of a kind of erotic warmth in his back and side muscles, where her butt and legs had weighed on him. Not a tease, because she hadn't been wiggling around or anything, but the feeling was there, and lingering.

He thought about Janey, probably home alone and lonesome. And he thought, *That would be wrong, Virgil.*

But would it really be wrong to bring a little warmth and comfort to a lonely woman? To help someone out who needed . . .

What a load of self-serving, hypocritical BS.

Mai Sinclair, he thought. *Pretty damn good.*

THE SCOUT sat in the back of a two-year-old white Chevy van, in a cluster of cars under a spreading oak, on Edgecumbe down from the corner at Snelling, watching John Wigge's house.

Waiting for the lights to go out. Waiting to go to bed. He'd been there waiting, for four hours, since Wigge got home.

The house was a single-story brick-and-shingle affair surrounded by a close-cropped lawn. A tough nut to crack. Wigge was an ex-cop, now the vice president of a high-end private security agency, and he'd taken advantage of the job: there were motion detectors, glass-break alarms, magnetic window sensors that would start screaming with any movement at all. The security panel, set into the wall near the back door, looked like it could launch the space shuttle.

Wigge had taken part in the meeting at Sanderson's, with Sanderson and Bunton and the unknown man in the backseat of Wigge's car. With Bunton on the run, Wigge was the next target—but he'd have to be taken outside the house. Inside the house, he had too many advantages.

Now, if he'd just go to bed, they could start again tomorrow.

THE SHOOTER was two blocks from the scout. He sat in silence, not moving. No iPod, no headphones, no book, though he couldn't have read in the dark anyway. He needed none of that, the artificial support, when he could simply run his memories, smile with them, cry with them, and all the time, all five senses could reach out over the landscape, looking for targets. . . .

Though, when he thought about it, had he ever used *taste*? He reached back through his memories . . . and was still there when the light came on in Wigge's garage.

That was one weakness in Wigge's security, and the scout had noticed it earlier and brought it to the shooter's attention. The garage was connected directly to the house, so Wigge could get out and into his car without being seen. But he had a garage door opener with an automatic overhead light. As soon as he touched the button to lift the door, the light went on. If he did that from the garage, rather than from inside the car, he'd be exposed, if only for a moment or two.

The shooter was in the back of the van, in a legal parking space, with the rifle on the floor beside him. When the light came on in the garage, he reacted instantly, dropping the window with one jab of his finger, swiveling the gun up . . .

The cell phone burped: no sign of life in the garage. The shooter picked up the phone, and the scout said, "He's in the car," and "He's moving."

And here it came, a big black GMC sport utility vehicle with a ton of chrome and gray-tinted windows of the kind popularized by the Blackwater mercenaries in Iraq. Wigge backed out, paused, watched the garage door all the way down, then backed into the street, aimed at Snelling, and drove away. The shooter waited until it turned the corner, then started after it.

His cell phone beeped, and he put it to his ear, and the scout said, "Straight up Snelling."

The shooter saw the truck again as it turned down the ramp onto I-94, headed east. He was ten seconds behind it.

JOHN WIGGE was a big red-faced man, bullet-headed and bullet-brained. He'd retired with a full pension from the St. Paul cops, where he'd spent most of his career working Vice. His nickname had been R-A, pronounced "ARR-AYY," which stood for Resisting Arrest. Sell dope in his territory without Wigge's okay, run a hooker without a nod from Wigge, and there was a good chance that you'd resist arrest and get your head busted, or an arm or a leg. He'd walked right up to the edge of criminal charges a few times, but he'd always walked away again.

A different proposition than Sanderson or Utecht. Sanderson was like a banty rooster, but a banty rooster was still a chicken. Wigge was not.

Still, the shooter could take him. There was no question about that. If he could get Wigge alone for thirty seconds, or even ten seconds. He had a gun, a lead-weighted sap, a roll of duct tape. Sometimes you had to take calculated risks; and sometimes, if you work at it hard enough, you get lucky.

Wigge merged left, leaving I-94 to take I-35 north, staying in the left lane, picking up speed. Going somewhere. The shooter settled in one lane to Wigge's right, and fell back until he could see only the top of Wigge's truck, and let the ex-cop pull him up the highway.

And they kept going, out of the metro. The shooter got on the phone, said, "He's past 694, still going north," and the scout came back: "I'm coming up behind you. I'll take it for a while."

The scout was in a new rented Audi A6, gave the shooter a wave as he went past. A minute later on the phone: "Okay, I've got him."

They rolled in the loose formation, through the night, then the scout came up again, "He's slowing down, he may be looking—I'm going on past."

The shooter slowed, slowed. The scout called, "I'm past him, still going away. He's definitely looking, he's going maybe fifty."

The shooter slowed to fifty, wondered briefly if Wigge had a trailing car. Well, if he had, there was nothing to be done.

The scout: "I'm off. I'll let him get past me. . . . Okay. He's still up ahead, still slower than anything else on the road. Look for a trailing car . . ."

The shooter couldn't see a trailing car. Couldn't see Wigge, either.

The scout: "I'm back on. I can see him, way up ahead. . . . I'm gaining on him, again." Then: "Okay, he's picking it up. He's picking it up. Really picking it up . . ."

They played tag, letting Wigge out of sight between exits, a delicate task made easier by the GPS video/map screens in the Audi. Thirty miles out of St. Paul; forty miles; coming up to fifty. The scout: "He's getting off. He's getting off at the rest stop. I have to go by, it's over to you. I'll come back quick as I can."

The shooter slowed again, back to fifty, and then moved onto the shoulder of the highway and stopped. He didn't want to pull into the parking lot, then have to sit in the truck without getting out. Wigge would be watching the vehicles coming in from behind, which was why the scout kept going. If the shooter waited, he might lose him, but he had to take the chance.

He made himself wait three minutes, then pulled back onto the highway. Another minute to the rest stop, two lanes, one for eighteen-wheelers, one for cars. The rest stop pavilion was a round brick building, sitting in a puddle of light, with a bunch of newspaper stands out front. A couple of kids were wandering around, and a couple of adults, killing time while somebody peed.

And there was Wigge, out of his truck, walking down the sidewalk, away from the pavilion, under a row of dim ball lights. Farther on, sitting on a picnic table, was the Indian, Bunton.

Jackpot.

THE SHOOTER called the scout: "We've got Bunton."

His mind was racing. There were a number of techniques for capturing two men, but the conditions here were difficult. He would need to run a dialogue on them; he would need to convince them that they might save their lives with cooperation. . . .

As he watched, looking at Wigge's back as Wigge strolled down the sidewalk, Bunton got up, stretched, and wandered away from him. The land east of the rest stop fell off into a ravine, and the edges were heavily wooded, oaks and a few maples. The two men moved at a leisurely pace toward the tree line, and Bunton turned his head, looked back, and disappeared into what must have been a trail.

A moment later, Wigge went in after him. The shooter waited, fifteen seconds, thirty seconds, then climbed out of the van. Behind the cover of the door, he tucked his pistol into the waistband of his pants, pulled on a University of Iowa baseball hat, and started after them, ambling along as easily as Wigge had.

Fifteen cars were spotted up and down the rest area, people coming and going, one whining kid, overtired, his parents urging him back to the car: "Only an hour to go," the father said as the shooter passed them.

The shooter walked past the point where Wigge had left the sidewalk, continuing all the way to the end of the parking area. He wasn't sure, but there appeared to be another pavilion back in the trees; not sure, but then a cigarette lighter flared. That's where they were. The shooter stepped into the trees, paused, watched, then began moving, quiet as a mink. Four steps, stop. A dozen more, always with a tree between himself and the targets. He heard voices then, two men talking, the sound low and urgent. He could take them both, right here. Have to be careful about Wigge—a former cop, a security guy, there was a good chance he'd be armed and know how to use the weapon. Another step . . .

"Hey!"

The voice came from behind and to one side, sharp, demanding, and hit the shooter like a thrown rock. He twisted and saw a tall man there, and the man had a gun in his hand and the gun was pointed more or less at the shooter. Without time to think, the shooter snapped the pistol up and fired four times, aiming at the man's eyes.

The shooter was a professional, shooting by instinct, and the man went down like a sack of gravel. But the gun, silenced as it was, wasn't silent, and the shooter heard "Jesus Christ!" and then Wigge was coming, and the shooter ran to meet him, needing to get the first shot, Wigge lifting a gun from his pants pocket, and behind him, Bunton had launched himself into the ravine.

The shooter shot Wigge in the knee and Wigge went sideways and fumbled the gun, tried to recover it, and fumbled it again, and then the shooter was there, the sap in his left hand, and he whacked Wigge behind the ear and Wigge went flat, groaning, and the shooter dropped on his shoulders and pressed the muzzle of the gun against Wigge's head and said, "Bunton. Who are the others? Two names. Who are the others?" As he asked, he could still hear Bunton, his footfalls diminishing, circling back toward the lights of the rest area. And he thought about the dead man, lying on the trail—anyone could look in here . . .

"Fuck you," Wigge said, and he tried to push himself up, a one-handed push-up, and the shooter's running tactical assessment took over and he half stood, lifted the sap, and hammered Wigge again, and the big man went flat and stayed there, his body slack.

The shooter ran back toward the rest area, hurdled the dead gunman, heard a motorcycle start, slowed to a stroll as he came out of the trail, saw Bunton firing out the exit lane. He hadn't tried to rouse the other people, hadn't tried to call the police. He'd simply fled. . . . The shooter watched him go, then put his head down and lifted the cell phone. "Where are you?"

"Just got back on, south of you, heading your way."

"When you get in, get all the way down to the end of the parking area. Car parking area. I'm back in the trees. I've got Wigge, but the Indian is on the loose, and if he calls the police, we'll have trouble."

"Three minutes . . . "

The shooter hurried back down the path, caught the dead man under the armpits, and dragged him into the heaviest clump of brush. He stepped back out on the trail and looked toward the body: almost, but not quite, invisible. Saw the dead man's gun, kicked it off the trail. If Bunton didn't call the police, he wouldn't be found until morning.

He continued back to Wigge, knelt next to him. Wigge was moaning, a quiet, steady sound, almost like a meditation vowel. The shooter stooped, grabbed him behind the shoulders, rolled him up and over, and then lifted him in an unsteady fireman's carry. He was fifty yards from the end of the parking area, through the brush. He walked steadily toward it, Wigge's weight crushing his shoulders and chest, but he kept going; and as he arrived, he saw the lights of a car rolling past the rest stop pavilion and continue to the end of the parking strip. He stood behind a thin screen of weeds until he saw the scout's car, then called, "Open the back door on your side."

His partner hurried to do it, and the shooter turned his head up the parking strip. He couldn't see anybody watching, not that there might not be somebody. Decision time, and a necessary risk. With Wigge still draped over his shoulders, he took five big walking steps across the grass verge to the car, stooped, and slipped Wigge into the backseat.

Stepped back, slammed the door, slapped his hands together, as if dusting them off. "I don't know how badly he's hurt. We might have to hold him for a while."

"If he dies . . ."

"Then we're in no more trouble than if he died here. We need to talk to him. Take him to the barn. I'll meet you there."

WHEN HIS PARTNER was gone, taking Wigge, the shooter walked back to the van. He'd killed an outsider, and that had broken the protocol. There'd been no choice—he'd fired in self-defense—but that might not make a difference. The unknown man was still dead. That meant that time was running out: if the unknown man wasn't found until morning, and if they hadn't connected him to Wigge until tomorrow afternoon . . .

They had to move on the Indian. They needed the last two names.

The whole game now shifted into the high-speed lane.

The protocol was gone. Now everybody and everything was up for grabs; and it was not too early to begin planning their exit.

A lot to do . . .

MAYBE TOO MUCH, the shooter thought later, his head in his hands. The years of killing had turned him into an animal—and then had tried to drag him down even further, turning him into a devil. Wigge, mostly conscious now, although the consciousness came and went, was spread on the rotting wood floor of the barn, a fluorescent lantern providing the only light, and Wigge was trying to scream.

Trying unsuccessfully, because of the lemon in his mouth, held in place with duct tape.

The shooter got up and slipped outside, into the cool of the night. Checking the countryside, looking for anything, for interlopers, for interference. For an ear, or an eye. And getting away from the sound of Wigge, whose moans sat heavily on his once-Catholic soul.

INSIDE THE BARN, Wigge humped against the electric spark, but did no more than hump against it: the scout had waited until Wigge was conscious, then had nailed his hands to the floor, seven-and-a-half-inch spikes right through the palms. Not out of cruelty, but to underline Wigge's helplessness, and the extent to which he would be mistreated if he did not cooperate. Wigge had passed out again as his hands were nailed down, but the scout was patient and efficient, and took off the big man's shoes and pants and underwear, then popped an ammonium carbonate capsule under Wigge's nose, and had started with the battery . . .

The interrogation might have gone on to daylight hours, but Wigge's heart quit a little after three o'clock in the morning and he died.

He'd given them one name.

The scout called the shooter, and the shooter said, "Maybe he really didn't know the last man."

"He knew," the scout said. "But he was a hard man. Harder than he looked."

"So now—we have the Indian and the Caterpillar man."

"And a dead man at the rest stop," the scout said. "Now we have to move, or we could be closed down."

"The thing that worries me is that the Indian has no ties—he might just leave, and if he's out roaming the highways, we might never find him," the scout said. "We should concentrate on him. The Caterpillar man has a home and family, if Wigge was truthful, and I think he was. The Caterpillar man will be there."

"The coordinator has an idea about the Indian," the shooter said. "We need to meet. You may have to work yet tonight."

"We've got no time," the scout said. "Everything has to go fast."

"Huh." The shooter looked at the dead man. "Poor soul," he said. "This poor soul."

The scout said, "Operationally . . . taking him to the monument is crazy."

"But necessary," the shooter said. "The sooner we do it, the better. We need the darkness. Call the coordinator from your car. I'll take this poor soul in the van."

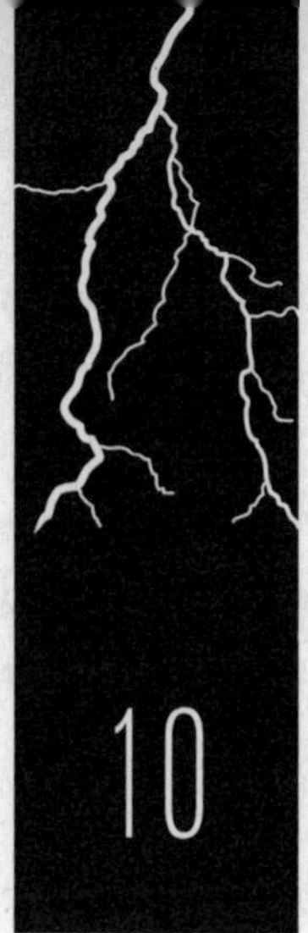

10

VIRGIL WAS in the shower, tired but feeling pretty good, the best he'd felt since Bunton had whacked him. He was washing his hair, taking care with the bruise behind his ear.

Whatever Mai had done, it had worked. He turned the heat up, let the water flow over his neck, did the second wash . . . and his cell phone went, and he said, "Shit," and almost simultaneously thought, *Mai?* and he dripped shampoo all over the bathroom and half the motel room going after it.

The caller ID said, "Bureau of Criminal . . ."

"Yeah? Flowers."

"Dan Shaver. I got the duty tonight." Shaver worked with the BCA. "You looking for a guy named Ray Bunton?"

"Yes. You find him?"

"No—but he's calling you," Shaver said. "He wanted your cell phone—I didn't give it to him, told him to call back. He said he's moving, but he'll call from somewhere else. Doesn't have a cell. Anyway . . . should I give him your number?"

"Yes. Absolutely. Did he say when he'd call?"

"He said he'd call me back in fifteen minutes," Shaver said. "That was two or three minutes ago. He said he had to drive to another phone."

VIRGIL JUMPED BACK in the shower, rinsed off, brushed his teeth, got dressed, stared at the phone. More than fifteen minutes: then the phone rang, and he looked at the caller ID: "Number Not Available."

He clicked it: "Virgil Flowers."

"Flowers?" An old man's voice, harsh with nicotine.

"This is Virgil. Is this Ray?"

"Yeah. Listen, man, some really heavy shit is going down," Bunton said; slang from the sixties.

"That's what I want to talk to you about, Ray," Virgil said.

"Fuck that. I don't know what's happening, and neither do you. I'm digging a hole. Anyway, what happened is, two guys got shot up at the rest stop on I-35. The one up past North Branch. The one on the side going north. Maybe . . . half hour ago. I was there, but I didn't have nothing to do with it. Some motherfucker come out of the woods with a fuckin' silenced pistol and started mowing people down. . . . Jesus Christ, it's like some kind of acid flashback . . ." And he made a *huh-huh-huh* sound as if he'd started trying to weep but couldn't get it done.

"Ray, Ray, stay with me, man. Two guys shot. Are they dead?" Virgil asked.

"I think so, man. I think they're gone. This motherfucker was a pro.

I ran for my life, got the fuck out of there. I'm going to Wisconsin, man, you gotta get this motherfucker."

"Ray, you gotta know what's going on," Virgil said.

"Fuck it, what I could tell you, that helps, is that the guy who got shot is John Wigge, he used to be a cop with St. Paul. Crooked motherfucker, too. Gone now. Gone now, motherfucker. They're way down at the end, off to the side, there's a, like, a shelter back in the woods. Dark, you can't see shit back there." After a second or two of silence, Bunton said, "I'm getting the fuck outa here."

"Ray, goddamnit, you gotta come in. We gotta talk. This looks really bad, man, you gotta . . ."

"Fuck you guys. I'll come in when you get this asshole," Bunton said.

And he was gone.

VIRGIL GOT on the line to the BCA: Shaver took the call.

"We may have a homicide. Bunton says two guys got shot at a rest stop on I-35 up past North Branch."

"Let me look on the map," Shaver said. Then: "Yep, I see it. Haven't heard anything. I'll talk to the Patrol, get somebody started. You going up?"

"I'm on the way," Virgil said.

VIRGIL WAS FIVE MINUTES from the I-35 junction in St. Paul, and fifty miles from there to the rest stop, running hard through the night, forty minutes, listening to Kid Rock singing "Cadillac Pussy."

Made him think of Mai: how in the hell could a woman who grew up in Madison, Wisconsin, as a dancer, for Christ's sakes, not know about Hole? Courtney Love had been every girl's hero—well, every girl of a certain kind, of which Mai was one. She must've been crying her eyes out when Kurt Cobain bit the big one. . . . Not know *Hole*?

Virgil looked at his watch on the way up: just after midnight. Fumbled out his cell phone, found Davenport's cell number, and punched it.

Davenport answered on the second ring. "You know what time it is here?"

"Washington? Should be just after one o'clock," Virgil said. "You're always up late—what's the big deal?"

"Nothing, I guess."

"You know the band Hole?" Virgil asked.

"Sure. Courtney Love. Pretty hot, twenty years ago."

"Thought you'd know," Virgil said.

Davenport said, "So—who's dead?"

"Bunton called me," Virgil said. "He and a former St. Paul cop named John Wigge apparently got together at a rest stop off I-35. He says some guy, who he describes as a motherfucker and an asshole, shot and killed Wigge and another guy, whose name he doesn't know. I'm on my way; we got the Patrol on the way."

"Where's Bunton?"

"He says he's gonna dig a hole in Wisconsin," Virgil said.

"Gotta dig him out."

"Thanks for the tip."

"You know Wigge?" Davenport asked.

"Yeah. Not well. He'd retired when I made detective. I ran into him a few times at crime scenes," Virgil said.

"I heard that Wigge might take a dollar or two," Davenport said.

"I heard that. Bad guy. That was my feeling. Made a lot of cases, though," Virgil said.

"He went to a security service . . ."

"Paladin," Virgil said.

"That's the one," Davenport said. "Armed-response guys, celebrity bodyguards. You know who Ralph Warren is?"

"The money guy? The real estate guy?"

"Yes. He owns Paladin. The word was, when Warren was building that shopping center / condo complex on the river, the lowlife was screwing up the ambience. So Warren sent in some of his security people to clean the place up, and Wigge covered for him. He got the job at Paladin as a payoff."

"Huh. I was probably still in Kosovo when that happened. How far did Wigge let it go? I mean, beating people up? Running them off? More than that?"

"Don't know. A couple of mean old street guys just . . . went away. What you heard was, they were screwin' with Warren, hanging out on the corner with 'Work for Food' signs. Wanted to be paid to stay away. Then they *went* away. Supposedly, if you ask Wigge about these old guys, he'll tell you they went to Santa Monica."

"Wonder if Utecht and Sanderson and Bunton were involved with Warren?" Virgil asked.

"A good detective would find that out," Davenport said.

"A good detective would call up Sandy and tell her to do the research," Virgil said.

"He would," Davenport agreed. They both thought about that, then Davenport said, "Listen, try to be a little careful about this. Warren's been throwing a lot of money at the Republicans, helping out with the convention. He hurried up a big block of condos at Riverside. He's providing them free for delegates. He's pretty political. I'm not telling you to back off, but be polite."

"I'll be good," Virgil said. Far up ahead, he could see flashing cop-lights. "Talk to you tomorrow."

"Hey—Virgil?"

"Yeah?"

"You're not pulling a boat, are you?"

"No. I'm not," Virgil said. "Swear to God."

"Good. Stay out of the fuckin' boat and on the case," Davenport said. "If there are really two guys down, and one of them is an ex-cop, you'll start taking some heat."

"Talk to you," Virgil said.

THE REST STOP ran a half mile or so parallel to the highway. A patrolman was parked at the entrance, half blocking the "cars" lane, waving cars into the "trucks" lane. He waved Virgil through, and Virgil went on down to the parking lot. A Chisago County sheriff's car was parked by the main rest stop pavilion, and four more cars, two patrol and two sheriff's, were parked at the far end of the lot, engines running, headlights aimed back into the woods along the edge of the rest area. The cop at the pavilion pointed Virgil toward the end, where Bunton had said the bodies would be.

Virgil parked, got a flashlight from his equipment bin, and hopped out. A highway patrol sergeant hustled toward him, carrying another oversized flashlight.

"Flowers?"

"Yeah. Two down?"

"One, at least. It's complicated. I'm Dave Marshall. Come on. I've got your crime-scene guys on the way, this belongs to the BCA."

"Did you find them, or had they already been found?"

"We found him, after your call." He gestured back up at the rest stop. "We've moved all the traffic into the truck lane, we're still letting people pee, but nobody comes into this area. I've got a guy back in the woods on the north side, keeping an eye on that."

THE BODY WAS that of a large man, lying on his back, in the trees, arms outspread. He had high, thick cheekbones and a linebacker's neck: a guy in good shape, carrying no fat, somewhere between thirty and forty. His pant legs had been pulled up when he went down, and his thick, hairy legs stuck down into incongruous red-striped white athletic socks. His mouth was open: no lemon.

"There's a Beretta, there, off the trail," Marshall said, turning the flashlight on it.

Virgil spotted it, nodded. "I'm gonna need to pick it up," he said. "You got any gloves in your car?"

"Yeah. You want them now?"

"You said there was some confusion. Tell me about the confusion."

Marshall nodded. "Look—this guy was probably shot right here." He pointed down to the flagstone path. "You can see blood on the stones, where he bled out, and then he was dragged back into the brush. See the scrapes? See the heel marks? And there's more of a blood trail. . . ." His flashlight spotted the blackish stripes of blood on the leaves of the trailside weeds.

"Now, look over here . . ." He led the way thirty feet down the path.

"Another patch of blood. Not as big as the first one, but significant. We thought maybe that the dead guy had been shot once and ran, but there's no blood on the path between here and there, and this puddle . . . patch, whatever . . . seems like it might have taken a few minutes to accumulate. Also . . ." He pointed the light back off the trail. "We have a second pistol, a Glock."

He continued, pointing the flashlight back into the brush: "Now, we've got a little track between here and the parking lot. Like somebody was trying to stay under cover. And we have more traces of blood. . . ."

"Maybe there was a shoot-out and the shooter was hit."

"Possible," Marshall said, "but the word we got from you, from your source, was that there was one shooter and two victims. What it looks like, to me, is that the one guy got killed. The other guy was wounded, and the shooter carried his ass over to the parking lot. He took *his* gun with him. There's another drop of blood on the sidewalk."

Marshall took him through the brush, spotting the blood trail. They carefully stayed off the trail itself so crime scene could work it, and at the parking lot, Virgil looked both ways and then at Marshall and said, "I'm buying your story."

"We put out word to local hospitals, for a guy with any kind of a wound where it's not clear where it came from . . ."

VIRGIL WENT BACK to look at the body, and Marshall went out to his car to get some gloves. When he came back, he said, "Your crime-scene guys might get pissed if you mess with the pistol."

Virgil said, "That's why they pay me the big bucks. To put up with crime scene."

He pulled the gloves on, knelt next to the Beretta, studied it for a moment, then gently lifted it, popped the magazine. Pressed down on the top round: the magazine was light one round. He worked the action and a round popped out of the chamber.

Sniffed the barrel, and smelled oil.

Okay. The dead man hadn't fired a shot, unless he'd reloaded after he was dead. Virgil slipped the magazine back in the butt of the pistol, replaced the pistol as he'd found it, and put the ejected round on top of it.

"So what does that tell you?" Marshall asked.

"That he didn't see it coming. That he didn't get a shot off. That the shooter wasn't wounded by him," Virgil said.

"I knew that," Marshall said.

Virgil went to the second gun, repeated the sequence: same story—an unfired gun.

"Two guys, plus one shooter. Your story looks even better," Virgil said. He pulled off the gloves. "You got any veterans' monuments around here?"

"Every town, just about," Marshall said.

"Start calling up the local cops—tell them to keep an eye out," Virgil said. "The killer's gonna dump the dead guy's body on a monument somewhere."

VIRGIL WALKED BACK up the parking lot, looking for surveillance cameras. Didn't find any. Asked the patrolman at the pavilion. "Don't think they've got any," he said. "Probably should."

"Doesn't seem right," Virgil said. "They've got them everywhere else."

He looked around a little more, found nothing, and was walking back toward Marshall when the crime-scene van rolled by. The head guy gave Virgil the required ration of shit about messing with the scene, then shut up, because he'd worked Homicide and would have done the same thing Virgil had done.

"Good to get the name as soon as we can," Virgil said. "We need to look at his place, make sure nobody's turning it over."

So they did the wallet first.

David Ross, thirty-two. Ross had a Virginia driver's license, but also a checkbook with an address in St. Paul.

"I'm going down there. You get *anything* . . . call me. I don't care how stupid it is," Virgil said.

BACK DOWN the highway, flying through the night, talking to the duty guy at the BCA, vectored into Wigge's house. Wigge lived in Highland Park, one of the nicer neighborhoods in town. The house was dark, but when Virgil walked toward the front door, two lights came on, spotlighting him on the driveway. He continued to the front door and knocked, and the instant he knocked, more lights came on inside.

Security systems. Serious security. Nobody came to the door.

The houses here were well spaced, with broad lawns. He looked left and right, saw a light come on in the back of the next house to the west. He walked that way, up the front walk, and knocked on the door and rang the doorbell. A voice inside: "Who is it?"

"Bureau of Criminal Apprehension."

The door popped open, on a chain. A worried woman looked

through the crack between the door and the jamb, and Virgil held up his ID.

"Can you tell me, does John Wigge live with anyone? Wife? Girlfriend?"

"We don't know him very well, but he lives alone," the woman said. "Has something awful happened?"

"Why would something awful happen?"

A man's face appeared at the crack: "Because you're beating on doors at two o'clock in the morning?" A St. Paul patrol car glided to a stop at the curb, and the man added, half apologetically, "We called 911."

Virgil said, "That's okay—I needed to talk to them."

He walked out to the curb, holding up his ID, called, "Virgil Flowers, BCA."

A St. Paul sergeant came around the car and said, "It's that fuckin' Flowers."

"That you, Larry?"

Larry Waters knew Wigge. "He's divorced. His old lady moved back to Milwaukee. I haven't heard that he was going out. He gone for sure?"

"The odds are pretty good. A guy who was at the scene, and knows him, says he was shot. We're missing the body, though," Virgil said. "He had a rep."

"Yeah, and he deserved it," Waters said. "Now he's got all these crazy gun-fucks coming in here, driving around in GMCs with blacked-out windows. He's contracting guys from all over the country, for security for the convention. There are some serious badass killers coming in."

"I talked to Davenport. . . . You know Davenport?"

"Sure."

"He says the security company, Paladin, is owned by Ralph Warren."

"Yeah, that's right. Between you and me, Warren's a bigger asshole than Wigge," Waters said. "He went bust about three times before he tapped into the city money and started building subsidized buildings all over town. . . . Probably as dirty as Wigge, but he was putting the money into the envelopes instead of taking it out."

"Paying people off?"

"Yeah. Wasn't any big secret. But it was subtle. He'd keep somebody in the public employee unions happy, and they'd talk to their friends on the city council, and things got done. He didn't just drop a load on somebody's desk. You weren't gonna get him on a camera."

Virgil talked to Waters for another couple of minutes, asked him to call some St. Paul guys to put some tape on Wigge's house until a crime-scene unit could get there or they found Wigge, whichever came second. Waters said he would, and Virgil headed downtown to David Ross's address.

ROSS LIVED IN an apartment that had once been a warehouse—another of Warren's projects. Virgil leaned on the mailbox buzzer for a minute, was surprised when a woman's voice asked, "Who's there?"

Jean Prestel was a schoolteacher, and looked like a schoolteacher, with short dark hair showing a streak of white over her ears—short and slender and earnest, and not somebody Virgil would have put with the dead, thick-necked David Ross. She was wearing a cotton nightgown with tiny teddy bears and little pink crossed ribbons on the breast, and she clutched her hands to her chest and asked, wide-eyed, "Oh my God, what happened?"

She fell to pieces when Virgil told her, and he sat on the couch with her and she wept, said, "What am I going to do now?" and "We didn't have any time" and "We were talking about getting married" and "Are you sure it was David?" and she showed him a photograph and he said that it was, and she rolled facedown on the couch and seemed to try to scratch through the seat cushions, weeping, weeping . . .

When he got her to the quiet, stunned stage, he asked about relatives, and she called her aunt, who said she'd come over. Her mother lived in Sioux Falls. And he asked her about Ross and what he'd been doing.

"He was working with John—I don't know exactly what he was doing, just, getting ready for the convention, I guess. But he got up every day at six o'clock and he'd go over to John's and pick him up, and he'd stay with him all day."

"How long had he been doing that?"

"Only a couple of weeks, and John said it wouldn't last very long, but that things were really intense now . . . and now David's dead? That can't be right. . . ." And she was gone again.

VIRGIL WAITED until Prestel's aunt arrived, then eased out of the apartment, leaving them with the misery.

He looked at his watch again: four-fifteen. Had to get some sleep.

Needed to talk to Ralph Warren, needed to track Ray Bunton. Needed sleep even more.

Talk to Warren in the morning, and start the hunt for Bunton, he thought.

He got an hour.

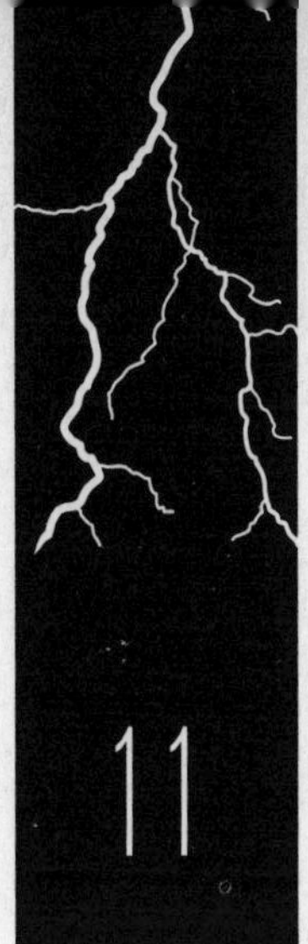

THE PHONE RANG.

Virgil was facedown on the bed: no coherent thought, just a lizard-like twitch. The phone didn't quit. He finally crawled across the bed and flipped it open, noticing, before he did it, that it was 5:23. He'd been in bed for a little more than an hour.

The duty guy: "Man, Virgil, I hate to do this to you."

Virgil groaned. "They found Wigge?"

"Yeah."

"It's bad, isn't it?" Virgil asked.

"Yeah, the lemon in the mouth, the whole thing."

"Where is he?" Virgil asked.

"You know up on Capitol Hill, the Vietnam veterans' monument by the Veterans Service Building? Not the name wall, but the green statue?"

"Ahhh . . . jeez." One of the best-known public spaces in the state, not ten minutes from where Virgil was lying.

"The St. Paul cops are there," the duty man said.

"Tell them that I'm on the way."

"Virgil . . . you know, the veterans' monument isn't the worst of it."

"Huh?"

"The St. Paul cops say it looks like Wigge, was, uh . . ."

"What?"

". . . was crucified."

THE VETERANS' MONUMENT is more or less on the front lawn of the enormous white state Capitol Building. The emerald-green lawn, the size of several football fields, stretched from the steps of the Capitol, down a broad hill dotted with monuments and flanked by government buildings, almost to the interstate highway that went through St. Paul, and looked toward downtown St. Paul and the Mississippi.

Virgil had taken two minutes to stand in the shower before he dressed and rolled out, hair still wet. In the parking lot, he found his truck hemmed in between a van and a sedan, so closely that he could barely get the door open without dinging the van: always something, he thought, when you were in a crazy hurry.

Wigge's body was beside the parking lot for the Veterans Service Building, and that's where he found the usual clump of cop cars. He waved his ID at the cop at the entrance to the parking lot, dumped the truck, and walked through the early-morning light down to a gaggle of cops gathered at the statue. Waters, the cop who'd met Virgil at Wigge's house, was among the dozen uniforms and three detectives, and he stepped over to Virgil and said, "This is bullshit, man. This is stickin' it right up our ass."

"Wigge for sure?"

"What's left of him," Waters said, his voice grim. "You're not gonna believe this. And there ain't no way we're gonna keep it off TV—it looks like he was nailed up, or something. Like Jesus."

WHEN VIRGIL had worked with St. Paul, he'd not known Wigge well, more to nod at than to talk to. When he looked down at the body, his first thought was, *Time passes*. Wigge was an old man. He hadn't been old when Virgil knew him, but he was old when he was murdered.

"Hell of a goddamned thing." Tim Hayes was a longtime St. Paul detective. A gaunt man, but with a small beer belly, he was watching the crime-scene people work over the body. "I understand you were looking for him up north."

"Yeah." Virgil pointed down the hill. "You see that building, that warehouse with the old painted sign on it? A guy who lives there was murdered off I-35 tonight and Wigge was with him, I think. There's some blood on the ground up there, and I think it was Wigge's. We'll match it."

"He probably spent some time wishing he'd died, before he did," Hayes said. "Look at this . . ." They edged up to the body, which had been planted under a bronze statue of a Vietnam veteran, and Hayes said, "Look at his hands."

He had no fingers or thumbs. The palms were all that remained, and in the center of each palm was a bloody hole. Virgil shook his head. "Ah, man. Ah, Jesus."

"See that sack?" Hayes pointed at an ordinary brown paper grocery sack, the kind that might have held three cans of beer. "His fingers are in there. They didn't just cut them off, they cut them off one joint at a time. With a pair of nippers of some kind. Brush cutters; tin snips. Something like that. I think there were, like, twenty-eight individual cuts. They tortured the shit out of him. He had bare feet, the bottom of his feet looked burned . . . they focused on his hands and his feet."

Crucified; but Virgil didn't think of Jesus, but of Jezebel, in 2 Kings 9:35, lying in the streets of Jezreel, and when the dogs were done, nothing was left but the palms of her hands and the soles of her feet.

Wigge was faceup; and between his gray lips, Virgil could see the yellow of the lemon.

"The shit's gonna hit the fan today," Virgil said, standing up, fighting the sour taste in his throat. "People are gonna be screaming for blood." He looked down toward the town. "Republicans gonna be here in a month, everybody's getting dressed up, and we got a crucified ex-cop on the front lawn of the state Capitol. Mother. Fucker."

He called Davenport: seven o'clock in the morning in Washington, and Davenport rarely got up before nine. Davenport answered with "It can't be that bad."

"It's worse," Virgil said.

DAVENPORT LISTENED as Virgil told him about the night, starting with the call from Bunton, through the murders off I-35, to the body at the Capitol. When he finished, Davenport said, "I'll call you back in five minutes or less."

Virgil walked around, looking at the scene, oblivious to the growing roar of cars on the I-35 as the rush hour started. The television crews would be here anytime, and the politicians would jump in with both feet.

Since there was nothing useful they could do, they'd start looking for somebody to blame. The whole thing would spin out of control. . . .

A cop came by: "What're you going to do about it?"

"What I *am* doing: try to find the guy who did this," Virgil snapped.

"Try harder," the cop said, squaring off a little. "Wigge was one of us."

"Why don't you go find the guy?" Virgil asked. "Gotta go write traffic tickets or some shit?"

Another nearby cop said, "Take it easy. . . ."

DAVENPORT CALLED: "I yanked Rose Marie out of bed, she's gonna do damage control," he said. "I'm coming back, but I can't get out until almost noon here. I won't be back until late afternoon. Listen: we're putting out the usual stuff to the media, Rose Marie will take care of it. But you gotta move. You gotta move, Virgil. What about Bunton?"

"I will get him today," Virgil said. "So help me God."

"I'll call Carol and tell her to get into the office. We'll start working the phones, we'll push everybody to find him. TV is gonna be all over us anyway, we might as well put it out there."

VIRGIL CHECKED the time, got a Minneapolis address for Ralph Warren, the owner of the security company, and headed that way. Found it, a white-stucco and orange-tile-roof Spanish-looking place off Lake of the Isles. Each square foot of the lot, Virgil thought, as he eased into the driveway, was worth more than his truck.

When he got out, a big man stepped out of the front porch, and then another came from the garage end of the driveway, both wearing black nylon windcheaters, both of them with their hands flat on their stomachs, as if they were holding in their guts. Actually, he knew, their hands were a quarter inch from a fast-draw weapon.

He called, "Virgil Flowers, Bureau of Criminal Apprehension, here to see Mr. Warren."

"Mr. Warren isn't up yet," said the man at the front door. Virgil was walking up the driveway, and the man said, "You should stop right there until we confirm your identity."

"Get Warren," Virgil said. He held up his ID.

The big man said something back into the house, and a third man looked out, nodded, and said, "Come on up to the porch."

Virgil walked to the porch, and the third man said, "Can I ask why you need to talk to Mr. Warren?"

"Because one of his vice presidents just got chopped into pieces about the size of a cocktail weenie, and that was after they crucified him," Virgil said. "Now, you wanna get him out of bed?"

"Who?" the man asked, but he was believing it.

"John Wigge."

"Are you shittin' me?"

"Can I talk to Warren, or what?"

VIRGIL WAITED in the entry, under the eye of the biggest of the three security men, while they got Warren. Warren was a man of middle height, an inch or two under six feet, with deep-set black eyes, a small graying mustache, and a gray scrubby-looking soul patch under his lower lip. He came out wearing a black silk dressing gown with scarlet Japanese characters on it, like the bad guy in a TV movie; if you squinted at him, he looked a little like Hitler.

"John Wigge . . ."

". . . and David Ross."

". . . and Ross, too?" Warren was astonished, but not astonished enough. Virgil thought, *He knows something.*

"They were ambushed at a meeting with Ray Bunton at a rest stop up north on I-35," Virgil said. "Do you know what they were talking about? Why they were meeting?"

"I don't know any Ray Bunton," Warren said. "Is this about the veterans thing?"

"If you don't know, how did you put that together?" Virgil asked.

"John told me. He said he knew the guys who were killed," Warren said. "That's why he had Dave Ross hanging out with him."

"But why are *you* stacking up with security?" Virgil tipped his head toward the bodyguard still in the room. The other two had moved back to their posts, wherever they were. "Three guys around the clock?"

Warren shook his head. "Nothing to do with that. I'm providing security for the convention. I've got two hundred guys in it, armed-response guys, bodyguards. I've got plans for the whole works right here in my briefcase, and the Secret Service requires, you know—they require that we keep it all under guard. The plans, me, everything."

"So this doesn't have anything to do with Wigge?" Virgil was skeptical.

"No, no. This is strictly the convention," Warren said. "You think this guy, the killer—you don't think he'd come after . . . people who know John?"

Virgil shrugged. "We don't know what he's doing, Mr. Warren. So the security is not a bad idea. But you're telling me that you didn't know about this meeting, about what's going on. Wigge never told you anything about it?"

"I think it might go back to his cop days—he said the Mafia might be involved," Warren said.

"The Mafia." Virgil let the skepticism show.

"That's what he said."

"In Minnesota?" Virgil asked.

"The Mafia is here," Warren said. "If you don't believe that, I can't help you."

"I know it's here—I know both guys," Virgil said. "Their average income last year was fourteen thousand dollars, from delivering pizza."

They talked for another five minutes, but Warren didn't know what was going on; he wanted a few details about Wigge's death, shook his head when Virgil told him about the torture.

"Why did they torture him?" he asked.

"They must think he knows something. They're trying to find something out. I don't know what that is."

"Well, I sure as shit don't—"

The conversation was interrupted by Virgil's cell.

Carol said, "We got a break, I think. I got a number for you, it's a cop out in Lake Elmo."

VIRGIL EXCUSED himself, walked out on the front lawn, and called Roger Polk, who was in Lake Elmo, all right, but turned out to be a

Washington County deputy sheriff. "The Liberty Patrol is on a run up to Grand Rapids for a funeral—"

Virgil said, "Wait, wait. The Liberty Patrol?"

"Bunch of bikers who provide security for the funerals of guys who get killed in Iraq. You know—they've got these antiwar church goofs who show up at the funerals to scream at the kid's parents? About how the kid deserved to die?"

"Yeah, I read something about that," Virgil said.

"The Patrol backs them off. Anyway, they met yesterday after work, and rode up to Duluth, sixty of them, about, riding in a pack. They're staying overnight in Duluth, and then they're heading over to Grand Rapids. One of the guys' wives is my sister-in-law, and she heard the thing on the radio, about Ray Bunton. She says that Ray Bunton was riding with them. She knows him. He's gone before."

"All right, all right. That's good, that's terrific," Virgil said.

VIRGIL SAID GOOD-BYE to Warren, trotted back to his truck, got out his atlas. Minnesota is a big state, but a good part of the northern third, where Bunton was heading, was vacationland: thousands of cabins on hundreds of lakes, surrounded by thirty thousand square miles of forest, bogs, and prairie.

As long as Bunton stayed on a highway, it'd be possible to locate him. If he were headed into the Red Lake reservation, as his uncle said he was, he'd be a lot harder to find. There was a history of animosity between the Red Lake tribal cops and outside cops, especially when it came to arresting tribal members.

And if Bunton weren't headed specifically to Red Lake, if he was planning to stop at one of the tens of thousands of cabins scattered all over hell, all off-highway, he'd be impossible to locate.

Best shot to catch him was on the highway and Bunton knew it—that was probably why he went up in a pack, using the other riders for cover.

VIRGIL GOT on the phone, talked to the highway patrol office in Grand Rapids. Because of the potential for trouble at the funeral, the Grand Rapids office knew where the Liberty Patrol was—still in Duluth. "They're eating down on the waterfront, making a little tour of it, picking up some Duluth guys."

"Do you have anybody traveling with them?"

"Nope. We're just talking to local deputies, who're passing them through," the Grand Rapids patrolman said.

"Have them take a look at the plates," Virgil said. He read off Bunton's plate number. "Don't be too obvious about it. We don't want to spook him."

"If your guy is in there, we'd have trouble pulling him out," the patrolman said. "Everybody's cranked about this funeral. We could have a riot here tomorrow, if those church people show up. We'd rather not have a riot tonight, busting one of the riders."

"So take it easy. I think he's riding up there as cover, so he can shoot the rest of the way up to Red Lake," Virgil said. "I'm coming up, I'll take him out. But keep an eye on him. If he makes a run for Red Lake, you gotta grab him."

"We'll keep an eye out," the cop said. "When'll you get here?"

"I'm driving and I got lights, so I'll be coming fast—but it's gonna be a while," Virgil said. "I won't catch them before they get there. Call me when you know anything at all."

"We'll do that."

HE CALLED Carol and told her where he was going; stopped at the motel, grabbed a change of clothes and his Dopp kit, but didn't check out; stopped at a Cub supermarket and bought some premade cheese-and-meat sandwiches, a six-pack of Diet Coke, and a sack of ice for his cooler. He packed it all up and headed north on I-35, lights but no siren, moving along at a steady hundred miles an hour, past the rest stop where he'd been at midnight—still cop cars where Wigge had been killed—almost to Duluth.

From there he hooked northwest through Cloquet toward Grand Rapids.

On the way, he got two calls. The first came an hour and ten minutes out of St. Paul, the highway patrolman reporting that Bunton had been spotted by a deputy who'd cruised the whole pack as they left Duluth. "Not sure it's him, but it's his bike."

"I'm coming," Virgil said. He was tired now, too long without sleep. Needed some speed, didn't have it.

When he was twenty minutes out of Grand Rapids, the Grand Rapids patrolman called again and said, "Your guy is still with the group. They just rode into town and we picked him out. It's the guy in your pictures. He's wearing a bright red shirt with a black do-rag on his head. Easy to track."

Tom Hunt, the state trooper, was waiting on the shoulder of the road just south of town. Virgil followed him into the patrol station, where Hunt transferred to Virgil's truck, tossing a shoulder pack in the backseat. "Saw him myself," Hunt said. Hunt was a sandy-haired man with wire-rimmed glasses, dressed in khaki slacks and a short-sleeved shirt. He looked more like a junior high teacher than a cop. "He wasn't trying to hide. He was like the third guy in line."

"Well, nobody ever said he was the brightest guy in the world," Virgil said.

Hunt looked out the side window and said, "Huh."

Virgil grinned. "So what you're wondering is, if he's so damn dumb, how'd he kick my ass?"

"Well, I figure, shit happens," Hunt said, being polite.

"Truth is, we were having a little talk—polite, not unfriendly," Virgil explained. "And he's an old guy. Got me looking in the wrong direction and sucker-punched me. He's old, but he's got a good right hand."

The Liberty Patrol had taken a block of rooms at an AmericInn, but after checking in had begun heading out to Veterans Memorial Park for an afternoon barbecue. Hunt directed Virgil through town to the park, which was built on the banks of the Mississippi. They left the car a block away, Hunt got the shoulder pack out of the backseat, and they ambled on down the street, cut through a copse of trees, onto a low mound covered with pine needles, the fragrance of pine sap all about them. Another guy was there, leaning on a tree. He turned when he heard them coming, and as they came up, Hunt said to Virgil, "Josh Anderson, Grand Rapids PD."

"He's still down there," Anderson said. "Got a beer, over by the barbecue."

The bikers were a hundred yards away, their bikes on one side of a pavilion, a few women clustered around a couple of picnic tables on the other side, the guys around two smoking barbecue pans. The afternoon breeze was coming at them, and Virgil could smell the brats and sweet corn, and the fishy scent of the river. Hunt unslung the pack, took out a pair of binoculars, looked over the gathering. After a moment, he said, "Huh," just like he had in the car. A rime of skepticism.

"What?" Virgil asked.

"There's a guy in a red shirt and a black do-rag . . . but he sort of doesn't look exactly like the guy I saw."

"Let me look." Virgil took the glasses and scanned the gathering, found the man in the red shirt, studied him, took the glasses down, and said, "We're too far away. We need a closer look."

Hunt asked, "You want more backup?"

"Ah . . . nah. If it's him, and he sees me, he'll either run or try to get the other guys to back him up. These other guys—they're not bad guys. I don't think they'll have a problem with an arrest for assault on a cop. And if he runs . . . we'll take him."

Anderson, the Grand Rapids cop, took a radio out of his pocket. "We've got a couple more guys around. We got a car across the bridge, we could block that."

"Do that," Virgil said.

ANDERSON MADE A CALL, then the three of them walked down to the pavilion. Something about cops, Virgil thought, got everybody looking your way. By the time they got to the group, most of the men were looking at them, but not the guy in the red shirt. He'd turned his back. Virgil let Hunt take the lead. He produced an ID and asked a guy, "Is there somebody in charge? We've had an issue come up. . . ."

While he was talking, Virgil walked over to the barbecue to get a closer look at the man in the shirt. As he walked around him, the guy first looked away, then glanced up. Not Bunton. But Bunton had been there—the way the guy looked at Virgil, half defiant, half placating, meant that he was wearing the red shirt and do-rag as a decoy. Virgil could see it in his eyes.

Virgil said, "Goddamnit," and turned and walked back to Hunt, who was talking to a gaunt, gray-bearded man who must have been pushing seventy.

"Darrell Johnson," Hunt said when Virgil came up. "He's the president."

Virgil stepped close to Johnson. "How long ago did he leave? Is he on his bike?"

Johnson's eyes shifted and he started, "You know . . ."

"Darrell, don't give us any trouble," Virgil said. "There's a felony warrant out on Bunton. I'm amazed you don't know—it's been all over the radio and television."

"We been ridin'. We didn't know," Johnson said.

"It's part of an investigation into the murders of four people—

including the three guys whose bodies got dumped on the veterans' memorials. You know about those? I guess the question is, are you guys only going to funerals? Or are you manufacturing them?"

Johnson sputtered, "What're you talking about? We didn't know Ray had anything to do with that. He said it was traffic tickets."

"It's murder, Darrell," Virgil said. "When did he leave?"

A couple more bikers had eased up to the conversation, including a woman with a plastic bowl of potato salad. Before Johnson could answer, one of the other bikers said, "I told you he was bad news. Something was up."

Johnson said, "Look, we came up here for this funeral. Those crazies are coming up, and we're gonna get between them and this boy who got killed."

Virgil said, "I'm a veteran, Darrell. I appreciate what you do. But we got four bodies. We gotta deal with that."

Johnson nodded, and sighed. "He got out of here probably fifteen minutes after we rode in. He went out the back. He said he was meeting a friend here."

"You see the friend?"

A few more of the bikers had stepped up. "I did," one of them said. "He was driving a piece-of-shit old white Astro van. Said something on the side about carpet service. Somebody's carpet-cleaning service. I think they put the bike inside of it."

Virgil nodded. "Thanks for that. Now, could you ask this guy in the red shirt to come over here? We don't want to disturb anybody, but we need to talk."

The guy in the red shirt was named Bill Schmidt. "He said he was dodging parking tickets," Schmidt said, not quite whining. "I don't know anything about any murders. He said the cops had a scofflaw warrant out for him."

Schmidt said Bunton was headed for the res, that a cousin had picked him up. He asked, "Are you gonna arrest me?"

"Not unless I find out you're holding something back," Virgil said. "This is serious stuff, Bill."

"He said *traffic tickets* . . ."

Virgil looked at Hunt: "He sucker punched me again."

VIRGIL LEFT Hunt and the others in Grand Rapids, put the truck on Highway 2 and headed northwest toward Bemidji, and called into the BCA regional office. The agent in charge, Charles Whiting, said he would touch base with every cop and highway patrolman between Grand Rapids and Red Lake.

"We can't play man-to-man, we've gotta set up a zone defense," Virgil said. "We need to get as many people as we can, sheriff's deputies and patrolmen and any town cops who want to go along, get them up on the east and south sides of Red Lake."

" 'Bout a million back roads up there."

"I know, but hell—he's trying to make time, he won't be sneaking around the lakes, he'll try to get up there quick as he can. If we flood the area up there, keep people moving, we should spot him."

"Flood the area? Virgil, we're talking about maybe twenty guys between here and Canada."

"Do what you can, Chuck. I'm thinking he probably won't risk Highway 2 all the way, there'll be too many cops," Virgil said. "He'd have to go through Cass Lake and Bemidji—I'm thinking he's more likely to take 46 up past Squaw Lake and then cut over."

"What if he's not going to Red Lake? What if he's going to Leech Lake?"

"Then he's already there and we're out of luck. But he's enrolled at Red Lake, that's where his family is, that's where they know him. . . . You get the people up there, I'm getting off 2, I'm turning up 46."

Virgil figured Bunton and his cousin had a half hour head start. They'd be moving fast, but not too fast, to avoid attention from cops.

Virgil, on the other hand, running with lights and occasionally with the siren, tried to keep the truck as close to a hundred as he could. He didn't know exactly how far it was from Grand Rapids to Red Lake, but he'd fished the area a lot and had the feeling that it was about a hundred miles by the most direct route. Longer, if you were sliding around on back roads.

Did the math; and he had to move his lips to do it. He'd take a bit more than an hour to get to Red Lake, he thought. If they had a thirty-mile jump on him, and were going sixty-five, and went straight through . . . it'd damn near be a tie. Even closer, if they were staying on back roads, where it'd be hard to keep an average speed over fifty.

Red Lake, unlike the other Minnesota reservations for the Sioux and Chippewa, had chosen independence from the state and effectively ran its own state, and even issued its own license plates and ran its own law-enforcement system, including courts, except for major crimes. And for major crimes, the FBI was the agency in charge.

In addition, the relationship between the Red Lake cops and the state and town cops had always been testy, and sometimes hostile.

Though it wasn't all precisely that clear, precisely that cut-and-dried.

Some of the reservation's boundaries were obscure, some of the reservation land had been sold off, scattered, checkerboarded. Sometimes, it wasn't possible to tell whether you were on the res or off . . . and sometimes, maybe most of the time, all the cops got along fine. A complicated situation, Virgil thought.

Virgil came up behind an aging Volkswagen camper-van, blew past, listened to the road whine; lakes and swamp, lakes and swamp, and roadkill. A coyote limped across the road ahead of him, then sat down on the shoulder to watch him pass, not impressed by the LED flashers.

WHITING CALLED: "Got all the guys I can get and a bunch of crappie cops will help out, stay in their trucks instead of hitting the lakes."

"Okay, but tell those guys to take it easy," Virgil said. "They're a little trigger-happy."

"Yeah, well—I'm not going to tell them that," Whiting said. "*You* tell them that."

"Chuck . . ."

"And listen, goddamnit, Virgil, you take it easy when you get up to Red Lake. We've got a decent working relationship with those folks, right now, and we don't want it messed up."

"Chuck, you know me. I am the soul of discretion," Virgil said.

"Yeah. I know you," Whiting said. "I'm telling you, take it easy, or I will personally kick your ass."

HE BURNED PAST Cut-Foot Sioux Lake, past Squaw Lake, made the turn at the Alvwood crossroads on Highway 13, which became 30 when he crossed the Beltrami County line, headed into Blackduck. Blackduck slowed him down, but he got through town, eating a sandwich from his cooler, drinking a Coke, paging through his Minnesota atlas, onto Highway 72 going straight north . . .

Worried some more: he was getting close, and nobody had seen Bunton or the van. Maybe they had ditched in a cabin somewhere, or back in the woods, waiting for nightfall to make the final run in.

Phone rang. Whiting: "Got them. Spotted them. They're ten miles out of Mizpah. Running to beat the band, heading toward Ponemah . . ."

"Let me look, let me look . . ." Virgil fumbled with his maps. "Who we got on him?"

"DNR guy, but he's pulling a boat, he's not gonna run them down," Whiting said.

"Ahh, I can't read this map," Virgil said; he was going too fast to track across the map pages.

"Where are you?"

"Uh, Highway 72, I went through Blackduck five minutes ago."

"Let me look on our maps . . . Okay. You're gonna come out right on top of him," Whiting said. "Let me give you a radio channel, you can talk to the DNR guy, and I've got a sheriff's deputy I can pull down there, I think."

They found a mutual radio channel and Virgil got the DNR guy, who was shouting into his radio, "Man, they're pulling away from me—they aren't stopping, they got the best part of a mile on me, I just passed Hoover Creek, we're not but five miles out of Kelliher . . ."

Virgil was six or seven miles out of Kelliher; Jesus, it was going to be close. And Virgil was cranked. What nobody ever told the civilians was, a good car chase was a hoot, as long as you didn't get killed or maimed, or didn't kill or maim any innocent civilians.

Sheriff's deputy came up. "I'll be in Kelliher in two minutes. Where is he, where is he?"

"We'll be there in one minute," the DNR cop shouted. "I can see it, goldang it, he's just about there, and with this boat, I'm all over the place."

Bunton's van busted the intersection—never slowed. Virgil saw lights coming both from the east and the north, and said, "I'm a minute out, guys, let's not run over each other. . . ."

The sheriff's car made the turn, then Virgil, with the DNR guy trailing. The deputy called, "We're about twenty miles off the res, depending on how he does it. We're asking for help there, but they're not too enthusiastic."

"So we're gonna have to push him off before he gets there."

The van was holding its distance, but Virgil closed on the deputy and said, "Let me get by here. If there's a problem, we can let the state pay the damage."

The deputy let him by, and Virgil slowly pulled away from him but hardly closed in on the van. Two minutes, three minutes, and then the van made a hard bouncing left, and Virgil almost lost the truck in the ditch, had to fight it almost to a complete stop before he was okay, and then he punched it and they were off again, and the deputy called, "Okay, there's only one way in from here, you got a hard right coming up, but if we don't get close before then, he's gonna make it across the line."

Virgil let it all out, traveling way too fast, right on the edge of control, and began closing up on the van. Another two minutes, three minutes, and now he was only a hundred yards behind, freaking out, when the van suddenly slowed again and cranked right. Virgil was ready for it, and came out of the turn less than fifty yards behind.

"Got another left," the sheriff's deputy screamed, and Virgil and the van went into the hard left and the deputy shouted, "They're almost there."

Up ahead, Virgil could see a truck parked on the side of the road— not blocking it— and two men standing beside it, safely on the ditch side, looking down at Virgil and the van. *That,* Virgil thought, *must be the finish line.*

He hammered the truck, closing in, and the van swerved in front of him, but Virgil saw it coming and went the other way, and with a quick kick he was up beside it, and he looked over at the other driver, who seemed to be laughing, pounding on the steering wheel, and Virgil said, aloud, "Fuck it," and he moved right and as they came up to the parked truck he leaned his truck against the van and the van moved over and he moved close again, so close that the mirrors seemed to overlap; he moved over another bit.

Waiting for the scrape of metal on metal: but the other driver chickened out, jammed on his brakes, tried to get behind Virgil, but Virgil slowed with him and in a dreamy slide, they slipped down the road to the parked truck and the van went in the left-hand ditch and Virgil was out with his gun in his hand, ignoring the two men in the parked truck, screaming, "Out of there, out of there, you motherfuckers."

Out of control. He knew it, and it felt pretty good and very intense, and if one of these motherfuckers so much as looked sideways at him he was going to pop a cap on the motherfucker. . . .

He could hear people yelling behind him, and then the driver got out of the van with his hands over his head but still laughing, and then Ray Bunton got out on the other side and began running across the swampy scrub, and Virgil turned and shouted, "Watch this guy," to whoever was behind him, and he took off after Bunton.

Virgil was in his thirties and ran on most nice nights. He liked to run. Bunton was sixty-something, had smoked since he was fourteen, and was wearing a leg brace. Virgil caught him in thirty yards, ran beside him for a second, and when Bunton looked at him, Virgil clouted him on the side of his head and the old man nose-dived into the dirt.

Virgil put a knee in the small of Bunton's back, with some weight, pulled the cuffs out of his belt clip, and wrestled Bunton's arms behind his back and cuffed his wrists.

"C'mon, dickhead," he said, and pulled Bunton to his feet. As they came back to the trucks, and the van in the ditch, the DNR cop was just pulling up, trailing his boat. Two Indian men, one older, in his fifties, the other young, maybe twenty-five, were standing between Virgil and his truck. Neither one wore a uniform, but both were wearing gunbelts. "Where're you going with him?" asked the older of the two.

"Jail," Virgil said, tugging Bunton along behind.

Bunton said, "Don't let him do it, Louis. I'm on the res."

"You can't have him, son," the older man said. "You're on reservation land."

"Sue me," Virgil said.

The two men stepped down to be more squarely between him and the truck, and the younger man dropped his hand to his gun and Virgil picked it up. "You gonna shoot me?" he demanded. He edged up closer to the younger one. "You gonna shoot me?" He looked at the sheriff's deputy still at the side of the road, with the DNR guy coming up behind. "If these assholes shoot me, I want you to kill them."

The deputy called, "Whoa, whoa, whoa . . ."

Virgil was face-to-face with the younger man. "C'mon, take your gun out and shoot me. C'mon. You're not gonna pussy out now, are you?"

"Son—" the older man began.

"I'm not your son," Virgil snapped. "I'm a BCA agent and this guy"—he jerked on Bunton's arm—"is involved in the murders of four people. I'm taking him."

"Not gonna let you do it," the younger man said, and his hand rocked on the butt of his pistol. "If I gotta shoot you, then I'm gonna shoot you."

Virgil was quick, and his pistol butt was right there. He had his gun out in an instant, and he stepped close to the younger man, who'd taken a step back, and he said, "Pull it out. C'mon, pull it out, Wyatt Earp. Pull the gun, let's see what happens."

"Wait, wait, wait, wait," the older man said, his voice rising to a shout. "You're crazy, man."

"I'm taking him," Virgil said.

"Louis . . ." Bunton said.

The older man's eyes shifted to Bunton. "Sorry, Ray. Little too much shit for a quarter-blood. Maybe if we had some more guys here . . ."

The younger man looked at Louis, said, unbelieving, "We're gonna let him take him?"

"Shut up, stupid," the older man said. "You want a bunch of people dead for Ray Bunton? Look at this crazy fuckin' white man. This crazy white man, he's gonna shoot your dumb ass bigger than shit."

He turned back to Virgil. "You take him, but there's gonna be trouble on this."

"Fuck trouble," Virgil snarled.

The younger man nodded. "I'll come down there . . ."

But the tension had snapped. Virgil said to Bunton, "Come on."

As they passed the sheriff's deputy, the deputy said, "That was pretty horseshit," and to Louis, "Man, I'm sorry, Louis. This is a murder thing. I hate to see it go like this, you know that."

Louis said, "I know it, but you got a crazy man there. Hey, crazy man—fuck you."

Virgil gave him the finger, over his shoulder without looking back, and heard Louis start to laugh, and Virgil put Bunton in the truck, cuffed him to a seat support, shut the door. Then he stepped back and put his head against the window glass, leaning, and stood like that for a moment, cooling off.

After a moment, he walked back to the two Indians and said to the older man, "I'll come and talk to you about this sometime. I drove from St. Paul to here at a hundred miles an hour—I'm not kidding. Hundred miles an hour, just to take this jack-off. He put me in the hospital a couple of days ago, and there really are four dead men down there, executed, shot in the head, and he knows about it. If you'd taken him on the res, you'd be up to your ass in FBI agents. This is better for everybody."

"Well, you were pretty impolite about it," Louis said.

"Yeah, well." Virgil hitched up his pants. "Sometimes it just gets too deep, you know? You can have the other guy and the van, if you want them. I'm not interested in him."

"Still gonna kick your ass," the younger man said.

"Keep thinkin' that," Virgil said, and clapped him on the shoulder before he could step back, and walked back to his truck.

The DNR guy was there, looking stoned, like most of them do. "That was way fuckin' cool," he said.

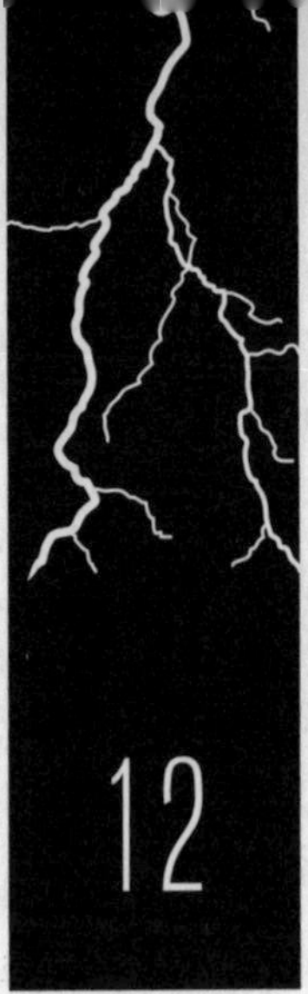

12

In the truck, Virgil backed in a circle, careful on the narrow road, held a palm up to the deputy, and headed back east, away from the reservation.

"Where're we going?" Bunton asked. One hand was pulled forward and down between his legs, almost under the seat, and Bunton was humped over and down.

"Bemidji. I'm gonna put you in a little dark room in the county jail and I'm gonna kick your ass. By the time you get out of there, you're gonna look like a can of Campbell's mushroom soup."

"Ah, bullshit," Bunton said. "Why don't you undo my hand? This is gonna kill my back, riding to Bemidji this way."

Virgil looked at him, sighed, pulled the truck over. "If you so much as twitch the wrong way, I'll break your goddamn arm," he said, and he got out, walked around the truck, unsnapped the cuff, and snapped it back onto the safety belt. As he was walking around to get into the truck again, the deputy rolled by, dropped his passenger-side window.

"If I were you, I'd get out of rifle range," he said.

"Think I'm okay," Virgil said.

The deputy shook his head. "Don't call me again," he said. "You might be okay, but I gotta roam around here on my own."

Virgil opened his mouth to apologize, but the deputy was rolling away. The DNR guy came up, dropped *his* window, and said, "You're the writer guy, huh?"

Virgil said, "Yeah, I do some writing."

"I read that piece on ice-fishing on Winni . . . Wasn't as bad as it might have been, but, anyway, you just weren't drinking enough." He said it with a smile.

"Well, thank you, I guess," Virgil said.

"We got a regional meeting up here in September, we're looking for a speaker . . ."

What he meant was *cheap speaker*. Virgil gave him a business card, told him he was available to talk if he could get the time off.

"We'll be in touch," the guy said. "Hell of a run; that's why I love this shit. But I gotta tell you, man, it's better in a boat."

"I hear you," Virgil said.

WHEN HE GOT BACK in the truck, Bunton had managed to dig a cigarette out of his shirt pocket and light it. Virgil said, "This is a no-smoking truck."

"I'll blow the smoke out the window," Bunton said.

"One cigarette," Virgil said, and he touched the passenger-window button and rolled it down.

Bunton nodded. "You lost. I made it across the line. You had to cheat to get me."

"Wasn't a race, Ray. There are four people dead now, and you know who did it," Virgil said.

"No, I don't."

"Ray, goddamnit, you know something. What I want to know is, are there more people gonna get killed? Are you gonna get killed?"

"Maybe," Bunton said. "But I need to talk to a lawyer."

"Fuck a bunch of lawyers. Talk to me. I'll give you absolution right here. Your sins won't count."

"How about the crimes?" Bunton asked.

"Those might count," Virgil admitted. "But you're obligated—"

Bunton cut him off. "Here is why I can't talk to you, okay? I'll tell you this."

Virgil nodded. "Okay."

Bunton thought it over for a minute, taking another drag on the cigarette, blowing the smoke out the side window. "I once did something that, if I tell you about it, I might get put in Stillwater. Not murder or anything. Not really anything that bad—not that *I* did, anyway. But if I go to Stillwater, I'll get murdered just quicker'n shit. I won't last a month, unless they put me in solitary, and even then, something could happen."

"Okay . . ."

"And if I don't tell you . . ." Bunton looked out at the low, crappy landscape. "If I don't tell you, and you don't catch this asshole who's killing us . . . then I might get killed. Shit, I probably will get killed. So I don't know what the fuck to do, but I got to talk to a lawyer."

"We'll get you a lawyer as soon as you heal up," Virgil said.

"Heal up?"

"From me puttin' you in that room and beatin' the crap out of you."

Bunton half laughed. "I had you figured out way back in the garage. You're one of those good-old-boy cops. Now, if you were John Wigge, I might tell you what I know, because if I didn't, Wigge'd get out a pair of pliers and start pulling off my balls."

Virgil thought about Wigge for a moment, and the cut-off fingers.

"Let me tell you about Wigge," Virgil said. "We found his body, but not at the rest stop. Whoever did this . . ."

He told Bunton about it, Bunton's face stolid, like it had been carved from oak. When Virgil finished, Bunton took another drag and said, "I just . . . shit. I gotta talk to a lawyer."

They rode along for a minute, and then Virgil said, "I'll have a lawyer waiting for you in Bemidji. But you gotta make up your mind quick. Things are happening."

"I'll tell you what, I might be fucked," Bunton said. They crossed a patch of swamp and he snapped his cigarette into it. "My best chance would be up on the res. If I was up there, they couldn't get at me. Even people who live up there, they can't find you if you don't want to be found."

Virgil said, "You said, 'this asshole who's killing us.' Can you tell me who 'us' is?"

Bunton shook his head. "Not until after I talk to the lawyer. 'Us' is part of the problem. 'Us' is why I want to get up in the woods."

He wouldn't talk about it anymore; he'd talk, but not about the killings. "I had enough dealings with the law to know when to keep my mouth shut," he said.

"Then you gotta know you're in some fairly deep shit, Ray. When you whacked me on the head, put me in the hospital . . ."

"The *hospital*? You pussy."

"Hey, I didn't ask to go. They took me in an ambulance, I was *out*."

"Didn't mean to hit you that hard," Bunton said.

"Shouldn't have hit me at all. Whacking me earned you two years in Stillwater, my friend. Ag assault on a police officer. And if you don't want to be in Stillwater . . ."

Bunton said, "It's not Stillwater—it's the guys who could get me killed in Stillwater. If you bust them, then Stillwater's okay. Sort of like having really good Social Security. I could get my teeth fixed, for one thing, and maybe even my knees."

"So you're saying that there are people *outside*, who could order you killed *inside*. Like dopers?" Virgil asked.

"Fuck you," Bunton said. "You're trying to sneak it out of me. I ain't talking to you anymore."

He did, but only about rock 'n' roll. "What's that shirt you've got on?" he asked. "Is that a band?"

Virgil looked down at his chest. He was wearing his KMFDM "Money" shirt: "Yeah, over on the industrial end," he said. "You know, they're the guys who became MDFMK? Then they went back to KMFDM. And I think a couple of them spun off and became Slick Idiot at some point."

That was more information than Bunton needed. "The only fuckin' slick I know is Gracie Slick," Bunton said. "Fuckin' ABC, DEF."

Bunton liked the old stuff, acid and metal, narrative music, Jefferson Airplane, Big Brother, middle Byrds, Black Sabbath up to AC/DC, and some of Aerosmith and even selected Tom Petty; and some outlaw country.

Virgil tuned his satellite radio to a golden-oldie station and Steppenwolf came up with "Born to Be Wild."

"That's what I'm talkin' about," Bunton said, slapping time on the dashboard with his free hand. "That's what I'm talkin' about, right there," and they got back to 72, and turned to head out on the highway, looking for Bemidji.

THEY CUT A DEAL after two hours in a small office on the second floor of the Beltrami County Jail. Bunton had the advice of a public defender, a tall, gray-haired, heavyset woman named Jasmine (Jimmy) Carter who wore a strawberry-colored dress and a scowl.

The arguments:

- Bunton believed he would be killed if jailed or imprisoned, for reasons he wouldn't divulge to anyone but the public defender. He refused to allow Carter to pass on the details, but did allow her to tell Virgil and Harry Smith, the Beltrami County chief deputy, that she thought Bunton's fears might have some basis in reality, although she couldn't say so for sure.

- Virgil, speaking for the state, said that Bunton was guilty of assault on a police officer, resisting arrest, and numerous traffic offenses, some of which might be felonies. And he was almost certainly guilty of conspiracy to conceal a number of felonies and accessory after the fact to four murders. He would be held in jail, where he'd almost certainly be safe, maybe. Virgil suggested that some accommodation might be arranged if Bunton talked.

• Carter said that any accommodation would have to be arranged by herself through the Beltrami, Chisago, Hennepin, and Ramsey County attorneys, where the alleged crimes had taken place. The deal would have to be approved by a judge.

• Virgil said that all the bureaucratic maneuvers would take a lot of time, in which time more people might be murdered, adding to the list of charges that Bunton already faced, and that in the meantime he'd be held in a jail, where he'd probably be safe, depending.

• Bunton said he needed a cigarette really bad, and Smith said that the Beltrami County Jail was a smoke-free facility, and Bunton said, "You gotta be fuckin' kiddin' me."

• Virgil wondered aloud what would happen if a police officer, acting on his own, made a deal with a prisoner, that he wouldn't use any incriminating information divulged by the prisoner against him, but instead would consider it information from a confidential informant.

• Carter said it might be too late for that, that arrests had already taken place. Bunton said, "Wait a minute, I could go for that."

Carter said, "You probably could, but it's probably illegal." Virgil said, "He's already up to his ass in alligators. He's gonna get bit—this would at least give you an argument. Fact is, I don't give a shit about Ray Bunton if I can stop the killing."

• Carter said, "Let me think about it for a minute."

She took Bunton to an interview room, where they talked for fifteen minutes, and then emerged and said, "This is the deal. It's all oral, no paper. You go for a walk with Ray, and talk. When you're done, Ray is released to the custody of the Red Lake police force, and he agrees to testify for you in court in return for dropping charges."

"That's a deal," Virgil said.

She shook her head: "We're all going to hell for this."

THEY GAVE Bunton his cigarettes and lighter, but kept his wallet and all of his money and ID, and when they got out the door, Virgil said, "I'll tell you what, dickweed. You best not try to run."

"I'm not gonna run," Bunton said. He lit a cigarette and blew smoke and said, "This fuckin' state. Whoever heard of smoke-free jail? Christ, you can only jack off so much. Then what're you going to do?"

"Keep that in mind," Virgil said. "Which way?"

Bunton tipped his head. "Let's go down toward the lake."

They walked over to the lake, south and east, along a leafy street, a cool wind coming off the water, Bunton smoking, Virgil letting it go, and finally Bunton said, "You know who Carl Knox is?"

Virgil did. "What does Carl Knox have to do with this?"

"I don't know, and I'm afraid to ask."

"Tell me."

"It started with a bunch of bulldozers in Vietnam . . ."

CARL KNOX, and more lately, his eldest daughter, Shirley, were the Twin Cities' answer to the Mafia—a kinder, gentler organized crime, providing financing for loan sharks and retail drug dealers. They neither sharked nor dealt, but simply financed, and earned a simple two hundred percent on capital.

Knox, now in his middle sixties, also ran the largest used-heavy-equipment dealership in the area, buying, selling, and trading mostly Caterpillar machines. He also—law-enforcement people knew about it only through rumor—bought and sold large amounts of stolen Caterpillar equipment, and moved it in Canada north of the Fifty-fifth Parallel.

"Half the stuff up in the oil fields came through Knox, one way or another," Bunton said. "I was right there at the beginning." His voice trailed off. "Jesus Christ, this is awful."

"Is he the guy you're afraid of?" Virgil asked.

"Damn right I am. He's the fuckin' Mafia, man," Bunton said. "He needs to get rid of us. He's got some shooters from fuckin' Chicago on our ass."

"You know this for sure?"

"Well—no. But who the fuck else is it gonna be?" Bunton asked. "Who else has the shooters?"

"Tell me about it," Virgil said.

"I DON'T KNOW all of it," Bunton said. "Back at the end of March 1975 . . . I'd been in Vietnam in '69 and '70, I'd been out for five years. Anyway, this guy calls me. John Wigge. Wasn't on the cops yet—he's just out of the service, Vietnam. I got no job, he's got no job—but he says he's got a guy who'll pay us twenty grand in cash for two weeks' work back in Vietnam. Two weeks at the most, but it might be a little hairy. Shit, we were young guys, we didn't give a fuck about hairy.

"The story was this guy, Utecht, the one that got killed—his father was this crazy guy who operated all over the Pacific, selling heavy equipment. He sold a lot of shit to the South Vietnamese. Anyway, this guy is in Vietnam, and the place is falling apart. The North Vietnamese were coming down, everybody was trying to get out."

"I've seen the embassy pictures, the evacuation," Virgil offered.

"Yeah, that was like a month later. Anyway, Utecht, the old man, is in Vietnam, and he finds this whole field of heavy equipment, mostly Caterpillars, D6s up to D9s, is gonna be abandoned there. Good stuff. Some of it is almost new. And everybody's bailing out.

"So he cuts some kind of crooked deal with the South Viets, and brings in a ship, and calls up his kid, and tells him to get some heavy-equipment guys together and get his ass over there. We're gonna take this shit out of the country."

"Steal it?"

"Well—save it from the North Vietnamese. The enemy." Bunton grinned at Virgil, showing the nicotine teeth.

"All right," Virgil said.

"So Utecht knows Wigge, and Wigge knows everybody else, and he starts calling people," Bunton said. "I could drive a truck, I could figure out a Cat if I had to. Twenty grand. That was a shitload of money at the time. Two years' pay. So six of us, young guys, Sanderson was one . . . we all flew out to Hong Kong and then right into Da Nang. Not all together, whenever we could get on a plane, but all within a couple of days."

"I've heard of Da Nang, but I don't know about it," Virgil said.

"Da Nang? Big base in Vietnam. Port city. So we flew in, and Utecht, the old man, picked me up at the airport, and what I did was, I drove a lowboy. There were thirty fuckin' D9 Cats sitting there and all kinds of other shit. . . . You know what a D9 is?"

"No."

"Biggest fuckin' Cat there was, at the time," Bunton said. He dropped his cigarette on the street, stepped on it, shook another out of the pack. "Maybe still are. They used them to clear out forest. Go through a bunch of fuckin' trees like grease through a goose. Anyway, there was thirty of them at Da Nang, and they were just sitting there, waiting for the NVA. So here we are, with this lowboy and a bunch of heavy equipment guys to get the tractors going and to run them—that was the other guys. I'd haul them out to the harbor, and they'd lift them onto the ship with this big fuckin' crane. One of the guys told me that they were headed for Indonesia, they had some oil fields going there. . . . I mean, some of these dozers were like fuckin' new."

"All the guys who've been killed were on this trip?" Virgil asked.

"Yeah. Anyway, what happened was, I dropped off the last load at the port, wasn't just these Cats, it was all kinds of shit. Everything they could get moving. After I brought in the last load, they even picked up the fuckin' lowboy and took that on board. Then Chester—"

"Utecht. Chester Utecht, the old guy."

"Yeah, that one," Bunton said.

"Okay . . ."

"He's dead now. Died about a year ago, in Hong Kong, is what Wigge told me," Bunton said. He had to think a minute, to get back to the thread of the story. "Anyway, Chester pulls up in this old fucked-up Microbus, and as soon as the lowboy was off the ground, going on the ship, we took off to get the other guys. This was about forty-five minutes each way, from the port to the equipment yard. Chester had airline tickets to get us out of there, spread over a couple of days, and two of the guys were going with the ship.

"So we got back to the yard, and what do we find? I'll tell you—these dumb fucks were all about nine-tenths loaded and they'd set this house on fire. . . . And they were fuckin' arguing with each other . . . I mean like, they were freakin' out about this house, and screaming at each other, and they had these M16s. Chester said, 'Fuck it, we're going,' and we went. Me and another guy, who I think was Utecht, the younger one, the kid, but this is so fuckin' long ago . . ."

"Okay . . ."

"Me 'n' Utecht, we flew out of there, to Hong Kong, and then back to Minneapolis, through Alaska. Wigge went with the ship, I think, because I didn't see him again, and somebody else went with him. Sanderson, I saw a year or so later. I asked him what happened with the house, and he said some chick got killed—that somebody started yelling at them from the house, I don't why, and one of the guys got pissed. He was already drunk, and somebody started shooting, and one of these guys went into the house with an M16 and shot the place all up and maybe some chick got shot and I guess some old man got shot. Maybe some other people."

Virgil said, "Ray—you're telling me some people got murdered?"

"Yeah . . . maybe," Bunton said. He shrugged. "Who knows? The fuckin' place was going up in smoke. Thousands of people got killed. Maybe . . . hell, maybe it was self-defense."

"So why is this gonna get you killed?" Virgil asked. "What does Carl Knox have to do with it?"

"One of the guys was Carl Knox," Bunton said. "When Utecht got killed, Sanderson called me up. He was freakin' out. He said Utecht had got Jesus, and called him a couple of times, after Chester died, and said Utecht was talking about confessing the whole thing."

"Ah, man," Virgil said.

"So I'm thinking, Carl Knox—he's not exactly the Mafia, but he knows some leg-breakers for sure. If he was the one who killed the chick, and he heard about Utecht, and if he needed a hit man, I bet he could find one. Get one out of Chicago. If he needed to kill someone in prison, he could get that done, too. If he did the shooting. I mean, if there was a bunch of guys who said he did murder . . . You see what I'm saying? He kills Utecht to shut him up, but then he starts thinking, these other guys will know why. . . ."

"There's this thing—the victims have lemons in their mouths," Virgil said. "Even Wigge . . . but not his bodyguard."

"Don't know about that," Bunton said. "But I believe it goes back to 'Nam."

"I've been told that when they executed guys in Vietnam, sometimes they'd stuff lemons in their mouths to keep them quiet," Virgil said.

"Don't know about that, either." Bunton crushed his second cigarette and lit a third. "All I know is, I want to stay out of sight until I know where this is coming from. If it's Knox. I want to stay out of jail, stay out of sight."

Virgil counted them off on his fingers. "There was you, and Utecht, and Sanderson, and Wigge, and this old Utecht, Chester Utecht, and Knox . . . that's it?"

"There was one more guy," Bunton said. "Damned if I know his name."

"When they tortured Wigge, maybe that's what they were looking for," Virgil suggested. "The last names. Your name and the other guy's name."

"So that's good for you, huh?" Bunton asked. "Can't be more than two more murders."

BY THE TIME they got back to the jail, it was almost dark. Smith, the chief deputy, and Carter, the attorney, were playing gin rummy, and Carter had a stack of pennies by her hand. She looked up when they came in and asked, "What happened?"

"We need to call the Red Lake guys," Virgil said. His cell phone rang, and he looked at it: Davenport. "I gotta take this," he said. "You guys call Red Lake. I'm gonna run Ray out there."

DAVENPORT SAID, "I'm on the ground in St. Paul. I'm told you're chasing Bunton."

"Got him," Virgil said. "But I'm letting him go. This is the deal. . . ."

He told Davenport the story, and when he was done, Davenport said, "I don't know if we can hold up our end of the bargain."

"Neither do I," Virgil said. "But hell with it—let the lawyers work it out. That's what they're for. What's happening down there?"

"Wall-to-wall screaming," Davenport said. "Crazy accusations and finger-pointing. Complaints about competence, threats about budgets. Questions from the Secret Service."

"So—the usual," Virgil said.

Davenport laughed. "Yeah. Tell you the truth, I think everybody likes it—gives them something to do, and they can go on TV. But it'd be best if we could catch the guy like . . . tomorrow."

"Well, if we can get to Knox," Virgil said. "Bunton thinks Knox has a finger in it."

"He's wrong," Davenport said. "I know Knox. Knox would never do anything like this. Not in a million years. I don't doubt that he could make people go away, but if he'd done it, there wouldn't have been a ripple. No lemons, no monuments—just gone."

"Still gotta find him," Virgil said.

"Get your ass back here. I'll have Jenkins and Shrake chase him down, but I want you here to talk to him. What about this last guy?"

"Don't know—maybe Knox will know."

THE RES WAS DARK, clusters of houses scattered along narrow roads radiating out from the town of Red Lake. Ray steered Virgil to his mother's house—"Her name is Reese now, so that won't give me away."

The two Indian cops were waiting in Reese's yard, sitting on a concrete bench, drinking from cartons of orange juice. Virgil hadn't been introduced when they were all down in the roadside ditch, and when they got out of the truck, Bunton pointed to the older one and said, "Louis Jarlait, who used to bang the brains out of my little sister, and Rudy Bunch, who's going to kick your ass someday."

"Fuck him if he can't take a joke," Virgil said. Then to Jarlait: "Thanks for doing this."

"What are we supposed to do with him?" Bunch asked.

"Keep an eye on him," Virgil said. "Keep an eye out for strangers who might be looking for him. He says he'll be safe here . . . hell, ask him. Once you get him talking, he won't shut up."

Jarlait looked at Bunton. "You okay with this?"

"Only goddamned way I'm gonna stay alive," Bunton said. "Even if you guys kissed me off this afternoon."

"We don't have to keep him or nothing?" Jarlait asked Virgil. "He takes care of himself, I mean, moneywise?"

"He stays with his mom, maybe you could have a guy hang with him. We can talk about compensation for your time, maybe later?"

"What about him puttin' you in the hospital?" Bunch asked.

"We've decided to let that go," Virgil said.

The two cops looked at Ray, who nodded, so Jarlait shrugged and said, "Okay by me, I guess, if it's okay with Ray."

"So we're good," Virgil said. "And we're all good friends."

Bunch grinned, a tight grin. "If I were you, I wouldn't park my car in Red Lake."

"Rudy, Rudy . . ."

Bunton took Virgil inside to meet his mother, who seemed nice enough, and they sat down to chat, and Virgil fell asleep. A gunfight woke him up, but it was on television. "You passed out," Reese said. She was a heavyset woman, wearing a fleece, though the room was warm.

"Tired," Virgil said. "Listen, thanks for lettin' me sleep." He looked at his watch. He'd been out for two hours.

Bunton came in from the kitchen, crunching on a carrot. "You outa here?"

"I am," Virgil said. "You take it easy, Ray. This thing's gonna wear itself out pretty quick now. If you keep your head down for a week, you'll be okay."

Late, running for home, probably wouldn't make it back until 2 a.m. Looking at the stars, listening to the radio, singing along with a country hit by the Rolling Stones, "Far Away Eyes" . . .

Two calls on the way back. The first from Mai: "I had a pretty good time last night."

"Slammed the door on my ass," Virgil said.

"If I hadn't, you would have been climbing on me like ivy," she said.

"Might possibly be true," Virgil admitted. "That was quite the neck rub."

She giggled, sounding girlish, and asked, "So why don't you come over? We can walk out and get a Coke."

" 'Cause I'm two hundred miles away," Virgil said. "Had to run out of town. Looking for that guy."

"Find him?" she asked.

"That's an official police secret," Virgil said.

"Pooh," she said. "So . . . when do you return?"

Virgil thought about it for a minute, then said, "I'm on my way right now. I'll get back really late. Need to get some sleep. How about tomorrow night?"

"Call me."

He thought about what she'd asked him. *When do you return?*

DAVENPORT, VERY LATE, lights of the Twin Cities on the far horizon. "Can't find Knox. He's crawled into a hole. Shrake talked to his daughter, and she says he's traveling. Says he's taken up art photography as a hobby, and nobody knows where he is. Says he never takes a cell phone, so people can't bother him and he can concentrate on his art."

"You believe her?" Virgil asked.

"No. He's hiding out," Davenport said. "We need to know why. Are you on the way back?"

"Coming up to Wyoming."

"Okay . . . Tell me about this Vietnamese chick."

So they talked about it, Davenport sitting in a leather chair with a Leinie's, Virgil rolling along under the stars, big fat yellow-gutted bugs whacking the windshield like popcorn.

A wonderful summer night, Virgil thought. Or, as Ray would have said, a wonderful fuckin' night.

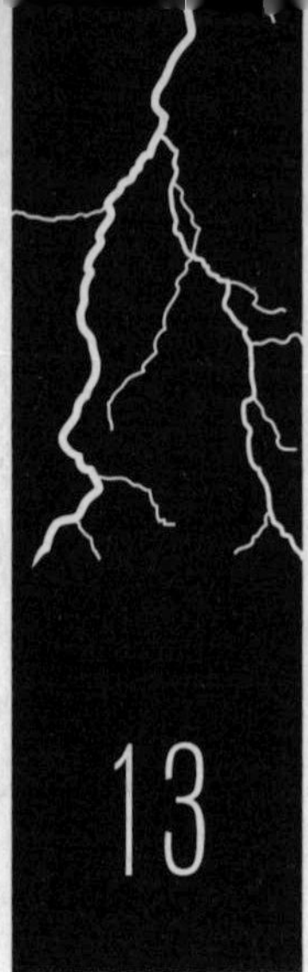

13

VIRGIL SLEPT until ten o'clock, when Davenport called. "Where are you?"

"About to leave the motel. I slept a little late," he said, sitting up in bed, scrubbing at his tangled hair.

"You gonna go talk to Shirley?" Shirley Knox was Carl Knox's oldest daughter.

"That's the plan," Virgil said. They'd worked it out the night before. First the push from Shrake, then another push from Virgil.

"I'll be running around with Rose Marie putting out brush fires," Virgil said. "We're pretty much guaranteeing people that it'll all be over in a week. They just don't want it to slop over into the convention."

"Good going," Virgil said.

"Hey, no pressure—if you can't produce, we can always turn it over to the FBI."

A USED Caterpillar 988B rubber-tire front-end loader, with a spade-nosed bucket, repainted and updated, sat on a patch of grass in front of Knox Equipment. A hand-lettered sign in the bucket said, in large black letters, "New Front Differential!" and under that, in smaller letters, "6000 hrs."

A hard-faced, dark-haired young woman was behind the counter. Virgil walked in, sniffing at the odor of diesel fuel, scuffing his boot heels. The woman had one yellow pencil behind her ear and another in her hand, and was focused on a stack of invoices and a hand calculator. On the wall behind her were two color portrait photos, with a sign that read, "Our owners." Under a picture of a square-faced man, a label said, "Carl." The other picture, of the woman behind the counter, said, "Shirley."

Shirley didn't look up for a minute as Virgil waited at the counter. Her lips were moving, and then she jotted a number on an invoice and looked up and smiled and said, "Sorry. You caught me in the middle. Are you Dave?" She had one slightly crooked front top tooth, and the smile and the tooth gave her a sudden snaky charm.

"Nope. I'm Virgil. I'm looking for Mr. Knox."

"Dad isn't here," she said. "If I could help you?"

Virgil shook his head, pulled his ID out, and said, "I really need to talk to him."

She looked vexed. "I talked to Officer Shrake yesterday. I explained all this."

"He's out taking photographs," Virgil said.

"That's correct," she said.

"Look—you, me, and all the wise guys on the corner, we all know that Carl is a big fat crook."

"That's not right . . ." She was sputtering, but faking it.

Virgil held up a hand. "I'm not recording anything, so you can save the act. We all know he's a crook, we all know he's hiding out because of these guys getting killed, and—I want to emphasize this, so you can tell him when you call him on your clean cell phone—we know why. Tell him we know all about the job in Da Nang, about stealing the bulldozers, and we don't care. Now. If he doesn't call me on my cell phone, we're going to put out a press release that says we're looking for Carl Knox in connection with these murders, and the TV stations will be on you like Holy on the Pope. So call him, tell him that, tell him Davenport doesn't think he's the killer, and tell him we need to talk."

"I'm telling you, I have no way of reaching him," she said, but she was lying through her teeth, and Virgil could see it, and she could see him seeing it. She smiled at him again, acknowledging all the knowing.

"Great. But when you call him, tell him that." Virgil snapped a business card down on the counter. "My phone number."

As Virgil turned to leave, she said, "He really is a photographer."

He stopped. "So am I. Is your dad any good?"

"Pretty good." She pointed to some big black-and-white prints hung along one wall, photos of old combines rusting in farm fields.

Virgil went over to look; they were okay, he thought, but not great. "Terrific shots," he said. He looked at them in a way he hoped was pensive, then drifted back to the counter and said, "Listen. I know you don't like us sniffing around, but I think your old man is in deep shit. Deeper than he might know. He better call us."

"I'm telling you . . ."

"Okay, okay—I'm just sayin'."

As he was going out the door, she called after him, "That Officer Shrake—does he work with you?"

"Sometimes," Virgil said. "He give you a hard time?"

"No, not at all. He was quite charming," she said.

"Shrake?"

"Yes. I was just thinking . . . what an attractive man he was."

KNOX EQUIPMENT was in the far northwest of the metro area, off I-94, the better to send stolen equipment up the line to Canada. Virgil fought the traffic back into town, and when he hit Minneapolis, pulled the phone out of his pocket and called the Sinclairs' apartment. No answer. He called Sandy and said, "I'll be at Wigge's house in twenty minutes."

"I'm in my car, on the way," she said.

A BCA INVESTIGATOR named Benson had been sent out to the house when Virgil reported the murders at the rest stop, had checked it for anything obvious, and had then sealed it. Benson had given the key to Sandy.

Sandy was sitting on the front porch with a white cat sitting next to her. The cat reflexively crouched, ready to run, when Virgil got out of his truck, but Sandy said "kitty" and scratched it between the ears, and the cat relaxed and stuck out its tongue.

"Virgil," Sandy said. She stood up, and the cat jumped down along the foundation, behind some arborvitae, and Sandy dusted off her butt. She was a latter-day hippie and carried an aura of shyness, which was starting to wear since she went to work for Davenport. She wore glasses, which apparently made her self-conscious, and when she was talking to Virgil she often took them off, which left her moon-eyed with near-sightedness. She was carrying a laptop. Virgil pulled off a seal, and she followed him through the door, and inside, they both paused to look around in the dry unnatural stillness. Owner dead. They could feel it coming from the walls.

"Must be a computer somewhere," Virgil said. They found a den, with bookshelves stuffed with junk paper—travel brochures, golf pamphlets, phone books, road maps, security-industry manuals and catalogs, gun books. The computer, a Sony, sat in the middle of it. Sandy brought it up, clicked into it. "Password," she said.

"Can you get into it?"

"Yeah, but I have to go around . . ." She began hooking the computer to her laptop, and Virgil started pulling the drawers on two file cabinets. In ten minutes, Sandy was going through the computer files and Virgil had found both a will and six years of income tax records.

Wigge had retired from the St. Paul force when he was fifty and had been with Paladin ever since; he was a vice president of the personal services division. In the previous year, he'd made $220,000 from all sources. One of the sources was better than two million dollars in investments, most of which were already in place in the earliest income tax records.

Someplace along the line, and it couldn't have been many years after leaving the police force, he'd had a windfall—but those years were the big tech-bubble years of the late nineties, so it was possible that he'd accumulated the money through either luck or intelligence.

His estate went to two sisters, one of whom lived in Florida, the other in Texas. Virgil didn't know whether they'd be notified of Wigge's death; notification wasn't his problem. Total estate, including the house, would push past three million.

"Not bad for a cop," Virgil told Sandy. "Anything in the computer?"

"Business e-mails. They did a lot of celebrity business. Concerts. Not much personal stuff. I haven't seen anything from your names—Utecht or Sanderson or Bunton or Knox."

"Anything that looks like anything—write the name down. Or print it."

Virgil began prowling the house and found a couple of phone numbers written on a Post-it pad next to the kitchen phone. One of the numbers was for Sanderson; the other was a northern Minnesota area code, and he got no answer when he called it. Red Lake? Had he been trying to reach Bunton?

He copied the unknown number into his notebook and moved on. Found a loaded .357 Magnum in a kitchen towel drawer. Found another one, identical to the first, in a side table in a bedroom that had been converted into a TV room, with a massive LCD television. A third one, just like the first two, in a bedstand in the master bedroom.

The bedroom also had a steel door, and a waist-high, pale yellow wainscoting on all the visible walls. When Virgil rapped the wainscoting with a knuckle, he found steel plate. So the bedroom, in addition to being fashionable, was also bulletproof. He pulled back the curtains and found a mesh screen over both windows. Wigge had been ready for a minor firefight, but the work wasn't new: he'd been ready for years.

Sandy called: "He's got an address book here. Contacts."

"Print it out."

He found a briefcase in the back hallway, looked in it: black address book, checkbook, pens, notepad, sunglasses, Tums, Chap Stick, a one-inch plastic ring-binder with upcoming security assignments.

He scanned the address book, but none of his names were in it. He found three numbers for Ralph Warren, owner of Paladin, Wigge's boss. Virgil put the phone book in his pocket.

THEY WORKED AT IT for three hours, piling up paper—Sandy running the computer files through Wigge's printer, the loose stuff through his tabletop Xerox machine. When they were done, they had a stack of paper three inches thick, everything from tax records to receipts.

"I'm not sure it means a thing," he told Sandy over bagels and cream cheese at a local bagel place. "The whole thing may fly back to Vietnam, right over the top of all this stuff with Warren. Just because he was a crook doesn't mean that had anything to do with him getting shot."

"Yes, it does," she said. "He went to Vietnam to steal bulldozers. He was a crook back then, and one way or the other, he got shot because he was a crook."

"You're such a charitable soul," Virgil said.

"In some ways," she said, and sort of wiggled her eyebrows at him.

"You know, Sandy, sometimes . . ." He thought better of it. "Never mind."

"What?"

"Ah, never mind."

"Chicken."

THEY SAT chewing for a moment, and then Sandy said, "If you think this Knox guy is moving around, then, you know, I don't know what you could do about it. But what if he has a place somewhere?"

"You mean, a hideout?"

"Sure," she said. "He's a rich crook, there might be people looking for him sometimes."

"Okay. How do we find a hideout?"

She shrugged. "If you've got a hideout, you pay property taxes on it. If you pay property taxes, and if you're greedy, you deduct the taxes from your income taxes, even if you want to keep the place secret. If you deduct from your income taxes, there'll be a tax form."

"Can we look at tax files?" Virgil asked.

"Absolutely."

VIRGIL CHECKED his watch when they got out of the bagel place: 1 P.M. What next?

"I'll drop you at your car, then I'm going to run around for a bit and then head back to the office to look at the phone numbers from Knox's place. Look at those tax records."

"Yup," she said. "Soon as I get back."

He dropped her at her car in front of Wigge's place. He called Sinclair, got no answer, and swung by, since he was so close. Rang the bell, still no answer.

"Shoot." Scuffed back down the sidewalk, looking up and down the street, hoping to see Mai, but didn't. He stalled, but finally got back in his truck and drove across town to the office.

AT DAVENPORT'S SUGGESTION, Virgil had a computerized pen register hooked into the phones at Shirley Knox's house, at Carl Knox's house, at the business, and for both of their cell phones; and had gotten a warrant delivered to the phone company for lists of calls made by the Knoxes' known phones.

Though, he thought, if they were really a bunch of crooks, they probably had unregistered phones, pay-as-you-go, which were cheap at Wal-Mart. Benson, the guy who'd sealed Wigge's house, was compiling the numbers from the Knoxes. Virgil stopped by his office: "Anything interesting?"

He shrugged, tapped on his computer for a moment, then printed out a list of numbers. "This is what we got. Numbers. It's a pretty big business—the numbers I've been able to find all go out to places that a heavy-equipment operator might call. But there are some that I couldn't tell you who the people are . . . but none of them's name is Knox."

Virgil checked the numbers against the number from Wigge's pad: nothing matched.

"Well, keep piling them up," Virgil said. "I'm done at the house, if you want to take a team over."

SANDY CALLED HIM on his cell phone as he was walking up to Davenport's office. "Where are you?"

"About thirty feet down the hall," he said.

She hung up and stuck her head out of Davenport's office. "Carl Knox has a cabin," she said. "What was that number you found at Wigge's? Was it up north?"

"Yup. You got Knox's number?"

"Yes, but it's not under his name—it's under one of his daughter's names, Patricia Ann Knox-Miller. But the cabin is his. He deducts the taxes."

"What's the number?" He opened his notebook as she read out the number for the cabin.

"That's weird," he said when she'd finished.

"What?"

"That's the number," he said. He looked up at her. "We found the hideout."

VIRGIL CALLED the number again, and once again failed to get an answer. Since he had the phone in his hand, he called the Sinclair number again, and this time, Mead Sinclair picked up the phone.

"I'd like to talk to you; I've got a Vietnam story for you," Virgil said.

"Always happy to hear Vietnam stories," Sinclair said. "Especially the ones where the American imperialist running-dogs get their comeuppance."

Virgil thought about that for a second, then said, "I bet you really pissed a lot of people off in your day."

"You have no idea," Sinclair said. "When are you coming over?"

"Right now."

"ARE YOU going north?" Sandy asked.

"Probably—but right now, I'm going over to the Sinclairs'. Could you get some plat books and spot Knox's place for me? Just send it to my e-mail."

"When are you going?"

"Don't know," Virgil said.

"I was thinking of going dancing tonight," Sandy said. "If you're around, we'll be at the Horse's Head."

"Sandy, you know . . ."

"What?"

"If I went dancing with you, I don't think Lucas would like it," Virgil said. "We're in the same group."

"Don't get your honey where you get your money," she said, one fist on her hip.

"I wouldn't put it that way," Virgil said. "But—think about it."

"I refuse to think about it," she said. "*You* think about it, when you're driving your lonely ass up to some godforsaken cabin in the North Woods."

"Sandy . . ."

VIRGIL WANTED to check with Davenport in person, but Carol, his secretary, said he was in his third crisis meeting at the Department of Public Safety downtown. "He'll be completely insane by the time he gets back. I know he wants to see you. He wants to make sure there's not a boat on the back of your truck."

"I'll be back," Virgil said.

In the hallway, he ran into Shrake, who was coming down the hall carrying a tennis racket with a cannonball-sized hole through the face of it, the strings hanging free. Virgil didn't ask. Instead, he said, "Hey—Shirley Knox sorta liked your looks."

"Yeah?" Shrake said. "I sorta liked hers, too."

"Gotta be careful," Virgil said.

"I'm cool," Shrake said. "So, uh . . . what'd she say about me?"

THE DAY WAS getting away from him, he thought, sliding from afternoon into evening as he got to Sinclair's apartment. Sinclair was barefoot, wearing white cotton slacks and a black silk shirt open at the throat. "Mai's not here," he said. "We should be able to talk in peace and quiet."

"She dancing?"

"Grocery shopping. She's running around somewhere, looking for a particular kind of food store. Some place that has seafood and weird spices."

"Gorgeous *and* a good cook."

Sinclair laughed. "She taught herself to cook fourteen things really well. Two weeks of dinners. Every other Wednesday, rain or shine, we have Korean *bulgogi*. Not bad. But today is okra gumbo day. Good gumbo, but you know, sometimes I'll wake up on gumbo day and I think I can't look another okra in the face. . . . I can't tell her that, of course." He led the way to the back porch and his stack of papers. "What's your Vietnam story?"

Virgil laid it out: the theft of the bulldozers, the shoot-out at the house, the deaths of the men in the circle of thieves.

"That's a great story, Virgil," Sinclair said, sitting back in a lounge chair, fingers knitted behind his head. "The business about the shooting in the house. The murders. That was a wild time—you think this could be a comeback?"

"I don't know," Virgil said.

"I did some research on you, you know, after you picked up that line from Virgil," Sinclair said. "You're a writer."

"I write outdoor stuff," Virgil said.

"Hey—I read that story about the moose hunt up in the Boundary Waters, and packing that moose out in the canoes. That's good stuff, Virgil. There's a great American tradition of outdoor writing, of exactly that kind. Teddy Roosevelt did it," he said, and Virgil got red in the face, flushing, pleased by the flattery, had to admit it.

Sinclair let him marinate in his ego for a moment, then continued: "Anyway, this Vietnam story, what you just told me. If you could get Bunton to repeat that, or any of them to repeat that, if they'd go on the record—and if there's a connection going back to those old days—I could put you in touch with a guy on the *New York Times Magazine*. They'd buy it in a minute."

"You think so?"

"I've been publishing for forty years in those kinds of magazines—they'd buy it," Sinclair said. "I mean, aside from the facts of the matter, it's a terrific story. A bunch of American rednecks flying into Vietnam as the place goes up in flames, to steal millions of bucks' worth of bulldozers? Are you kidding me? Keep your notes, buddy."

Virgil nodded. "But what do *you* think about the story?"

Sinclair ran his tongue over his lower lip, then shook his head. "I've worked with the Vietnamese for a long time. They can be a subtle bunch of people and they know how to nurse a grudge. On the other hand, they can be the biggest bunch of homeboy hicks that you could imagine. So I suppose it's *possible* that there's a Vietnamese connection . . ."

"But you don't believe it."

Sinclair shrugged. "I didn't say that. Millions of people were killed back then. *Millions.* Whatever happened in that house, however bad it was . . . was nothing. And the lemon thing. That's pretty obvious. It's like a flag to attract your attention. Have you thought about the possibility that it's coming from another direction?"

"Yeah, I have," Virgil said. "I've even got a guy I'm thinking about. But I don't want to take my eye off the Vietnamese connection, either."

"Which is why you were harassing Tai and Phem."

"Checked them out—they seem like they're on the up-and-up," Virgil said. "That's what the Canadians tell us, anyway. But who knows? They could be some kind of crazed Vietnamese hit team."

Sinclair nodded. "They could be. On the other hand, they could just be a couple of gooks who got lucky and were born in Canada instead of a reeducation camp."

"You still pissed about that?" Virgil asked.

"Yeah." He chuckled. "And they're still pissed at me. They don't believe that I didn't tell you about them."

Mai came back carrying two big grocery sacks, plunked them on the counter; she was wearing a simple white blouse and blue jeans, and looked terrific. She even looked like she *smelled* terrific, but when Virgil sniffed, he smelled raw crab. She asked, "Can you stay for dinner?"

Virgil thought about the okra. Okra is essentially a squid that grows in the ground instead of swimming in the ocean. He said, "I can't. I'm looking for a guy. Wouldn't mind walking you around the block, though."

"You should ask my daddy if it's okay."

"REALLY BORED," she said. They ambled along, and somewhere down the block she took hold of a couple of his fingers, and they went the rest of the way hand in hand. "St. Paul would be a nice place to live if you had something to do. I don't have anything to do."

"There's always sex," Virgil said. "You're away from home, where nobody knows you. You could indulge all your sexual fantasies and nobody would ever find out."

"But who would I sleep with?"

"We could put a notice in the paper, ask for volunteers."

"Did you ever find that guy you were looking for?" she asked.

"Yes, I did. He told me a strange story, which I just told to daddy. Something weird is going on. But I'll crack it," Virgil said.

"You think?"

"These things have a rhythm," Virgil said. "You get something going . . . it's like a plot in a novel. You start out with an incident, a killing, and there are millions of possibilities, and you start eliminating the possibilities. Pretty soon, you can see the line of the story and you can feel the climax coming. We're not there yet, but I can feel it. It's taking form."

"Be careful," she said. "This whole thing is pretty creepy."

BACK AT THE apartment, inside, at their door, she said, "You're sure you can't stay?"

"Got to move along," Virgil said; but he took a minute to kiss her. Didn't exactly catch her by surprise, but he felt a second of what might have been resistance, which surprised *him*, because they'd been getting along and he rarely miscalculated in these kinds of things—Sandy, for example, you wouldn't feel *her* stiffen up—and then Mai melted into him and the kiss got long and his hand drifted to her backside. . . .

"We gotta find a place," she said. She patted his chest. "The other night when I was sitting on your back . . . I got pretty warm."

"Well, I know a cabin over in Wisconsin," Virgil said. "We could go up for the day . . . but today and tonight, I'm working. I'm hunting for this guy—"

"Wisconsin. Let's go soon. I mean, I really *need* to go soon."

VIRGIL LEFT HER at the door and headed back to the motel, checked his e-mail.

Sandy had sent along a PDF file of a large-scale plat map, with an arrow pointing at the precise location of Knox's cabin on the Rainy River outside of International Falls, two hundred yards from Canada. A strange place for a cabin, for anyone else—but maybe not for a guy who did a lot of business there and might want to cross over without all the bureaucratic hassle of the border.

He called Davenport to tell him what he'd found out during the day.

When Virgil had finished, Davenport said, "I can't deal with this anymore. I got a tip that some real trouble is headed this way, and I need to work it. Nothing to do with Knox or your killings."

"Okay. Well, it's gonna break, I think."

"You going to International Falls?"

"Yeah. You know it?"

"I played hockey up there a few times when I was in high school," Davenport said. "It's a long way. Maybe you oughta see if you could get the Patrol to fly you up there—rent a car when you get there."

"Ah, I'm thinking about driving up tonight," Virgil said. "Get a few hours' sleep. The day's shot anyway, might as well drive. I could hit Knox's place first thing in the morning."

"Your call," Davenport said. "I got problems of my own. Just get this thing done with."

VIRGIL SET HIS alarm clock, and crashed. He woke at nine o'clock, scrubbed his mouth out, got his stuff together, and headed for the truck.

He always had fishing gear with him. He could drive for five hours, bag out at a backwoods motel, rent a boat at a resort in the morning, get in a couple hours on the water, and still make it to International Falls before noon.

Another good night to drive.

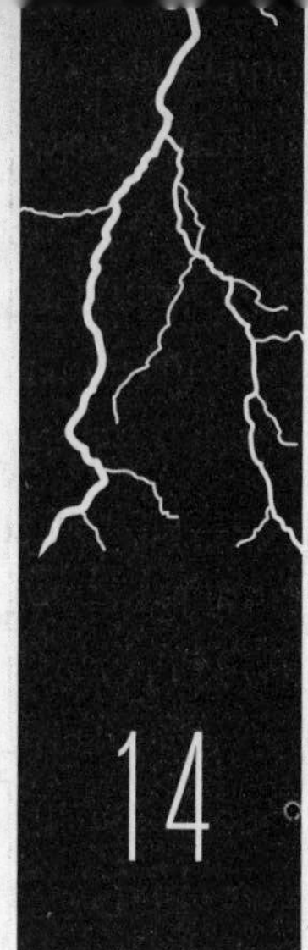

14

THE SHOOTER was city, not country.

He wore comfortable, low-heeled shoes with pointed toes made of delicate Italian leather, summer-weight dark-blue wool pants, a short-sleeved cotton shirt, and a black cotton jacket. One of two things would happen that evening, he thought, because of his citiness: he'd either be eaten alive by mosquitoes, or he'd freeze.

The scout had spotted Bunton's hideout and had delivered both precise GPS coordinates and a satellite map that would take the shooter to a little-used, dead-end trail that ended at a marshy lake a hundred yards from Bunton's. From there, the scout suggested, the shooter could walk in. He'd be coming out of the deep woods, in the night, a direction that the Indian wouldn't expect, even if he was on his guard.

"I couldn't hang around, but I got good photographs. There's no security system that I can see. There's not even a motion-detecting garage light. The only wires going in are electric. No phone. The TV comes off a satellite dish, so there's no way for a remote alarm system to call out. . . ."

The shooter hadn't even driven past the Bunton place, hadn't even given them that much of a chance to spot him. He'd come from the opposite direction, from off the res, and had taken the trail down to the lake, where there was an informal muddy canoe launch. He pulled off into the weeds, checked the GPS, got his pistol and his sap, and called the scout.

"Going in."

The scout hadn't walked it himself in the daylight, because he'd been afraid to give it away. So the shooter was on his own going in—and within fifty feet of the car, he was slip-sliding through stinking mud and marsh, and kicking up every mosquito in the universe, spitting them out of his mouth and batting them away from his face, until he was driven into a jog just to stay ahead of them.

But the bugs dropped on him like chicken hawks when he came up to the house, and he'd eventually pulled his jacket over his head, blocking out everything but his eyes, retracting his hands into the coat sleeves.

Then they went after his eyes. . . .

BUNTON'S HIDEOUT was in a cluster of five small suburban-style houses that might have been built during the sixties, all facing a narrow wooded road from town. His house was the second from the end—the one with a cop car parked in the driveway.

The shooter called the scout: "I'm in, but he's got protection from the Indian police."

"Let me call," the scout said. He meant to call the coordinator. Three minutes later, the phone silently vibrated in the shooter's hand as he got back to the car.

"Take him alone if you can," the scout said. "If you can't—we've already broken the protocol. We need these two as fast as we can."

"Of course," the shooter said. He was in the back of the van, going through the garbage he'd accumulated during the drive up from the Twin Cities. "So if I need to take a police officer . . ."

"If we have no choice, we have no choice."

The shooter rang off, risked a light, found what he'd been looking for—two plastic grocery sacks. He put the sacks in his jacket pocket, then took off his jacket. Using his penknife, he cut out the rayon lining.

He could lose Bunton while he did all of this, he knew, but he also knew that he couldn't tolerate even a half hour in the wood, with the insects. When the lining was free, he carefully wrapped it around his head, mummylike, until nothing was open except a small breathing hole and his eyes. He got his sunglasses off the passenger seat and stuck them in his jacket pocket with the plastic bags.

When he was ready, he got his equipment and walked back through the woods to Bunton's house, slipping and sliding in the oily slime at the edge of the marsh. By the time he got there, he was wet and muddy to the knees, and his Italian shoes felt as though they were about to dissolve.

He sat at the end of the woods and listened, then quietly pulled the plastic sacks over his hands to fend off the mosquitoes. Moving slow as a glacier, he crept through the woods to a point directly behind Bunton's house, watched, listened, waited, then crossed the dark backyard to the outer wall of the house.

NO AIR-CONDITIONING, nothing between the shooter and the target but some screens—and two other people. A television was going inside, and two men and a woman were talking a rambling, desultory conversation as they watched a rerun of *American Idol.* At one point, the woman said, "Hey, Ray? Could you get that?"

The shooter didn't know what *that* was, but there was at least one Ray in the house. He settled down to listen, against the wall of the house, like a lump, or a boulder, next to the electric meter, listening. The mosquitoes came for his eyes: he put on the sunglasses and bunched the fabric around them. He couldn't see much, but there wasn't much to see. A few cars went past, but not many. There wasn't much down the road. The woman inside, he learned, was named Edna; Ray called her Ma. The other man was Olen.

The shooter wondered if there were poisonous snakes in Minnesota. . . .

SOME TIME LATER, he wasn't sure how long, but long enough to get stiff in his bones, he heard Ray say something about "Going to get some toilet paper. Want anything else?"

"Oatmeal, for breakfast . . . maybe some eggs, if you want scrambled eggs."

The shooter broke cover, eased around the back of the house, crawled up the far side, watching the end house, looking for people who might glance out a window. Two of the windows had no curtains, but the others were closed off. He saw no one, no movement.

He made it to the front of the house, the side next to the garage. He'd been there two minutes when the front door opened, and Ray and the cop came out on the porch, and the cop stretched and said, "Cold," and Ray said, "Let me get my jacket," and he went back inside the house. The officer lit a cigarette and ambled down to the car, and the shooter processed it all: two men, one dark street, getting darker as it went through the woods. No traffic.

If he took them here, he had to think about the woman: if she saw him, he'd have to take her, too. It wouldn't be the odd dead officer, it'd be a massacre. The bodies were already beginning to stack up, beginning to get intense coverage from the media.

He decided, and turned, and moved as silently as he could back down the garage wall, across the backyard and into the trees, and then, using a tiny button flash, he ran as best he could through the trees toward the van. Behind him, he heard the police car start, and he ran faster, and he heard the car door slam and he crossed the trail to the lake, ran down to the van, climbed in, tore the jacket from his head, and threw the van into a circle and banged back to the main road.

The cop car was taking it easy, and the shooter caught them a mile down the road, in the dark, coming up fast. On the way, he'd called the scout: "Come in now," he said. "North on that road." Nothing to identify location.

When he caught them, he began flashing his high beams, blasting them through the cop car's back window, and the cop turned on his flashers and pulled over, and the shooter pulled in behind him and jumped out of the car and ran to the police car, as if he were looking for help, and the cop, not thinking, cracked the door and the shooter shot him in the head and yanked the door open and pointed the gun at Ray's face and said, "Get out. Get out."

The cop had collapsed in his seat and now slid out the open door, and Ray, eyes staring, fumbled at the door handle. The shooter kept the gun on him, the muzzle pointing at his eyes, and pushed the door open, and the shooter, fast as a snake, vaulted the hood of the car, sliding across it, to Ray's side.

Ray lurched back into the car and slammed the door and fumbled at the cop and the shooter realized he was going for the cop's gun and he fired two quick shots through the window into Ray's legs and then slid across the hood again and thrust the pistol into Ray's face and said, "I'll kill you now. Get out."

Ray said, "I'm hit."

"Get out. Get out."

Ray got out, holding on to the door, and screamed when his feet hit the ground, and he called, "I'm hit; shit, I'm hit bad."

When Ray was well clear of the door, the shooter pulled back and ran through the headlights, keeping the gun trained on Ray, who was holding himself up on the far door, and the shooter came around and said, "Walk to the van."

Ray said, "I can't walk."

"Then crawl."

Ray turned to look at the van, and the shooter stepped closer, worried that he was about to fall, and then Ray slammed the door and charged him, head down, legs working fine, and Ray caught the shooter's shirt in one hand and yanked on him and the shooter thrust him aside and Ray twisted and came back for him and the shooter fired and hit him in the heart and Ray went down and died.

THE SHOOTER was counting time in his head. The whole thing, at this point, had taken perhaps thirty seconds, from the time he killed the cop until he killed Ray. He needed time to move. He ran back around the police car, pushed the cop back inside, scanned the controls, killed the light bar. The car was still running, and he shifted it into gear and pushed it farther to the side of the road, got it straight, turned off the engine, and slammed the door.

Bunton.

He spent five seconds looking up and down the long dark road: nothing but the lights of his own van. He dragged Bunton to the van by the collar of his jeans jacket, threw him in the back.

Wiped his hands on his pants: what was he forgetting?

Nothing that he could think of.

Except the error. Another mistake. Another dead man, but no name. These people were tougher than he'd been led to believe. Utecht had been soft and easy, and that had misled them.

Cursing, he got on the phone. "Abort it. Two down. Coming out."

THE SHOOTER rolled through the dark, fast but careful, putting Red Lake behind him. Only one name left now. The scout had needed to speak to Bunton. Needed to isolate him, to work on him. But what could you do in a place like this? The scout had told him that if he spent one hour on the res, in the open, everybody would be looking at him, everybody would know the van.

The group had one more target that they knew of: the next target they had to isolate, they had to talk to, or the game was over.

He followed his headlights through the dark, now sickened by the smell of raw blood in the back. He reached across to the grocery sack on the seat, took out the lemon, scratched the rind, held the lemon to his nose to kill the scent of the blood.

The lemon didn't work.

The smell of blood, the shooter realized, had soaked into his brain: it was there forever. He would never escape it. Never.

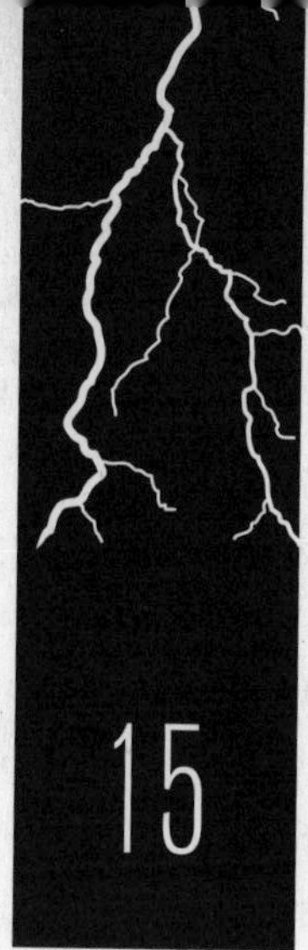

15

THE NIGHT was full of stars and night lights, like a Van Gogh painting, and Virgil followed the red taillights of a million cars headed toward cabin country. He got off at the I-35 rest stop where Wigge had been shot and David Ross was killed, to take a leak at the restroom and to look at the scene again. There was no sign of a murder, and a young couple and two children were sitting at the pavilion in back, near the murder scene, eating white-bread sandwiches in the light of a fluorescent camping lantern.

On the way out the exit ramp, a tall thin blond kid with a backpack stuck his thumb out, and Virgil pulled over and popped the door. "Where you going?"

"Duluth. Trying to get a ship out."

"I can take you most of the way," Virgil said.

The kid looked at all the lights on the dash as he settled down and asked, "Are you a police officer?"

"Yeah."

"I know I'm not supposed to hitchhike along here—"

"Don't worry about it," Virgil said. "Not many roads out here that I didn't hitchhike over."

The kid, whose name was Don, had come off a farm outside of Blooming Prairie, had done a year at the University of Minnesota, working nights at UPS, throwing boxes, and finally realized that the whole thing wasn't for him.

"I was too tired to read, and the university . . . the place is sunk in bullshit," he said. "I tried to figure out how long it would take me to get through, and it might take me six years, going full time, because there's so much bullshit that you can't even figure out ahead of time what you need to take to graduate."

Virgil had gone to the university, and they talked about that and looked at the stars, and the kid confessed that he had all three volumes of John Dos Passos's *U.S.A.* in his pack, and had read them so often that they were falling apart, and that he had just started Conrad's *Heart of Darkness* and that he couldn't get over the second paragraph.

He quoted part of it from memory: "In the offing the sea and sky were welded together without a joint, and in the luminous space the tanned sails of the barges drifting up with the tide seemed to stand still in red clusters of canvas sharply peaked, with gleams of varnished sprits. A haze rested on the low shores that ran out to sea in vanishing flatness. The air was dark above Gravesend, and farther back still seemed condensed into a mournful gloom, brooding motionless over the biggest, and the greatest, town on earth."

"London," he said. "I'd give my left nut to go to London."

"You got a ship for sure?" Virgil asked.

"I got a guy who says he's got one, for sure. I'm probably gonna be lifting weight, but I don't care—heck, I grew up on a dairy farm. There's no ship that could be harder than that."

Virgil thought he was probably right, and wished for a moment that he was going with him.

He dropped the kid at the I-35 intersection east of Moose Lake and cut cross-country to the west, thinking about the lakes he knew, and where he might bag out for the night, and still get a good couple of hours on the water before he had to move in the morning.

The lights of Duluth were fading off the far eastern horizon when his cell phone rang. He glanced at it, saw that it came from the northern Minnesota area code, thought *Ray,* and then *Ray's gonna tell me something . . .*

He flipped open the phone and a man on the other end said, "Virgil Flowers? This is Rudy Bunch. The Red Lake cop?"

The young one. Virgil said, "Hey. How's it going?"

"Not so good, man. We're in deep shit up here. We've got a dead cop and Ray's gone."

Virgil peered into the dark; it was something like an embolism—part of his brain shut down for a minute. Then: "What?"

"Somebody shot Olen Grey on the side of the road. He was watching Ray. Ray's gone," Bunch said.

"Ray shot him?"

"We don't know what happened, but . . . I think maybe somebody took Ray. We're calling both the state and the feds. Where are you at? St. Paul?"

"No, no, I'm heading your way, I'm over by Grand Rapids," Virgil said. He was still befuddled. "Man, what're you telling me here? When was this? Have you closed down the roads?"

"No. We're pretty sure it happened an hour and a half ago. Olen and Ray were going to buy groceries and Ray's mom saw them leave. Then a guy named Tom Broad was driving out and he saw Olen's car sitting kind of in a ditch, and he thought that was strange, but it was a cop car, so he didn't do nothin'. Then he was driving back out to his house and saw the car still sitting there, so he stopped and looked and he could see Olen dead in the front seat. He called us, and . . . that's what happened. There's blood on the passenger side and there's bullet holes in the passenger-side window, and shit, I think somebody took Ray."

"Goddamnit. Listen, have you got a veterans' memorial there?"

"We got a flagpole with an MIA flag," Bunch said.

"Have somebody check it, see if they can find a body," Virgil said. "You say you've got the state coming in? You mean us? The BCA?"

"Yeah, the crime lab," Bunch said.

"Okay, freeze it. . . . I'll be there quick as I can."

"What about Ray?"

"I think Ray's gone," Virgil said.

CHARLES WHITING, the BCA agent-in-charge at Bemidji, said he'd sent the crime-scene crew and had been about to call St. Paul looking for Virgil. He said he would call the local cities, to have them check and then watch the veterans' monuments.

"We can do the crime scene, but this is gonna be a federal case. The FBI has two guys on the way from Duluth," Whiting said. "There might be some question about why we arrested Bunton and then turned him loose, and he gets killed the next day. . . ."

"I've got some questions about that myself," Virgil said. "I haven't been to Red Lake for five years, but unless it's changed, it's a mess of roads and tracks, and *how in the hell* did the killer find him? How? The whole point of going up there is that *nobody* could find him if he didn't want to be found."

"Well—I don't know. You left him at his mother's house."

"Yeah, but, she has a different last name," Virgil said. "They didn't look him up in the phone book."

"No. She doesn't have a wired phone, anyway, so that wasn't it. You know, Virgil, I don't *know* how they found him. But I will start pushing that question with the Red Lake cops."

"Do that," Virgil said. "Bunton had to be under observation. I thought the deal was everybody could spot an outsider in a minute."

"I'll push it. How far out are you?"

"I don't know exactly, I'm somewhere out in the dark, on 2, south of Grand Rapids. Coming fast as I can . . ."

"You be careful up there in Red Lake. Olen Grey was a pretty popular guy, and they . . . you know. They're gonna be looking for somebody to blame," Whiting said. "We've had some problems, even before your stunt the other night. Some of the drug task-force guys went up there, undercover, and got their asses kicked out. They were told if they came back, they'd be arrested."

"I'll take care."

ANOTHER TEN MINUTES, and Rudy Bunch called: "Nothing at the flagpole. Nobody's seen anything there."

"Okay. Chuck Whiting is calling the other towns around, telling them to keep an eye out," Virgil told him.

"If we don't find him, that's good, right? There wasn't too much blood in the car, on the passenger side. Ray might not have been hurt that bad."

Virgil thought about the bag full of Wigge's finger joints. "I don't know, Rudy. I don't know. I got a real bad feeling."

HE WENT THROUGH Grand Rapids with lights and siren and never did slow down, heading northwest in the dark, and then Whiting called again. "They found him. Here in Bemidji. At the veterans' monument on Birchmont Drive. Got the lemon in the mouth. Shot in the heart and the legs."

"Any sign that he was interrogated?"

"No; he's got some fingernails ripped loose, but it looks like he was fighting. Looks like he got the killer by the coat."

"DNA?" Virgil asked.

"Don't know. Don't know anything but what I told you. I'm in my car, on the way over there. You know, the other night, when you guys went for the walk?"

"Yeah?"

"You must've walked right past the monument," Whiting said. "It's right there, where you guys were."

VIRGIL WENT and looked at the body, another puddle of light with cops, but there was nothing to see other than Bunton's distorted face. A local television reporter tried to get him to talk, but he referred everything to Whiting, said good-bye to the agent, and headed on north to Red Lake. As he crossed the line, he called Rudy Bunch on his cell phone, and Bunch said that Louis Jarlait would meet him in Red Lake.

JARLAIT FLAGGED HIM down outside the Red Lake Criminal Justice Center, said, "Follow me," got in his own truck, and led Virgil through a profound darkness into the woods. Two or three miles out of town, Virgil saw the lights coming up: ten or fifteen cars lined up along the road, cops standing around.

They parked and climbed out, and Jarlait had a lollipop in his mouth and asked, "You want a sucker? Chocolate?"

"Sure." Jarlait got a Tootsie Pop out of his truck, and Virgil unwrapped it as they walked toward the house.

Jarlait said, "I heard about Ray."

Virgil: "Yeah. . . . Who's here?"

"Most of us Red Lake guys. Some of your people here from Bemidji we invited in. FBI is still on the way, they probably won't get here till morning."

"Anybody have any ideas about who did this? Strange cars, strange guys—how in the hell could he come in here and just do this?"

"White van," Jarlait said. "It might have been a guy in a white Chevy van. We got people coming through here all the time, but there was a white van going kind of slow around, and one of our guys, Cliff Bear, passed it, and he, uh . . ."

Jarlait paused, and Virgil said, "What?"

"Well, he said the guy was an Indian man," Jarlait said. "So he didn't pay much attention."

"He didn't recognize him? Or the van?"

Jarlait shook his head. "No. Here's the thing—Cliff thought he was an Indian man, but not one of us. He thought he looked like an Apache."

"An Apache."

"Yeah. You know, those skinny string bean little assholes," Jarlait said. "BIA has a lot of Apache cops for some reason. They get sent up here sometimes."

A half-dozen Red Lake cops were looking down at them as they walked up the road, working on the suckers, and one of the cops, Rudy Bunch, broke away from the group. Virgil noticed a man sitting on the side of the road, weeping. Jarlait walked over to him and squatted down next to him.

"Did you stop and see Ray?" Bunch asked.

"Yeah. Shot in the legs and head. Probably killed here, transported down there," Virgil said. "What's the situation with your guy?"

"Shot in the head. Cold. Looks like he was sitting right at the wheel. Looks like a .22."

"That fits," Virgil said. "Any reason that he'd be here?"

Bunch pointed back up the road. "Well, you were at Ray's place, Ray's mom's place, it's about a mile up that way. She says Ray and Olen was going into town. Looks like they got this far. . . ."

Virgil scratched his head, looking up and down the road. "So . . . what'd he do? Flag them down? Fake an accident?"

"Olen never called in, so that's not it," Bunch said. "If he'd seen an accident, he would have called. I don't know why he stopped, but he did, and here he is."

"Would he have called for something like a flat tire?" Virgil asked.

"Ah, probably not. He didn't . . . but who knows?"

Virgil looked up and down the road, shook his head. He didn't know why Olen Grey had stopped, but he suspected that whatever happened, neither Grey nor Bunton had taken the situation as seriously as Virgil had. Maybe, Virgil thought, he hadn't pounded it home hard enough. Ray had been frightened but had seemed to think once he got across the line into Red Lake, he'd be safe. As though that, alone, would be enough.

Then he'd gone to his mother's house. . . .

VIRGIL WALKED OVER, looked in the car. A white guy was working with gloves and a UV light on the far side; on the street side, Grey sat slumped in his seat, his safety belt still looped around his chest. He turned back to Bunch: "If an Indian man did the shooting—Louis told me somebody saw a guy who might be the shooter—that'd mean, what? That it's somebody with connections up here?"

Bunch shrugged. "That was Cliff Bear who saw him—but he didn't recognize him, and he would have recognized him if the guy was from up here. He could be from the Cities. . . ."

"There are some drug connections between here and some Indian people down in the Cities, the way I understand it," Virgil said. "Was Ray tied into that?"

"Not as far as I know. Ray used to do a little reefer, but you know—nothing serious," Bunch said. "He wasn't dealing or anything. Not up here, anyway."

"It seems like Ray had to be fingered somehow," Virgil said. "How would a guy who doesn't know this place find his way back to Ray's mom's house, then shoot a cop who never even took his pistol out?"

Another Indian cop had edged over to listen, and now he chipped in: "You're thinking what I'm thinking?"

"What are you thinking?" asked Virgil.

"That Olen recognized the guy who flagged him down? Didn't think it was a big deal because it was another Indian guy?"

Virgil nodded at him. "Actually, I wasn't thinking that, but it's a good thought."

Bunch said, "We got some assholes up here, and I'm not saying there aren't people up here who wouldn't shoot a man, because there are. So if Ray turned up dead, and you say, okay, Red Lake did it, I'd think about it. It's possible. But this lemon deal? What about all these other people killed with lemons? You think Indian people did all of them?"

Virgil said, "No. I don't. What I'm thinking is, they were killed by somebody who had the connections to get a killing done up here."

The second Indian cop said, "Have to be drugs, then. That's the only kind of organized crime we've got. Everything else is disorganized."

THE GUY who'd been working in the car stood up, walked around the car, and asked Virgil, "You're Virgil?"

"Yes."

"Ron Mapes. I'm with the Bemidji office." He was a balding, ginger-haired man wearing surgical gloves. "I just talked to our guys in Bemidji at the veterans' memorial. They say that Bunton may have slashed him with his fingernails. Got some blood and a little skin."

"That's terrific. Get it to the lab quick as you can."

Mapes nodded. "Of course. Not much up here, so far, except footprints."

"Yeah?"

Mapes led the way back down the road, pointed out two footprints marked with little orange plastic flags.

"Can you tell anything from them?" Virgil asked.

"Couple things—he's got a small foot. Size eight or nine, I'd guess," Mapes said. "The shoes had no cleats or even ripples—they were flat leather bottoms with low heels. Like loafers. They weren't boots of any kind, or sneakers. More like dress shoes."

"So a small guy," Virgil said.

"Yeah. The ground is damp and he didn't sink in too deep. Put that with the small foot, and I'd say a small guy with small feet. We figure—the officers here figure—that he had the Bunton house under surveillance somehow, which means that he had to be parked back in the woods somewhere. There's a boat landing road a hundred yards or so from the Bunton place; it's possible he was back in there. We'll check in the morning when it gets light—can't see much with just a flash."

"What do you think you'd find?"

Mapes shrugged. "Well, I'm hoping for a matchbook that says 'Moonlight Café, St. Paul, Minnesota,' and inside is written, 'Call Sonia.'"

"That'd be good," Bunch said.

Virgil was patient. "What," he asked, "do you think you'll find?"

"Best case? More blood. If he was doing surveillance from up close, he was walking through heavy brush in the dark. If he scratched himself . . . But that'd be best case. More likely, a little fabric, which we might be able to match with some of his clothing, if we find him. If he fell, maybe a handprint. Or maybe he did drop something—who knows?"

"Find any .22 shells on the street?" Virgil asked.

"Nope."

"So if he's using a silencer—we think he might be using a silencer—he either took the time to pick up the ejected shells, or he had some kind of little catch basket rigged on the side, or he's really good at hand-capturing them."

"That seems likely," Mapes said. "You could silence a single-shot, but this isn't a single-shot. These people were shot in a hurry."

"He's a professional," Bunch said.

"That's right," Virgil said.

VIRGIL STAYED until four in the morning, hoping against hope that they might find something. They went back to Bunton's place, where his mother sat in a rocker staring at a wall, and looked at what Bunton had left behind: a motorcycle saddlebag with a few shirts and a pair of jeans, but not a single piece of paper.

At four o'clock, he told Jarlait and Bunch that he was heading back to Bemidji to get some sleep.

"Let me ask you something," Jarlait said. They were off by themselves, leaning on Jarlait's truck. Up and down the street, people were standing in their yards, watching the cops at Bunton's place. "We've been talking about the white van and the Indian man, and dope. I know goddamn well that the dope people in Minneapolis got shooters. Or they could get them if they needed them. And when we started talking about dope, you were thinking about something. Do you know something? Do you know where the connection is? Between all the lemons and Ray? That has to do with the dope people?"

Virgil thought about Carl Knox. Carl Knox had put money into dope dealers, the BCA's organized-crime people said, but nobody had been able to prove it, because he'd never dealt dope himself. All he did was provide financing, and then only at four or five levels above the street. His return was smaller, but also safer.

"Virgil?"

"It's something I gotta think about," Virgil said. "I've got a guy . . . I can't talk about it, really . . . but there's a guy in all of this who was a moneyman for dope dealers. Might still be."

"We need to know this shit, because that's one of our friends sitting back there dead in that cop car," Jarlait said. "Ray . . . Ray was okay, but this was gonna happen sooner or later, one way or another, with Ray. He was gonna ride his bike into a phone pole, or he was gonna piss off the wrong guy. But Olen . . . Olen didn't deserve anything like this. He was a good guy."

"Like I said, I got a guy," Virgil said. "I don't know if he's involved, but I'm going after him."

"Like soon?"

"Like tomorrow morning," Virgil said. "You guys: stay in touch."

"We will. You stay in touch with us, too," Jarlait said. "If something happens, and we can get in on it, we want in."

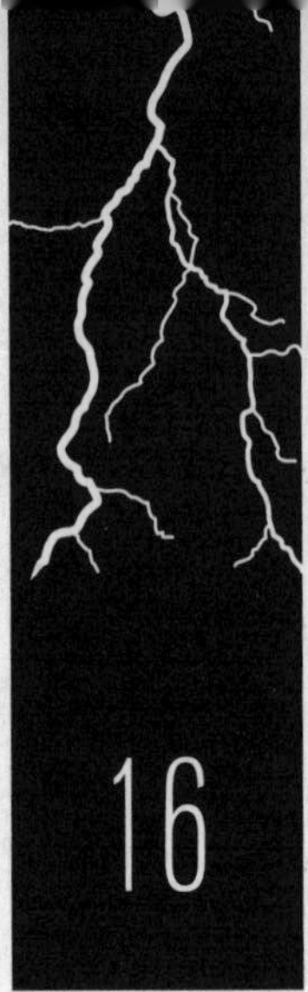

16

VIRGIL FOUND a bed at the RootyToot Resort on Candi Lake, a place with tumbledown brown-painted fake log cabins and beds that were too short, and mattresses that were too thin, and pillows that were flat and hard and smelled like hair and Vaseline; but that also rented fourteen-foot aluminum boats with 9.9-horse Honda kickers, that came with the cabin and he could take out anytime.

Virgil had stayed there twice before and didn't mind having a beer or two with the resort's alcoholic owner, Dave Root, though at five o'clock in the morning, Root was unconscious and Virgil took a key out of a mailbox, left a note on Root's door, and checked himself in.

He lay in bed and thought about God and the people who were dead on this case, and who'd died years ago in Vietnam, if Ray Bunton had been telling the truth, and wondered what all that was about, and how somebody like the dumb-ass preachers on TV could think this could all be part of God's Plan.

God didn't have a plan, Virgil believed.

God had His limits, and one of them was, He didn't always know what would happen; or if He did know, He didn't care; or if He cared, He was constrained by His own logic and couldn't do anything about death and destruction. Virgil believed that God was actually a part of a rolling wave front, hurtling into an unknown future; and that humans, animals and, possibly, trees and chinch bugs had souls that would rejoin God at death.

Which brought him to Camus' big question, and he didn't like to think about Camus, so he went to sleep.

He woke up at eight, bone-tired, rushed through a shower, got his musky rod out of the car and his emergency tackle box and walked down to the boat, pushed it off; heard a man yelling at him, looked back and saw Root, standing on the grass shore, barefoot, in black Jockey shorts and a white T-shirt.

Root shouted, "Hey, big ballplayer," and he heaved a perfect, twenty-yard spiral pass and Virgil plucked a bottle of Miller Genuine Draft out of the air, ice cold. "Back in an hour," Virgil called, and he headed across the lake, into the wind, to the far shoreline, where he set up a drift and began casting along the edge of a weed bank.

The water was clear and the sun was on his back and he could see into the water as though it were an aquarium, and it all smelled wonderful, like pine and algae and fish, and nothing at all like a blood-soaked car. In forty-five minutes, in three drifts, he caught two hammer-handle northerns, threw them back, and had a follow from a decent, but not great, musky. He was happy to see the fish in the water and he worked a figure eight, trying to get it to strike, and finally gave up, sat down, and cracked the Miller.

The beer was pretty much dog piss, he thought as he drank it, but not bad on a morning that was cold on the verge of turning hot. He finished the beer and dropped the bottle in the bottom of the boat. He felt like a horse's ass for doing it, but took out his cell phone and checked for messages.

Two: Davenport and Carl Knox.

He stared at the Knox call for a moment, then clicked through to the number, and sat there on the bench seat looking at a woman and a small girl fly-fishing on the far shore, the woman showing the girl how to roll a cast out over the water, and Knox answered after two rings.

"Virgil Flowers, BCA, returning your call," Virgil said.

"Flowers—where are you?"

"Bemidji," Virgil said.

"Then you know about Ray," Knox said.

"Yeah—how did you know about it?"

"Have you looked at a TV this morning?" Knox asked.

"All right. We need to talk," Virgil said.

"Yeah. But I've got myself ditched where this asshole can't find me, and I've got my own security," Knox said. "I'm pretty far from Bemidji, but I can get there. We need to meet someplace . . . obscure."

Virgil scratched his head, looking in toward the RootyToot. "Okay. Where are you coming from?"

Hesitation. Then: "Down south of you a couple of hours."

Liar, Virgil thought. "Okay. There's a broken-ass resort northwest of Bemidji on Highway 89 about four miles north of Highway 2. It's called the RootyToot."

"Wait, wait, let me look at my atlas . . . page seventy-one . . . okay, I see it, south of Pony Lake."

"That's it," Virgil said. "There's a Budweiser sign right on the highway. See you when? Noon?"

"Noon. Be there right on the nose. I ain't hanging out."

TWO HOURS and a little more; he could spend more time on the water, and he did, until the sun started cooking his nose. He had some suntan lotion in his tackle box, but he didn't want to get started with that; he needed to go in and shave. He called Sandy and said, "I want you to do something for me. You heard that Ray Bunton got killed?"

"Yes. It's everywhere. All the TV people are flying up there, wherever you are," she said.

"Okay. What I need is, I need you to do research on Ray Bunton, and see if you can spot his mother's house without knowing her name. If there's a way to track Bunton through the res, somehow, and get to that house."

"I see what you're getting at," she said. "I'll start right now."

HE CALLED Davenport before he started the motor, and Davenport came up and said, "What happened?"

"You probably know as much as I do—or, if you don't, call Chuck Whiting. What you don't know is, Carl Knox called me and we just negotiated a meet-up north of Bemidji. He says he's coming up from the south, but he's lying—he's coming down from International Falls."

"You gonna bust him?"

"I've got nothing to bust him with. He says he's hiding out from the shooter. But he wants to meet because he's got something. We're set up to meet at a place called the RootyToot Resort, whatever the heck that is. I gotta get my atlas out and find it, I'm heading up there to scout it out."

"Careful, Virgil. This might be a place that he's got locked down," Davenport said.

"You don't think he'd pull anything? With a cop?" Across the lake, the woman with the fly rod had hooked into a panfish of some kind, probably a bluegill, and handed the rod to the little girl, who played it in. And far down the lake, he could see the white line that meant a bigger powerboat was headed his way.

"No. I've talked to him a couple times," Davenport said. "He's an asshole, but, you know . . . he'll talk to you. He knows where things are at."

"All right. Listen, I gotta run. I'll call you as soon as I hear something," Virgil said.

"Stay in touch. I'll talk to Ruffe over at the *Star Tribune,* let him understand that things are breaking, that we should have something pretty quick. Maybe he could drop in a story that would take some pressure off."

In another thirty seconds, Davenport would hear the powerboat in the background. Virgil said, "Okay, I'm running. Talk to you."

Virgil stuck the phone back in his pocket and smiled: what Davenport didn't know wouldn't hurt him. Or Virgil. He cranked the motor and headed into shore, the water smooth as an old black mirror.

WHEN HE WAS cleaned up, wearing a fresh but ancient white Pogues T-shirt, and a black cotton sport coat over his jeans, he went off to the bar to talk with Root, who'd had a couple eye-openers, getting up a morning shine so that he could drift painlessly through the afternoon before getting totally crushed in the evening.

"Virgil fuckin' Flowers, " Root said. There were three other men in the bar, two facing each other across a table, the other sitting at the bar, all three with beers. Root introduced Virgil: "This is my friend Virgil Flowers, the famous outdoor writer, who is also a cop and is up here investigating that murder in Bemidji, I bet. Is that right?"

Virgil nodded, and said, "Good morning, David. I see the lake is empty of fish, as usual. Give me a Diet Coke."

"Empty of fish," Root said. "If you knew a fuckin' thing about fishing . . . whoops . . ." He grimaced at his own language, and Virgil turned and saw the fisherwoman and the little girl walking past the screen windows, and a moment later they came inside.

The woman was probably forty, Virgil thought, thin, small-breasted, with a sprinkling of freckles across her nose, and nice brown eyes. She had a fisherwoman's tanned face and arms, with a small white scar on one of her arms, and Virgil felt himself slipping over the edge into love.

She glanced at Virgil and smiled and then said to Root, "We need a cream soda and an ice cream cone," and Root got a soda from a cooler behind the bar and the little girl fished an ice cream cone out of a freezer by the door, the woman paid, and they took the soda and the cone to a corner table.

Root said to Virgil, "So what happened to this Indian dude?" and the three drinking men bent his way.

Virgil shrugged and said, "Well—I know about what you do. The killer's the same guy who killed those guys down in the Cities, and the guy in New Ulm. We know that. Now it's just . . . working through it."

"What are the chances of getting him?" one of the men asked.

"Oh, we'll get him," Virgil said. "The guy's asking for it, and he's gonna get it. The question is, will he kill anybody else before we get him."

"That is a question," Root said. "The answer is, I think I'll have a beer."

So they sat and talked about murder, fishing, hunting, and boats; and after a bit, the woman finished her cream soda and she and the girl left, the woman raising a hand to Root, saying, "See ya, Dave," and he said, "See ya, El," and when she was gone, Virgil asked, "Who was that?"

"Her name is Loren; everybody calls her El, like the letter *L*. She and her husband got a place down the lake," Root said. "He works in the Cities four days a week, comes up here three. Four days, though, she's sorta . . . untended-to."

"Untended-to, my ass," one of the men said. "You tend to her, her old man'll blow you up, that's a fact."

"You know him?" Virgil asked.

"Asshole," the man said. "Big shot at Pillsbury."

"How does that make him an asshole?" Dave asked, the beer bottle poised at his lower lip.

"I dunno. He's an asshole because he's married to her and I'm not," the guy said. "I'm sitting in a dogshit tavern at eleven-fourteen in the morning drinking beer."

"But that's a *good* thing," Dave said.

THEY SAT UNTIL almost noon, adding women to the list of murder, fishing, hunting, and boats, and then Virgil excused himself and wandered off. His cabin was in easy sight of the driveway. He thought about it for a minute, then went to his truck, fished around under the seat, got his pistol and a leather inside-the-waistband holster, and tucked the gun into the small of his back.

Then he sat on the top step of the cabin's stoop, where he could be seen from the driveway. The woman and the girl were down at the dock, messing around in a boat, and Virgil watched for a couple of minutes, then a Jeep rolled into the parking lot and parked. The two men who got out weren't fishermen, Virgil thought, and he stood up, and as they looked around, he nodded and they walked over.

"Virgil?" The two looked like bookends: tall, dark-haired men with bent noses and an air of competency, both wearing black sport coats and khaki slacks and L.L. Bean hiking shoes and black sunglasses.

"That's me. But neither one of you is Carl," Virgil said, remembering the portrait photo at the dealership.

"No, Carl's coming in, he'll be here in a minute or two," the man said. He looked down at the lake, and the half-dozen boats tied to the pier, and the woman and kid. "Sal, why don't you go get a few beers."

Sal nodded wordlessly and walked down to the bar.

Virgil said, "You're security."

"Yeah, sorta."

"Where'd you get your nose bent?" Virgil asked.

The man grinned, and Virgil suspected all of his short glittering-white teeth had been capped by a very good dentist. "Chicago, actually." He looked down at the pier. "You know the chick?"

"I asked about her, they know her in the bar," Virgil said. "And the owner didn't know I was coming until this morning—I sorta dropped in."

"All right. Woman with a kid, they make a good recon team, you know?" the guy said. "You got a woman with a kid on the street, who'd think they might be wired-up?"

Virgil said, "I'll write that in my notebook."

The man said, "You do that." Then he tapped Virgil's chest. "The Pogues. Goddamn good band. I'm Irish myself."

"You didn't say what your name was," Virgil said.

"Pat. O'Hoolihan. Pat O'Hoolihan."

"You're shittin' me."

The man showed his teeth again. "Yeah. I am."

Sal came back with two cold six-packs: "Four drunks talking about bait. I thought my ears was gonna fall off, and I was only there for two minutes."

"Gotta learn to relax," Virgil said. "Get in the flow of the conversation."

Sal popped his gum. "I'd rather be dead."

The man who wasn't named Pat O'Hoolihan got on his cell phone, dialed a number, and said, "We good."

KNOX ARRIVED in a black GMC sport-utility vehicle with an unnecessary chrome brush guard on the front, and two little tiny chromed brush guards on the back taillights, and Virgil said to Sal, "These taillight brush guards look kinda gay."

Sal popped his gum. "I hadn't thought about it, but you're right."

Knox climbed out of the passenger seat, and another bent-nosed guy from the driver's seat. Knox was a large man, balding, with a fleshy face and a heavy gut, who looked like he might deal in bulldozers. He was wearing khaki cargo pants, a white shirt, a black sport coat, and more L.L. Bean hiking shoes.

He walked down to Virgil's place and said, "Mr. Flowers." Not a question.

Virgil shook hands with him and said, "Why don't we go inside?"

Knox looked at the cabin and shook his head. "Nah. I hate enclosed spaces that I don't know about. Let's go find a stump." To the security guys, he said, "Why don't you guys hang out?" and to the one who wasn't named Pat, he said, "Larry, come on with us."

Virgil said, "Yeah, come on, Larry."

Larry said, "That'd be Mr. Larry to you, Virgil. Let me get one of those six-packs."

THE THREE OF THEM strolled down to a picnic table behind one of the cabins, out of sight of the bar, out of sight of the driveway. The mom and daughter were kneeling on the dock, peering into the water, and Larry said, "Nice ass," and Knox said, "C'mon, man, she's only eight," and Virgil had to laugh despite himself. They all took a beer and settled on the picnic table bench. Larry faced away from them, looking up at the cabins; the other two men were wandering around the driveway.

"So what's the deal?" Knox said. "I understand you've been talking to my daughter."

"The deal is, somebody is killing people—and all the people who are dead went to Vietnam in '75 and stole a bunch of bulldozers. The last guy to get killed . . ."

"Ray."

"Yeah. Ray. Ray told me a story. He said that while you guys were stealing the bulldozers . . ."

"Weren't stealing them," Knox said. "It was more of a repo."

"Whatever. When you'd finished taking the bulldozers, there was a nasty shooting incident. Murders, is what it was. Ray said that Chuck Utecht was talking about a public confession about the killings, and somebody needed to shut him up. But by then, Utecht had talked to Sanderson, and Sanderson had talked to Ray, and it was all getting out of control. The killings are professional. So we asked ourselves, 'Who is still alive, who might be able to find some bent-nosed killers from someplace like Chicago to come in here and clean up his mess?' I guess—well, hell, we thought of you."

They were sitting facing the lake, their legs away from the table, their elbows back on it. When Virgil stopped talking, Knox said, "You hear that, Larry? You're a bent-nosed killer from Chicago."

"I resent the hell out of that characterization," Larry said. He burped beer. "I have many fine qualities."

The repartee, Virgil thought, was a cover: Knox was thinking about it. Then he said, "This was a really long time ago, and I didn't have anything to do with it."

"That's what Ray said—he didn't have anything to do with it. He said he was driving a lowboy back and forth, and when he got back the last time, some house was burning down and somebody had gotten shot."

More silence. Then: "It wasn't one. It was four. At least. And that wasn't all. . . ." He shook his head.

"You want to tell me?" Virgil asked, pushing.

"Yeah. I can't prove it, but I might even be able to point you at the shooters," Knox said. "But they'll have deep cover. Deep cover. And if you go after this guy, you better get him . . . and I got a few more things I want."

"Like what?"

"I might have some evidence," he said. "You need to say you took it off Ray. Somehow found it in Ray's shit. Not from me."

Virgil said, "I don't know if I can do that."

"Then, hey—maybe I can't find it. . . . It's not because I'm trying to avoid responsibility," Knox said. "It's because I don't think you'll get this guy. Even with the pictures. And if you don't get him, there's a good chance he'll take me out. Or my kid, or my ex-wife, because he's fuckin' crazy. I know you and Davenport think I'm some kind of big crook, but honest to God, I never had anybody killed in my life. I wouldn't even know who to ask. I sell bulldozers."

Virgil felt the ice going out: Knox *knew.* He went back to the essential point: "You got pictures. . . ."

"Yeah. Not with me, but I can get them."

"So tell me the story. . . ."

IN 1975, with Vietnam coming apart, old man Utecht found the bulldozers. He called his kid, who called Wigge, and Wigge called Knox. Knox was another ex-GI, who'd been stationed in Germany, and had been trained as a heavy-equipment operator. "I fit with their plan—we all knew heavy equipment, one way or another, and we were all ex-military, except Utecht, and Ray was the truck driver."

He flew to Vietnam with Chuck Utecht, and they were picked up at the airport by Chester Utecht, who drove them out to the equipment yard.

"Some of the stuff was new, but was already in trouble because it'd been sitting there for a couple years, and the jungle was eating it up. The fuel lines were all clogged up and the fuel filters had turned into rocks, and some of the rubber hydraulic lines were eaten by squirrels, or something—these little red-bellied fuckers, they'd eat anything. Anyway, there was more stuff than you could believe. . . ."

The crew went to work, restoring one machine at a time, getting them moving, and then Ray arrived and began hauling the bulldozers away. "We had a big truckload of spare parts, I don't know where Chester got them from, but they were all new. We were sweatin' like dogs out in the sun, there was no shade in the yard, it was about a million degrees out there, bugs as big as my thumbs. We had these whole pallets of Lone Star beer . . . we didn't have access to safe drinking water, so we were drinking like three or four gallons of beer a day just to stay hydrated.

"Anyway, there was this big house just down the way . . . across this dirt road, and it had a water pump outside, one of those old pump-handle things, and Chester said if we drank it, we'd get dysentery, but it was all right to rinse off with it, to cool down, and we'd go down there and pump water into a bucket and throw it on each other. It was cool . . . but there was this old man there, he'd come out and scream at us. . . . Screaming in French, didn't know what the fuck he was talking about."

Knox drifted away for a couple of minutes, then said to Virgil, "You know something, Flowers? This one time, I was delivering a used Cat over in Wisconsin, the west side of Milwaukee. They were building a subdivision, they were going to beat the band. And I was there, and they had these guys working in a trench, putting down a water line, and the trench fell on them. Sand and clay. Six or seven guys, but four guys went under, and we all jumped in there and started tearing up the dirt with our hands . . . and all four guys died. When we got them out, they were like sitting there, with their mouths full of dirt and their eyes open, but all covered with sand, deader'n shit. I don't think about that but once a year. And hell, it was an accident, you know. . . .

"This thing in Vietnam, I don't go two hours without thinking about it. For more than thirty years—"

Virgil said, "Somebody's across the lake with a high-powered rifle, and you're gonna say, 'The asshole's name is—' and pop! The killer nails you. So could you give me his name? Just in case?"

Knox made a *huh-huh* sound, which was his kind of big-guy chuckle. "Warren."

"Ralph Warren?"

"Yeah. I assumed you knew that," Knox said. "His name, anyway."

"I never got to anybody before they were dead, except Ray, and he didn't know who Warren was."

Knox laughed again, a short half grunt, half laugh. "Well . . . who else do you know who could import a bunch of bent-nosed, cold-eyed killers?"

"But one of the cold-eyed killers got killed," Virgil said.

"Yeah? That guy up at that rest stop?"

"Yeah. Ex-military, special forces," Virgil said.

"Probably Wigge's man. Probably an accident. Warren wouldn't have wanted Wigge to see it coming, because Wigge was a hard-ass himself. They've been tangled up forever—ever since Vietnam, anyway."

"So—what happened in Vietnam? Warren did the killing?"

Knox nodded. They'd gotten as much equipment as they could onto the ship—even though that meant that some perfectly good stuff would be left behind—and called it a day. But when the last truck left, Knox said, and they knew the truck itself would be lifted onboard the ship, Warren and Wigge produced a couple of bottles of rum that they'd bought the day before from some Cambodian security guards, and they started mixing up rum and Cokes.

"Cuba libres, they called them back then. Goddamn, they were good when it was hot outside," Knox said. "So we're sitting around drinking and we'd already had two or three gallons of beer, and we're gettin' pretty fucked up, and Warren says he's gonna take a bath. We're all laughing at him and giving him shit, and he pulls off his shirt and walks down to this house. Probably a hundred meters away. Pretty nice house, older, palm trees around it. Looked French, and this old guy used to yell at us in French, so maybe it was.

"Anyway, there was this chick down there, we'd seen her a couple of times, coming and going on a bicycle, but . . . mmm . . . Warren goes down there carrying this gun—Chester gave us a couple of M16s, just in case—and he starts taking off all his clothes until he's buck naked, and he's drunk, and he gets under this water at the pump . . . and this chick comes along on the bike and she doesn't see him until she's already off it, and she tries to run around him, and he comes after her, and grabs her ass, and he's drunk and sort of rubbing himself on her and laughing . . .

"So the old guy comes out, and this time he's got a rifle, and he points it up in the air and fires off a round and we're all, like, 'Jesus Christ,' and the girl runs into the house past him and he comes running down from the porch screaming at Warren, and Warren is like picking up his clothes, but the old man keeps coming and he gets too close and Warren throws his clothes at him and grabs his gun and *boom*. Then he runs in the house after the chick, and there's more shooting, like bam, bam, bam-bam-bam, and we're all running down there, but not too fast, because of the shooting, and we only got the one other gun.

"We get there, and there's this dead guy in the yard. And we all freaked out. We all stopped, and I remember Chuck saying, 'I'm getting the fuck out of here,' and then there was some screaming from the house, and we can hear Warren yelling, and we're all like going, 'What the fuck?'

"Then there's nothing. We're yelling, 'Ralph, Ralph,' and he yells, 'I'm okay,' and we go in there, look in there, and there's these dead kids in the hallway, these two dead little kids, and we can hear this . . . this . . ."

He stared away, across the lake, and Larry said, "Jesus Christ," and Knox went on: "I went through that and I went into the next room, and here was Warren, and he was fuckin' this chick. He was fuckin' her, and I could see she was dead, or she was dying, but he was crazy drunk and he was just fuckin' her. . . ."

"Pictures," Virgil said.

Knox nodded. "I had this Instamatic. Like this little Kodak pocket camera. I was wearing fatigue pants, and, shit, I had this bad feeling that I could get blamed, that we could all get blamed, and Warren was banging her like mad and Sanderson was yelling at him and he wouldn't stop, and Sanderson ran away and I took a shot of Warren banging this chick, and then I took off, but I took a shot of the kids, and the old man, and then I went running out of there. I was thinking if they tried to blame all of us we could use the pictures as evidence against Warren, who did the whole thing."

"But nothing ever happened?" Virgil asked.

"Nah. We didn't really understand it all at the time, but that whole country was going crazy. People were stealing everything that wasn't nailed down, people were trying to get out, they were stealing boats and robbing stores for money, it was crazy. Chester, when he found out about the killing, he freaked out. He said we had to get the fuck out of there and keep our mouths shut. That's what we did. We all got jammed in that van and we took off for the airport, and we camped out there for four days before I could get out, but some of the guys—Warren, I think, and maybe Sanderson—went with the boat."

"Ray said he saw Sanderson back at home just a couple months later, so he didn't go with the boat."

"Well, shit, they just took them to Indonesia," Knox said. "That's only, like, three or four days away."

"I don't know anything about that part of the world," Virgil said.

They all sat there, staring at the lake, then Virgil said, "I'll see what I can do about the photos. About attributing them to Ray. But . . . I don't know. I'm gonna have to have them, and if we have to argue about it in court, Warren's gonna know where they're coming from anyway."

Knox bit his lip and then said, "What if I tell the guys from Chicago to put a bullet in your head and walk away?"

"I'm heavily armed," Virgil said.

"That won't work, then," Knox said. He dipped into his jacket pocket and handed Virgil an envelope. "What I did was, I scanned the negatives and then I printed them out. I really don't have the negs with me—if you can get him with these, I'll bring the negs around as the final nail in the coffin. But I'm not giving them up. They might be the only thing between me and Ralph. As long as he doesn't know where the negs are . . ."

"When Wigge was killed, his fingers were cut off. He was tortured," Virgil said. "If Warren was his good buddy, why'd he do that?"

Knox said, "Because he's nuts."

"But that's worse than nuts—it's unnecessary. The pro they brought in, he might be willing to kill some people, but he's not gonna risk his neck so somebody can get his rocks off slicing a guy up."

Knox rocked back and forth on the bench for a moment, then said, "After Sanderson got killed, I sent Warren copies of the pictures. Didn't say who had them, I just said, 'Back off or the police get the pictures.'"

"Ah, man. He's been looking for the pictures," Virgil said.

"That's what I think." Knox turned his head to Virgil. "I'll tell you what, Mr. Pogues-Boy, I don't think you're gonna get him. He's too well-connected. It was all too long ago. I don't even know who could prosecute it as a crime. The Vietnamese? You think he'd get a fair trial? I don't think anybody would send him back there. . . . I mean, I just think . . . I think he got away with it."

"Then why all the killing?"

"Well—they couldn't hang him for it, but if these pictures got out, that'd be the end of him, businesswise. Look at those little kids he gunned down. Look at him fuckin' the dead woman. Nobody would touch him. He'd be like Hitler."

Virgil made Knox walk through it again, then said, "You think you're okay where you're at? For the duration?"

"Couldn't find me in a million years," Knox said.

WHEN THEY were gone, Virgil called Davenport.

"I got a killer," he said. "Might not be able to get him, because it was all so far away and long ago, but I've got pictures of the crime in progress."

"Anybody I know?" Davenport asked.

"Yeah."

Long moment of silence, and then Davenport said, "Virgil, goddamnit . . ."

"Ralph Warren," Virgil said.

Longer moment. Then: "I gotta see the pictures. How fast can you get back?"

"I'm heading out now," Virgil said. "I'll be back by dinnertime."

"Then come to dinner at my place. Six o'clock," Davenport said.

"See you then."

VIRGIL GOT his gear out of the cabin, threw it in the truck, and went to get a beer to drink as he headed south. The fisherwoman was putting the little girl in a new Mercedes station wagon, and she nodded at Virgil and asked, "Was that some kind of *meet?*"

"What?"

"Well, they told me in the bar that you're a state investigator, and a writer, but you were up here on that awful murder, and all of you guys were wearing black sport coats like you're covering up guns, and I could tell that those other guys were hoodlums of some kind." The woman had a small handhold on his heart, and it was getting stronger. The way she could roll that fly line out there . . .

"A meet. That's what it was, I guess," Virgil said. "I'd be happy if you kept it under your hat."

"Mmm. I'll do that. Virgil Flowers? Is that right?"

"Yes, ma'am." She had little flecks of gold in her eyes.

"Are you armed right now?"

"Yes, ma'am," Virgil said.

"Huh. Well, my name is Loren Conrad."

"Pleased to meet you, ma'am."

She walked around the car and stopped before opening the door. And the little girl, maybe ten, was looking at Virgil out through the glass of the passenger-side window, solemn, as if something sad were about to happen. "Maybe if you come up again, during the week, we could go fishing."

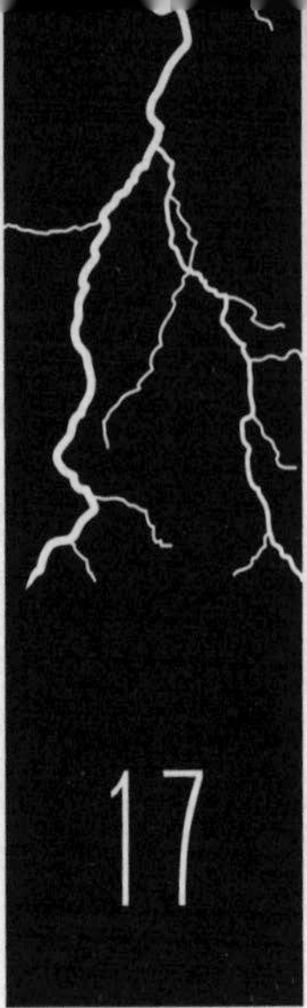

17

VIRGIL THOUGHT about the woman and daughter as he drove back. Had Mom been hitting on him, just the lightest, mildest of hits? What was the sadness in the small girl's eyes? Had she seen other men spoken to when Dad wasn't there?

The whole thing seemed less like an invitation to romance than an invitation to a story of some kind. Not journalism, a short story. Something Jim Harrison might write.

Virgil had had an interest in short stories when he was in college, but journalism seemed more immediate, something with its claws in the real world. The older he got, though, the wider he found the separation between reported facts, on one hand, and the truth of the matter on the other hand. Life and facts were so complicated that you never got more than a piece of them. Short stories, though, and novels, maybe, had at least a shot at the truth.

He was so preoccupied by the idea that he almost ran over a mink that crawled out of a ditch, poised for a dash across the road. He dodged at the last minute, wincing for the crunch as the animal went under the tire, felt nothing, looked in the wing mirror and saw it scurry across the tarmac, unhurt.

A small blessing.

THE WORLD was little more than a month past the summer solstice, so the sun was still high in the sky when he got off I-94 and turned south on Cretin Avenue in St. Paul, past the golf course with all the rich guys with their short pants and stogies, and farther south, hooked west on Randolph, then over to Davenport's house on Mississippi River Boulevard.

He parked on the street so he wouldn't block the three cars already in the driveway, and as soon as he stepped out, smelled the barbecue, heard the people talking in the back. He walked around the garage and pushed through the back gate, and Weather, Davenport's wife, spotted him and called, "Virgil Flowers!"

Davenport was there, with a former Minneapolis cop turned bar owner named Sloan, and his wife; and fellow BCA agent Del Capslock and his pregnant wife; and a spare, bespectacled woman named Elle, who was a nun and a childhood friend of Davenport's; and Davenport's ward, a teenager and soon-to-be-gorgeous young woman named Letty; and Davenport's toddler, Sam.

Weather came over and pinched his cheeks and said, "It's about time you got here, you hunk."

He gave her a little squeeze and asked, "Why don't you run away with me?"

"Then you wouldn't have a job and I'd have to support you," Weather said.

"Then he'd be dead and you *wouldn't* have to support him," Davenport said.

"Still, couple good days at a Motel 6 in Mankato . . . might be worth it," Virgil said to her.

Davenport said, "Yeah, it would be. When you're right, you're right."

Elle, the nun, amused, said, "You guys are so full of it."

"The shrink speaks," Del said. Elle was a psychologist.

"Give the poor boy a hamburger, Lucas, and then let's hear his story," Elle said to Davenport. She patted a chair next to her in the patio set. "Sit next to me, so I can ask questions."

DEL HAD BEEN doing counterculture intelligence for the upcoming Republican convention, and had been out of the loop on Virgil's investigation. All the others had read about the killings in the newspapers, but knew nothing else. Davenport told him to start at the beginning, with Utecht, and let it all out. Virgil did, all the details he could think of, ending with the conversation with Knox.

Then they wanted to see the pictures, and Virgil went out to the car to get them, and Davenport looked through them and handed them to Del and Sloan, and Elle got up to look, and Letty wanted to see, but Davenport snapped at her, "Get your nose out of there."

"It's not fair," and she sat down and put on a pout; Weather patted her on the leg.

"If that's actually Mr. Warren, then he is a very troubled man, with the kind of trouble you don't cure yourself of," Elle said. "If he did this, I would not be surprised to learn that he did similar things, here, over the years."

"Really," Virgil said. He put the pictures back in the envelope. "What would we be looking for?"

"If he's a smart man . . . maybe dead prostitutes. Perhaps dead prostitutes in other cities. Bigger cities that he knows well, or that attract prostitutes, or an anonymous population of women. Brown women—Latinas, Filipinas, Malaysians, Vietnamese. Miami, Los Angeles, Las Vegas, New York, Houston."

"Tortured?" Virgil asked. He was thinking of Wigge.

She shook her head. "Not as such. Not coldly. Not calculated. He'd kill them in an excess of violence. Beat them. Strangle them. A violent show of dominance and sexuality."

Virgil looked at Davenport. "Miami, Los Angeles, Las Vegas, New York, Houston."

Davenport shook his head. "There's so much background noise, we'd never sort them out."

"DNA," Sloan said. "If he's raping them, they'll have DNA in a DNA bank. Get some DNA from Warren, send it out there. Hell, circulate it everywhere."

"YOU THINK Knox was really scared?" Del asked. Del knew Knox better than any of them.

"Not scared—careful," Virgil said.

Del nodded. "That sounds like him. Where'd he get those guys?"

"One of them told me Chicago—Chicago came up a couple of times during the conversation," Virgil said. "There was a woman there, fishing, who told me when I was leaving that they looked like hoodlums. I guess they sorta did."

Del said to Davenport, "When we find him again, it'd be good to get some surveillance shots of these guys. If they're heavy-duty, it might tell us where Knox's connections go."

"We can do that," Davenport said. To Virgil: "What kind of vibe did you get from him? From Knox? Does he know more than he's telling us?"

"Don't think so," Virgil said. "The guys he had with him, they were definitely working. They were looking out for somebody. Knox thinks Warren's coming for him."

"Maybe," said Sloan's wife, "Warren's afraid not so much of . . . of . . . what happened back then, but what it'd tell you guys. That you'd get DNA from him, based on the pictures, and then something *would* pop up."

Davenport said, "Hell of a thought."

Sloan said, "Warren has been walking along the edge for years—he's got a full-time lawyer who does nothing but yell at city inspectors. Some of those places over on the riverfront, in Minneapolis, you could punch your fist through the walls."

"That's a long way from being a killer, though," Davenport said.

"But he *is* a killer," Virgil said. "We know that for sure. I got it from Ray, who knew there'd been killing, and I got it specifically from Knox, and I don't think Knox was lying. That isn't Knox in those pictures."

ELLE SAID, "Virgil, I'm very interested in the older Utecht. Chester. Am I wrong to think that he's actually the beginning of the sequence of deaths?"

"Well—that'd be one way to look at it," Virgil said. He hadn't looked at it that way. "I didn't ask, but I get the impression that he was an old guy who died, you know, a while back. Like a year or so. Nobody ever said it wasn't a natural death, so I assumed that it was."

She had cool, level eyes. "The circumstances of his death—they would be interesting to know."

"Yeah. Now that you mention it, they would. I'll check. Anybody know what time it is in Hong Kong?"

"Early morning, I'd guess," Davenport said.

"I'll try to call somebody before I go to bed," Virgil said. "The embassy maybe? There must be some kind of police liaison in the embassy."

Elle said, "I have another . . . interest. This man Sinclair. If I understand you correctly, he would be almost exactly as old as the murder victims. And we know he was in Vietnam at that time, or around that time. Where was he when these murders took place in Vietnam?"

Virgil pulled on his lip, shook his head. "All right. That's another thing I can check. I'm friendly with his daughter; maybe I can start with her."

THEY WORKED through it, and Davenport asked, "How'd they get to Bunton? There's a mystery for you. An Indian hitter? An Apache?"

"Geronimo returns," Del said.

So they sat and ate hamburgers and hashed it all over, and drank some beer, and Virgil lay back in a wooden recliner, looking at the stars that peeked out from behind the shine of city lights, and Letty came over and perched on the end of the recliner and was very cute and tried to wheedle the photos from him. He told her that she was too young, and she went steaming off.

Davenport had been watching from the corner of his eye and gave Virgil the thumbs-up. Virgil stood up and stretched and said, "Think I'll go call China," which was something that he'd never done.

BACK AT the motel, he sprawled on the bed and started by calling the phone company to find out how he called Hong Kong, and whom to call.

What he needed, it turned out, was the American consulate. After some switching around, he was told that the man he needed to talk to had gone to lunch and would be back in an hour. Virgil asked the woman how hot it was there, because he had the impression that Hong Kong was a hot place, and she said that it was eighty-four, and Virgil said that Minneapolis had been ninety that day, and the woman didn't have a comment about that, so Virgil said he'd call back in an hour.

He gave it an hour and a half, twelve-thirty in Minnesota, then talked to a man named Howard Hawn, who actually seemed interested in Virgil's question, and explained that he spent quite a bit of time getting puke-covered American tourists out of the drunk tank. Hawn said that he had some contacts who would know about Utecht's death, and he would find one and get a name back to Virgil.

"But it probably won't be until late in the afternoon—it's hard to get people at this time of day. Lot of people take a break."

"Leave a name and number on my phone," Virgil said, and Hawn said he would.

"Pretty cool in Minneapolis today?" Hawn asked.

"No, it was ninety—but I was up north yesterday, and it was cool at night, probably forty."

"Good sleeping weather," Hawn said. "It was about eighty-seven here when I came in." After that, there wasn't much more to say, and Hawn said he'd leave a name and number when he got them, or have somebody call him directly.

Virgil set his alarm clock for 7 A.M. and thought about Mead Sinclair, talking to two of the victims that night at the vet center, who spent all that time in Vietnam. Sinclair caused an itch, and had since Virgil first met him.

And the nun, Elle, who knew a lot about crime and criminals, had picked him out of the whole circus to ask about . . . and she'd asked about Chester Utecht, and now that Virgil thought about it, Sinclair had shown up here in St. Paul shortly after Chester Utecht died in Hong Kong. He'd apparently taken leave from the University of Wisconsin, one of the great universities in the country, to work part time at Metro State? Now that he thought about it, that seemed passing strange. . . .

The thoughts all tumbled over each other, and he got nowhere. He cooled out by thinking briefly about God, and considered praying that there wouldn't be another murder and another middle-of-the-night call. He decided that praying wouldn't help, and went to sleep, and dreamed of the fisherwoman with strong brown arms and gold-flecked married eyes.

VIRGIL WAS picking the day's T-shirt, undecided between Interpol and Death Cab for Cutie, when he remembered to check his cell for messages—there were none. Maybe Hawn hadn't made the connection, or maybe the Chinese didn't care, or maybe the request was bouncing around the halls of bureaucracy like a Ping-Pong ball, to be coughed up after Virgil was retired. He'd think about calling again later in the day.

He slipped into the Death Cab for Cutie shirt, a pirated model sold by street people outside shows, checked himself in the mirror, fluffed his hair, and headed out into the day.

Early and cool. Jenkins and Shrake would be helping with the surveillance on Warren, but they wouldn't be around until 10 A.M. or so, and Del Capslock had suggested an early start with a real estate consultant named Richard Homewood, who, Del said, would be at his office anytime after six in the morning.

Homewood worked out of a business condo on St. Paul's west side, off the Mississippi river flats beside the Lafayette Freeway. Virgil called ahead, mentioned Del's name, and Warren's, and Homewood, who might have provided the voice for Mr. Mole in *Wind in the Willows,* suggested that he stop at a Caribou Coffee for a large dark with plenty of milk, and come on over.

Virgil got the coffees, and found Homewood's office by the street number: there was no other identification. He rang, and Homewood, who could have *played* Mr. Mole—he was short, chubby, bespectacled, long-haired, and bearded—answered the door, took the coffee, sipped, said, "Perfect," and invited him in. The office was a paper cave, with bound computer printouts stacked on floor-to-ceiling shelves that completely covered the walls except for two windows and a gas fireplace. The center of the big room was taken up by three metal desks, each with a computer and printer and office chair, but there was no sign that anyone worked there but Homewood.

Homewood sipped, pointed Virgil at an office chair, asked, "How's Del?" but didn't seem too interested when Virgil told him about Del's wife being pregnant; and then he asked, "Are you really looking at Ralph Warren?"

"Yes—but not the way you probably think," Virgil said. "This is not a corruption investigation."

"Then what?"

Virgil said, "I can't give you all the details, but a group of men went to Vietnam a long time ago, when they were still young, and this group is now being murdered. The men whose bodies are being left at the veterans' monuments."

"The lemon murders. The lemons in the mouth."

Virgil frowned. "Where'd you hear that?"

"Television, last night, and this morning. The papers must have it. The lemon murders."

"Damn it. We'd held that back," Virgil said.

"Well—it's on the news now. So, Warren, how's he tied in?"

"He was one of the guys," Virgil said.

Homewood leaned forward, hands on his knees, intent. "Wait a minute. You think Warren's a killer?"

"We don't think anything, other than this killer is killing these guys. There are only two left alive, and I'm going to talk to Warren. Del told me you might have some background that I couldn't get anywhere else."

Homewood leaned back, looked around the jumble of the office, and then waved a hand at it. "I'm a real estate consultant, Virgil. Nobody knows as much about real estate in the Twin Cities as I do. I know what the values are, what the values should be, what the values *will* be. Ralph Warren has made a living by selling pie in the sky to a dozen city councils. Bullshitting them into providing taxpayer financing, buying council votes when he had to, buying planners and inspectors, threatening people. Makes a hash out of my values: I tell you, I can *see* what's going to happen. He sold the city on one deal, twenty years ago, it's now in its twelfth refinancing; the city's still on the hook for eight million dollars, sixteen million if you count all the interest over the years, all so Ralph Warren could take out a mil. I mean, the guy—if you'd told me that he's a killer, I'd say, *probably.*"

"Who's he threatened? That you know for sure?"

"Me," Homewood said. "I testified for the Minneapolis Planning Board against a ridiculous, absurd proposal for low-income housing—and I'm in favor of low-income housing, don't misunderstand me, but this was a fraud. A straight-out fraud. We came out of the hearing and Warren was laughing, and he came over to me, joking, and he said, 'Don't fall off no high bridges,' like it was a joke, but it wasn't a joke. I kept a gun in my desk drawer for six weeks after that. Every time I heard a sound at night, I jumped."

"But he never did anything," Virgil said.

"People don't believe me when I tell them what's going to happen," Homewood said. He shrugged. "Warren figured that out. If I'm not going to have any effect, why worry about me? People believe what they *hope* will happen, and that's what Warren peddles to them—hope that something good will happen. Something good does happen, but only for Warren. And then the taxpayers wind up holding the bag, just like they have with Teasdale Commons."

"So he's an asshole," Virgil said.

"More than that." Homewood shook a finger at him. "He's a criminal and a sociopath. How often do you have one of those, in the same . . . environment . . . as a bunch of crazy awful murders, and he didn't have anything to do with them?"

"That's a point," Virgil said. "That's a point."

JENKINS AND SHRAKE were throwing a Nerf football around the BCA parking lot when Virgil pulled in, and Virgil took a pass and the three of them threw it around for a few more minutes. The NFL preseason was around the corner, and as they headed inside, the three of them agreed that the Vikings were screwed this year.

Inside, they borrowed Davenport's office again and Virgil briefed them on Ralph Warren. "I'm going to get Sandy to research him, but to tell you the truth, I don't think we're going to find anything in research. We'll find it in some kind of action. He'll do something. So we watch him. If nothing happens for a couple of days . . . we might try a sting."

"What do we have to sting him with?" Jenkins asked.

"I've got some photos from Vietnam, of him raping a dead woman. Or a dying woman, anyway," Virgil said. "If somebody were to call him, and offer them for sale, and if that guy were an out-of-town hoodlum like Carl Knox might hire . . . it might have enough credibility to get him to act."

"Yeah, and if he's as bad a dude as you think, his action might be to blow somebody's head off," Jenkins said.

"There're ways around that. We could work that out," Virgil said. "But we'd have to work it so that he talked about it."

"So let's watch him for a while," Shrake said. "Just the three of us?"

"Just the two of you, for today," Virgil said. "I'm running around poking sticks into things. You can talk to Lucas and see if he can give you somebody else."

"What're you poking your stick into?" Shrake asked.

"I'm going to ask a woman up to Davenport's cabin for the day and I'm gonna try to get her on the couch so that . . ." He spun and looked at the big map of Minnesota on Davenport's wall.

Jenkins said, "You gonna get this chick on the couch so that . . . what?"

"So I can betray her," Virgil said. "I need to get some stuff out of her about her father. Without her knowing what I'm doing. So I can fuck with her old man."

They all thought about that for a while, then Shrake said, "Well, shit. We're cops."

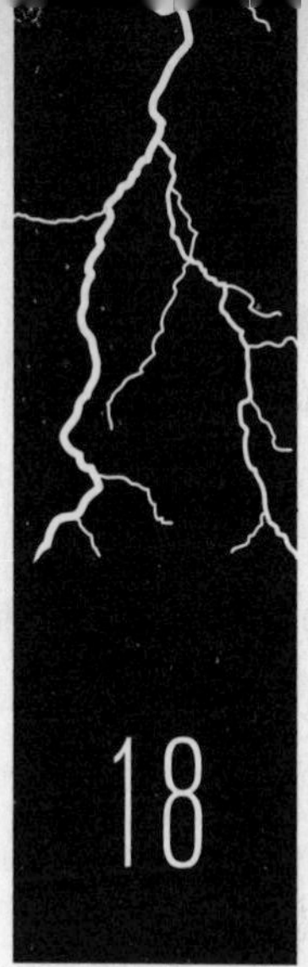

18

MAI WAS HAPPY to hear from him: "I'm standing outside an ice cream parlor on Grand Avenue, thinking about eating a giant ball of fat and sugar, so my ass will blow up to the size of a dirigible."

"Want to go fishing?"

"Sure. Where?"

"My boss has a cabin up north—two hours from here," Virgil said. "It's pretty far, but we could be there by early afternoon, go fishing, go for a walk, whatever, and be back here by bedtime."

"There's this restaurant at Grand and Victoria that makes good sandwiches and desserts," she said. "I'll go get some. You can pick me up outside—if that's not too quick for you."

"Fifteen minutes," Virgil said, and he was running.

DAVENPORT'S CABIN was twenty miles east of Hayward, a bit more than two and a half hours from the Cities, but they ate lunch in Virgil's truck and never slowed down and made good progress. Mai had never been in a police vehicle before, other than Virgil's, and wanted to know what all the pieces were, and for a while, when nobody was around on Highway 70, Virgil ran with lights and sirens to give her the feel. Mai was wearing blue jeans and a black cotton blouse, and her physical presence was all over the truck, her high-pitched girly voice, a tendency to giggle at vulgar jokes, a flowery scent.

"Peach blossom," she told him.

"I thought perfumes were called 'Sin' or 'Obsession,'" Virgil said.

"Eh, that's so inane. Do you wear a scent?"

He smiled at the word. "Aftershave sometimes, 'Big Iron Panzer Diesel.' It makes me feel more masculine."

They talked growing up in the Midwest, about going to Big Ten rival schools in Madison and Minneapolis. She confessed to never having gone to a Wisconsin football or basketball game, though she'd once gone on a date to a wrestling match, Wisconsin against the University of Iowa. "We got crushed," she said. "I mean, they got crushed. I personally didn't wrestle."

"I bet that disappointed everybody."

"Especially my date," she said, and patted him on the thigh.

Virgil said, "Have I told you about my illustrious baseball career?"

"You haven't mentioned it."

"The salient fact is, I couldn't hit a college fastball. I could hit the covers off a high school fastball, but not a college fastball. Anyway, I played for a couple of years and we went down to Madison three or four times a season. I'd hang out on the Terrace, eat ice cream, try to pick up women at the Rat . . ."

"Successfully?"

"Well—college successfully," Virgil said. "Never got laid, but we got some to talk to us."

She asked him how he felt about shooting people. He'd shot two people in his life, and had shot around a couple more. Of the people he'd shot, one man and one woman, he'd killed the man and had shot the woman in the foot. The same woman, as she lay wounded on the sidewalk, had been shot and killed seconds later by a second woman.

"Does it make you feel bad? Shooting people?" She was genuinely curious; the question wasn't a hidden accusation.

"Yes. Of course. People, you know . . . Neither of those people I shot had children, and here they are, at the end of millions of years of evolution, ancestors lived through the ice ages, hunted bison and mammoths, and here it all ends in a puddle of blood on some street, or out in a weed field. Their whole line, whatever potential they may have had in the centuries ahead of us . . ."

"That sounds pretty dry and intellectual."

"Because I've thought about it a lot. Intellectualized it. At the time, I felt pretty bad. I find you feel less bad the further you get away from it—but I dunno, it could come back on you later."

She said, "It'd be a pretty big load, killing people," she said.

"Yeah, well, you are what you do," Virgil said. "That's my take on it. I'm officially a killer. I think about it."

He asked why her father, big shot that he was, a leading antiwar critic, environmental activist, full professor at the University of Wisconsin, deigned to take a year to teach at Metro State.

"Burnout. Pressure to perform all the time," she said. "Always had to be out front on every issue. Maybe just getting old—things didn't work out the way he thought they would. Also, maybe, he didn't impress anybody at Wisconsin anymore. His big days are gone. He still impresses people at Metro State."

"Why didn't he get one of those fellowships or foundation grants and go live in New York or Paris or something? Go for long walks."

She shrugged. "Some people are teachers and take it seriously. He does. That's what he is—a teacher. So he looked for a job where he could stay in touch with things at Wisconsin."

"And you came with him," Virgil said.

"I'm trying to break the Madison spell—I've gotta get out of there. If I'm going to do anything with my life, I've got to start figuring out what it is. I can't take dance lessons forever. I've pretty much figured out that my answer isn't to dance with small repertory companies—and I'm not dedicated enough to make it with a big New York company. So I'm trying to figure out what to do."

"And what have you figured out?" Virgil asked.

"I'm thinking . . . Don't laugh . . ."

"I won't."

"Medicine," Mai said.

"Oooh. That could be tough. But my boss's wife is a surgeon, and she is really fascinated by it, really into it."

"I could handle the academics," she said confidently. "It's just sometimes . . . you think, I'll do all that work, years in school, and then . . . that's it? That's my life?"

Shrake called: "These guys around Warren—we've been watching them all day. These guys are heavy hitters. They're all wired up, they're talking to each other—there's a whole net around him. And he was down talking to John Crumb, who's like some big deal with the Republicans, and Crumb's got his own net, and they all knew each other. Man, this is tough stuff. Who are all these guys? I've never seen them before."

"He's piping them in from someplace," Virgil said. "Borrowing people, I guess—maybe all these security guys know each other or something."

"We can't stay too close to him," Shrake said. "I don't know what good we're gonna be able to do, Virgil. He's just got too many guys."

"WHO WAS THAT?" Mai asked.

"We're watching a guy—a suspect. I really . . . can't talk to you about it. I mean, I really can't."

"All right," she said. "Gives me a little tingle, mysterious cop stuff."

DAVENPORT DID MOST things well, Virgil thought, and among the things he'd done well was his lake cabin. The place was built of planks and cedar shingles and native stone, with a big fireplace and a comfortable living room and efficient kitchen, and two small comfortable bedrooms, all on one level.

The place was surrounded by a patch of overgrown fescue; off to one side, a giant white pine loomed over the water's edge; and Davenport had paid a deer-stand builder to build him a treehouse up in the pine, a deck with a few chairs and a roof, all up above the mosquitoes. A stone walk led to a forty-foot floating dock. A Tuffy fishing boat with a ninety-horse Yamaha outboard sat on a boatlift next to the dock.

Virgil recovered the guest key from a fake rock next to a stone wall along the driveway, and they went inside, into the dimly lit living room, and Virgil pulled the drapes and let the sunlight flood in.

"I don't know much about fishing," Mai said. "I've *been* fishing, but only with a bamboo pole."

"You're a jock. You've got reflexes. It'll take you two minutes to get a good start," Virgil said. "Lucas keeps his stuff in the storeroom."

He took out two seven-foot light-action musky rods and a box of baits, humming to himself, and sat her down and showed her how to rig them, did it himself, then took it apart and made her do it. They were still doing it when his phone rang again. He dug it out, looked at it, said, "Huh," and answered.

The voice actually sounded far away and satellite-fed: "This is Harold Chen with the Hong Kong Police Force. Is this Virgil Flowers?"

"Yes, it is. . . . Hang on just one second."

Virgil said to Mai, "I gotta take this, it's from China. . . . I'm gonna run outside, sometimes you can drop the calls inside here."

He went back to the phone as he walked toward the door. "Yes, Mr. Chen, thank you for calling me back. I'm looking for information about Chester Utecht, a man who died there a year or so ago. I've got the details in my notebook—"

"I'm quite familiar with Mr. Utecht's case." Chen sounded like he'd just left Oxford. "Could I ask why you're inquiring after him?"

"We've had a series of murders here. . . ." Virgil told Chen about the murders in detail, and about the possible tie to Vietnam.

When he was done, Chen said, "Well. Vietnam. I should tell you that Mr. Utecht was something of a character. One of the last of the old-time soldiers of fortune, so his death was . . . noticed. He had been suffering from a series of debilitating diseases in his final days. Both his liver and kidneys were failing. However, his death hadn't appeared imminent when he saw his internist a few days before he died. The pathology suggests that he may have taken his own life, or perhaps accidentally overdosed, on pain pills and alcohol."

"Ah. A suicide," Virgil said. "Nobody told me that on this end."

"There was no official finding of suicide," Chen said. "The cause was recorded as 'unknown.' However, the pathologist, who is quite competent, told me privately that Mr. Utecht had some bruises on his arms above his elbows, and around his ankles, that would be consistent with restraint."

"Restraint."

"Yes. But restraint by who, or what—or even if there was any restraint—is unknown. We looked for something, but couldn't find anything at all. The fact is, he was elderly, alone, sick, probably dying, and running out of money. The easiest answer is suicide or accident; however, I wasn't entirely satisfied by that. I looked for anyone who might have had any animus toward him. Anyone who could have carried out such a sophisticated murder, or would have any reason to. I found nothing; and frankly, Utecht was not important enough to be the object of such a murder. Now you say there was a murder in Vietnam, that he was involved, and that others who were involved are also being killed."

"Yes, that's what I'm saying," Virgil said.

"That may give me a few more questions to ask. But I can also tell you this: we are quite certain that Mr. Utecht had connections with your

CIA in his past. He didn't work for them, he wasn't paid, but he had . . . connections, if you see what I'm saying. He helped them when he could, and they helped him when they wished."

"You don't think the CIA is killing these people?"

"I think nothing in particular," Chen said. "But who really knows what happened in the last minutes before the victory? The whole business of the ship, this sounds like too complicated an operation for one man. If it were a CIA operation that had gone bad, if, as you say, you have photographs of a man raping a dead woman, if babies were killed . . . Well, this is an ugly thing. With the controversy about the CIA, perhaps they wouldn't like to have this float up from the past. Especially if the men were willing to talk about it."

They let the satellite idle for a moment, then Virgil said, "Mr. Chen, if you're curious, I will call you and tell you how this works out. I would deeply appreciate it if you would ask your questions and let me know the answers. I don't like the sound of this CIA connection. I don't like that."

"Yes, because what could you do? Your hands would be tied."

They talked for a few more minutes, details and phone numbers, then Virgil rang off, and as he walked back to the cabin, he could hear Mai talking. He stepped inside, and she smiled and said, "Daddy . . . I will be home when I will be home. We're just going out fishing. I will see you when I see you. Good-bye."

THEY DROPPED the boat in the water and headed out, a good blue day without wind, the water like green-black Jell-O, not quite still, but jiggling from the distant passings of small motorboats. Virgil found a weed bed, and explained about musky fishing. "There's a cliché about musky—that they're the fish of ten thousand casts. Hard to catch. Which means, when you go musky fishing, you probably won't actually have to deal with catching one."

He tied a black-and-orange-rubber Bull Dawg lure onto one of the rods, flipped it out, retrieved it, showed her how the tail rippled at a certain speed, showed her how to cast with her arms and her back instead of her wrists, steadied her in the boat with a hand on her waist and back and occasionally her butt. Twenty or so casts out, the lure was hit by a small northern pike, two feet long, which hooked itself and then flipped once out of the water and gave up, and she reeled it in. Virgil wet a hand in the lake, grabbed the fish at the back of its head, unhooked it, and dropped it back in, looked up to see her watching in fascination.

"You threw it back! That's the biggest fish I ever caught!" she said.

"Shoot . . . hmm, I didn't think you'd want it. Besides, if you want one, we'll catch more."

"Well, I guess I don't really want one. I like fish . . . but . . ."

So they went on around, and she caught two more northerns, which were easy, and lost a fish that Virgil thought might have been a small musky.

"You fish for a while; I'm going to drink a Coke," she said.

So he fished as she sat in the boat, and then she said, "Is that a thunderstorm?"

He looked off to the southwest, over his shoulder, and saw the anvil of cloud coming in. "Yeah . . . gotta be thirty miles away. We got time."

"Until you reminded me . . . I hadn't thought about the Terrace for years—I was never that much for it. Too busy. Now that I look back, I wonder what I was busy at. I should have had some lazy friends, you know, just sit out there with root-beer floats and watch the sailboats. But what the heck did I do?" She stared at the water, and Virgil flipped the lure into a niche in the weed line, twitched it a few times, and she said, "You know what I did? I worked. But I worked at all this art stuff. Dancing. Photography. Writing. All the time. Obsessively. I hardly ever went and sat and laughed with friends."

"Madison is the best place in the world if you want to hang out," Virgil said. "You see these old gray-bearded guys on their rusty bikes, they've been hanging out since the sixties. Never quit."

"Yeah, but . . . ah, I don't know. And the Rat. What a dump; that's what I used to say. What a dump. Just too busy . . . busy, busy, busy . . ."

So they floated and talked and she cast some more, and once almost tipped over the side, and he said, eventually, "If you cast any more, you're gonna be sore in the morning. You're going to feel like this muscle"—he rubbed his knuckles up and down the big vertical muscle just to the left of her spine—"is made out of wood."

She'd caught five fish at that point. "One last cast."

"No point. You never catch anything on the last cast."

She cast, and didn't catch anything. "All right. I submit to your greater knowledge, although it doesn't make any statistical sense."

"Sure it does—if you catch something, that's never your last cast," Virgil said. "You always keep going for at least ten minutes. So you never catch anything on the last cast."

He sat next to the motor, saw a distant flash of lightning, counted the seconds, and then said, "Six miles, more or less. Better get off the lake."

They got off, cranked the boat out of the water, pulled the plug, tied on the canvas cover, walked up to the cabin, washed their hands, got a couple of beers, sat on the lakeside porch, and watched the storm coming in.

When the first fat drops of rain hit around them, she said, "We probably ought to go jump in bed."

"Probably," he said.

SHE SAT on the edge of the bed and let him take her clothes off; he did it from behind her, kneeling on the mattress, with his face buried in the pit of her neck, his hands working the buttons on her blouse and jeans.

"Ah, God, this is where I can't stand it," he said. He popped the hooks on her brassiere.

She giggled with the stress. "What? You can't stand it?"

"It's always so wonderful . . ." He popped her brassiere loose and let his hands slip up her stomach and cup her breasts.

"It can't *always* be wonderful," she said.

"No, no, it's *always* wonderful," he said. "It's just like opening your Christmas presents when you're eight years old. Ah, jeez . . ."

Then it was underpants and she was pulling on Virgil's jeans, which still smelled a little fishy from one of the northerns they'd caught, and then they were all over the place, and somewhere during the proceedings, though Virgil didn't bother to check the time, she began to make a low *ohhhh* sound and then Virgil lost track, but not for long.

WELL, HE THOUGHT as he lay on his back, the sweat evaporating from his stomach, he'd thought it would be pretty good, and it had been. And would be again in about, hmm, seventeen minutes.

She said, "Why . . ." She giggled. "That was so crazy—all of a sudden, I realized, this afternoon, before we went out, you said you got a phone call from China. From China? You get calls from China?"

"No, it's this case. Trying to go back in time. There was a guy killed in Hong Kong a year or so ago, and there's a question of how exactly he died. He's connected with the guys here. The Chinese are going to look into it, see what they can find out."

"All the Chinese? That's a lot of Chinamen."

"The Hong Kong police force."

"Really. Indians, Chinese, Hong Kong, the North Woods."

"Yeah . . . I gotta tell you, when I brought you up here, I was mostly thinking about this . . ." He slipped his hand up her thigh. "But I worry about your father and you. You don't know anything about this case, do you?"

She propped herself up on one elbow. "Why would I know anything about it? Why would you ask?"

"Because your father, you know, he was talking to Ray and Sanderson, and when I asked what they were talking about, he didn't have much to say. The thing is, if this killer even *thinks* your father was involved, he might go after him. And if you're in the way . . . Look, I really, really don't want you to get hurt, and if your father's involved, you could be in the line of fire."

"Oh . . . Virgil. You don't really think so? I mean, my father . . ." She trailed away.

"Was he in Vietnam in 1975?"

"He's been there a lot. When I was a child, it seemed like he was gone all the time, but that was in the eighties. As I understand it, the Vietnamese really thought they had allies with the American people, and that he was one of them. So he was there during the war, and right after it, and later, he was there more. . . . He was there a lot. But 1975, I don't know."

"I'm amazed he was never busted," Virgil said.

"Busted . . ."

"Arrested. By the feds . . . you know, 'giving aid and comfort.'"

"Well, when he went, he went as a journalist," Mai said. "So that gave him some status."

"Still. You gotta ask him about it," Virgil said. "If there's anything, he's got to talk to me."

"How many more killings do you think—"

"I don't know. . . . I'll tell you something, but you gotta promise not to tell."

"All right, sure," she said.

"The last one, the killer was probably seen, and he was an Indian guy. Ray was an Indian guy. Some of these guys were living on the edge, and there's a question of whether there was a dope deal going down somewhere. So . . . it's all really confusing."

"Do you know who the other targets might be?"

"Yeah, I talked to one the other day. I can't really tell you his name—it's, like, a legal thing. But he's out there traveling around. He told me he's safe. He's got a security guy who travels with him, he says the president couldn't find him. But hell, it's possible he's involved somehow."

"You'll figure it out. Dad says you're a pretty smart guy," Mai said.

"I don't feel so smart; I feel like my head is stuffed full of cotton. Something is going on, and I don't know what it is."

She squeezed him. "Feels like something is going on down here."

"I know what *that* is," he said. "I have that *completely* under control."

"Right. Mr. Control." She gave him a yank. "How many women have you slept with, Mr. Control?"

"I have a list on my laptop," Virgil said. "I'd hate to say without consulting my list."

"Just names, or . . . talent, as well?"

"Everything. Names, photographs, résumés, criminal records. I give them all grades, too. For example, a couple of women might call me up, and I don't remember them that well in the fog of *all* the women, but I've got to make a decision. So I look at my computer records, and one of them I've given a B-minus, and the other a C-minus. So the decision is clear."

"What'd I get?"

"You got a B-plus," Virgil said. "You could easily move up to an A, if you play your cards right."

"Lying in bed," she said. "Joking."

"Ah, well . . ." He sat up, looked down at her. "It's what happens when you become a cop. Something curdles your sense of humor. My problem is not really that I sleep with so many women. My problem is that I fall in love with them."

She was lying facedown on top of the sheet with her face turned toward him, and he ran his hand down her back and over the rise of her butt. "Women don't understand how beautiful they are. They don't understand it. They get beauty all confused with personality, or charisma, or a nice smile . . . but they really don't see the simple beauty of this . . ." and his hand glided again over her bottom. "It's a goddamn tragedy that you can't see it. But you can't; I know you can't. And it's just so beautiful."

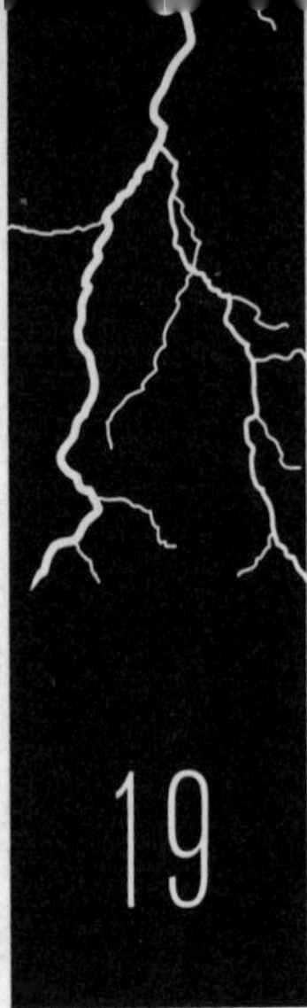

19

VIRGIL WAS moving early the next morning, out at dawn, heading southwest out of the Twin Cities, still feeling the glow of the afternoon and evening with Mai. He'd spoken with Shrake the evening before, after he'd dropped Mai, and Shrake said that he and Jenkins had spotted several more bodyguards working the streets around Ralph Warren's home.

"We gave it up. We were staying *way* back, but they were still going to see us. We can get on him again tomorrow, but it seems like he's moving at night, if he's doing these killings. We need to do something electronic with his truck, to follow him, or something—this ain't working."

Virgil spoke to Davenport, and they agreed that Shrake and Jenkins would resume the surveillance in the morning, just tight enough to keep track of Warren's general location. "We ought to try the sting, see what happens," Virgil told Davenport. "We need an undercover guy who Warren wouldn't know, and between him and his pals, they'll know a lot of cops around town."

"I'll make some calls," Davenport said. "I've got an ex-cop in Missouri who could do it. He'd be perfect for the job."

SO VIRGIL got up early, headed back to Mankato, his home base, with ten pounds of dirty clothes. He lived in a compact 1930s brick house on the edge of downtown, on a block with trees and quite a few kids. When he bought it, the house had belonged to an elderly widower whose children were moving him to a nursing home. The old man had been a mechanic before he retired, and had restored cars as a hobby. His two-and-half-car garage was nearly as big as the house, and provided good room for both Virgil's truck and his boat.

He left the truck in the driveway, checked the place to make sure everything was okay, stuck the dirty clothes in the washing machine, collected his mail, paid bills, and walked downtown and dropped them off at a mailbox. He got an early-morning cup of coffee and a croissant at a coffee shop.

Eating the croissant as he went, he walked back home, put the clothes in the dryer, and made a phone call to Marilyn Utecht, hoping he wasn't waking her up; but she was an early riser, and said, "Come on ahead." He got in the truck and headed to the town of New Ulm, which had at one time been the least ethnically diverse town in the United States—everybody had been of German ancestry.

UTECHT WAS working in her still dew-wet yard when he got there, digging dandelions with a paring knife, tossing them into a bucket.

"How're you doing?" Virgil asked as he crossed the lawn.

She said, "Okay," and stood up, and "I got a job."

"Good. Get you out and about," Virgil said.

She smiled and said, "It's not much of a job . . . part time at a day-care center. But I always liked little kids, and I don't really need a lot of money."

"Don't you get diseased?"

"Oh, yeah. Keeps your immune system going, that's for sure," she said. "So, Virgil—what's up? You want a root beer or anything? Or is it still too early?"

"Sure, I'll take a root beer."

THEY SAT in lawn chairs in the backyard, a pool of uninflected grass surrounded by a white board fence, and drank root beer, and Virgil said, "You've been reading about what's going on."

She shivered and said, "I can't believe it. I just . . . can't . . . believe it. Are you going to catch him? Whoever's doing it?"

"Hope so. He's a psycho, whoever he is, and I think he's compelled to do this," Virgil said. "We've got one suspect, who we're watching, and one fellow who we know is a target, who's protected, and sooner or later, something is going to crack open. I hope we're in a position to move when it does."

"I should hope," she said. "I still cry about Chuck, poor guy. I'll be standing by the sink, and I'll start crying."

"You were married a long time."

"Yup," she said, and took a sip of root beer.

"What do you know about Chuck's dad, Chester?" Virgil asked. "When he died, did you guys go over?"

"Chuck did—just to see . . . well, there wasn't much of an inheritance. Eighteen thousand dollars, that was about it. He had an annuity, but that was gone the minute he died. Chester was cremated, and they put his ashes in the ocean, so . . . there wasn't much left."

"I talked to a guy from China. A Hong Kong cop. He said that Chester might have had some contact with the CIA."

Utecht's eyebrows went up, and she said, "You know, I wouldn't doubt it. We used to joke about him being a spy. We even asked him once, and *he* joked about it—but when he was joking about it, his eyes didn't look funny, if you know what I mean."

"I do."

"Chester was all over that area when he was young, after World War Two—Hong Kong, North Vietnam, South Vietnam, Laos, Cambodia, Thailand. He knew a lot of French people from North Vietnam," Utecht said. "He even spoke French. He stayed here a few times when he was in the States, and once he was joking about having kids in Thailand, but I'm not sure *that* was completely a joke, either. How does all of this figure in?"

Virgil told her about the bulldozer heist and she said, "I knew about that. Chuck . . . it was the big adventure of his youth, but it was in seven or eight years before we got together, so I didn't know the details. Do you really think all of this"—she waved her hand, meaning the killings—"could have anything to do with *that?*"

"I'm pretty sure it does," Virgil said. "I'm just not sure how. Have you ever seen or heard the name Mead Sinclair in any of Chuck's papers, or did he ever mention that name?"

She thought a moment, then said, "No, I don't think so. Odd name. I can look, if you want. We've still got a lot of stuff."

"Well, if you see anything . . ."

"Who is he?"

So he explained about Mead Sinclair. She said, "If Sinclair was an antiwar activist, and Chester had contact with the CIA . . . do you think they might have been enemies or something? That this man is running a revenge feud?"

"I don't know. Honest to God, I keep going around in circles. My problem is, I've got two things in my head. One loop involves the guys getting killed here, because they did something that one of them is trying to cover up. The other loop involves Mead Sinclair and the CIA and people getting killed in Hong Kong, maybe, and God only knows what that motive would be. If I could put the two loops together, I might have something. And it seems like there should be a fit somewhere."

"Be careful," she said. "Don't get hurt."

BACK IN Mankato he picked up his dry clothes, repacked, and headed north to the Cities again. So Chester may have worked with the CIA, he thought. Which meant that there may have been more to the bulldozer heist than was apparent—and more to the Vietnam killings than was apparent.

Or not.

Damnit.

He got on his cell phone and called Sandy. "Are you working today?"

"Uh, I've got a class, but I could do a couple hours."

"I need to find out if Mead Sinclair had any direct clashes with the CIA, or has ever said anything about the CIA coming after him, or about CIA killers in Vietnam, or any kind of intelligence agencies doing anything to him, or about him, or bringing charges against him . . . anything like that."

"I'll call you," she said. "Or I might be around the office this morning, before lunch."

"I GOT A bunch of stuff," Davenport said when Virgil checked in at the BCA at ten-thirty. "I've got a meeting I can't miss, so I won't be around. Andreno just called in, he's on his way from the airport. He'll be here in fifteen minutes or so. I'll send him down to you—I got you John Blake's office while he's on vacation."

"What's the guy's name? Your friend?" Virgil asked.

"Micky Andreno. I told him to bring a gold neck chain. Also, I got the Secret Service and the FBI asking about you—they want to know what the status is, they're getting a little worried about the killings, especially after Wigge. Too many important people are going through town to have a psycho running loose, so you need to call a couple people and give them status reports."

"Pressure starting to build?"

"Of course. I'm not unhappy with what you've done, but these people don't want to know about processes, they want the problem to go away," Davenport said. "If you don't get something quick, they may want to *help*. As in, use a bunch of their own people."

"That'd slow things down pretty good," Virgil said.

Davenport nodded. "Absolutely. Anyway, that means if Warren is a legitimate suspect, then let's squeeze *now*, and *hard*. Get it done."

VIRGIL MADE calls to the FBI and the temporary Secret Service office that had been set up to protect the Republican National Convention. The agents he'd talked to seemed cool and skeptical, and when he was done, Virgil threw the receiver at the desk set and said, "Fuck you."

Shrake and Jenkins came by: "We gonna do it?"

"Yeah. Our setup guy is on the way from the airport. We gotta round up Dan Jackson, I want to get the whole thing on video if we can, and get the guys in tech services to wire up Andreno, if we can pull this off today. . . ."

"Where're we going to do it?" Jenkins asked.

"Gotta be some place public or Warren won't buy it," Virgil said.

"Be best if it was our choice," Jenkins said. "We could set up in advance. With the security guys he's got, if *they* pick location, they'll spot us coming in to monitor the place."

Shrake: "How about Spiro's on University, in Minneapolis? That's fifteen minutes from Warren's place, and he's had projects on University, so he'll probably know it. That might ease his mind a little. And the neighborhood is cut up, so we can monitor a little easier."

"All right. You guys set that up, I'll wait for Andreno. Lucas wants us to push it, hard. Go for something right now."

SANDY CALLED. "Where are you?"

"John Blake's office."

"I'll be right down."

She had a file in her hand when she came through the door, and she passed it to him and he popped it open: anonymous stuff copied in a variety of fonts from different Web sites.

"Something I find very interesting," she said. "Starting in the sixties, Sinclair had a lot to say about the CIA. They were assassins, they were counterproductive, they destabilized progressive countries, they propped up right-wing dictatorships, blah-blah-blah. All the usual stuff, nothing specific. Nothing you didn't read in the newspapers. It sort of tapered off in the eighties and the nineties. But then . . ."

Big smile.

"What's the big smile?" Virgil asked.

"Six years ago, a man named Manfred Lutz from Georgetown University wrote an article for *Atlantic* in which he said that Mead Sinclair basically made his reputation in the sixties counterculture by writing two lefty antiwar pieces, very well researched, very insightful, in *Hard Times Theory* magazine and another in *Cross-Thought* magazine, which Lutz says were small but influential magazines on the political left."

"I think I knew that," Virgil said. "I saw those names somewhere."

"But did you know that Lutz claims that both *Hard Times* and *Cross-Thought* were CIA-sponsored vehicles?"

Virgil took that in for a few seconds, then he said, "I didn't know that. Was he saying that Sinclair was a CIA agent?"

"No. Not exactly. He just lists Sinclair as among the people who benefited from publication in the magazines. Then, when that started a brouhaha, Sinclair apparently threatened to sue, and that shut everybody up. Sinclair's position is that he didn't believe that they were CIA vehicles, because they published too many progressive and hard-left articles, but even if they were, he didn't know it at the time. They were leading left-wing publications who were willing to publish his articles, and to pay him for them, and that's all he knew. He even joked that maybe they were CIA, because they were about the only left-wing magazines that actually paid anyone."

"Where can I find Lutz?"

"He lives near Washington. I wrote his office phone number on the article," she said.

"You're amazing," Virgil said. "I'll call him right now."

LUTZ HAD A dark, gravelly voice with a New York accent. "How'd you find me?" he asked when Virgil identified himself.

"One of our researchers did," Virgil said.

"How do I know you're who you say you are?"

"You could look up Minnesota Bureau of Criminal Apprehension online, call the number, and ask for Virgil Flowers."

"How do I know the CIA hasn't put up a spoof?"

"What's a spoof?"

Lutz thought about the question for a minute, then said, "Ah, hell. I stand by my story, even if you are the CIA. The CIA sponsored those magazines. Period. End of story. I'm not talking about a little clandestine support—I mean, they were CIA fronts. They cranked out these mind-numbing leftist proclamations and articles, mind-numbing even for the time. In return, they had entrée into all the left-wing intellectual circles of the time, both here in the U.S. and in Europe."

AT THAT MOMENT, a man stuck his head in the door: he was chunky, square-faced, with short, curly hair and a bald spot at the crown of his head. He had small black eyes, fight scars under them, a nose that had been hit a few times. Virgil said to Lutz, "Hang on a minute," and asked, "Mickey?"

The man showed some completely capped white teeth. "Yup, Virgil?"

"Sit down, I got a guy I gotta talk to."

"I gotta shit like a shark, man."

"Down the hall to the left. . . ."

VIRGIL WENT BACK to the phone. "Okay, where were we? Listen, you not only suggest that the magazines were CIA fronts, you hint that Mead Sinclair and a couple of other guys were agents. Not dupes, but agents."

"I'm still of that opinion," Lutz said. "I can't get it printed, because Sinclair says that it will harm his reputation and that he'll sue. That scares everybody off, because I can't provide any documentary proof. But that's my opinion."

"So how'd you get to that opinion?"

"Mostly because of the . . . smoothness of his arrival. One day you never heard of him, the next day he's all over the place, publishing articles, giving speeches. And it's not only that, it's also the quality of the response. Sinclair would say something, and somebody in the government would actually respond to it, they'd debate him instead of ignoring him. That put him right in the heat of the battle—this terrific-looking blond guy with big ideas, who was willing to risk going to North Vietnam, to Hanoi, in the middle of the war.

"He gets arrested at demonstrations, but he's always pretty quick to get out. Always the terrific PR photos. And if you look at it, and you're cynical enough, you can see that it was certain congressmen and some people in the Johnson and Nixon administrations who actually made him into a lefty big shot. Because they gave him attention. And when you look at those people, you can see that every single one seems to have a tie to the intelligence community."

Virgil didn't say anything for a moment, and then, finally: "Interesting."

Lutz said, "Yeah," with a skeptical tone right there. "What are you going to do with it?"

"I don't know," Virgil said. "I'm trying to solve some murders that seem to go back to Vietnam."

"If you solve them, and they do go back, I'd like to hear about it. I'd like to write about it," Lutz said.

"Keep an eye on the news. The whole story is out there right now, and it's getting bigger. I'll give you my number."

Virgil gave him his number, and Lutz said, "Virgil Flowers. That's an operator's name if I ever heard one. You're really CIA, aren't you? You're gonna bug my house and my office and my car . . ."

"We don't have to," Virgil said. "We already replaced your fillings with microphones."

Lutz laughed and said, "Maybe that's why old ABBA songs keep running through my head."

"Jesus Christ, we're not that cruel," Virgil said.

ANDRENO WAS wearing tan slacks and a powder-blue golf shirt, a thick gold chain around his neck. He chewed gum. Virgil looked at him and thought, *Perfect.*

"How ya doin'?" Andreno asked, shaking Virgil's hand. His hand was still damp—from the water faucet in the restroom, Virgil hoped.

"Let's get the other guys."

They gathered in Virgil's temporary office, Jenkins and Shrake and Andreno, and Virgil showed them the copies of the photographs.

"That's pretty crude of old Ralph," Jenkins said. He held one of the photos close to his face, studying the rape photo. "That's him, all right."

Shrake was looking at the other photos, took the rape photo from Jenkins. "But what if he just flat denies it—says he never went to Vietnam, that it's not him. . . . It *could* be somebody else."

"Probably can't get him for Vietnam," Virgil said. "Too long ago, there's only one witness still alive, and he probably wouldn't testify anyway. We need to shake him up—Warren—freak him out. Get him to argue. We need to get him to give us something."

"That's gonna be tough," Andreno said. "If he's smart, he'll keep his mouth shut. Deny, deny, deny. Imply a deal, acknowledge a deal, wink and nod, but not put it in words."

"He's a psycho," Virgil said. "You gotta stick a sliver under his fingernails. You got to get him to cook off a couple of wild shots."

"I can get into my wise-guy mode, give him some shit about rapin' dead women," Andreno said. "But if this guy is really smart . . ."

"What if he just doesn't buy it?" Shrake asked. "This is pretty thin stuff."

"The photos aren't thin," Virgil said. "Knox sent him some xeroxes and didn't hear anything back. So it's him, and he knows it. And maybe they wouldn't work in court, but if they got out there, started making the rounds, he'd be finished, socially, politically. You could stick a fork in him. We gotta hope they set him off."

"I need to take a look at this restaurant ahead of time," Andreno said. "If he's really got top-end security guys, they're gonna have some electronic gear. They're gonna check me for a wire."

"We're not gonna wire you," Shrake said. "We got something way more cool. We'll show you downstairs."

Andreno nodded, snapped his Juicy Fruit, and looked at Virgil. "What's my story?"

THE STORY, they'd decided, was that Andreno had been hired by Carl Knox to provide security against whoever was killing the people involved in the bulldozer heist, who Knox suspected was Warren. But Andreno and Knox had a falling-out. Knox was at his cabin up north, and Andreno had been out in the woods with mosquitoes and blackflies and ticks all day, and that wasn't his scene. There'd been an argument, and Knox had fired him and refused to pay his fee.

"So you knew where the pictures were, which was inside a fake book, and you took them on the way out. You want money for them—you were supposed to get five thousand bucks a week toward a guarantee of twenty-five thousand, plus expenses, and that's what you want: thirty thousand. If he doesn't want to buy the pictures, you'll see if anybody else does."

"You have to tell Warren that you *know* that he's behind the killings, you have to make him believe that you believe," Virgil said. "You have to convince him that you don't care about that, that Knox doesn't care, maybe even that Knox approves, to get rid of witnesses. Also, you gotta suggest to him that you'll tell him where Knox's hideout is."

Andreno said, "What about the negatives?"

"You don't know anything about the negatives," Virgil said. "If Knox has negatives, then Warren's got another problem—but who knows if he's got any? Warren's gotta solve the Andreno problem first. Get *these* pictures out of the way."

DAVENPORT SHOWED UP as they were working out the details, had a backslapping reunion with Andreno.

"Don't get my boy shot," Davenport said to Virgil after Virgil told him how they'd work the approach.

"Yeah, don't get his boy shot," Andreno said.

"We should be okay—we'll have it scouted, we'll be inside, it'll all be on tape," Virgil said. "We'll make movies of everybody coming and going."

"What could possibly go wrong?" Jenkins asked.

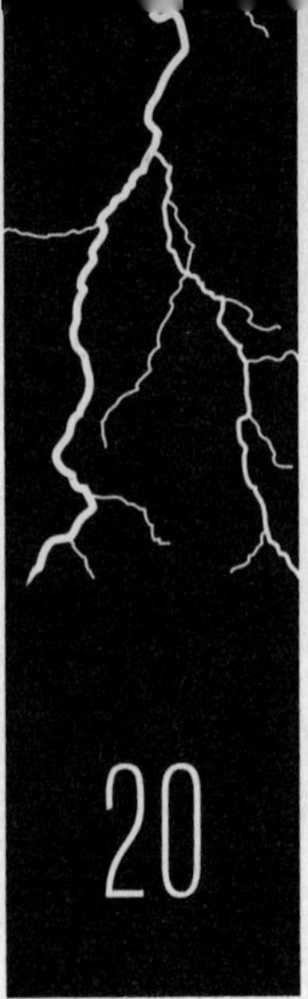

THE "WAY MORE COOL" surveillance device was a laptop computer, brought in by the film guy, Dan Jackson. The computer had two battery slots, one of which had been replaced by a high-definition digital video recorder with four tiny cell-phone cameras, four tiny microphones, and a transmitter.

"The way it works is, you hit F-10. The computer doesn't come up, but it starts the recorders and transmitter. It'll pick up every word within ten feet, and it records wide-angle photographs in all four directions, and transmits," Jackson said. "You're gonna want to sit away from the kitchen . . . it really picks up plates and silverware. And you're gonna want to set the computer so one of the lenses is looking across the table at Warren and one of them is looking at you. They got wireless there, so you could have it open and be working on it, so they know it's really a working computer. When he shows up, you get offline, and close the lid, and shove it off to the side."

"Why's that better than a wire?" Andreno asked.

"Because everything is so much bigger, they can jam more shit into it. Get better sound, you get movies, you get a better radio, and a bigger battery," Jackson said. "But the main thing is, a bug-detection device will pick up a computer every time. If they scan you, they'll pick up the laptop. And they make an allowance for it. And the computer works, if they want to see it work. The trick is, it really *is* a bug."

Andreno looked skeptical. "Maybe I should just take a wrist radio."

Andreno would give Warren color xerox copies of the photos, saying that the actual photos were nearby. "He won't believe it if you just hand over the originals," Virgil said. "Or, if he does believe it, why would he give them back to you? It's not like you're gonna shoot him right there in the restaurant."

ANDRENO PRACTICED with the laptop a bit, put in his own e-mail address and figured out how to call it up. When they were satisfied that he knew what they were doing, they headed out, across town, to the restaurant, a sandwich-and-pie place, and they all got coffee and a piece of pie and worked out the seating arrangements.

When they were done, Virgil asked, "You happy?"

Andreno nodded and said, "I am. It's almost noon. Let's make the call."

They went out to Virgil's truck, gave Andreno a clean cell phone, which Shrake plugged into the microphone attachment on the laptop, and Warren's cell-phone number.

Andreno sat in the passenger seat, hunched over the phone, cleared his throat a couple times, and dialed. The phone call lasted a minute, and they replayed it from the recorder.

ANDRENO: "Ralph Warren. I'm an ex-employee of a very old friend of yours, going back to the sixties. I need to talk to you."

"What friend? Talk about what?" Warren had a high-pitched, reedy voice on the phone. "How'd you get this number?"

"We need to talk about all these dead people with lemons in their mouths. Your old friend figures that you might know something about it, and he's very nervous. Therefore, he's hiding out. The thing is, he took some pictures way back then, in that house, the one where the trouble started. He sent you copies. I had a little problem with your friend, and he canned my ass, so I lifted the pictures and here I am. All I want is my fee. Thirty thousand dollars. Then I go away."

"I don't know what the fuck you're talking about, pal."

"Okay. Well, then, don't show up," Andreno said. "I'm gonna be at Spiro's Restaurant, which is three blocks west on University from your Checkerboard Apartments, at one o'clock. If you're not there by ten after one, fuck it, I mail the pictures to the television people and go on back to Chicago. See you there, or not. I know what you look like . . . from the pictures. Oh—if you want to know where your pal is, I can tell you that, too. 'Bye."

"Wait . . ."

But Andreno had hung up.

"He bit," Shrake said from the backseat. "He'll be there."

JACKSON SET UP three hundred yards away with a camera lens as long as his arm. The rest of them stayed on the street, sitting in the backseats of plain-vanilla state cars, behind lightly smoked glass, each with a radio. For the first half hour, they saw nothing at all. Then the radio burped and Jenkins said, "Look at this guy. Red Corolla. He's five miles an hour too slow and he's checking everything."

"Can't see his face," Shrake said. Virgil was at the end of the line, watched the Corolla as it passed, but was on the wrong side of the street to see the driver's face. He watched as the car made an unsignaled right turn off University. They'd driven the neighborhood before taking their parking spots, and there wasn't much down that street—a crappy old industrial street with no residential.

A minute later, the Corolla poked its nose back onto University and turned toward Virgil. "Corolla's on the way back," he said. "He's probably our guy."

The car rolled past: the driver was a big guy, wearing a steel-gray suit, wine-colored necktie, and sunglasses. He looked like one of Warren's security people: good physical condition and too big for the Corolla.

"Got another one," Jenkins said. "Look at the Jeep."

Red Jeep Cherokee, a few years old, slowed and turned into the parking lot. The Jeep made a slow tour, parked at the far end, sat for a moment, then slowly came back out. "I think they're taking down the tag numbers on the cars," Jenkins said. "It'd be interesting to know who's running the numbers for them."

"Let's figure that out," Virgil said. "Let's get the numbers on the plates ourselves, see who ran them."

The Jeep rolled out of the parking lot, turned back into traffic, drove a hundred yards up the street, then did a U-turn and parked two cars behind Shrake. "This isn't good," Shrake said.

"Maybe they'll get out when Andreno shows or Warren shows," Jenkins said.

"Hope so. Makes me nervous to have them right on my back."

THEY ALL SAT, and waited, and got hot, and Andreno showed up at ten minutes to five, showing the Illinois tags, and turned into the parking lot. Shrake was watching the guys in the Jeep, through the windshield and rear window of the car behind him, and called, "They made him. They picked him out. As soon as they saw him get out of the car, the driver was on his cell phone."

Andreno went inside. Three minutes later, he said, "I hope you guys can hear me."

Virgil called him on his cell phone and said, "You're loud and clear."

WARREN SHOWED UP at one o'clock in a black Cadillac Escalade, got out of the passenger side, brushed the seat of his pants. Virgil said, "There he is, the guy in the black suit."

Warren was wearing wraparound sunglasses and took them off and dropped them in his jacket pocket. One of his security people had been driving, and he checked out the parking lot, his eyes lingering on Andreno's Crown Vic. Then he nodded at Warren and they disappeared into the restaurant.

They heard Andreno say, "Mr. Warren."

Warren: "What's your name?"

"Ricky."

Warren must have sat down, Virgil thought. Warren said, "Call in," apparently to his security guy, and then said to Andreno, "We're checking in with my security people."

A new voice said, "Yeah, we're in. He's here."

Then Warren said, "What's this about pictures?"

Andreno: "You want my story, or you just want the pictures, or you want the pictures first and the story later?"

"Let's see the pictures."

SHRAKE CALLED: "The Jeep guys are moving."

The Jeep moved out into traffic, then turned into the restaurant parking lot and parked. A moment later, the Corolla rolled down the street, made a turn, and parked next to the Jeep.

ANDRENO WAS SAYING, "I've got color xeroxes. The actual pictures are . . . close. But I want to see some money."

"The money's close," Warren said. "Let's see the pictures."

There was a moment of silence, then Warren said, "That's not me. That's just not me. Sorry about that, but it's not me. That might be my head, but they Photoshopped it onto somebody else's body."

"Well, you know, it sorta looks like you, asshole," Andreno said, putting a little New Jersey into his voice. "Quite a bit like you. And there's at least one guy still alive who'll tell the cops it *is* you. Anyway, if it ain't you, fuck it, I'll take my pictures and hit the road."

"Where's Knox? I want to talk to him," Warren said.

"I don't want to talk to him," Andreno said. "We had a pretty serious disagreement."

"About what?"

"About I was supposed to bodyguard him, but when I get up there, he's in some fuckin' cabin on this fuckin' lake and he wants me out in the woods with the fuckin' ticks and mosquitoes and these little fuckin' flies. . . . They were chewing my ass up, and I sez, I gotta get out of there, and he sez, we gotta have you up in the woods, Ricky, and we went around about it, and I went back out in the woods, but when they went out—they went out a couple times a day—I lifted the photographs and took off. All I want is my money."

"Your deal is with him, not with me," Warren said.

"Yeah, but you're the guy I fuckin' got," Andreno said. "You can get the money back from him: believe me, you don't want these things rolling around out there."

"Five thousand," Warren said. "That's all they're worth."

"Bullshit. You killed those people in Vietnam and Carl said this other guy, this first guy you shot here, was feeling guilty and was going to the cops and that's why you killed him, and then you had to kill everybody."

"That's wrong. Carl's killing people, not me. Carl's the one who killed those people in Vietnam."

"Horseshit, I've got the pictures," Andreno said.

"Five thousand . . ."

"Five thousand, kiss my ass, that won't buy gas to Vegas."

A third voice, the first time the other man had spoken: "Shouldna bought that piece-of-shit Crown Vic. What you get, a mile to the gallon?"

"FUCK HIM," Jenkins said.

Shrake: "He's right. Can't shoot him for that."

ANDRENO: "Twenty. I gotta have twenty."

"Well, fuck you," Warren said. "You're lucky to get five, and I gotta get back to work. You want the five, or what?"

"You gotta come up from that or I'm walking," Andreno said. "Five is the same as nothing."

"ANDRENO IS good at this," Jenkins said.

WARREN SAID, "Last offer. Ten. You can have it in one minute. You get it when I see the photographs."

Long pause. Then Andreno said, "Gimme the ten."

WARREN MUST'VE nodded at the third man. He said to Andreno, "If you know what's good for you, you won't be back. I'm providing ninety percent of the security at the convention, and if I tell somebody you're a risk, you're gonna go away. So I better not see your face again."

"What the fuck convention? What convention?" Andreno whined.

"The Republican National Convention. What, you don't know what convention is coming here?"

"What the fuck do I give a shit about a bunch of political shit."

As they were squabbling, the third man left the restaurant, unlocked the back of the Cadillac, leaned inside, did something. . . .

"Getting some money," Virgil said. "They had more than ten thousand."

When Warren's security man had the money, he walked quickly to the red Jeep, said something through an apparently open window, then hurried back to the restaurant.

"Something happening?" Shrake asked. "Maybe they're gonna try to lift him."

Virgil started his truck and said, "Get ready to move."

Inside the restaurant, the third man's voice came up. "Ten. Count it if you want, but keep it under the table."

Another pause. Andreno: "Okay. Lot of money for a picture that isn't of you."

"Fuck you," Warren said. "Where are the pictures?"

"Here . . ."

The third man said, "He's got the money, we've got the pictures."

Virgil asked, "What's that? What'd he say?"

Andreno said, "What'd you say?"

The third man said again, to somebody unseen, "He's got the money, he's got the money."

IN THE PARKING LOT, two guys got out of the Jeep and a third from the Corolla, and Virgil called, "Something's happening, we gotta move," and Shrake called back, "Hey, that second guy, that second guy is Dave Nelson, he's with Minneapolis, he's a cop."

"I know the third guy, he's with Minneapolis, I know his face," Jenkins said, "Hell, they're cops! They're gonna bust Andreno."

Virgil said, "God . . . damnit. They were wired. Mother . . ."

HE PULLED INTO the parking lot and stopped at the door, but all three of the men were inside and he hurried to catch up. He turned one corner inside, blowing past the hostess, who was looking after the Minneapolis cops anyway, and when he turned the next corner the three were crowded around Andreno and he could see Warren's face, sneer playing across it, and Andreno was saying, "Wait a minute, wait a minute . . ."

All the customers in the restaurant were looking, some half standing for a better view, and then Virgil turned the last corner and one of the cops was telling Andreno to get out of the booth and Andreno settled back and said, "Look that way."

The cop turned his head and saw Virgil coming, and then Shrake and Jenkins, and Virgil dropped open his ID and said, "BCA. You just busted our show."

The lead Minneapolis cop looked from Virgil to Jenkins to Shrake and said, "Ah, shit."

THEY ALL BOILED into the parking lot, Warren screaming-angry, ripping a wire from under his shirt. He tossed it at a Minneapolis cop and then pointed a trembling finger at Virgil. "You motherfuckers. You're all done. You're all gonna be unemployed in two fuckin' hours. You don't know what getting fucked is like until I fuck you. . . ." Spit was flying from his mouth, and his face was heart-attack red and the Minneapolis cops were shaking their heads.

Virgil got tired of it and said to Warren, "Shut up. I'm tired of hearing it. So get us fired. Go do it. In the meantime, I'll take the photographs."

"You're not taking any photographs."

Warren put his hands up, and Virgil said, "You touch me, I'll put you on the ground, and after we pull your teeth out of your throat, we'll charge you with assault. Now, give me the photographs: they're state evidence."

The lead Minneapolis cop, whose name was Randy, said, "Give him the photographs. You gotta give him the photographs."

"The photographs," Warren said. "The photographs . . ."

He kept backing away, Virgil a step away from him, and Randy tried to get between them, but then Warren had his back against Virgil's truck and Randy said, "Mr. Warren. Give him the photographs. This is enough of a screwup without you going to jail. If you push the man, I can tell you, you're going to jail."

"The photographs . . ." Warren was so angry that his entire body shook, but he put his hand in his pocket and pulled out the envelope of photographs and gave them to Virgil. Virgil stepped back, checked them, put them in his pocket. "If I see those fuckin' things on TV . . ."

"You won't see them on TV until they're admitted into evidence somewhere, and then you can argue with the judge," Virgil said.

"If you let those out . . ."

"What're you gonna do?" Jenkins asked. "Fire us some more?"

"Keep laughin' motherfucker."

"You call me a motherfucker one more fuckin' time and I'm gonna break your head like a fuckin' cantaloupe," Jenkins said.

Randy: "Hey, hey . . . Mr. Warren, you better take off."

"We'll be back in touch," Virgil told Warren. "We're taking evidence from a witness to the murders shown here, who says that you committed them. If the evidence is found to be credible, we will turn the photos over to the responsible federal authorities, and they can decide what to do," Virgil said. "In the meantime, stay away from Carl Knox."

Warren erupted again. "Knox is the one! Knox is the one! Knox did all this shit! He was right there! Right there! He's the guy who did all this shit—he's the one who's killing everybody, he's the goddamn Mafia, you moron. Why do you think I've got security guys all over the place? It's Knox, you dummy!"

Virgil said, "We want some DNA from you. A blood sample. We have some DNA from the killer. You want to give us some?"

"Fuck you."

"We're also considering charges of willful obstruction of justice and possibly accessory after the fact to murder—I have notes from our first interview, when you said that you didn't know the other men who went to Vietnam, and we have photos that say you knew them very well. Your obstruction may have resulted in the death of Ray Bunton."

Warren's attitude stepped down. "My obstruction . . . I'll give some DNA. I'll give some blood. Not to you, asshole, because you're gonna get fired. But I'll give some DNA to whoever fills your job."

"I'm taking you at your word," Virgil said. "We'll have a guy come around tomorrow."

"Fuck you." Warren pulled his shirt cuffs down, adjusted his tie, turned to his security man, and said, "We're outa here."

WHEN THEY WERE GONE, Randy said, "This ain't going down in the annals of fine police work. For any of us."

They all half laughed, and Virgil said, "He sounded for real. When did he get in touch with your guys?"

THEY FIGURED OUT that he'd called Minneapolis a half hour after Andreno had called Warren. "So they talked it over," Virgil said.

"For a while," Randy said. "We had to run like hell to set this up. Jesus—we had like twelve minutes."

"But by calling you in, he's putting the pictures in the hands of the cops," Virgil said, confused.

"Maybe he figured the pictures were gonna get out there. Maybe he figured he could finesse the pictures," Shrake said. "Pictures from Carl

Knox are gonna be a little shaky. If Knox would even testify. And without him testifying, the pictures don't mean jack-shit."

"How about this?" Andreno said. "Maybe he thought he could find out where Knox is by squeezing me."

"Maybe," Virgil said, fists on his hips. "Ah, man, it's all screwed up. I gotta have some time. I gotta think."

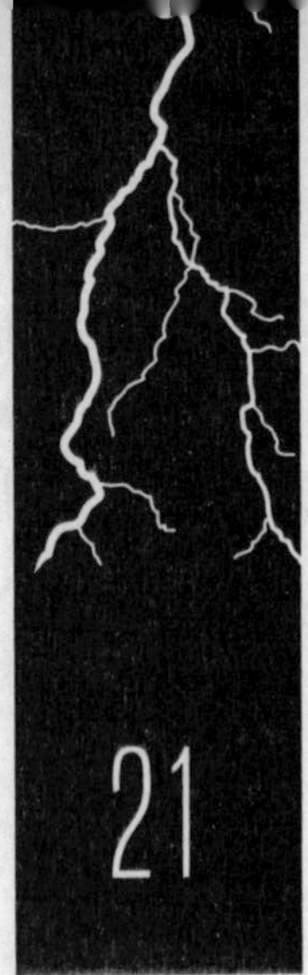

21

VIRGIL CALLED Davenport and told him what happened. Davenport said, "You're fired."

"Yeah, well . . ."

"Do get the DNA. We'll run it through every bank in the country," Davenport said. "Chances are small, but if he's really nuts . . ."

"I don't care about that. Wait a minute—I do care about that. What bothers me is, I bought everything that Knox said about Warren," Virgil said. "Warren's an asshole. But you know what? I bought everything Warren said about Knox, too. I don't think you could fake it."

"But we've established that Warren's a killer," Davenport said. "That's one fact to keep in mind."

"I'll keep it in mind," Virgil said. "You got anything else for me?"

"As a matter of fact, I do," Davenport said. "Some advice."

"Like what?"

"Go fishing. I know a guy who lives out on the St. Croix, about a mile south of the I-94 bridge. He's got a twenty-foot Lund and he hardly ever uses it. I can borrow the boat for you."

Virgil thought it over for a second, then said, "Not a bad idea. I've got all these snaky ideas in my head. If I could get out on a river for a while, maybe I could shake something loose."

"I'll call him."

"What about Warren?" Virgil asked.

"Rose Marie knows him," Davenport said. "There's a cocktail party this evening at the Town and Country Club, for the Republican arrangements committee. Warren'll be there, because he does the security, Rose Marie's gonna be there, the governor's giving a welcome talk. We'll get Warren in a corner and hammer down the rough edges."

"He's pissed," Virgil said.

"Well—you get that way when the necrophilia cat gets out of the bag," Davenport said. "If this goes public, he'd be in trouble. Can you see the headlines on CNN: 'Necrophiliac Runs Republican Security'?"

"How would that be a change?" Virgil asked.

"Funny. I'm laughing myself sick," Davenport said.

Virgil: "Tell me this: why did he bring in the cops on the photos?"

"Maybe he thought he was being set up—that Knox was out there with a gun."

"But Knox . . . never mind. I was gonna say, Knox isn't the killer," Virgil said. "*But Warren maybe believes that he is.* I can't seem to focus on that: and if Warren really believes that Knox is the killer—then Warren isn't."

"You need some time on the water," Davenport said. "Work it out."

DAVENPORT'S FRIEND called Virgil and said that he was standing on the sixth tee at Clifton Hollow golf course and that he wasn't planning to be home soon. "If you walk around to the back of the house, the porch door will be open, and if you look up on the beam, you'll see a nail with one of those pink plastic floats on it. That's the boat key. Fold up the boat cover and leave it on the dock under the bungee cord. Lucas said you'd have your own fishing gear."

"Yeah. I'm heading down south of the Kinnickinnic, see if I can pick up some smallies," Virgil said.

"Throw a musky lure when you're down there. There's muskies in there; I've been trolling the whole river the last couple years. I've taken two forty-inches-plus just south of the Narrows, on the Wisconsin side around behind the hook, and I saw one that went maybe forty-eight."

"Thanks. I'll leave a twenty for the gas, if that's enough," Virgil said.

"That's good—just stick it back up there with the key."

DAVENPORT'S FRIEND lived in a rambling cedar-shake and stone house down a long single-lane road on a bluff above the St. Croix River. Virgil left the 4Runner in the driveway, walked around back, found the key, and carried three rods and his emergency tackle box down eighty steps to the beach and a dock. The boat had a dried-on foam line that suggested it hadn't been out for a while. He stripped off the canvas cover, snapped it under the bungee cord on the dock, dropped the motor, and fired it up.

No problem. One minute later, he was a half mile down the river. Glanced at his watch: just three o'clock. He'd been up since five, but still, the day seemed like it was rolling on forever.

The high Wisconsin bluffs on the St. Croix are such a dark green that in bright afternoon sunlight, they seem almost black. Virgil puttered through the Narrows, then hooked around behind the sandbars in back. With the sun hot on his shoulder blades, he set up a drift, faced into the east bank of the river, started dropping a lure a hand span from the bank, yanking it back in a quick retrieve.

And he thought:

Give me an anomaly that I can hang my hat on. There's got to be one back there somewhere. Something that can't be easily explained . . .

He thought about Sinclair, and the two Vietnamese, Tai and Phem—but the fact was, Virgil had gone looking for clues at a place that dealt largely with veterans who'd had problems in Vietnam, where he'd encountered a man who'd spent his life dealing with Vietnam and the Vietnamese. What did he expect, Latvians?

They were persons of interest, but at least temporarily opaque.

He worked through the sequence from his first moments at Utecht's death scene, through the drive out to look at Sanderson, to Wigge, to Bunton, to . . .

Bunton. The thing about Bunton was, how did they find him? How did they find him that quickly? He could understand that somebody might find Carl Knox. With sufficient insight into how public records and computers worked, it was simply a matter of pounding paper . . . or electrons, or whatever it was that lived inside of computers.

But Bunton was out in the woods. How did they even know that he was there? They probably got his name from Wigge or Utecht—

Sanderson had been dead too quick to give up anything—but how did they come to Bunton's mother's house, which wasn't even in the phone book?

He hooked into a smallmouth, a fifteen-inch bronze-backed fish that fought like a junkyard dog against the small tackle. He lifted it out of the water, unhooked it, slipped it back in.

Hooked another, slipped it back.

Worked his way through the sandbars and shallows and into deeper water, threw a few bucktails, looking for a musky, saw nothing but black water. A cigarette-like boat powered past at sixty miles an hour, rocking him, rolling him.

He was a mile south of the Narrows, sitting behind the wheel of the boat, drifting, letting the sound of the river carry him along, when a small niggling thought crept into his head.

He tried to ignore it and failed. Looked at the sun: the sun was still high, fishing would get nothing but better as evening came on. Still . . .

Goddamnit.

One last cast, nothing—you never catch anything on the last cast—and he reeled in, fired up the motor, and was moving, and moving fast. The Narrows was a no-wake zone, with a half-dozen beached cruisers taking in the afternoon sun, and people screamed at him as he went through at forty-two miles an hour, which was all he could squeeze out of the Lund.

At the dock, he took care to tie up and cinch the cover down, but then he ran up the steps to the house, put the key and a twenty up in the rafters, hustled around the house to the truck.

And he stopped and looked at it.

The idea was goofy, but there was no driving it out of his head, and it made him sick. He walked away from the truck and called the BCA duty officer.

"I've got a question for you."

FIVE O'CLOCK.

They worked silently through the truck in the BCA garage. One guy changed the oil and hummed to himself, while the other guy worked it over with a bunch of electronic gear, then snapped his fingers at Virgil and pointed outside.

"You got a microphone in there somewhere, and there's a wire splice going up to your GPS antenna off your navigation screen—it's probably broadcasting your location, like one of those LoJack things."

"You can hear it broadcasting?" Virgil asked.

His heart was going like a trip-hammer, the anger surging into his throat. *He'd* given away Bunton. He'd been chumped.

"No, but it might be broadcasting on demand," the tech said. "Or it might be broadcasting on a schedule, every half hour. That's no problem with the new gear. Anyway, you definitely have a microphone in there. I could find it if you want me to, but it might let them know that we're looking for it."

"You think it's a voice recorder?" Virgil asked.

"For sure. If it was just sending out the GPS, they wouldn't need a microphone. What it probably is is a voice-activated microphone, hooked up to a digital recorder. Every little while, or maybe once an hour, it uploads whatever it's recorded. They could do that with a cell-phone connection. Anything you said on a cell phone or a radio, they'd know about. They wouldn't know what was coming from the other end, unless it was coming through a loudspeaker . . . but they'd hear you."

"How big would the package be? The bug?" Virgil asked.

"Depends on the power supply. They either have to have a pretty good battery or they've tied into your twelve-volt system," the tech said. "If they tied into the car, it could be pretty small. Maybe . . . twice the size of a cell phone."

"Get a flashlight and see if you can spot it. They'd have to put it in pretty quick. I'd just like to see if it's Motorola, or Ho Chi Minh Radio Works."

The tech found the package after five minutes of looking; it was jammed under the front-left turn signal, taking power out of the lines coming into the light.

"No telling where it's from," the tech said when they were outside again. "But it's sophisticated. You saw how small it was—that's way smaller than our stuff, and our stuff is pretty good."

"Could be Vietnamese?"

"Don't have to go that far," the tech said. "Could be CIA."

THE CIA: Sinclair.

Or maybe not. Why the hell would the CIA go out to kill a bunch of old-timey vets and general dipshits?

Answer: The CIA wouldn't. Virgil didn't even believe that the CIA killed people, not in civilized countries, anyway. Maybe they hired mercenaries in the Middle East, but they really wouldn't go around killing people on the streets . . . would they?

His fuckin' truck.

Burned him.

HE WALKED THROUGH the mostly empty building to his temporary office, shut the door and lay down on the floor behind the desk, closed his eyes.

Sinclair . . .

He thought about Sinclair: about Sinclair making the phone call from the cold phone to Tai and Phem. Why'd he do that? Why didn't he have a cold cell phone? You could buy them over the counter. . . .

Christ.

Tai and Phem. Were they working with Sinclair, had Sinclair fingered him somehow? But he'd only talked to Sinclair once, for any amount of time. It'd take testicles the size of basketballs to hook that electronics package into Virgil's truck, when it was parked almost outside the door. If Virgil had gotten up and walked out at some point, Sinclair wouldn't have had time to get them out.

They had to do it some other time, but when?

In the motel lot? But he never told Sinclair where he was staying.

Though he'd told Mai.

HE'D FELT himself circling around her. Great girl, but . . . how in the *hell* did a hot young dancer-woman grow up in Madison, Wisconsin, in the nineties and not know what *Hole* was? How was that possible?

When he'd suggested to her that you could have a good time at the University of Wisconsin, out on the Terrace or down in the Rat, she seemed uncertain. But how could you be a hot young dancer chick from Madison and not know about hanging out on the Terrace or down in the Rathskeller? Then, when he'd gone outside to talk to the guy from Hong Kong, he'd come back to find her talking to her father, to Sinclair. Or to somebody she'd said was Sinclair. Out on the lake, a few minutes later, she'd pushed the conversation to the Terrace, to the Rat, as though she were proving to him that she knew about them.

She'd been covering herself, Virgil thought.

He remembered a few times when her turn of phrase seemed off, or unusually formal; remembered because he was a writer and the words she'd used seemed tinny on his ear. She'd once asked him, "When do you return?" instead of, "When ya comin' back?"

He said to himself, "No goddamn way."

HE LAY ON THE FLOOR for another three minutes, then climbed the stairs to Davenport's office. Carol's office was out in the open, in a cubicle, and he rifled her Rolodex and found the home phone number and cell phone for Sandy.

He caught her at home, on the way out: "I've got a date," she protested. "Me and some people are . . ."

"I don't care if you're going out to fuck Prince Charles, get your ass in here," Virgil snarled. "Where are you?"

She was intimidated, sounded frightened. "I live over by Concordia."

"Ten minutes, goddamnit. Be here in ten minutes."

Virgil couldn't stand it, went out and walked around the parking lot, looked at his traitorous truck, kept checking his watch. She took fifteen minutes coming in, and during the interval, she'd gone from intimidated to pissed.

"You know what? I'm pretty gosh-darned upset," she said. Her glasses were glittering under the lights from the streetlamps. "You have no right to talk to me like that. I've done nothing but help."

"Walk while you're talking," Virgil said, and he set off toward the building entrance. Looked at his watch: almost six.

She caught up and took a breath and said, "Okay. Something happened. Are there more dead people?"

"Sandy . . . I need to get into the Wisconsin driver's license bureau, whatever it's called, and I've got to retrieve a license and look at the photograph."

"I can't do that."

"You're gonna have to find a way. Talk to a friend in Wisconsin, talk to somebody." He stopped short and stepped next to her and said, "Sandy, you gotta help me. I don't know this shit, and I'm desperate."

She put her hands on her hips: "Neither do I. If it was the middle of the day and I had some support . . ." Then her eyes slid sideways behind her glasses, and she said, "You know, the duty guys coordinate with Wisconsin. Maybe they could get it?"

"Atta girl. See, I didn't think of that," Virgil said. "C'mon, keep talking, let's go. Who do you know in Canada?"

WHILE SHE WAS working the phones and the computers, Virgil went back to the floor of the office, eyes closed, looking for anything. Finally crawled to his briefcase, found his phone book, fished the phone off the top of the desk, lay down again, and called Red Lake.

Now that things were starting to crack up, the luck was running with him. Jarlait was off duty, but had stopped at the law-enforcement center to shoot the shit with a friend. He came up, and Virgil said, "You know that Apache dude that your friend saw on the reservation the day Ray was killed?"

"*Could* have been an Apache."

"Look, you got basically two kinds of guys up there—Indian guys and white guys. Maybe a black guy every once in a while, but not too often. So if you see a guy who isn't white and isn't black . . ."

"Spit it out," Jarlait said.

"You think your pal could have seen a Vietnamese and thought he was an Apache?"

Long pause. Then: "Huh. You know? I know some Vietnamese, and some of them do look like Apaches. Yeah, you get the right-looking Vietnamese . . ."

THE STUFF FROM Canada got back quicker than the stuff from Wisconsin. The Canada request was apparently routine for the Canadians, who turned around a couple of passport photos for Tai and Phem. Tai and Phem were definitely of Vietnamese heritage, small slender men with dark eyes and good smiles, and neither one of them was the Tai or Phem that Virgil met at the hotel.

"Ah, man."

"This is getting a little scary," Sandy said. "This woman, Mai . . . do you know her?"

"Yeah, we've talked," Virgil said.

"Does she seem pretty nice?"

"I guess," he said. "Goddamnit, I was a fuckin' chump."

"Hey, how often do you deal with spies?" she asked.

Mai photos came in. She was nice-looking, round-faced, pleasant, and not the Mai that Virgil knew.

"Now what?" Sandy asked.

"Now I gotta go talk to somebody," Virgil said.

"Let me tell you something sincere before you go talk to somebody," she said.

"Okay . . ."

"You smell like a fish."

FUCK A BUNCH of fish. Virgil was in the truck two minutes later, running with lights, rolling down to I-35 and then left on I-94 across town to Cretin, south on Cretin to Randolph and over to Mississippi River Boulevard, to Davenport's house. There were lots of lights, and Virgil parked in the driveway and walked up and pounded on the front door. Davenport popped it open, standing there in a tuxedo with a satin shawl collar, his tie draped around his neck, untied, and he said, "There's a doorbell, Virgil."

"Man . . ."

"Come on in."

They went and sat in Davenport's living room, and Virgil laid it out: Sinclair and Tai and Phem and Mai. "They're not here by accident. And I had to wonder about Sinclair, a couple of the things he said. . . . I mean, he led me straight to them, making that phone call. What do you think if you're doing surveillance on a guy, and he walks out to a cold phone and makes a call like that? You think he's got something going on. And he calls right in to Phem and Tai . . . like he was pointing me at them."

"Maybe not. I've had some dealings with these kinds of people," Davenport said, "Their problem is, they're smart, but they're not smart enough to know that they're not as smart as they think they are. It gets everybody in trouble."

"What I can't get over is that they used me, and the truck, to locate Bunton. At least Bunton. Maybe gave them a lead on Knox, maybe gave them a lead on Warren—Christ, they heard everything I said when we were setting Warren up."

And the more he thought about it, the more pissed he got.

WEATHER CAME DOWN the stairs, wearing a frilly black cocktail dress that skillfully showed off her ass. She said, "Hi, Virgil. . . . Say, you smell like a fish."

"Ah, for Christ's sakes." To Davenport: "What do I do?"

"What do you want to do?" Davenport asked.

"Go beat the shit out of Sinclair," Virgil said. "Find out what's going on."

"Well, God bless you, Virgil."

"You think I should?" Virgil asked.

"Yup. That's what I would do," Davenport said. "I'll have my cell phone with me—let me know what you find out."

Weather had taken Davenport's tie from around his neck, fit it around his collar, and began tying it. She said, "Give us a little time to party, though."

Virgil said, "Even though you insulted me about my fish smell, I gotta say, that dress does good things for you."

"I was afraid it made my ass look big," she said.

"Ah, no, no," Virgil said. Her ass was right at his eye level. "Not at all."

Davenport nodded. "Virgil is correct. And observant."

VIRGIL SLAPPED his thighs, stood up, and said, "Well, I'm gonna go chain-whip Sinclair. I'll probably drag his ass down to the lockup. Mai, too. I gotta believe that Mai isn't American, or even Canadian. She's some kind of spy, and that means they gotta know something about these killings. We can hold them for a couple of days until we get something back from the State Department. Man, this is gonna hurt, picking her up."

Weather finished with Davenport's tie, patted him on the chest, and Davenport said, "Find Shrake and Jenkins—or see if Del's around. Take some backup. Then go get these Vietnamese guys, too. Put them all inside until their status is figured out. They must be traveling on bad documents. We'll get DNA from all of them. They'll be a risk to run, so there won't be any bail."

"You think we need a warrant?"

"No. We've got probable cause," Davenport said. "If they invite you in, you see anything lying around . . ."

"All right. Goddamnit. This—"

"Hey," Davenport said. "You cracked it, man. Not even a week. What the fuck do you want?"

"Wash your hands before you go," Weather said. "You don't want to arrest somebody when you smell like a fish. There's some Dove on the kitchen sink."

"All right." He moped off toward the kitchen.

Weather called after him, "Say, Lucas said you were taking a friend fishing up at the cabin. It wasn't this Mai person, was it?"

"Ah, jeez . . ."

He started back toward the kitchen, heard Davenport mutter something to his wife, and he turned back and caught them suppressing smiles, and he asked, "*What?*"

"Nothing," Davenport said.

"He said, 'At least Virgil wasn't the only one who got screwed,'" Weather said.

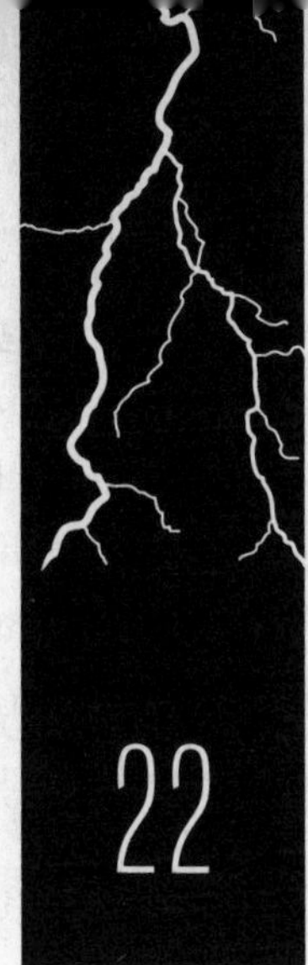

22

MAI AND PHEM sat in the back of Tai's rented Toyota Sequoia, a huge tank of an SUV, and Phem unwrapped the rifle, pulling gently at the soft gray foam that had cushioned the weapon from road bumps and motor vibration.

Mai was looking at the target with a pair of night-vision glasses: there was enough ambient light to clearly illuminate the entire target area, and she could see the security men orbiting through the kill zone every few minutes.

"Lot of guns," she said in Vietnamese.

"Of course," Phem said. "But they won't expect our reach."

Phem had the rifle free of its wraps: an accurized Ruger .338 bolt-action rifle in a black synthetic stock, with a twenty-four-inch barrel, and fitted with a new U.S. Army–issued third-generation starlight scope that had gone astray in Iraq.

Phem had worked up the gun himself, firing in a backwoods quarry in Michigan's Upper Peninsula. He could reliably keep the first round from a cold gun in a one-inch circle at two hundred yards, with the starlight scope. Not an easy thing.

The .338 was a powerful gun, chosen for its ability to bust through Level IV body-armor plates, the heaviest armor ordinarily worn. Phem had supervised the machining of the solid bronze slugs he'd be using.

Phem started to hum tunelessly, his body rocking a bit as he sat cross-legged in the dark, the rifle across his thighs.

Mai said, "Yama—you can do this."

"Yes, but no more after this trip," Phem said. "No more trips."

"You know what these people did."

"Of course. I wouldn't have agreed if I hadn't known; and also as a tribute to your grandfather. I would do anything he asked now," Phem said. "In the future, maybe not. I might want to, but I think . . . sometimes, I think I couldn't do it. My brain would boil up, and I'd be done."

"Tai seems fine?"

Phem nodded and smiled. "Oh, Tai is always fine. He does his research and slips around like a ghost, and the life pleases him."

"Well, be at peace," Mai said. "You are working wonders."

She went back to her glasses. At the bottom of the hill, past some oak trees and through a chain-link fence, three hundred and twenty-two meters away, as measured by a laser range-finder, she could see the front door of the country club: Republicans gathering to congratulate themselves on their preparations for the national convention.

"I haven't seen Tai," she said after a while, making conversation.

"You won't until he gets back to the truck. He's a ghost."

THEY SAT IN silence as more people gathered, men in black and white, women in every color in the universe, laughing among themselves, kissing, hugging. Mai was amazed at her sex, sometimes, because of the female ability to enjoy power, status, position. Not the ingrown satisfaction shown by males, but an overt celebration, a genuine *happiness.*

"Do you expect to see Virgil?" Phem asked.

"I'm done with Virgil," she said. She smiled at him in the dark and let her smile seep into her voice. "What are you asking, you old gossip?"

"Nothing whatever; we all know that the mission comes first," Phem said.

"Ah, the mission. Well, I can tell you, Virgil got about as much of this mission as he could possibly tolerate," she said.

Phem giggled. "I think he gave as good as he got. You seemed . . . your aura was very smooth when you returned."

"You are worse than your mother," Mai said.

"My mother . . ." Phem said, and his voice trailed away. Then: "When they find the electronics on the truck, they will be . . . amazed."

"Who knows, maybe they'll never find it," Mai said.

"Oh, I think they will. If Sinclair is correct, Virgil is a smart man," Phem said. "When you vanish, when the investigation is curtailed, he'll begin to think. He'll find it eventually."

"He is smart, but not that smart, I think," Mai said.

MAI LAY BACK in the truck and thought about the mission so far. If they had been sent simply to remove the men, there would have been no problem; but that's not the way the mission had been briefed. Simple death would not have brought the necessary satisfaction.

Not to Grandfather, anyway.

The mission had begun to evolve after Chester Utecht had gotten drunk with several old friends, including one who'd long been paid by the Vietnamese government to keep an ear on the Chinese in Hong Kong. The informant—not a spy, but simply a man who listened, and who occasionally found an envelope with three or four thousand yuan under his door—had told a strange tale of a man who'd stolen a ship full of bulldozers at the end of the war, just before the final victory.

And with the theft, there'd been murder. The story came out of a drunken fog, and back in Hanoi had rung no bells at first. Instead, the story of the bulldozers and the murder circulated simply as a tale . . . and then an old man, high in the government, heard it. Heard it almost as a joke. Within a day, he'd followed the story back to its source and had identified Utecht.

The Vietnamese had no desire to disturb the sleep of the Chinese, and so they moved carefully, lifted Utecht, and visited him with a moderate amount of pain before the old man told the story again. But he had only two names other than his own; and one of those names was his son, a name he gave up in croaking horror and despair.

He'd been left in an alley, dead, and full of alcohol. There'd been no stir at all, no ruffle in the leaves of the Chinese peace.

The ear had gone to his funeral, with twenty thousand crisp new yuan in his pocket; had seen the younger Utecht, had chatted with him and taken down the details, and sent them along.

Another twenty thousand, in gratitude, and the investigation moved on.

Details were difficult to develop. Then, fortuitously and fortunately, an agent in Indonesia, on an entirely different mission, had found indications of an al-Qaeda effort in San Francisco, with (perhaps) critical munitions shipped from Jakarta through the Golden Gate.

It was all very foggy, but the Americans' Homeland Security was needy, in a time of declining budgets and controversial war. An exchange had been made, a liaison forged, one that would be both reliable and deniable. He was a well-known former radical activist with ties to the Vietnamese government, but who'd actually been an active CIA agent from the beginning—a man who could see his comfortable end-life ruined by disclosures from either the American government or the Vietnamese. Further, a man with a daughter, now working in Europe, who could be held over his head, an implicit, unspoken threat . . .

A man who could be grasped and twisted into the necessary shape for the job.

A CAR WENT BY at high speed, followed by another car, down the hill, cutting in toward the country club; gathering Republicans turning to stare. Mai watched through the glasses, then lifted a walkie-talkie—an ordinary plastic walkie-talkie that Tai had bought at a sporting goods store—and clicked it four times.

Two seconds later, listening, two quick clicks.

She said the same word three times: break break break.

Phem looked up when he heard the critical abort code, then down the hill at the country club. "What?"

"We have a problem," Mai said. She pointed down the hill and said, "See that long blond hair?"

"Virgil," Phem breathed.

One minute later, Tai slipped into the driver's seat.

Mai said, "Go."

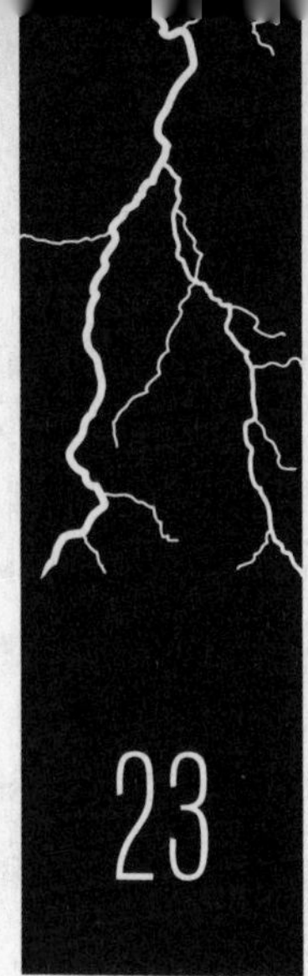

23

SHRAKE WAS on a date and nobody knew where, and Jenkins said that he never took a cell phone with him because somebody might call him on it. Jenkins had been in a sushi bar, eating octopus and drinking martinis out of a flask, though he said he was totally sober and could be there in ten minutes. Del's wife was pregnant and going to bed early, so Del had no problem and could be there in fifteen.

Two extra guys, Virgil thought, should be enough. They agreed to meet at the Pomegranate, a once-trendy salad-and-dessert place seven blocks from the Sinclairs' condo. Virgil had forgotten to eat, and suddenly realized that he was starving. He got an apple salad and a piece of carrot cake and wolfed them down, saw Jenkins go by in his Crown Vic, looking for a parking place, and then Del in his state Chevy.

They arrived together. Jenkins got a chocolate mousse and Del said he wasn't hungry, and Del asked, "What're we doing?"

"We need one guy on the back, by the porch. I can point it out from the back side of the house—the condo's an old house, and it's got porches on the ground floor. It's almost like a bunch of town houses. The other two of us go to the front door. The back-door guy is whichever one of you can run fastest."

Del looked at Jenkins and said, "You're pretty quick on your feet."

"Yeah, I can do it."

Virgil said, "There's a possibility that these guys are involved in the lemon killings . . . a good possibility. They at least know something about them. So we gotta take care. Know where your weapon is; somebody's a professional killer. Stay on your toes."

"You think . . ." Del's eyebrows were up. "Maybe some armor?"

"If you want, but I don't think it's necessary," Virgil said. "It'd be weird if there were any shooting right there. I mean, this guy is semi-famous."

"But the daughter is an impostor," Jenkins said. "Maybe she's another Clara Rinker." Clara Rinker had been a professional killer working for a St. Louis mobster, who'd been taken down by Davenport's team a few years earlier. She was believed to have killed thirty people.

"Look—do what you're comfortable with," Virgil said, gobbling down the last of the carrot cake. "My sense is, we won't be doing any shooting. But know where your weapon is. If we go in, and there are a couple of Vietnamese guys there . . . then take care. Take care."

THEY CIRCLED Sinclair's block and Virgil pointed out the back of the condo, the porch where Sinclair was working. "There's somebody in there," Jenkins said.

Virgil dug out his binoculars and put them on the lighted porch.

Sinclair was there, bent over a laptop. "That's him," Virgil said. As Virgil watched, Sinclair sat up and stared straight out into the night for three seconds, five seconds, and then went back to the laptop.

The house that backed onto the condo was also lit. Jenkins said, "I'm gonna knock on the door there, tell them what's up, so they won't be yelling at me and calling St. Paul when I sneak through their yard."

"All right. Call me when you're set," Virgil said.

Del followed Virgil around the block and they parked, facing in opposite directions in case they had to move quickly, and they met at the walk going up to the condo, waited, and Virgil took the call from Jenkins: "I'm crossing the fence now. I'll be in position in ten seconds. Sinclair is still in the window."

Virgil looked at the names on the mailboxes outside the apartment, picked another one on the first floor, and buzzed. No answer. He waited ten seconds, then buzzed a second one, labeled "Williams." A moment later, a woman answered: "Yes? Who is it?"

"Virgil Flowers and Del Capslock. We're agents of the state Bureau of Criminal Apprehension. Could we speak to you for a minute?"

"What's happened?" she asked, a streak of fear in her voice. "Did something happen to Laurie?"

"We just need to speak to you for a minute, ma'am," Virgil said.

She buzzed them and Virgil pushed through, and a moment later a door opened to their right and a woman looked out. Virgil put his finger to his lips, showed her his ID, and said, "We're here for another apartment. If you could go back inside, please. Everything should be okay."

The woman's eyes flicked to Del. Del had taken his pistol out and was holding it along his pant leg. "You're sure . . ." and she was backing away.

Virgil put his finger to his lips again, breathed "Shhh . . . ," and he and Del moved down the hall as the woman closed the door.

"You want to take the door, or do you want to try knocking?" Del asked.

"Knock first. If he doesn't answer, I'll kick it," Virgil said.

Del knocked, and they both stepped back sideways from the door. They heard steps inside, and Del ticked his finger at the door, and Virgil put his hand on his pistol at the small of his back.

The door opened, and Sinclair looked out. "Took you long enough," he said. "Come on in."

SINCLAIR WAS dressed in faded blue jeans, a soft white shirt, and sneakers, the gold tennis bracelet still rattling around his wrist. Virgil followed him into the apartment as Sinclair backed away. Virgil said to Del, "Get Jenkins in here. Clear the place."

"She's gone, Hoa is gone," Sinclair said. "I don't think she's coming back—you spooked her."

"Hoa?"

"It means 'flower,'" Sinclair said. "Mai means 'cherry blossom.' Quite the coincidence, huh?"

Jenkins came in through a back door in the kitchen, and he and Del did a quick run-through of the apartment. Sinclair said to Virgil, "Come on the porch and we can figure out what we're gonna do. Your friends can sit in."

"I *know* what I'm going to do," Virgil said. "I'm taking your ass down to jail and I'm charging you with murder."

"That's not a bad idea, except that you've got nothing to convict me with," Sinclair said. He pointed at the circle of chairs on the porch, where his laptop sat in a circle of light. "And there would be some serious fallout that I'm not sure you'd want to deal with. But: If you are willing to deal with the fallout, it's an option, and we should talk about it."

DEL HEARD the last bit of the conversation, and he said to Virgil, "Apartment's clear," and then to Sinclair, "What's up with you? You're pretty calm for a guy who's looking at thirty years without parole."

"Never do thirty years," Sinclair said. "My family's programmed to die at eighty-five. I wouldn't do more than twenty."

Jenkins said to Del, "The man's got a point."

"If anybody wants a beer, we got some Leinenkugels in the refrigerator," Sinclair said. To Virgil: "You want to sit down?"

Virgil sat. "What the hell is going on?"

Sinclair said to Jenkins, "If you're gonna get a beer, could you get me one?" He said to Virgil, "This is complicated. But one thing that's going to happen, if it hasn't already, is that this Warren guy is probably gonna get killed tonight."

"Warren's at a big political party," Virgil said.

"Blowing him up at a big political party would just about make Hoa's day," Sinclair said. Jenkins handed him a beer, and he said thanks and took a sip.

"Blowing him up?" Virgil said. He was digging his cell phone out of his pocket. "They've got a bomb? Jesus . . ."

"No, no, not literally. They're going to shoot him," Sinclair said. "I don't know any details, but I believe they're going to shoot him. The shooter, who's the guy you met named Phem, doesn't do bombs. But I'm told he's a marvelous shot. Olympic quality. And Tai, who's a researcher, an intelligence operator, an interrogator, doesn't do assassination. He might tear you apart with a pair of pliers, but he won't try to snipe you. He doesn't have that cold temperament—he gets all excited when he's killing somebody. That's what I'm told."

"What about Mai?"

"Hoa—she's the coordinator. She's the one who can pass as American. Got all the right American accents. You oughta hear her Valley Girl."

VIRGIL WAS on the phone, and Davenport answered: "What'd you get?"

"There are three Vietnamese, two men and a woman, and they're planning to kill Warren. I'm told that nothing would make them happier than killing him at your party. To do it in public. They got a shooter with them. I don't think it's a suicide run."

"It won't be—no suicide," Sinclair interjected.

"I'm told it's not a suicide, so they've got to get in close or do him with a rifle," Virgil said. "You better tell his security to get tight."

"I'm on it and Warren's here," Davenport said. "This place is crawling with security—I'll light them up. Can I tell Warren?"

"Yeah, yeah, he has nothing to do with the lemon killings," Virgil said. "It's a Vietnamese hit squad, going back to the war days. That whole murder thing."

"Where are you?" Davenport asked.

"At Sinclair's. He's telling us a story. It's complicated, man."

"You better get over here. I'll get St. Paul SWAT, but that's gonna take a while. They're probably up on the golf course looking down at us. . . . If we can get SWAT around the edges of the course, we might chase them out."

"What about Sinclair?" Virgil asked.

"Whatever you think—I'll get with Warren, call me when you're close."

VIRGIL RANG OFF and said to Del and Jenkins, "We're going. My truck is bugged, Sinclair and I will ride with Jenkins. We're gonna bring in SWAT and see if we can corner them on the golf course."

"They've got night-vision gear." Sinclair said. "They'll see you coming."

"Ah, shit." Virgil got Davenport back on the line.

"What?"

"Sinclair said they've got night-vision gear . . ."

"And a starlight scope," Sinclair added.

"And a starlight scope," Virgil said. "Maybe it's better to put the guys out on the perimeter of the golf course, keep bringing people in until it's completely blocked, and wait for daylight."

"Let me think about it," Davenport said. "Get down here."

"We're coming."

IN THE CAR, Virgil took out his cuffs and cuffed Sinclair's hand to a loop of the safety belt in the backseat. They were five minutes from the golf course, running without lights.

"Tell me," he said to Sinclair, and Jenkins's eyes flicked up in the rear-view mirror. Storytelling time.

A LONG TIME AGO, Sinclair said, when college kids thought they were the spearhead of a revolution, when fifty-five thousand Americans were dying in Vietnam, when ghettos were burning in most of the major American cities, when women started burning their bras and hippies were dropping out and turning on, he'd been a student in American studies at the University of Michigan.

"I loved this country. My grandparents were immigrants, my father and all my uncles fought in the Second World War, and I wanted to do something for the country," Sinclair said. "My history prof knew that, the jolly old elf that he was, and knew just what to do: he put me in touch with the CIA. He said there was no point in going to Vietnam and dying as a second lieutenant. Anyone could do that."

So Sinclair took some tests, went to Langley, was trained, and then dropped right back into his most natural environment: the University of Michigan.

"I was there when the Students for a Democratic Society got going, I knew all of the early Weathermen. . . . You know about the town house explosion in Manhattan? No? Never mind. Anyway, I started going to Vietnam," he said. "I dodged the draft with the help of the Agency, made a lot of contacts with Vietnamese who were moving up in the government over there."

By the time the war ended, he said, he had radical contacts everywhere in Asia and Europe. He did the last interview with Ulrike Meinhof in April 1976, a few weeks before Meinhof either hanged herself or was murdered in her German jail cell.

"I don't know who you're talking about," Virgil said.

"I suppose not. You'd have been a baby at the time. . . . Ulrike was the coleader of the Baader-Meinhof Group, one of the so-called Red Army groups, the Rote Armee Fraktion," Sinclair said, sputtering through the German with an academic's enthusiasm. "Big radical deal at one time."

"So you were hot."

"Yup. But like all good things, the nonsense stopped, and there I was. I'd gotten my PhD, and to tell you the truth, I'd been in academia for so long that I had pretty much adopted the points of view of a lot of people I'd opposed at the start. That the Vietnam War was a waste of time and blood, a tragedy—"

"Yeah, yeah, so much for old home week," Virgil said. "What about these assholes? What about Mai, or whatever her name is?"

"Hey—let me tell it. So I told the Agency what I was thinking. You know, that I was tired and, worse than that, a liberal. And they just let it go . . . quite a few liberals in the Agency, actually. I retired. I was doing pretty well as a teacher and a writer, I still had contacts in Vietnam—I'd married my Vietnamese woman, though I met her here, in the States—and I started doing some work on trade deals and so on. I'd still get a call from the CIA guys every once in a while, and I was happy enough to talk to them. Then Chester Utecht got drunk and told everybody in sight about stealing bulldozers in Vietnam."

Vietnamese intelligence picked it up. In the way of the world, the father of the woman raped and murdered that day in Da Nang was now an eighty-five-year-old first-tier government official in the misty realm where intelligence and the military overlapped. He heard the story.

He could have his revenge, his peers agreed, as long as it didn't upset the trade apple cart.

As it happened, Vietnamese intelligence had also picked up a line on an al-Qaeda plot that came out of Indonesia. Whether it was real or not, they got in touch with somebody at Homeland Security and suggested that the information was available. In return, they wanted the relevant layers of U.S. intelligence agencies to look in the other direction during a short, violent operation in Minnesota.

The people who would die were all known killers and rapists. The people who would die on the West Coast—and there would be many more of them, if al-Qaeda had its way—were innocents.

A deal was cut—and a deniable contact was needed between Washington and Hanoi.

"You," Virgil said. They were on Cretin Avenue, headed north toward the golf course, just a few blocks away now.

"Me. I speak Vietnamese, have contacts in both places—though the Viets were a trifled surprised about the CIA," Sinclair said with a grin. "I talked to an old friend over there who thought it was hilarious—turns out he was a member of *their* intelligence service, and he'd been playing *me.* One thing about the Vietnamese—they got a pretty goddamn good sense of humor."

What wasn't so funny, he said, was what happened when he tried to turn them down. The people from Homeland Security pressed on him the urgency of the case, and said something to the effect that the

Vietnamese had already researched him . . . and knew where his daughter was.

"It was a threat," Sinclair said. "I didn't really believe they'd do anything to her—family is pretty important in Vietnam. But I wasn't sure. So here I am."

"You set me up to see Tai and Phem," Virgil said.

"Of course; and they were seriously pissed. I'll tell you what—the real Tai and Phem would be astonished to hear about it. They're in town all the time, you know. Don't stay at the Hilton. But if you'd called somebody at Larson to check their bona fides, they would have told you that Tai and Phem were outstanding citizens and enthusiastic followers of the capitalist road."

JENKINS TURNED the corner on Marshall, headed down the hill toward the clubhouse at the Town and Country Club. The place was lit like a Christmas tree, people all over the entry and parking lot.

"Do you have any idea of exactly what Hoa's doing?" Virgil asked.

"No. But I believe it's a gun, I believe it's Warren. All I get is what seeps through from phone calls that Hoa makes. I've also got the feeling that they may have a line on the last man. One thing I didn't tell you—they've got a direct connect, I think, with somebody in Washington. I don't know where. Homeland Security, probably. They have access to every record you can think of. I got Hoa's laptop password, not without a lot of trouble, I can tell you, and signed on when she was gone with you. If you get your hands on it, you'll find documents that you won't believe. The U.S. government vectored them right in on Utecht and Sanderson."

"So why tell me now?"

"Because we're at the end of this," Sinclair said. "My daughter will be okay—the Viets will have what they want, so they'll be done with us. I just might be able to fuck with the people who did this to me, the guys over here. Depending on what you want to do."

A guy in a black tuxedo, accessorized with a Beretta 93R with the twenty-round mag, was flagging them down and Jenkins slowed and held up his ID. Davenport called, "That guy's okay," and they went through. Sinclair said, "I wonder if that's his dress gun?"

DAVENPORT MET Virgil in the street: "We've got people coming in on the corners: they'll do it all at once, when they isolate the streets." He looked at Sinclair, still cuffed in the backseat, then asked Virgil, "What's the deal?"

"I'm not exactly clear on that," Virgil said. "But Professor Sinclair has been talking up a storm. Things have gotten a little out of my pay grade."

"So maybe I should hear his story," Davenport said.

"Little out of your pay grade, too. And Rose Marie's," Virgil said.

"So whose pay grade are we talking about?" Davenport asked.

"Dunno—maybe the president."

Rose Marie Roux was walking toward them in a political orange dress the size of an army tent.

"Got to be quite a story," Davenport said to Sinclair.

"Oh, it is," he said. He nodded across the room at a cluster of men in front of a fireplace. "Is that the governor? I'm sure he'd be fascinated."

THEY TOOK Sinclair into the women's locker room. Davenport spoke quietly with Rose Marie, who got another glass of something and tagged along.

"First piece of business," she said to Sinclair. "We're not talking about a machine gun or a rocket or a bomb?"

Sinclair shook his head. "They're operating under pretty strict guidelines: nobody dies except the people involved in the original rape and murder. There were actually five killed back then: the woman, her two young children, three and two years of age, the woman's grandfather, and a housekeeper. These people, Hoa and her team, messed up when they killed Wigge's bodyguard. That wasn't supposed to happen. That was a lapse. The cop up in Red Lake was an even bigger lapse, but I think by that time they didn't care so much. They were making the final run."

"My God," Rose Marie said. She looked at Virgil. "You knew this?"

"Not the details—the outline," Virgil said. "I was getting pieces."

Rose Marie said to Jenkins, "Go get Warren."

When Jenkins had gone, Davenport asked Sinclair, "How many more people are on their list?"

"Warren and one more. Six altogether, or seven, if you count Chester Utecht. The last guy—I don't know the name—lives on a lake somewhere. They were having a hard time tracking him down, exactly, but I think their . . . outside . . . contacts came through on that."

"He means Homeland Security," Virgil said to Davenport and Rose Marie. "The guy they were looking for is Carl Knox."

WARREN WALKED IN a minute later, followed by Jenkins and a security man. Rose Marie said, "We've identified the people who are trying to kill you. Agent Flowers has information that they will attempt to shoot you, probably with a rifle. We're putting officers around the golf course, where we think they are. If you wish, you could go out the back unseen."

Warren bobbed his head. "I'll do that. I'll be at home. I've got some serious protection there. Call me when you get them." He glanced at Virgil, his upper lip rippled, and he left, followed by his security man.

Sinclair said, "There goes the worst man in this whole episode, dressed in a tuxedo and patent-leather shoes, untouched by human hands."

Davenport said to Sinclair, "All right—we've got ten minutes before we drop the net around the golf course. Tell the rest of us what happened."

At that moment, the governor walked in, shadowed by Neil Mitford, his personal weasel. The governor smiled at everybody, said, "Ah, that fuckin' Flowers. How are you, Virgil?" He shook Virgil's hand. "Love the cowboy boots. I just bought a pair myself. What's up with all you people? Are we going to be assassinated, or what?"

Rose Marie said, "Governor, I'm not sure you want to be here."

"That's what I said," Mitford muttered.

"Better than making small talk with a guy who wants more ethanol subsidies." He looked around. "I haven't been in a women's locker room since my junior year at Princeton." He chuckled. "Anna Sweat, I swear to God she had . . . Never mind." He peered at Sinclair. "So—let's hear it."

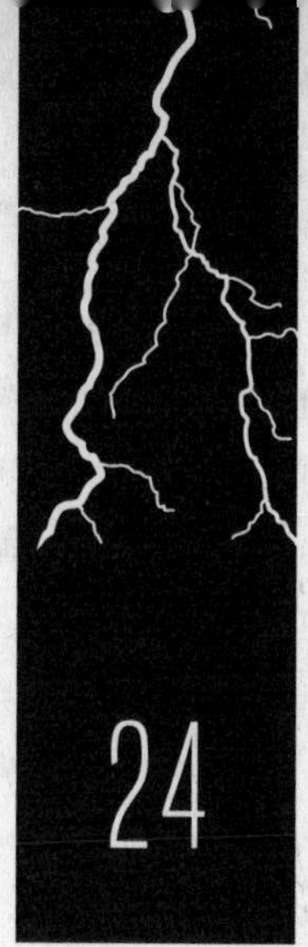

24

A WONDERFUL, soft summer night: when Mai returned to Vietnam, she would take with her, she thought, the memory of these nights. There was nothing quite like them in Hanoi, where the sea was always close and dominated the weather. Here, the nights could be both cool and soft, or warm and soft, with the air resting on your skin like a feather, scented with flowers, and without the overriding tang of salt and seaweed.

She and Phem lay on the edge of the lake, deep in the brush, dressed all in black except for the olive-drab head nets that Tai had found in a sporting goods store. They'd be heading north after they killed Warren, and Phem had sworn that he wouldn't go back without what he called "country equipment."

They had no excuse for being where they were at: if they were seen, or found, then the person who found them would die. Mai had a silenced Beretta pistol, fitted with a strap, hanging on her back; Phem had the rifle, and a pistol as well.

Tai was four hundred meters away, where he would have a better view of the approaches to the target. Phem eased forward and sideways, moving an inch at a time, so that his face was only inches from Mai's. "No wind," he whispered quietly. "Look at the water."

The water was smooth as a piece of silk, doubling the lights across the way as shimmering upside-down reflections.

"Perfect," she said. They were whispering in Vietnamese.

After another moment, he said, "I wonder what happened?"

"Virgil must have figured something out," she whispered. "I can't imagine that he was there just to help with security."

"Maybe he was there for Warren."

"I don't think so. He came so fast—he felt so urgent . . . he discovered something."

"If he did, do you think he took Sinclair?"

"I don't know. There are too many possibilities."

THE EARBUD in Mai's right ear clicked and she saw Phem put a hand to his ear. Mai slipped out the walkie-talkie and said, "Yes."

"Four cars coming, convoy."

"Yes."

Phem moved away from her, and though she couldn't see him well, she felt him extending the rifle toward the target and then stripping off the head net. He'd bought a bag of beans to use as a rifle rest, and she heard that crunch as the forestock wiggled down into it, and a click as the safety came off. If the target appeared, there wouldn't be much time—maybe only a second or two.

Mai put her glasses on the house; looking through them was like watching something on a black-and-white television screen, except that the image was green-and-black. There was enough ambient light that the entire target area looked like a daylight scene.

She took the glasses down, a bit night-blind after looking through the glasses, put the radio to her lips, clicked it once, and said, "Still coming?"

Tai: "Yes. They will be at the turn in ten seconds."

She looked that way, counted, saw the headlights at the corner. She said to Phem, who was concentrating on his scope, "Headlights at the corner. I think it could be them. Here they come, they're coming this way. One-two-three-four vehicles . . ."

Phem was unmoving; she could see a ring of green light where it slipped past his eye from the tube inside the scope. She called it for him, whispering: "Fifty meters. Thirty meters. They're slowing, it's them. Ten meters, the first car turns, I think he will be in the second car, Tai says he always rides in the second car."

The first car drove up the driveway and went all the way to the back, where it faced a garage, but the garage doors didn't go up—the walk from the garage to the back door of the house would be longer than the walk from a car in the driveway to the house.

They were apparently going to minimize the exposure. . . .

The second car turned in, pulled even with the back of the house. The third and fourth stayed in the street, one blocking the driveway.

Two men got out of the first car and walked to the back of the house.

Two more got out of the second car. They looked around, then the man on the driver's side, the side closest to the house, opened the back door of the car and stood beside it.

Warren got out and took a step toward the house, stepped just for a second out from behind the man holding the door. . . .

Phem fired, and Mai saw a muted flash and was slapped by the loud *whack,* and Phem said, "Go . . ." and they were scrambling along behind the screen of bushes and Mai could hear a distant shouting and then gunfire, but couldn't see the gun flashes and had no idea where the bullets were going. . . . They crossed the street as planned, running hard, and cut across a lawn and then between two houses, around a pool and over a fence, Mai clicking the radio button as they went, never stopping, to a side street, and there was Tai, backing up, reversing down the street, and they were in the back of the truck and it was rolling away.

Tai asked, "Good shot?"

"Good shot," Phem said. "I make no guarantees, but it felt good going out."

Mai knew that Warren was dead. She asked, "Are you okay?"

Phem smiled at her. "You *are* like my mother. I am okay."

Mai turned on the radio, to an all-news station, and they headed north through the welter of streets. They would take I-94 to a twenty-four-hour Wal-Mart store on the northwest edge of the Twin Cities, where Tai would move to another car.

From there they would continue north up most of the length of Minnesota and along the eastern edge of North Dakota toward Canada, before they cut back into Minnesota for the last page of the assignment.

The second car was needed should they be stopped by a highway patrolman or a local police officer. They would kill the officer and abandon the known car for the second vehicle.

After that, they would have no backup.

But there was no reason that they should be stopped. Both cars were rentals, taken under completely clean IDs from California.

The entrance ramp came up, and they were gone.

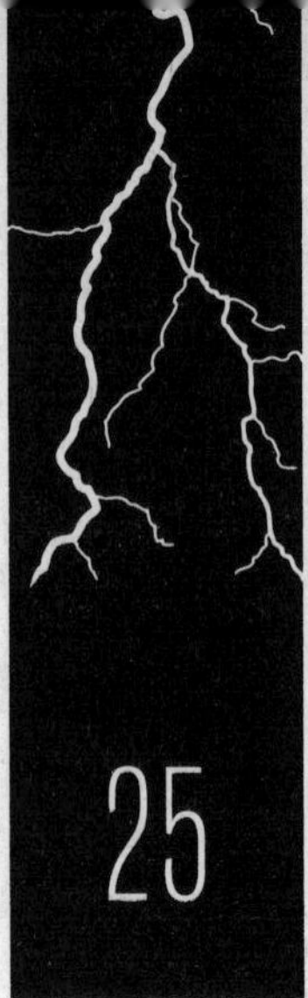

25

THE ST. PAUL cops came out of the woodwork, from staging areas a block or so back from the golf course, and took up stations along the streets at the perimeters. A deputy chief named Purser said, "A goddamn rat couldn't get out of there on his hands and knees."

Virgil, Davenport, and Rose Marie were inside, looking through the windows up at the hillside golf course. A minute passed, two, without any incoming reports. Virgil said to Davenport, "They're not up there."

Rose Marie asked, "How do you know?"

"I'm not getting the right vibration," Virgil said. "When they saw St. Paul coming in, they should have moved. Instantly, before everybody got set. They should have made a break for it. They should have had a backup plan. They should have had somebody on the outside . . . they should have done something."

Davenport nodded. "They're gone—if they were ever here."

Virgil dug out his notebook, flipped it open, found Warren's cellphone number.

"What?" Warren's voice was positively noxious.

"I've got a bad feeling here," Virgil said. "We dropped the net and nobody made a move. You gotta take it easy. They could be coming after you at your house."

"I'm three blocks out," Warren said. "I got three guys inside and they're okay, I just talked to them. I got guys patrolling the neighborhood. Nothing going on. We'll be there in one minute."

"Keep your guys awake until we get them," Virgil said.

"Yeah. And you know what, Flowers? You can still go fuck yourself."

Virgil laughed as he shut his cell phone, stood up, looked out through the front windows at the dark hillside and the golf course. "Guy picked the right job—professional asshole."

Davenport said, "You might want to stand back from the window in case they're still out there. If they've really got a sniper scope . . . They might be a little pissed at you."

"What about Sinclair?" Virgil asked.

"I don't know. I suggest that we put him inside and give him his phone call. He says that's an option, and after we do it, we should get some kind of response from somebody. Find out who's in charge, in any case."

"What if—" The phone in his hand rang, and he looked down at the LCD: Warren. He flipped it open. "Yeah. Flowers . . ."

The guy on the other end was shrieking. "We're taking fire, we're taking fire. Warren's down, Warren's down, he's dead, we got Minneapolis cops coming, we got medics coming, but we, shit, you better get here."

"Ah, man—you're taking fire right now?"

"Right now. Right now. I'm in the driveway, I'm under the car, I can hear a fucking machine gun, man, can you hear that?" The guy was shouting again. "Christ, it's a nightmare, they got fuckin' machine guns. . . ."

"Warren's down?"

"I'm looking at him, man, his whole fuckin' head is gone, man, he's gone, he's gone, I got blood all over me, I'm drowning in blood, man . . ."

"We're on the way, we're on the way. . . ."

Virgil looked at Davenport. "They just hit Warren. They're talking machine guns. Warren's dead in his driveway."

THEY TOOK Davenport's car, and Davenport pushed it hard, out to the interstate, into Minneapolis, Del trailing behind in the state car. Warren's neighborhood had been shut off, and two helicopters were picking through the brush with searchlights. They found a place to park, and Virgil, Del, and Davenport walked down the street to Warren's place, where a dozen cops were milling around in the yard. Eight or ten cop cars were parked along the street and on the other side of the lake, and two hundred people from the neighborhood were out in the street, standing in clumps, watching.

They found a Minneapolis captain named Roark who'd taken charge of the scene, who nodded at Lucas, checked out his tux, asked, "Is that the new BCA uniform?" and said, not waiting for an answer, "I hear you guys are involved."

Lucas nodded. "This is the lemon killings. The killers are three Vietnamese, a woman and two men. We can get prints and DNA anytime we need them—on the woman, anyway. Probably on all three. They're running."

"Any idea on their vehicles?"

Virgil shook his head. "No. But they'll have an exit plan, so they're twenty miles from here and moving. Or they're getting on a plane somewhere."

Del asked, "You know what happened?"

"They got him when he was uncovered for one second, getting out of his car," Roark said. "His bodyguard swears it was one second. They don't know where the shot came from, but we think it was from across the lake. We sent some guys over there with a flashlight, and they found a matted-down place in the brush, and a mosquito net thing, you know, a head net, and a beanbag that was probably used as a rest."

Virgil looked. "Easy shot, if you know guns."

"I talked to one of the bodyguards, he said they never thought about the other side of the lake. The lake was like a barrier, but it's only about a hundred and forty yards."

"Goddamnit," Davenport said. "They might never have been at the golf course. If they knew he was coming out tonight, that would have been enough to wait here."

"What about machine guns?" Virgil asked Roark. "We talked to a guy . . ."

Roark was shaking his head. "One of the bodyguards freaked

out and hosed down a ceramic statue. Blew it up, said he thought the guy had ducked for cover, so he put a couple more magazines into it."

"So no machine guns?"

"We think it was one shot," Roark said. "Big gun. Warren never knew what hit him. Blew out a good piece of his head. He was dead before he hit the ground."

Davenport looked at Virgil. "You think they'll try for Knox?"

"Yeah. They don't know that we know where he is—in fact, they think we *don't* know where he is."

"Better get your ass up there," Davenport said. "I'll get you a plane, get some guys from the Bemidji office. Take some heavy shit with you."

"I gotta get back to my truck. . . ."

"We're not doing any good here. Let's go."

ON THE WAY OUT, Virgil got on his phone and called Louis Jarlait at Red Lake. "Louis, We figured out the lemon killers. Three Vietnamese, two guys and a woman. They're headed your way; they're going after a guy up on the Rainy River, outside of International Falls. I'm flying into International Falls tonight, but I could use a little help—guys who know their way around in the woods."

"I could get Rudy and go up there," Jarlait said.

"Man, I'd appreciate it. We're gonna get some guys from the BCA office in Bemidji, but they'll be investigator types. We need some guys with deer rifles."

When he was off the phone, he said to Davenport, "You should talk to Sinclair tonight. I'm wondering if he told me what he did to flush Warren out in the open. To make a predictable move."

"I'll do that. You take it easy up there."

As they came up to his truck, Virgil said, "I'm going to call you in about one minute—they're probably still monitoring my truck, and I'm going to tell them I don't know where Knox is. You might get a little pissed about that."

"I'll play," Davenport said.

IN THE TRUCK, headed down to the BCA office, Virgil got on the phone to Davenport, shouting: "Warren's dead. They shot him at his house. . . ."

Davenport: "Have you found Knox? Where the hell is Knox?"

"I don't know. His daughter says he does photography, that he might be out in North Dakota somewhere. Maybe I could put out a BOLO on his car, maybe with the North Dakota guys. I don't know where to take it. . . ."

"How are these Vietnamese finding this shit out?" Davenport demanded. "Where are they getting their information?"

"Good fuckin' question," Virgil said. "I'll talk to Sinclair about that."

"You said he wasn't home."

"He's not. I don't know where the hell he is," Virgil said. "He's not answering his cell. Maybe he's with the Viets—he was some kind of fruitcake left-winger. . . ."

"So what're you gonna do?"

"I'm going to put Shrake outside Sinclair's house. If he comes back, we nail him. I'm gonna head down to the office, start working the phones. Honest to God, we gotta find Knox. Maybe tomorrow morning we could drop something in the media, something that would get him to call in."

"If he sees it," Davenport said. "Man, you gotta do better than this. You just gotta do better than this."

THEY SOUNDED pretty good, Virgil thought after he rang off. He'd have bought it.

Virgil stopped first at the BCA office, transferred his outdoors duffel to a state car, including head nets and cross-country ski gloves, good for shooting and fending off mosquitoes. From the BCA equipment room, he got armor and an M16 and five magazines and two night-vision monoculars. Driving the state car, he stopped at the motel, picked up a jacket, and traded his cowboy boots for hiking boots.

Davenport called: "Got you a plane. They'll pick you up at the St. Paul airport. They're starting three guys to International Falls from Bemidji, but it's a ride. It'll take a while."

"It'll take Mai longer, unless they're flying," Virgil said. "If they're flying, they still won't be that far in front of us. I'm gonna try to call Knox, too. Tell him to get the fuck out."

"Tell him to leave the lights on," Davenport said. "Tell him to leave a car in the driveway. We need to pull them in there. We need to get this done with."

VIRGIL CALLED Knox, and this time the phone was answered. Virgil identified himself and was told that Knox was in bed. "Then get him out of bed," Virgil said. "I need to talk to him, now."

Knox came up a minute later. "What happened?"

"Warren got hit. He's dead. The killers are a Vietnamese intel team, apparently after revenge for the '75 murders."

"I had nothing to do with that," Knox said with some heat.

"Well, they don't know that—or they don't give a shit," Virgil said. "Anyway, they're headed your way. They know where you are."

A few seconds of silence, then; "How would they find that out?"

"Hell, man, I put our researcher on it, and she found your place in an hour," Virgil said. "You pay taxes on it and deduct them from your income tax. That is, if you're on the Rainy River, outside of International Falls."

"Sonofabitch." A moment of silence. Then: "You don't think they're here yet?"

"Not yet. Not even if they're flying," Virgil said. "I'm flying up now, I've got guys started up from Bemidji and Red Lake, and we're gonna ambush them. I need to know how to get into your place."

Knox gave him directions, right down to the tenth of the mile. "It's dark out here. If you get lost, you stay lost."

"I'll find it. I got GPS directions to the end of your driveway. I just wasn't too sure about the roads out there," Virgil said. "In the meantime, you oughta get out of there."

"Think so?"

"Yeah. There's nothing you can do at this point," Virgil said. "Don't use your cell phones, they might have some way to track them. Just go out somewhere to a resort and get a place for overnight."

"I'll leave a guy here, tell you about the security systems," Knox said. "He can help you out."

"That'd be great," Virgil said.

"Okay, then. Good luck. I'm outa here."

And he was gone.

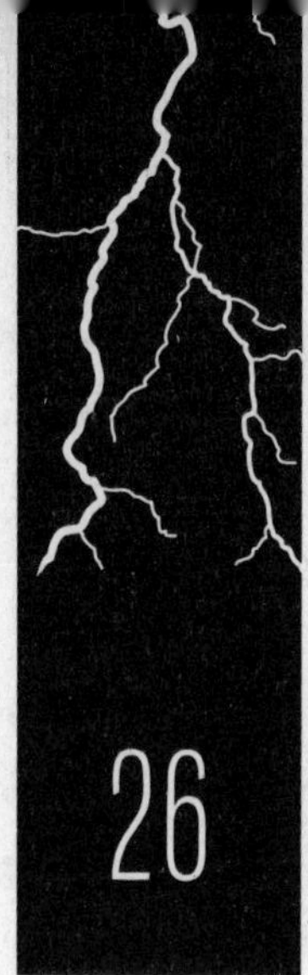

26

THE PILOT'S name was Doug Wayne. He was a small, mustachioed highway patrolman who looked like he should be flying biplanes for Brits over France; he was waiting in his olive-drab Nomex flight suit in the general aviation pilots' lounge at St. Paul's Holman Field.

Virgil came through carrying a backpack with a change of clothes, the ammo and the nightscopes and a range finder and two radios, a plastic sack with two doughnuts and two sixteen-ounce Diet Pepsis, and the M16 in a rifle case.

Wayne said, "Just step through the security scanner over there. . . ."

"Place would blow up," Virgil said. "We ready?"

"How big a hurry are we in?"

"Big hurry," Virgil said. "Big as you got."

WAYNE WAS flying the highway patrol's Cessna Skylane, taken away from a Canadian drug dealer the year before. International Falls was a little more than two hundred and fifty miles from St. Paul by air, and the Skylane cruised at one hundred forty-five miles per hour. "If you got two bottles of soda in that sack . . . I mean, I hope you got the bladder for it. We're gonna bounce around a little," Wayne said as they walked out to the flight line.

"I'll pee on the floor," Virgil said.

"That'd make my day," Wayne said.

"Just kiddin'. How bad are we going to bounce?"

Wayne said, "There's a line of thunderstorms from about St. Cloud northeast to Duluth, headed east. We can go around the back end, no problem, but there'll still be some rough air."

They climbed in and stashed Virgil's gear in the back of the plane and locked down and took off. St. Paul was gorgeous at night, the downtown lights on the bluffs reflecting off the Mississippi, the bridges close underneath, but they made the turn and were out of town in ten minutes. Looking down, the nightscape was a checkerboard of small towns, clumps of light along I-35, the lights growing sparser as they diverged from the interstate route, heading slightly northwest.

"Gonna take a nap if I can," Virgil said.

"Good luck," Wayne said.

Virgil liked flying; might look into a pilot's license someday, when he could afford it. He asked, "How much does a plane like this cost?"

"New? Maybe . . . four hundred thousand."

He closed his eyes and thought about how a cop would get four hundred thousand dollars—write a book, maybe, but it'd have to sell big. Other than that . . .

The drone of the plane and darkness started to carry him off. He thought about God, and after a while he went to sleep. He was aware, at some point, that the plane was shuddering, and he got the elevator feeling, but not too bad; and when he woke up, his mouth tasting sour, he peered out at what looked like the ocean: an expanse of blackness broken only occasionally by pinpoints of light.

He cracked one of the Pepsis and asked, "Where are we?"

"You missed all the good stuff," Wayne said. "Had a light show for a while, off to the east. We're about a half hour out of International Falls. You were sleeping like a rock."

"I've been hard-pushed lately," Virgil said. He looked at his watch: nearly one in the morning. Took out his cell phone: no service.

"You won't get service until we're ten minutes out," Wayne said. "We're talking vast wasteland."

VIRGIL TRIED AGAIN when they could see the lights of International Falls and Louis Jarlait came up. "We're just out of town," Jarlait said. "Where do you want to hook up?"

"Pick me up at the airport. We got some BCA guys coming up from Bemidji."

"I talked to them. They're probably a half hour behind us, they had to get their shit together."

"Okay. I'll get them on the phone, bring them into Knox's place," Virgil said. "We need to check at the airport and see if they had any small-plane flights in the last hour or so with some Vietnamese on board."

"I'll ask while we're waiting for you."

"Careful. You might walk in right on top of them."

Virgil couldn't reach the BCA agents from Bemidji: they were still too far out in the bogs.

WAYNE WAS going to turn the plane around and head back to the Cities. Virgil thanked him for the flight, and he said, "No problem. I love getting out in the night."

Louis Jarlait and Rudy Bunch were waiting when Virgil came off the flight line: "No small planes, no Vietnamese," Bunch said.

"So they're traveling by car. That was the most likely thing anyway," Virgil said. "They won't be here for at least a couple of hours."

They loaded into Bunch's truck, Virgil in the backseat, and Virgil asked, "What kind of weapons you got? You got armor?"

"We got armor, we got helmets, we got rifles. We're good," Jarlait said. "Goddamn, I been waiting for this. I can't believe this is happening."

"You've been waiting for it?"

"I was in Vietnam when I was nineteen—coming up on forty years ago," Jarlait said. "We'd send these patrols out, you could never find shit. I mean, it was their country. Those Vietcongs, man, they were country people, they knew their way around out there." Jarlait turned with his arm over the seat so he could look at Virgil. "But up here, man—this is *our* jungle. I walk around in these woods every day of my life. Gettin' some of those Vietcongs in here, it's like a gift from God."

"I don't think they're Vietcong," Bunch said.

"Close enough," Jarlait said.

"Yeah, about the time you're thinking you're creeping around like a shadow, one of them is gonna jump up with a huntin' knife and open up your old neck like a can of fruit juice," Bunch said.

Virgil was looking at a map. "Take a right. We need to get over to the country club."

"Nobody gonna creep up on me," Jarlait said. "I'm doing the creeping."

THE DRIVEWAY into Knox's place branched off Golf Course Road, running around humps and bogs for a half mile through a tunnel of tall overhanging pines down to the Rainy River. The night was dark as a coal sack, their headlights barely picking out the contours of the graveled driveway. Not a place to get into, or out of, quickly, not in the dark.

"Weird place to build a cabin," Bunch said. "You're on the wrong side of the falls—if you were on the other side, you'd be two minutes out of Rainy Lake."

"He didn't build it for the fishing," Virgil said. "I think he built it so he and his pals can get in and out of Canada without disturbing anyone. The rumor is, he deals stolen Caterpillar equipment all over western Canada."

Knox's house was a sprawling log cabin, built from two-foot-thick pine logs and fieldstone; the logs were maple-syrup brown in the headlights. The house sat fifty yards back from the water on a low rise, or swell, above the rest of the land. A pinkish sodium-vapor yard light, and another one down by a dock, provided the only ambient light. Across the water, Virgil could see another light reflecting off a roof on the Canadian side.

"How far you think that is to the other side?" he asked Bunch as they parked. He was thinking about Warren, and how he'd been shot across the lake.

"Two hundred and fifty yards?"

"Further than that," Jarlait said.

Virgil fished his range finder out of the backpack and, when they stepped out of the truck, put them on the distant roof. "Huh."

"What is it?" Bunch asked.

"Three-eighty from here to the house over there."

"Told you," Jarlait said.

"I meant that the water was two hundred yards."

"Yeah, bullshit . . ."

Virgil said, "The main thing is, I think it's too long to risk a shot. They'll have to come in on this side—they can't shoot from over there."

"I shot an elk at three-fifty," Bunch said.

"Guy's a lot smaller than an elk . . . and there're enough trees in the way that they can't be sure they'd even get a shot. If they're coming in, it'll be on this side."

A MAN SPOKE in the dark: "Who are you guys?"

He was so close, and so loud, that Virgil flinched—but he was still alive, so he said, "Virgil Flowers."

He saw movement, and the man stepped out of a line of trees. He was carrying an assault-style rifle and was wearing a head net and gloves. "I'm Sean Raines, I work for Carl. Better come in, we can work out what we're gonna do."

Inside, the place was simply a luxury home, finished in maple and birch, with a sunken living room looking out across the river through a glass wall, and a television the size of Virgil's living-room carpet. Raines was a compact man wearing jeans and a camouflage jacket. He peeled off the head net to reveal pale blue eyes and a knobby, rough-complected face; like a tough Kentucky hillbilly, Virgil thought.

Virgil asked, "What about the windows?"

"Can't see in," Raines said. "You can't see it from this side, but they're mirrored. How many guys you think are coming?"

"Probably three," Virgil said. "Two guys and a woman. They've got a rifle—hell, they probably got anything they want."

"They any good in the woods?"

"Don't know," Virgil said.

"It's gonna be just us four?" Raines asked.

"We got three more guys coming from Bemidji, oughta be here pretty quick." As he said it, Virgil pulled his phone from his pocket and punched up the number he'd been given.

He got an answer: "Paul Queenen."

"Paul, this is Virgil Flowers. Where are you guys?"

"Fifteen, twenty minutes south of town on 71," Queenen said.

"Stay on 71 until you get to Country Club Road."

VIRGIL GAVE THEM instructions on getting in and then Raines took the three of them to an electronics room to look at the security system. "We got some deer around, so we keep the audio alarms off most the time, but I've got them set to beep us tonight. . . ."

Knox had a dozen video cameras set out in the woods, feeding views into three small black-and-white monitors, all of which were a blank gray. "When you hear an alarm, you get a beep and an LED flashes on the area panel," Raines said. He touched a ten-inch-long metal strip with a series of dark-red LEDs in numbered boxes. Above the LED strip was a map of Knox's property, divided into numbered zones that corresponded to the LEDs. "When you get a flash, you can punch up the monitor and get a view of the area . . . you almost always see a deer, though we've had bears going through. Sometimes you don't see anything because they're out of range of the camera."

"But in the dark like this . . ."

"The cameras see into the infrared, and there are infrared lights mounted with the cameras," Raines said. He reached over to another numbered panel, full of keyboard-style numbered buttons, and tapped On. One of the monitors flickered and a black-and-white image came up: trees, in harsh outline.

"You'll notice that there isn't as much brush as you'd expect—Carl keeps it trimmed out pretty good. The trees are bigger than you'd expect, because he has them thinned. He wants it to look sorta normal, but when you get into it, you can see a lot further than if it was just untouched woods."

"How does it pick up movement?" Bunch asked. "Radar?"

"They're dual-mode—microwave and infrared to pick up body heat."

Raines had worked through a defensive setup. "Whoever's covering the system has to know where our guys are at. You don't want to be turning on the lights if you don't have to, because you've got your own guys moving around. If somebody's coming in with high-end night-vision goggles, some of those can see into the infrared. It'd be like turning on a floodlight for them."

Virgil looked at his watch. "I don't think they'll get here until daylight anyway," he said. "Not unless they flew, and then they'd still have to drive."

They got a beep then, and Raines switched one of the monitor views, and they saw a fuzzy heat-blob moving across the screen. "It's small—probably a doe," he said. He flicked on the infrared lights and they saw the doe, wandering undisturbed through the trees.

"Hell of a system," Virgil said.

TWO OR THREE minutes later, as they were headed back to the living room, the security system beeped again and they went back to look at the monitors. "Car coming in," Raines said. He touched one of the monitors and they saw a truck coming toward them, down the driveway.

"Bemidji," Bunch said.

"We oughta put the trucks in the garage—too many of them, they'll get worried. If they spot them," Jarlait said.

THE THREE AGENTS from Bemidji—Paul Queenen, Chuck Whiting, Larry McDonald—brought assault rifles, armor, and radios. With the handsets that Virgil already had, there'd be enough for everyone. They gathered in Knox's den, where he had a Macintosh computer with a thirty-inch video display, and Virgil called up Google Earth and put a satellite view of Knox's property on the screen.

"Overall, I see two possibilities," Virgil said, touching the screen. "First, they come in by water, which wouldn't surprise me if they've looked at this picture, and they probably have. They could grab a boat, or bring one—a canoe or a jon boat—throw it in the water, and drift right along the shore. They'd probably come in from the south, but they could come in from either direction, so we have to watch both. The second possibility is that all they've got is a car, or a truck, and they come in from the highway . . . but they won't want to park in the open, so they'll have to ditch the truck here or here."

When he finished, one of the Bemidji agents said, "You know, there're only two highways in here." He tapped the screen. "If you put roadblocks here and here . . . they gotta hit them. If you had some guys hiding off-road, south of the roadblocks, and if somebody turned and ran, they could block them south. Trap them."

"I thought of that," Virgil said. "One problem: we'd have some dead cops. These people have no reason not to fight. They've already killed seven or eight people, they're here illegally, and they could be considered spies. Probably would be. If we catch them, they'll go away forever. So if they're suddenly jumped by a roadblock, my feeling is that they'd go for it—they'd try to shoot their way through. And they might have any kind of weapons.

"The other problem is, we've got Canada here." Virgil traced the border on the satellite view. "They could literally swim to a country where we have no authority, if they could shoot their way to the river. If they get to Canada, I have a feeling we lose them."

"Probably would," another of the agents said. "Their crimes are federal capital crimes. Canada wouldn't extradite. We'd have to make some weird kind of deal. I don't think the politicians would go for it—let Canada tell us what we could do."

"One more thing," Virgil said. "They've been working this operation for a year. They're not stupid; they'll have alternative plans. I thought about things like, what if they ditched all their weapons down in the Cities and flew into Fort Frances? They walk through Canadian customs, pick up a prepositioned weapons cache and a boat over there, cross the river, hit Knox, cross back, and head out."

They all looked at the map, then Jarlait chuckled and said, "Wish you'd mentioned that sooner. If they did that, they could be here right now."

"No. Not on the alarm system," Raines said. "We'll see them coming—might only have a minute or two, but we'll see them."

"Maybe they've got invisibility cloaks," Bunch said.

Raines said, "Well, then we're fucked."

VIRGIL SAT staring at the map until Bunch prodded him and asked, "What do we do, boss?"

Virgil said, "Our biggest problem is that we don't know the territory, and we don't have time to learn it. Can't see in the woods, but we can't help it, because if they're coming at all, they're coming tonight. By tomorrow, they've got to figure they'll be all over the media. That Knox will know that they're coming and will get out. And I've set them up to think that I don't know where this house is . . . if they're still monitoring my truck. So: I think they'll come in fast, but there aren't many of them."

He looked at Jarlait and Bunch. "I want you two guys at the corners of the property, on the river, looking for boats." He touched the two corners on the video map. "I want you deep under cover, I want you to literally find a hole, and then, not move. Nothing sticking up but your head. They've got starlight scopes and night-vision glasses. If they come in, I just want a warning so we can reposition everybody else."

To the Bemidji guys: "I want you three on the land side." He pointed at the video display: "Here, here, and here."

"I want everybody on the ground, hidden. Your main job will be to spot these guys so we can build a trap as they come in."

"You mean, ambush them," Whiting said.

Virgil nodded. "That's what it comes to. I'm going to ask Sean to monitor the security system. If anybody sees or hears anything, you call on the radio. Bunch of clicks and your name. That's all. When they come in, you let them past and then get ready to close from the back. Sean will vector you in behind them. If they come in spread out, that means they'll be hooked up by radio. If they're operating as a sniper team, I expect at least two will come together, a spotter and a shooter. Gotta watch out for the third one.

"If they come in from the river, I want the land-side guys to rally down here on the house; if they come in from the land-side, I want Jarlait and Bunch to rally up to the house," Virgil said. "I'll be here with Sean until something pops up, and then I'll go out to face them. By staying here, I can go in any direction."

"And stay out of the mosquitoes," Bunch said.

"And drink beer and watch TV," Virgil said. He looked at his watch. "I want to get us out and get spotted right now. So get armored up, get warm, get your head nets on, get plugged into the radios. Find a comfortable place to lie down and then check in with us."

Raines said, "Best if it's in a ditch or low spot, someplace that will minimize your heat signature, in case they have infrared imaging capability. Get low."

"If everything works perfectly, if they come in and we drop the net around them, I'll try to talk to them," Virgil said. "If they make a run for it, well, stay down and make sure you know what you're shooting at. Anybody running has got to be them. Got that? Nobody runs. We don't want any of us shot by any of us."

He looked around. "If anybody gets hurt, call it in if you can, and we'll make you the first priority. First priority is 'Don't get hurt.' Catching these people is the second priority, okay? Don't get your ass shot."

He turned to Raines. "You know where the hospital is?"

Raines nodded.

"Then you're in charge of making the hospital run if anybody gets knocked down. Them or us," Virgil said. "One thing to remember is, they're coming in here expecting to be on the offensive. They've got to come to us. We don't have to maneuver; we just have to snap the trap. Okay? So let's put your armor on and get out there."

To Raines: "One more thing: if there's shooting, and I can't do it, I want you to call the sheriff's office and tell them what's up. Tell them that it's a BCA operation. We don't want any locals to come crashing through and get mixed up with us, or with the Vietnamese."

VIRGIL AND Paul Queenen moved the BCA truck into the garage, and on the way back in, Queenen looked up at the overcast sky and asked, "What if they don't come in?"

"Then they don't. But if they're monitoring my truck, and they should be, it's been like the ace in their hand . . . then they know we've tumbled to them. They know when people start watching TV, everybody in the state will be looking for them. If they don't move tonight, they'll have to give it up." Virgil looked at his watch again. "They've got to be getting close."

"If they come."

"They will," Virgil said. "I talked to the woman a couple days ago. Mai—Hoa. Told her I didn't know where Knox is hiding. I said it again tonight, in the truck. So—this is their last chance."

"Why did you tell her that? Did you already know she was in it?"

"No." Virgil thought about it for a minute, then said, "I don't know why I told her that."

FIFTEEN MINUTES LATER, all five men were at their stands. All five were deer hunters, they were all camouflaged and armored and netted and settled in, earbuds operating.

Virgil piled his armor in the hallway leading to the electronics room. He slipped into a soft camo turkey-hunter's jacket, put a magazine in each of four separate pockets so they wouldn't rattle, another one seated in the rifle, a shell jacked into the chamber. He jumped up and down a few times to make sure that nothing rattled, then piled the jacket and rifle next to the armor and walked around the house turning off lights.

When the place was dark, he pulled a couple of cushions off the couch in the living room, got a towel from the kitchen, and carried them to the electronics room, where Raines was sitting in a dimmed-down light, watching the monitors.

Virgil tossed the cushions on the floor, lay down on them, put the towel across his eyes, got out the second bottle of Pepsi, took a sip. "Everybody spotted?"

"Yes. I can barely see them, even on the infrared. They got themselves some holes."

A moment of silence, then Virgil asked, "How'd you get this job?"

Raines said, "Got out of the Crotch, couldn't get a job, so a guy got me a shot as a doorman at a club. You know. I met some guys doing security for rock stars, thought I could do that, and that's what I did."

"What rock stars do you know?"

He shrugged again. "Ah, you know. I don't *know* any of them, but I've ridden around with most of them one time or another. I'm the guy who gets out of the limo first."

"What'd you do in the Crotch?"

"Rifleman, mostly—though the last year I spent mostly on shore patrol."

"Yeah? I was an MP," Virgil said.

"Tell you what," Raines said. "I was in Iraq One. I did a lot more fighting as an SP than I ever did in Iraq. Especially those fuckin' squids, man. When the fleet is in, Jesus Christ, you just don't want to be there."

"I was in Fort Lauderdale once when a British ship came in," Virgil said, relaxing into the time-killing chatter. "The people that came off that boat were the pinkest people I ever saw. Absolutely pink, like babies' butts. You could see them six blocks away, they glowed in the dark. I went down to a place on the beach that night, you could hear the screaming a block away, and then the sirens started up, and when I got there, here was twenty buck-naked pink British sailors in the goddamnedest brawl. . . . Man. They were throwing *cops* out of the club."

So they bullshitted through an hour, and once every fifteen minutes or so Raines would start calling names, getting a click from each.

Raines said, "We looked you up on the Internet. Me 'n' Knox."

"Yeah?"

"Saw that thing about the shoot-out, that small-town deal, with the preacher and the dope. Sounded like a war," Raines said.

"It *was* like a war," Virgil said. The towel on his eyes was comfortable, but not being able to see Raines was annoying. "Close as I ever want to come."

Raines said, "But here you are again, automatic weapons, body armor . . ."

"Just . . . coincidence," Virgil said. "I hope."

THE VIETNAMESE came in.

Fifteen clicks, a solid, fast rhythm, and one muttered word, "Bunch," carrying nothing but urgency.

"It's Bunch," Raines said. "I don't see shit on the monitor." He picked up a radio and said, "That's Bunch clicking, folks. Bunch: one click if by land, two if they're on the water."

Pause: two clicks.

Raines: "Bunch. One click if it's likely some fishermen. Several clicks if it's likely the Viets."

Pause: several clicks.

Raines: "Click how many there are."

Pause, then: five slow clicks.

Virgil had crawled into the hallway and closed the door against the light, pulled the armor over his head, patted the Velcro closures, pulled on the jacket, pulled on the head net and the shooting gloves. His eyes were good, already accustomed to the dark. He could hear Raines talking to Bunch.

Raines: "We got five clicks. Give us several clicks if that's correct."

Pause: several clicks.

Raines: "One click if they're still outside of your position. Several clicks if they're past your position."

Pause: several clicks.

Raines said through the door, "Bunch says they're inside his position, but I've got nothing yet. We got a bad angle to the south. . . ."

Virgil plugged in the earbud, said, "I'm going."

Raines said, "It could be a fake-out. A diversion."

"I don't think they've got enough people for a diversion. Tell the other guys to hold their positions until you're sure. I'm going out to face them."

Raines said, "Wait—wait. I got heat. I got heat, right along the bank, they're two hundred yards out, they're all together, they're running right along the bank."

"I'm going," Virgil said. "I'll lock the door going out. Keep your piece handy."

He went out the back door, moved as slowly as he could across the parking area, onto the grass, through a carpet of pine needles, along to the edge of the woods, almost to the river. When he sensed the water, he turned left, into the woods, where he ran into a tree. He couldn't use the night-vision glasses because they'd ruin his night sight. Just have to take it slower. He moved, inches at a time, taking baby steps, one hand out in front, through the edge of the trees.

Raines spoke in his ear. "They're landing. They're seventy-five yards south of you—or west, or whatever it is. I'm going to pull the guys on the land side, bring them down to the cabin. If you've got a problem with that, click—otherwise, go on."

Virgil moved deeper into the woods, felt the land going out from under him. A gully of some kind, a swale, running down toward the water. He moved down into it, felt the ground get soggy, then he was up the far side: couldn't see anything.

At the top of the swale, he found another tree, a big one. The position felt good, so he stopped.

Raines: "Virgil, I've got you stopped. If you're okay, give me a click."

Virgil found the radio talk-button and clicked it.

Raines's voice was calm, collected, steady: "I got a heat mass moving out of the boat, one still in it. Now I got two, okay, they spread out a little, I've got four heat masses moving up on the bank. They're grouping again. They're stopped. Bunch, you're behind them. You'll be shooting toward Virgil if you shoot past them—see if you can move further away from the river and toward the house. Looks like they're gonna stay along the bank. One guy is still in the boat."

Raines: "Bemidji guys, you're right on top of each other, do you see each other? Give me a click if you do." *Click.* "Okay, spread out, we want a line between the west edge of the house running down to the river . . . that's good . . . now moving forward. . . . Careful, you got Jarlait closing in along the bank. Jarlait, you might be moving too fast, take it easy."

Raines kept talking them through it, the Bemidji cops and Jarlait closing on Virgil, the heat signatures by the river hardly moving at all. Raines finally said, "Okay, everybody stop. I think these guys are waiting for a little light. Bemidji guys, Virgil's about fifty yards straight ahead of you. Virgil, the four who got out of the boat are still in a group, they're maybe fifty yards straight ahead of you. Bunch, you're good. Wait there, or someplace close. Looks a little lighter out there . . . sun'll be up in an hour."

THEY WAITED, nobody moving, soothed by Raines. "Everybody stay loose, stay loose . . ."

Virgil first imagined that the sky was growing brighter, then admitted to himself that it wasn't: a common deer-hunting phenomenon. Then it did get brighter, slowly, and Virgil could see the tips of trees, and then the tips of branches, and then a squirrel got pissed somewhere and started chattering, and the woods began to wake up.

"They're moving," Raines said. "They're coming in two plus two. Two are going further up the bank, two are coming right at you, Virgil. They're closing, you'll see them, if you can see them, in about a minute. . . . Rest of you guys, don't shoot Virgil. Bunch, the second two are as high on the bank as you are, you're behind them, they're moving toward the cabin. . . . Virgil, you should see them anytime."

Virgil sensed movement in front of him, thumbed the radio button, said as quietly as he could, "Rudy, I'm gonna yell. Your guys may move."

"I think they heard you—they stopped," Raines said in Virgil's ear. "Christ, they're not more than twenty-five yards away."

From out in front of him, a woman's voice said quietly, "Virgil?"

Virgil eased a little lower down the slope of the gully, thumbed the radio button so everybody could hear him, and said, "Mai—we're looking at you on thermal imaging equipment, and on visual cameras up in the trees. We can see all of you. We've got you boxed, and there are a lot more of us than there are of you. Give it up or we'll kill you."

There was a heavy thud as something hit the far side of Virgil's tree, and Virgil realized in an instant what it was, and flopped down the bank and covered his eyes and the grenade went with a flash and a deafening blast, and a machine gun started up the hill and Virgil thought, *Rudy,* and he rolled up and a burst of automatic-weapon fire seemed to explode over his head, coming from where Jarlait should have been, and he heard somebody scream and then there was a sudden silence and he could hear Raines talking: "Rudy, he's up above you, circling around you, back up if you can, back up, you see him, you see him?"

More gunfire, and then Bunch shouted, "I got him, but I'm hit, I'm hit, ah, Jesus, I'm hit . . ."

Raines said, "Virgil, you've got one not moving in front of you, one moving away."

Jarlait: "I got the one in front of Virgil, I had him dead in my sights."

Raines: "We got one moving down to the water, Jarlait, if you move sideways down to the water you might be able to see them, you might have to move forward. . . . Virgil, you can move forward. . . . Paul, can you and your guys get to Rudy? Can you get to Rudy?"

Queenen said, "I can hear him, but where's the other guy, is he still there?"

"He's not moving, he may be down, I'm going to illuminate with the

IR . . . okay, I can see him, he looks like he's down, he's on his back, if you go straight ahead you should get to Rudy. . . . Rudy, I can see Rudy waving . . . Rudy, the guy above you is moving, but not much. He's crawling, I think, can you see him?"

And Queenen said, "Is Rudy moving? Is Rudy crawling, I can see a guy crawling—" Rudy shouted, "No," in the open, and Queenen opened up, ten fast shots, and Raines, his voice still cool, said, "I think you rolled him."

JARLAIT SHOUTED, in the open, "I can't see them."

Virgil moved. The light was coming up fast, and he went forward, and Raines said in his ear, "Virgil, I can't tell if the guy in front of you is down, but he's not moving at all. The other one is down at the water."

Virgil moved again, fast dodging moves from tree to tree. Raines called, "You're right on top of him, he's just downhill."

Virgil saw the body: Phem, with a rifle. He was lying on his back, looking sightlessly at the brightening sky, the last he would ever have seen; his chest had been torn to pieces.

Virgil could hear Mai's voice, calling out to somebody, the tone urgent, well ahead, but couldn't make out what she was saying. Vietnamese?

Queenen: "Okay, the first guy's dead. . . . Larry, watch me, I'm moving over to the left, you see me? Watch right up the hill there . . . I'm gonna make a move here."

A few seconds, then Queenen: "Okay, the second guy is dead. Rudy, where are you?"

Raines called: "They're moving, they're on the water . . . they're moving fast . . ."

Virgil heard somebody crashing along the riverbank, assumed it was Jarlait, and then a long burst of automatic-weapon fire, interspersed with tracers, chewed up the riverbank and cut back into the woods and he went down.

Raines: "Louis, are you okay?"

"I'm okay. Jesus, they almost shot me." His breath was hoarse through the walkie-talkie; another old guy.

Another long burst, then another, and Virgil realized that somebody—Mai?—was loading magazines and hosing down the woods as thoroughly as possible, keeping them stepping and jiving until they could get down the river, in the boat, to wherever their vehicle was.

He left Phem and hurried forward through the trees, crashing around, knowing he was noisy, and another burst slashed and ricocheted around him, and he went down again, and somebody shouted, "Man," and then, on the radio, "That last one . . . I'm bleeding, but I don't think it's too bad."

Virgil thought, *Shit,* turned back to help out, then heard Jarlait yell to the wounded man, "I see you. I'm coming your way, don't shoot me, I'm coming your way."

Virgil turned and jogged through the woods, fifty yards, a hundred yards, Raines calling into his ear, "I'm gonna lose you in a minute, Virgil, they're already off my screens . . . I'm losing you . . ."

Virgil ran another fifty yards, to a muddy little point, risked a move to the water. The morning fog hung two or three feet deep over the water, wisps here and there, and Virgil saw only a flash of them, three or four hundred yards away, heading into the Canadian side, around another bend in the river; they disappeared in a quarter second, behind a screen of willows. No sound—they were using a trolling motor. He put his aim point a foot high, where he thought they'd gone, and dumped the whole magazine at them. When he ran dry, he kicked the empty mag out, jammed in another, and dumped thirty more rounds into the trees about where the boat should have been.

He thumbed the radio and shouted, "I'm coming back, watch me, I'm running back."

When he got back to the house, Jarlait was there, standing over McDonald, as one of the trucks backed across the yard toward them. Jarlait looked at Virgil and said, "Rudy's hit in the back. He's hurt. This guy's got a bad cut on his scalp, but not too bad. Needs some stitches."

VIRGIL SAID, "So what are you up to?"

"What?"

He nodded down to a canoe, rolled up on the bank. "There's a chance I hit them, or one of them. I'm going after them."

"Let's go," Jarlait said. "Fuckin' Vietcong."

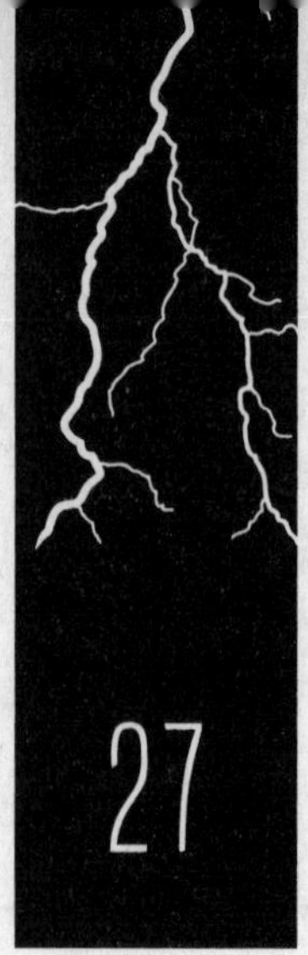

27

THE CANOE was an old red Peter Pond, rolled upside down with two plastic-and-aluminum paddles and moldy orange kapok life jackets stowed under the thwarts. Virgil twisted it upright, frantic with haste, chanting, "C'mon, c'mon," and they threw it in the river, and clambered aboard with their weapons and Virgil's backpack.

Whiting had backed the truck down to McDonald and was helping the wounded man into the truck; McDonald had a scalp gash that must've come from a wood splinter. Queenen saw them manhandling the canoe to the river and shouted, "Virgil, that's Canada," and Virgil saw Raines spinning out of the driveway in the other truck, running to the hospital with Bunch, and Virgil ignored Queenen and said to Jarlait, "If we roll, that armor will pull you under. Grab one of those life jackets," and Jarlait grunted, "Ain't gonna roll," and they were off. . . .

They slanted upstream, paddling hard, Virgil aiming to land a couple of hundred yards north of where he'd seen the jon boat disappear. If they were caught on the open river, they were dead.

They crossed in two minutes or so. Jarlait jumped out of the front of the boat, splashed across a muddy margin, and pulled the canoe in. Virgil stepped out into the shallow water and lifted the stern with a grab loop as Jarlait lifted the bow, and they dropped it fully on shore. A muddy game trail led back into the trees, and they took it for thirty feet, and somebody said in Virgil's ear, "Virgil, the local cops are coming in."

Virgil lifted the radio to his face and said, "Keep them off the place until we get back. . . . Don't be impolite, but tell them that the crime scene is all over the place and we need to get a crime-scene crew in there."

Jarlait said into his radio, "You guys shut up unless you see these people and then tell us. But shut up." To Virgil, he said off-radio, "Let's go."

THE CANADIAN SIDE was a snarling mass of brush, and they walked away from the river to get out of it. Virgil said quietly, "That topo map showed a road straight west of here—they've probably got a car back in the trees. Gotta hurry."

They ran due west, quietly as they could, but with some inevitable breaking of sticks and rustling of leaves, and after two hundred yards or so, saw the road ahead. With Virgil now leading, they turned south, parallel to the road, inside the tree line, and ran another hundred and fifty yards, where a field opened out in front of them. They could see nothing across the field, and Jarlait asked, "Are you sure they're this far down?"

"Yeah, a little further yet. There might be farm tracks between those fields right down to the trees."

He started off again, back toward the river now, running in the trees, off the edge of the field. They spooked an owl out of a tree, and it lifted out in absolute silence and flew ahead of them for fifty yards, like a gray football, then sailed left through the trees.

At the end of the field, they turned south again, and Jarlait, breathing heavily, said, "I gotta slow down a minute. I can taste my guts."

"Gotta slow down anyway—we're close now."

They moved slowly after that, stopping every few feet to listen, moving tree to tree, one at a time, covering each other, back toward the water.

If he'd missed them completely, Virgil thought, and if the car had been right down at the water, it was possible that they were gone. On the other hand, if he'd hit them, it was possible that they were lying dead or dying down at the waterline.

When they got to the river, they squatted ten yards apart and listened, and then began moving along the waterline, both crouched, stopping to kneel, to look, one of them always behind a tree. A hundred yards farther along the bank, Virgil saw the tail end of the jon boat. They'd dragged the bow out of the water, but there was no sign of anyone.

Virgil clicked once on the radio to get Jarlait's attention, mouthed, "Boat," and jabbed his finger at it, and Jarlait nodded and moved forward and farther away from the water, giving Virgil room to wedge up next to the boat.

They were in a block of trees, Virgil realized—trees that might run out to the road. The field they'd seen was now actually behind them. No sign of a truck or a car track.

They moved a step at a time, until Virgil was right on top of the boat. When he was sure it was clear, he duckwalked down to it and saw the blood right away. He risked the radio and said, quietly, "Blood trail."

Jarlait, now fifteen yards farther in, looked over at him and nodded.

THE BLOOD looked like rust stains on the summer weeds and brush. There wasn't much, but enough that whoever was shot had a problem. The blood was clean and dark red, which meant the injured man was probably bleeding from a limb but hadn't been gut- or lung-shot. Still, they'd need a hospital, or at least a doctor—something to tell the Canadians if Mai and the second man were already gone.

Virgil went to his hands and knees and crawled along the blood trail, grateful for the gloves; Jarlait worked parallel to him. They were a hundred and fifty or two hundred yards from the road again, Virgil thought, but he didn't know how far from wherever the Viets had left a vehicle. He could see no openings in the treetops, so it must be some distance out.

He picked up a little speed, risked going to his feet, while Jarlait ghosted along to his right. The trees thinned a little, the underbrush got thicker. There were still occasionally drops and smears of blood, but as the plant life got softer, less woody, Mai's trail became clearer.

"Man, we sound like elephants in a cornfield," Virgil said. "We gotta slow down."

From up ahead—a hundred yards, fifty yards?—Virgil heard a *clank* and both he and Jarlait paused, and Jarlait asked, "What do you think?" and Virgil said, "It sounded like somebody dropped a trailer."

They both listened and then they heard an engine start, and Virgil started running, Jarlait trying to keep up. At the end of the trail, they found a vehicle track through shoulder-high brush, an abandoned trailer sitting there, and then the end of a pasture, or fallow field, and on the other end of the pasture, a silver minivan bumped over the last few ruts and pulled onto the road a hundred yards away.

Not a hard shot.

Virgil lifted the rifle and put the sights more or less on the moving van and tracked it and picked up the house in the background, said, "Shit," and took the rifle down.

They were gone.

And though Virgil didn't know which one of the Viets was hurt, who had been bleeding, he believed that he'd caught something of Mai in the driver's-side window, at the wheel.

VIRGIL GOT on the radio and called a description of the van back to Queenen, who was holding the fort on the other side of the river. When they walked back past the trailer, they saw, sticking out between a spare wheel and the trailer frame, a manila envelope. Virgil looked at it and found "Virgil" scrawled across it.

Inside were ten color photographs—crime-scene photos, in effect, of the house at Da Nang, apparently taken a day or so after the killings. Flies everywhere, all over the corpses. Two little kids, one facedown, one faceup, twisted and bloated in death. A woman, half nude, flat on her back, her face covered in blood. Another woman lying in a courtyard, apparently shot in the back. An old man, out in front of the house . . .

Jarlait kept going back to the picture of the kids. "Little teeny kids, man. Little peanuts," he said.

"Bunton knew about it. So did all the others," Virgil said. "They couldn't have stopped it, the way they tell it—Warren did all the killing. But they all kept their mouths shut."

They thought about that for a few seconds. "Little kids," Jarlait said. "I can see them coming over, to get the killer. But they killed Oren. Oren didn't do shit. . . . Oren was a nice guy."

"The guy you shot on the other side. He's the guy who shot Oren," Virgil said.

"All right," Jarlait said. "So we're all square with him. . . . Wonder how they happened to have the pictures with them?"

"They were going to leave them on Knox's body, to make their point."

NOT YET DONE, not by a long way.

As they crossed back over the river, Jarlait said, "Now we've broken two laws—illegal entry into Canada, then illegal entry into the States."

"Probably best not to emphasize that when we're talking to people," Virgil said.

VIRGIL CLIMBED OUT of the canoe and helped Jarlait drag it on shore, then Jarlait said, "I gotta find out about Rudy." Queenen had been standing at the end of the driveway, talking on a cell phone, when he saw them land, and came jogging down the slope toward them.

He took the phone down as he came up and asked, "Anything new?"

"Just what I told you on the radio. We hit one of them, though. There's blood in their boat and there's a blood trail up through the trees." He held up the manila envelope with the pictures. "They left this for us."

Jarlait asked, "How's Rudy?"

Queenen said, "He's at the hospital. Raines said they're gonna do some surgery, but it's basically to clean out a hole. Shot went under the skin by his armpit, and then back out. My guy's getting his scalp sewn up, but he won't need surgery."

Virgil: "The three Viets . . ."

"Yeah. They're all dead," Queenen said. "All with multiple wounds. Rudy shot one of them when the grenade went off, and then he and the other guy shot each other, and I shot the second guy. The third guy, I guess you guys . . ."

"Louis," Virgil said. "Phem threw a flash-bang and tried to come in behind it. It hit a tree and bounced off and I was right there. Almost knocked me on my ass. . . . If Louis hadn't been ready, they'd of had me."

"Well—what are you gonna do?" Queenen asked. He looked away, across the river. "I wish we'd gotten the other two assholes."

"I gotta get up to see Rudy," Jarlait said. "His mom is gonna kill me."

Queenen said, "Virgil, you gotta come up and talk to these deputies. They're getting antsy as hell. The sheriff's on his way in."

Virgil nodded and said, "Let's go." To Jarlait: "Get your truck, head on out, but stay in touch."

BEFORE THEY TALKED to the deputies, they took a quick detour through the woods so Virgil could look at the bodies: Phem, Tai, and another Asian man he didn't know. Had there been some other way to do this? Or had he really *wanted* to do it after being used around by the Viets? He'd think about it some other time.

"Lotta blood," he said to Queenen.

ON THE WAY up the driveway, Virgil got on the cell phone and called Davenport. "What happened?" Davenport asked as soon as he picked up the phone.

"We had a hell of a gunfight," Virgil said. "We got three dead Vietnamese, and two got away, into Canada. We need to call the Mounties . . . hang on." He turned to Queenen. "Did you call the Canadians?"

Queenen said, "I called the office, they're gonna get in touch."

Virgil went back to the phone. "I guess Bemidji's getting in touch. There might be a little dustup coming there."

"Virgil, tell me you didn't cross the river," Davenport said.

"I didn't cross it by very much," Virgil said. "I was in hot pursuit."

Davenport pondered for a moment, then said, "You thought that if these desperate killers encountered any Canadians, they'd ruthlessly gun them down to cover their escape, and so, throwing legal nit-picking to the wind, you decided to put your own body between the murderers and any innocent Canucks."

"Yeah—that's what I thought," Virgil said.

Davenport said, "We had a good talk with Mead Sinclair. We put him in Ramsey County overnight until we decide what to do. I don't think he'd run. But—we've got a couple of guys coming in from Washington to speak to us."

"Who's us?" Virgil asked.

"Rose Marie, me, you, Mitford, hell, maybe the governor," Davenport said. "They'll be here this afternoon. You gotta get down here. I'm going to call around, see if I can get you a plane out of International Falls. You got somebody you can give the scene to?"

"We've got a crew coming up from Bemidji, and there are two Bemidji guys here. There were three, but one got a scalp cut. . . . One of our guys from Red Lake got dinged up . . ."

Virgil told him the whole story, a blow-by-blow. When he was done, Davenport asked, "Where's this Raines guy?"

"Still at the hospital, I think. There were gunshot wounds, so he might be talking to the International Falls cops."

Davenport said, "Okay . . . listen. Go talk to the deputies. Tell them to secure the scene. Keep them out of the house. Keep everybody out of the house. Then go in there and take a little look around. You were invited in . . . are there any file cabinets?"

Virgil said, "You're an evil fuck."

Davenport said, "Call me when you can move. I'll find a plane."

VIRGIL DID ALL THAT: brought the deputies in, made them feel like they were on top of things. Let them look at the bodies; kept them out of the house. Got Queenen to talk to the sheriff when he arrived.

A little over an hour later, Virgil was climbing into a Beaver floatplane that taxied right up to Knox's dock. The plane felt like an old friend: Virgil had flown over most of western Canada in Beavers and Otters, and he settled down, strapped in. The pilot said her name was Kate, and they were gone.

Virgil hadn't found much in Knox's house. The big computer was used, apparently, for photography and games. There'd been another small desk in the main bedroom, with a satellite plug and a keyboard, and Virgil decided that Knox must travel with a laptop. In a leather jacket tossed on the bed, he had found a small black book full of addresses and phone numbers. There was no Xerox machine in the place, but he went and got his bag, took out his camera, and shot a hundred JPEGs of the contents, to be printed later. When he was done, he put the address book back in the jacket and tossed it back on the bed.

When Davenport had called about the plane, he'd asked, "How things go? You know?"

"Not much, but, um, I found like three hundred names and addresses in a private little book."

"Not bad," Davenport said. "For Christ's sakes, don't tell anybody about it."

"Get me a plane?"

"Yup. Got you a bush pilot," Davenport said.

VIRGIL TRIED TO chat with Kate, who was decent-looking and athletic and outdoorsy and had a long brown braid that reminded Virgil of all the women in his college writers' workshop; but Kate, probably shell-shocked by being hit on by every fly-in fisherman in southwest Ontario, didn't have much to say.

So Virgil settled into his seat and went to sleep.

KATE PUT him on the Mississippi across the bridge from downtown St. Paul. Davenport was waiting; Virgil threw him the backpack, thanked Kate, climbed up on the dock, and pushed the plane off: Kate was heading back north.

Davenport asked, "You okay?"

"Tired," Virgil said. "Still alive. Anybody talking to the Canadians? Anybody seen Mai and the other guy?"

"We're talking to them, they went down and recovered the boat, they've got some guys working the other side. But not too much."

"Goddamnit," Virgil said. "We were too goddamn slow getting across."

"Nothing works all the time," Davenport said. "On the whole, you did pretty damn good. Knocked it all down, settled it. Now, if we can get the Republicans in and out of town without anybody getting killed, we can all go back to our afternoon naps."

Virgil handed him the manila envelope.

"What's this?"

"Something to think about," Virgil said.

DAVENPORT LOOKED AT the photos as they walked out to his car. When they got there, he put them back in the envelope and passed them across the car roof. "Hang on to these until I can figure something out."

They were meeting the two guys from Washington in a conference room off Rose Marie's office at the Capitol. "They want to talk about Sinclair—that's all we know," Davenport said.

"Is Sinclair still in jail?" Virgil asked.

"No. We let him out this morning. Put a leg bracelet on him, told him not to go more than six blocks from his house. He's at his apartment now," Davenport said. "There are some very strange things going on there—I'm not quite sure what. Some kind of inter-intelligence-agency pie fight, the old guys from the CIA against the new guys in all the other alphabet agencies."

"Who's Sinclair with?"

"The old guys, I think, but I'm just guessing," Davenport said. "The thing is, he hasn't asked for an attorney. He's actually turned down an attorney, though he says he might ask for one later. He thinks the fix is in."

"Is it?"

"Well, we're having this meeting—"

"You can't just throw dirt on the whole thing."

"Maybe you can't—but maybe you can. Who knows? Not my call."

"We got bodies all over the place."

"And we got three dead Vietnamese. There's your answer for the dead bodies. If nobody mentions the CIA, why, then, should anybody get all excited about mentioning them?"

Virgil looked at Davenport and asked, "Where do you stand on this?"

Davenport said, "Basically, at the bottom of my heart: if you do the crime, you do the time. And I don't like feds."

ON THE WAY across the Mississippi, Davenport said, "You need to get over to Sinclair's place. If you look behind the seat, you'll see that laptop that Mickey carried into the meeting with Warren."

Virgil twisted in the seat, saw the laptop, picked it up.

Davenport said, "Take it with you. What I want you to do is, while we're all real hot, I want you to go into Sinclair's place with the laptop turned on. You can stick it in your pack with those photographs—they ought to distract him from thinking too hard about you being bugged—and talk to him for a while. He seems to like you for some reason. Find out what *he* wants. Find out what he'd do. What he'd admit to. Might get him, you know, at home, when his guard's down a bit."

"Is that why you turned him loose?" Virgil asked.

"Maybe."

"Did they take the bug out of the truck?" Virgil asked.

"Not yet, but what difference would it make? There's nobody to listen to it."

"Mai's still out there," Virgil said.

"So yank it out—but go see Sinclair first."

"OK."

"Did that truck thing do any good?" Davenport asked. "You know, pretending you were still with the truck?"

"I think it killed three people," Virgil said. "They bought the whole thing."

"You are a shifty motherfucker," Davenport said.

"Yeah, I know. I remind you of yourself when you were younger."

"Not much younger," Davenport said.

Virgil made a rude noise and they rolled through St. Paul to BCA headquarters, and Davenport dropped Virgil beside his truck. "The meeting with the Washington guys is in an hour, or an hour and fifteen minutes, so you don't have much time," Davenport said. "Do what you can."

AT THE TRUCK, Virgil lay down beside the front fender, looked up at the transmitter. A couple of wires led into the turn signal box, and he yanked one of them out of the transmitter. That would kill it; creeped him out to think about the thing giving up Ray Bunton.

Ten minutes to Sinclair's. He parked in the street, turned on the laptop recorder, slid it into the pack, put the envelope on top of it, threw the pack over his shoulder, and walked to Sinclair's place.

He pushed the doorbell, and Sinclair answered immediately, as though he'd been waiting for it: "Who is it?"

"Virgil."

The door buzzed and he went on through, and Sinclair was waiting at the open door to his apartment.

"What happened to Hoa?" he asked.

"Made it to Canada," Virgil said.

Relief showed in Sinclair's face. "I couldn't help liking her," he said. "What about the other guys?"

"Phem and Tai, whatever their real names are, are dead," Virgil said. He was thinking of the recorder. "So's another guy that I never met. Another guy got out. Either he's wounded, or Mai is. We found a blood trail, but it was in Canada, and they had an exit route all set up. We called the Canadians with a description of the vehicle, but they haven't seen it yet."

"Phem and Tai. Not bad guys, actually, for a killer and a torturer," Sinclair said.

"I'll quote you when I write my article for the *Atlantic,*" Virgil said.

"Yeah, right. *Fur 'n' Feather* is more like it. . . . When did you get back?"

"Ten minutes ago," Virgil said. "I talked to my boss on the phone, and he told me you were here."

THEY'D MOVED through the apartment, talking, out to the porch. Virgil tossed his pack on the table, undid the quick-release buckles, pulled out the envelope of photographs, left the end of the laptop hanging out, one of the tiny camera lenses facing Sinclair.

He handed the envelope to Sinclair: "They left them for us. Deliberately, I'm sure."

Sinclair slid them out of the envelope, thumbed through them, then looked at them carefully, one at a time. He looked up and said, "That's bad—and they're real. I've had some training in this stuff. If they're not real, they're better than anything we could do."

"They're real," Virgil said. "We got some shots from the last guy they were looking for. Carl Knox. He took some right at the time of the shootings. The bodies look the same, the way they landed. No way to fake that."

Sinclair leaned back and said, "What are you guys planning to do?"

Virgil shrugged. "It's not up to me. There's a big meeting, forty-five minutes from now—I've got to go—with some guys from Washington.

I suspect we're about to shovel a whole bunch of dirt over the whole thing."

"That's one way to handle it," Sinclair said. "What about me?"

"Hard to avoid the fact that you were helping out," Virgil said. "People already know . . . lots of cops, probably some newspeople. Gonna be hard to make it go away. I suspect what will happen is that you'll wind up on trial in one of those intelligence courts, the secret-testimony ones, and then . . . what it is, is what it is."

Sinclair bared his teeth. "I could get really fucked, if that happens," he said.

Virgil spread his hands. "Shouldn't have signed up with them."

"There was pressure. I told you about my daughter," Sinclair said. "They were gonna fuck me over with that whole thing about the agency. I'd lose my job at the university . . . I'd be cooked."

"Shit happens," Virgil said.

Sinclair grinned and said, "You're a lot rougher than you look, Virgil. You look like some kind of rockabilly, straw-headed, woman-chasing country punk."

Virgil said, "Thank you."

"But you went and broke down the program, and shot a bunch of people up, and here you are, looking me in the face and telling me that I might be going to prison."

Virgil stood up. "I gotta go. I wanted to tell you about Mai."

Sinclair said, "Wait a minute. Sit down for two more minutes. Let me tell you what I know about this whole thing. Maybe we can work something out. . . . You owe me, after I gave you Phem and Tai."

"You knew you were giving them to me?"

"You knew the Virgil quote—I thought there was a good chance that you'd be smart enough to pick up on me."

"Weird way to do it."

"I needed something absolutely deniable." Sinclair grinned at him. "You got the information, I got the deniability. Deniability is the Red Queen of American intelligence."

VIRGIL PLAYED THE TAPE for Rose Marie Roux, for Davenport, and for Neil Mitford, the governor's aide. Roux, who'd been a cop and later a prosecutor before she went into politics, said, "He's willing to testify that Homeland Security—some officials at Homeland Security—cut this deal knowing that a bunch of people would be murdered."

Virgil nodded.

Rose Marie tapped a yellow number two on her desktop, then looked at Mitford and asked, "The governor's on the way?"

"He should be in the building if traffic isn't too bad." Mitford was another lawyer.

"Get down there and brief him. We've got to go." Two Homeland Security people were in the conference room, waiting.

THE HOMELAND SECURITY guys looked like the security people that Warren had been bringing in, but with thinner necks. They were sleek, tanned, confident, smiling, gelled, and their neckties coordinated with both their suits and their eye color; one of them checked out Virgil's cowboy boots and backpack when he came in and frowned, as if he suspected that he might not be talking to the BCA's upper crust.

Rose Marie sat everybody down and introduced the two, James K. Cartwright and Morris Arenson, to the BCA agents. She said, "Virgil has just come back from a firefight up north. Three of the Vietnamese were killed, and two escaped into Canada. We are asking for Canadian assistance in tracking them down."

Arenson threw back his head and said, "Ah, damnit."

"I thought that would be good news," Rose Marie said.

"Anytime things go international, they become harder to control," Cartwright said. "Was one of the dead Viets a young woman?"

"No, that was Mai," Virgil said. "Or Hoa. She and another guy got away."

Cartwright looked around the table and said, "Thank God for small favors. Her family is right at the top of the totem pole in Hanoi."

Davenport asked, "Whose side are you guys on, anyway? We've been—"

Before he could finish, the governor pushed through the door, smiling, trailed by Mitford. The governor said, "Glad I could make it. Glad I could make it."

When they were introduced, Arenson looked at his colleague and then at Rose Marie and the governor and said, "I'd thought that we were keeping this on an Agency level."

The governor said, "I like to keep up."

THE TWO Washington men, Mitford, the governor, and Rose Marie then went through a couple minutes of name-dropping and bureaucratic hand-wringing, and the governor finally said, "Look, I came all the way down the hill to hear this. I have other things to do, so let's cut the horse hockey and get down to it." He turned to Virgil: "Virgil, tell me what you know about all this."

Virgil said, "Well, from what I'm able to tell, six Minnesotans went to Vietnam just before the fall of Saigon and stole a bunch of Caterpillar tractors and other equipment that was being abandoned by the military. While they were there, one of them, Ralph Warren, killed a number of people, including a couple of toddlers, and raped a woman who was, at the time, either dying or dead."

"Disgusting," the governor said.

Virgil continued: "A year or so ago, the Vietnamese found out who'd done it—found a couple of names, anyway. The murdered people had family who are now high in the Vietnamese government. The family decided to get revenge.

"To do that, they contacted an American intelligence agency and offered a trade: they had information about an alleged al-Qaeda plot coming out of Indonesia. They would turn over the information to Homeland Security, if Homeland Security looked the other way—and provided some direct informational support—for a hit team."

Virgil continued: "A deal was made, and the Viets sent a gunman, a torturer, and a coordinator over here to kill the six people involved in the '75 murders. They'd already killed one man in Hong Kong, I believe. They only had two or three names for the people here, and had to gather the others as they went. That's why John Wigge was tortured before they dumped his body on the Capitol lawn.

"An American, Mead Sinclair, who may have been a CIA agent but who was well-known as a political radical with contacts in Vietnam, was coerced into working as a contact between the Vietnamese and the intelligence agencies here in the U.S. The idea was, he was deniable.

If he talked, the old intelligence agencies could point to the fact that he was a longtime radical friend of the Vietnamese and had no credibility. Sinclair didn't want to do it, but threats were made against his daughter—"

"Let's stop there," Cartwright said. "Most of this is just speculation. I don't doubt that Virgil here did a bang-up job in tracking these people down"—Virgil thought he detected a modest lip-curl with the compliment—"but that American intelligence agency stuff is fantasy."

The governor looked at him for a moment, then said, "Virgil?"

Virgil said, "Well, you all know most of the rest of it. The Viets killed Warren last night. I'd discovered that they'd bugged my car, with a bug that looks like it was designed right here in the good ol' USA. I used the bug, which was still operating, to convince them that I didn't know where the last man was. Then we flew to the guy's place and set up an ambush. The Viets walked into it this morning, three of them were killed, and two escaped to Canada, one of them wounded. So here we are."

"And that's just about nowhere," Arenson said.

Virgil said, "We've got Sinclair. We've got him cold. He's willing to turn state's evidence."

Cartwright looked straight across the table at Virgil. "That won't happen."

"Already happened. I accepted his offer, and he gave me a brief statement," Virgil said. "I recorded it."

Arenson pushed back from the table and said in a mild voice, "I don't think you folks understand quite what is going on here. We represent the Homeland Security Agency. We're not *asking* you what we're going to do. We're *telling* you what we're going to do. What we're going to do is, we're going to smooth this whole thing over. The Vietnamese provided us with a key contact—"

The governor broke in: "Wait a minute. A whole bunch of Minnesotans are dead. Two were completely innocent. Five, maybe, were involved in a crime thirty years ago, but they get a *trial.*"

"Governor, in the best of all possible worlds, that's the way it would work," Arenson said. "Post-9/11, some things have changed, and this is one of them. I'm authorized, and I'm doing it—I'm classifying this whole matter as top secret. We will help you develop an appropriate press release."

"You can't . . . this is our jurisdiction," the governor began.

"There's been a tragedy, but a minor one," Cartwright said. "What was done was necessary. We may have saved hundreds of lives. If the al-Qaeda plan had gone through . . ."

The governor said, "I can't accept—"

Arenson snapped: "Let me say it again, in case you didn't get it the first time: we're not *asking* you, we're *telling* you. What part of *telling* don't you understand?"

THERE WAS A moment of silence, then the governor cleared his throat and said, "Rose Marie, Neil, Lucas, Virgil, let me talk to you in Rose Marie's office for a moment." He stood up and said to the two Washington guys, "Just take a moment. I think we can come to a satisfactory resolution of this."

The governor led the way out the door and down the hall to Rose Marie's office, closed the door behind Virgil, the last one in, then turned and bellowed, "Those *MOTHERFUCKERS* think they can come into *MY* state and kill *MY* people and they tell me that *THEY'RE* saying how it is? They don't tell *ANYBODY* how it is in *MY* state. . . . *I* say how it is—they don't say a *FUCKIN' THING.*"

The governor raged on and Virgil looked away, embarrassed. The tantrum lasted a full thirty seconds, then the governor, breathing hard, red-faced, looked around, looked at Rose Marie, looked at Mitford, and Mitford smiled and said, "Glad we got that cleared up."

"What are we going to do?" the governor asked him, his voice rough from the tantrum.

Mitford shrugged. "You're a liberal, God bless your obscenely rich little soul. How does it hurt you to go up against a bunch of fascists from Homeland Security?"

"Uh-oh. What are you thinking?" Rose Marie asked.

Mitford said to the governor, "You don't have much political runway left here in Minnesota. What will you do when you're not governor anymore?"

"I thought I'd just be a rich guy," the governor said. "If somebody dies, I could run for the Senate."

"Will that make you happy?" Mitford asked.

"Neil, skip the dime-store psychology," the governor said. "What are you thinking?"

"We could arrest these two guys and charge them with conspiracy to commit murder in the planned execution of five Minnesotans, with two more murdered in the process. Before anybody has time to react, you have a press conference. You give an Abe Lincoln speech about protecting our precious freedoms, about how we don't turn our laws over to a bunch of Vietnamese killers. You'd take some heat, but by this time next week, you'd be a national name. You're on the cover of *Time* magazine. You'd be a hero to a lot of people in the party. Play your cards right over the next four years . . ."

The governor looked at him a long time, then said, "What's the downside?"

Rose Marie said, "They arrest you for treason and you're executed."

The governor laughed and said, "Really." That didn't worry him; he was far too rich to hang.

Davenport turned to Virgil: "You did turn off that recorder, didn't you?"

Virgil said, "Jeez, boss . . . I forgot."

Davenport: "Wonder what they're in there saying?"

"They already said enough," Virgil said. "But . . . I wouldn't be surprised if they said a few more things. Being in there by themselves."

THEY ALL contemplated him for a few seconds, then Rose Marie shook her head, turned to the governor, and said, "Neil raises an interesting possibility. But you *would* take some heat. A lot of people think security is all-important—they'd absolutely throw six or eight people overboard if it might stop an al-Qaeda attack. As long as it wasn't them getting thrown."

"That can be handled," Mitford said. "That's all PR. Our PR against their PR, and we'll have a big head start. Do it right, and they'll be cooked before they can even decide what to do. We're talking televised congressional hearings."

The governor mulled it over, then cocked an eye at Mitford. "A national name by next week?"

"Guaranteed."

Rose Marie said, "A national name isn't the same as a national hero. Lee Harvey Oswald is a national name. Benedict Arnold—"

Mitford snarled, "You think I'm so lame with the PR that we'd wind up as Benedict Arnold? For Christ's sakes, Rose Marie, I ran the negative side in the last campaign."

"I'm just saying," she said.

The governor said, "Let's sit here and think about it for two minutes. All right? Two minutes."

At the end of the two minutes, the governor covered Rose Marie's hand with his own and said, "Weren't you getting a little bit bored? How long has it been since we've been in a really dirty fight?"

"You got me there," she said.

THEY TROOPED BACK into the conference room, where Arenson and Cartwright were slouched in their chairs, barely containing their impatience. The governor said, "Virgil?"

Virgil said to Cartwright and Arenson, "Well, guys, I've got some bad news."

Cartwright: "What's that?"

Virgil threw his arms wide, gave them his best Hollywood grin, and said, "You're under arrest for murder."

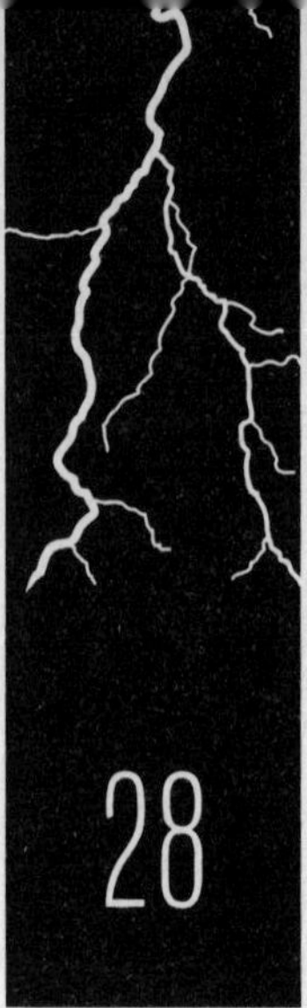

28

THE CONSPIRACY-to-murder charges were filed with Ramsey County, although, when he learned the circumstances, the Ramsey County attorney got nauseous and had to be excused to a quiet place, where he could curl up with his blankie.

Mitford put together the PR package in two hours, and the press conference was held in the rotunda of the Capitol, with an oversized American flag, borrowed from a fast-food franchise, hanging in the background. The governor gave the Abe Lincoln speech, provided family photos and testimonials from the loved ones of the two innocent men who were killed, as well as crime-scene photos of the five men executed by the Vietnamese for the crime in Vietnam.

Davenport tipped friends at TV stations and the newspapers, and after the press conference—a sensation that quickly spread from Minnesota to the evening talk shows in Washington—they'd perp-walked the two Homeland Security guys, something that was never done, so there was lots of film available.

After the perp walk, they gave the two guys the mandatory phone call.

THE U.S. ATTORNEY served a habeas corpus on the Ramsey jail six hours after Cartwright and Arenson went inside, and put them on a plane to Washington, where they became unavailable for comment.

Mitford had a package of the local crime scenes and family photos on an earlier plane, to the same destination, a half hour after the governor's press conference. When the Homeland Security fanboys went on the Washington political shows, they were greeted with the photos and "How do you explain this?"

A few tried to float the idea that although this was a fantasy dreamed up by a longtime opponent of the administration, that if it *hadn't been* a fantasy, it would have been a pretty good deal, giving up these six criminal Americans while saving all those hypothetical lives somewhere on the West Coast.

That didn't fly worth a damn. How many hypothetical people died, anyway? Then an Internet guy in Indonesia learned that one of the Indonesian al-Qaeda plotters ran a lawn service, and posted a photo showing the man pushing an ancient Lawn-Boy. There was an international guffaw at the expense of Homeland Security.

Blah-blah-blah-blah.

In the end—after two weeks, anyway—Mitford was proven correct. The governor was a national figure, both admired and reviled, who further confused the issue by giving a rousing pro-gun, anti-Vietnam-killers speech at the NRA convention.

A good time was had by all.

MEAD SINCLAIR went back to the University of Wisconsin, where, it turned out, nobody much cared about what happened in the sixties. A week after he got back, though, he was spit upon by an aging hippie while he was walking down State Street, and Sinclair punched the hippie in the head and knocked off his glasses, which broke when they hit the sidewalk.

Sinclair was later taken to the hospital for observation after a possible heart attack, but the heart attack was not confirmed. A student photographer, arriving too late for the actual fight, got the hippie to put his glasses back on the ground where they'd fallen, then took a neat photo of them with the light shining through the cracked lens, with a drop of dried nose blood, and the cops in the background. The photo ran in the student paper, the unannounced "reconstruction" was revealed in a letter to the editor, and the student was fired by the newspaper.

JANEY SMALL told Virgil that their night of passion couldn't happen again, because it was too depressing. Virgil agreed, which set off an argument, and he fled to Mankato.

While he was there, a man named Todd Barry called from the *New York Times Magazine* and said he'd talked to Sinclair about it, and that they could use twenty-five hundred words each for two articles, to run sequentially, on the Great Caterpillar Heist & Vietnam's Revenge. Virgil told him he could have the stories in two weeks. Barry asked him if he was sure he could get permission from all the sources. Virgil said, "Fuck a bunch of permission," and Barry said, "We could get along."

THEN MAI called from Hanoi.

When she called, Virgil was sitting in a country bar talking to a woman named Lark, an opium addict who was accused of boosting thirty thousand dollars' worth of toddler jeans out of a Wal-Mart supply truck as the truck had sat unattended overnight in a Wal-Mart parking lot. According to the local cops, Lark had driven her boyfriend's Ford F-350 Super Duty up beside the tractor-trailer, cut her way through the side using a Sawzall run off a Honda generator, and then filled up the longbed pickup with the toddler clothing. She was not believed to have had time to get rid of the loot, but nobody could find it. They were hoping that a thoughtful threat from Virgil might help, since Virgil had at different times arrested her boyfriend, father, and brother.

When Virgil's phone rang, he looked at it, saw the "Caller Unknown," opened the phone, and said, "Yes?"

"Virgil?"

He picked up her voice and turned away from Lark, into the booth. "Mai? Where are you?"

"Hanoi. In a pastry shop."

"Who got shot?" Virgil asked.

"He was a college boy who supplied the boat and the vehicles," Mai said. "He was supposed to go back to school, but now he'll have to find another school. He's here."

"Hurt bad?"

"The bullet broke his leg," she said. "I had to carry him. When we were in the truck, I looked back at you and saw you aim, but you didn't shoot."

"Ah, there was a farmhouse in the background. I couldn't see what was behind you."

After a moment, she giggled and said, "You could have thought of something more . . . I don't know. Sensitive? Romantic? You didn't shoot me because you thought you might hit a cow?"

"Well, Mai, I was pretty . . . intent," Virgil said. "I would have put your little round butt in jail if I could have."

"Mmm. How is Mead?"

"Mead's fine."

"I could not believe your governor's press conference," Mai said. "I was in Victoria when I began to see news stories about it. I couldn't believe it."

"Get you in trouble back home?" Virgil asked.

"No. You know, here, what's done is done. Then you go on. I would have liked to have told you about the people who were killed in Da Nang," she said. "The old man was my grandfather. The woman was my aunt, the little children were my cousins. I never knew any of them. My father, in his whole life, was insane with the grief of them dying. They went through the whole war, and then, just as the victory arrives, they are killed by American criminals. When this chance came, well, our whole family took it. Justice too long delayed."

She waited for a reaction. Virgil finally came up with "There would have been a better way to handle it."

"Well—my great-uncle is dying," Mai said. "Nothing but old age, and he is famous here, the head of our family, so his life is good enough.

But this justice was his one last wish. We didn't have too much time; he will die this autumn, I think."

"So what do you want from me?" Virgil asked.

"Closure. Say good-bye. I liked dancing with you, Virgil. I liked sleeping with you. We'd be friends if we could be, but we can't."

"Mmm," Virgil said.

"So when you get rich and start to travel, if you ever come to Hanoi—give me a ring," she said. "Or even a good neutral country. China."

"I wouldn't go to China if I were you. To Hong Kong," Virgil said.

Another bit of silence. "Virgil—what did you do?"

"I talked to that Chinese cop again," Virgil said. "He's a little annoyed that Vietnamese intelligence came into Hong Kong and murdered a guy without even a courtesy card."

"Oh, Virgil. Goddamnit. He knows who I am?"

"Yeah, we squeezed that out of Mead," he said. "So, if I were you, I might hesitate before going in there. For a while, at least."

Then she laughed. "Virgil . . . you were a surprise."

"So were you, Mai."

"Good-bye," she said.

And she was gone.

"OLD GIRLFRIEND?" Lark asked. She had her legs up on the opposite seat, two empty Grain Belt bottles by her elbow; clicked her front teeth with her silver tongue stud after asking the question.

"Not exactly," Virgil said. "Now, Lark, about these goddamn baby pants . . ."

THE TAIL END of August was hot. Davenport got in a lot of trouble working a new case, and called for help. Virgil went north, in the night, and found the entire east side of St. Paul in darkness. Some cog or gear in the power system had given up under the strain of the hundreds of thousands of screaming air conditioners, and popped.

The BCA was a puddle of light, minimal services—not including the air-conditioning—running off an emergency generator. He checked in with the duty man and was told that Davenport, Del, Shrake, and Jenkins were out on the street somewhere, looking for a crazy guy in a wheelchair. "You're welcome to wait in Lucas's office, but I don't think he's coming back. Not soon, anyway."

Virgil went up to the office, walking down dark hallways; only the emergency lights were working in the halls. Davenport still had some power. Virgil got a fan going, pointed it at Davenport's chair, turned on Davenport's small flat-panel TV, and sat back in the chair.

The convention had arrived. The parties had started, the champagne was flowing, the Young Republicans were barfing in the Mississippi, the anarchists were flying the black flag in Mears Park, and Daisy Jones was anchoring the street action. She was so excited that her glitter lipstick was melting.

He was taking it all in when Sandy leaned in the door. "God, it's hot," she said. She had a plastic bottle of Coke in her hands, sweating with condensation.

Virgil said, "Get yourself a fan."

"You've got the only fan in the building. Who has fans in an air-conditioned office? Lucas, that's who." She was barefoot, wearing a T-shirt and a taffeta girly-style skirt. She looked a little dewy, and pretty good.

"What are you doing here?" he asked.

"Research," she said. She took off her glasses, put them on a bookcase. "Can't believe this heat. It's still eighty-five out there, and it's midnight."

"You heard that Mai called me?"

"I heard," she said. She twisted the cap off the Coke, took a drink, leaned back against the doorway, and rolled the cold bottle against the side of her face and neck.

"Hot," Virgil said.

"Yeah, screw it," she said. She put the bottle on top of the bookcase, pulled her arms through the sleeve holes of her T-shirt, popped the back snap on her bra, pulled the straps over her hands, pushed her hands back through the sleeves, and then pulled the bra from under the shirt and put it on the bookcase next to the glasses. "That's better."

"Gotta be comfortable," Virgil said. "That's the important thing."

"Damn right," she said.

Virgil stood up and stretched, yawned, said, "Where'd you get the Coke? The machine's still working?"

"Yeah."

They ambled down the hallway together to the canteen room, where Virgil got a Diet Coke, then back toward Davenport's office. She said, "I don't think there's anybody else in the building except the duty man."

They were under the glass skylights when they caught the brilliant flash to the west, and lingered there, elbows on the banister over the courtyard, looking up through the glass at the clouds churning above the bright city lights.

"You get strange cases," she said, looking up at him. Without her glasses, her eyes looked as large as moons.

"I do," he said.

They both thought about it, standing shoulder to shoulder, and she took a hit of her Coke and said, "I like working them. I'm a hippie, God help me, and I like chasing down rat-fuckers."

Virgil laughed and stood up, and could see the line of her spine through the thin cloth of the T-shirt, and without thinking, ran his middle knuckle up her spine. She wiggled, and slipped closer, her hip against his. They got another flickering flash off to the west.

"Heat lightning," she said.